D1478990

False Riches

To: Tracy Hawthorne

False Riches

John Paul Miller

"There's only one sure thing..."

Charleston, SC
www.PalmettoPublishing.com

First Edition

Hardcover ISBN: 979-8-8229-2640-0
Paperback ISBN: 979-8-8229-1861-0
eBook ISBN: 979-8-8229-2641-7

To my wife, Judy.
Until I met you, the only thing I knew about
horses was what I had seen on TV.
Thanks for letting me immerse my life in
your world of thoroughbred horses.

Chapter 1

"There's only one sure thing." I spoke softly, and BigOilRig studied me with his wise brown eyes as I brushed his mane. "Nothing's going to happen to you. If anything, we'll go out together." The Texas sky was dark through the bars in his stall window.

Lucky took off barking down the shedrow, and I ducked under the webbing. It was Dos, probably wanting tips on the race today. He walked up from the far end of the barn and looked over his shoulder at the security camera. Pulling a small white towel from his back pocket, he wiped the rain off his goatee and bald head. Lucky rushed closer, barking and growling. He was the kind of dog that liked everybody, except guys like Dos.

Most people would let their hand be smelled, but Dos stood still as a fence post. He kept his hands in the pockets of his khakis. Lucky smelled his feet and his brown leather sandals. I shook my head. Who would wear sandals around horses?

I whistled, and Lucky went over and lay down by GunShy, who sat by the office door, watching everything. They had become pretty good buddies in the past four days since SkyMan had showed up. He was getting his next horse ready. Dos gave him a long, hard look as I approached.

"Who's the new guy?" Dos asked, as if SkyMan couldn't hear.

"He's from the Zia racetrack over in Hobbs."

SkyMan kept Dos in his sights, almost challenging him with his dark brown eyes.

Dos motioned for me to move away. "Where's Charlane? It's 6:30. I can't be here when the windows open. I need her to make two important bets today."

"Charlane's riding for a new trainer in Barn5 this week. Coming in this afternoon."

Dos studied me. "How 'bout you? You'll do it, won't you?"

He took out a marker and crossed out her name, wrote my name on a scrap of paper torn off a brown paper bag, and handed me four 100's and four 20's.

~~Charlane~~ *Amos*
Race 4 HorseShoeDowns
2, 6, 10, 3, 7
$2 Superfecta Box $240 each ticket
Two tickets $480 total
Friday 3/26

Our horse, 8, wasn't on his list.

"What about 8—BigOilRig?" I asked. "You left him out?"

Dos tapped the paper. "2, 6, 10, 3, 7. I got good info on this one. Here, I'll loan you $120, and you can get a one-dollar super ticket for yourself."

Now he had my attention. He was the kind of man most people didn't want to be associated with, but I said, "Okay."

"Don't mess up like that time Charlane said she got shut out at the betting window—cost me a lot of money."

"Don't worry, I'll make the bets." I thought Charlane had probably lied that she didn't get the bet down and had kept the winnings.

Satisfied, Dos walked to the stall with the card "BigOilRig" on the door. He raised his right hand to rub the horse's muzzle, maybe to show he cared about horses, too, not just gambling. The horse in the stall was actually NoCashRefund, a gray stakes winner. He pinned his ears back and showed the whites of his eyes, not wanting anything to do with Dos. The dogs barked and bolted at him, as if to protect NoCashRefund, which made SkyMan head over, too.

NoCashRefund bared his teeth and lunged to take a bite out of Dos's arm, but Dos jumped back. "Dammit, that's why I didn't put 8 in today. You oughta scratch him." He brushed his arm as if it had dirt on it. The pink flamingos on his cheap long-sleeve Hawaiian shirt reminded me of the flamingos at Hialeah Racetrack. When I was six, Daddy went to the barns at Hialeah to get tips and almost got bit by a horse.

"Well, you oughta put 8 in your ticket," I said. "I ride him every day. He's gonna be right there. He's a strong finisher."

"Nah. Not today." He stood there looking at the horse he thought was BigOilRig. For a second, I wanted to take the money out of my pocket and give it back, but instead, I squeezed those bills so they wouldn't contaminate my pocket.

He turned back to me. "Don't tell anyone where you got those numbers."

Buster, our trainer, came out of the office. "Aren't you supposed to be getting the next set ready?"

He was so superstitious, almost paranoid, when someone like Dos came around on a day we had a horse entered. He was sure it was bad luck.

Dos gave me a thumbs-up and went back down the shedrow as Lucky gave him a goodbye growl.

"Why can't they keep those guys out of the barns?" Buster asked, staring after him. "What's he doing here?"

"Lookin' for Charlane. He has a tip, but he left BigOilRig out."

"Must not be a very good tip. BigOilRig is ready to go today. Let's get the next set ready." He headed back to the office.

As I started tacking my next horse, SkyMan came up to help. He had stoic brown eyes, a few wrinkles, and thick black hair pulled back in a braided ponytail, tied in a knot at the end with a piece of smooth rawhide. Probably up in his fifties, but as fit as anyone here. He had a natural way with horses.

"What's that guy do?" he asked.

"Dos? He has a Mexican restaurant in South Fort Worth," I said. "He's Charlane's friend, always wanting tips. He bets a lot."

"How about you? You bet?"

"Oh yeah. Some people around here think I'm a professional gambler and do this horse thing for information. Let's say I'm way ahead, which, for a bettor, is unusual. All gambling is a sucker's game. Got my daddy. Chewed him up and spit him out."

He nodded. "Yeah, guys like that back home can't stay out of the casinos. They put casinos on Indian land—the tribe, the state, they get their cut. We know who pays for it—the losers."

I was momentarily hurt he would refer to my daddy as a loser—he never knew him. But SkyMan was right. Daddy lost everything, and therefore he was a loser.

"Here we are, you and me, up at dawn, busting it," I said. "Riding these horses. Risking our lives. For what? Twenty-five dollars a mount. If we get hurt, they get another rider."

"We can't play it safe," SkyMan said. "Gamblers can't play it safe. We're no different from them. Even the bettors, all they care about is cashing tickets."

"We care about these guys," I said, sliding my hand down my horse's neck. "Buster does too; he was a pretty good exercise rider back in the day. Some veterinarians and trainers care about us. Others only care about their invoices and day rates and full barns. At least now, there's NESPA—you know, the National Equine Safety Protection Authority is a check and balance. They're working to tighten the safety protocols, something I've been fighting for, too."

It was still raining when SkyMan and I rode out to work the two horses in the next set. We got back to the barn, wet from the rain, and I was glad I was able to share a ride with someone like SkyMan instead of Charlane. I looked at the past performances of the horses in race 4 in my *DRF*, the *Daily Racing Form*. I was excited about BigOilRig's chances. He was picked by two handicappers to be second or third, not like the long shots on Dos's list.

SkyMan had been riding NoCashRefund the past five days since Charlane had been off, and he asked, "How come NoCashRefund and BigOilRig switched stalls?"

"Oh, Buster's superstitious," I said, setting down the *DRF*. "Since BigOilRig is in a race today, I moved him to stall #12 last night, right across from the office."

NoCashRefund, who had been anxious when Dos was here, was calm as SkyMan got him ready for the next set. SkyMan had a special way with horses. I often wondered what he was saying as he talked in his native language to his horses. He whispered a few words while he pulled NoCashRefund's black mane back and rubbed his neck up to his ears.

I got FlyByNite ready, and we left the barn to work the next set on the main track. SkyMan looked up, his eyes following a raven until it landed on the top rail of the fence beside us and flapped its wings. SkyMan said, "You know, ravens are messengers; they mean lots of things, like changes."

"Don't some people think ravens are bad luck?" I asked.

"Luck is neither good nor bad."

As the horse's hooves hit the ground, it reminded me of my mother pounding on the kitchen table, telling Daddy about his luck. It was never good and almost always bad. He blamed luck. She blamed him.

Lucky and GunShy had the drill down pat as they scampered beside us all the way to the track and stayed with Buster under the outside rail. From there he clocked the horses and watched with his binoculars.

"Just gallop these two around twice," he said. "Keep them side by side."

A light drizzle continued. Skyman smiled, raised his eyes overhead, and said, "A great day to ride."

We trotted around the track once and began our first gallop. FlyByNite floated over the muddy track. It was a combination of speed and the smooth magical rhythm of an athletic horse.

Coming down in front of the grandstand, NoCashRefund started tossing his head. SkyMan pulled on the reins, trying to steady him. "Something's wrong," he called.

FlyByNite and I slowed down. I had flipped to a clean pair of goggles when I saw Skyman was out of balance. He was coming off.

NoCashRefund took two bad steps. SkyMan shifted his weight and grabbed the mane at the same time as his inertia yielded to gravity. NoCashRefund's front legs buckled, and as he went down on one knee, SkyMan came off in a free-fall tumble. Grunts and groans of air whooshing out of his lungs alternated as gasps went back in. The track, still damp and covered with hundreds of muddy hoofprints, lay quiet, almost waiting for him to bounce, or roll, and then finally land.

I didn't want to watch as his head snapped in the other direction, but it happened too fast to look away. I watched for the millisecond I was beside him.

Mother Earth greeted him when his shoulder slammed into the track.

The rain was like tears in my eyes. Everything was blurred as I jumped off my horse. The screeching horn broke the silence and all training stopped. We were right by the main gate. Lucky and GunShy ran up and stayed right beside SkyMan. NoCashRefund had scrambled to his feet, and Buster caught him and held the reins.

I knelt beside SkyMan. He was a pile of muddy jeans. For a moment, there was complete silence. Then he moaned. I pulled his goggles up on his helmet and said, "Don't move. Everything's gonna be okay." He blinked a few times. By the look on his face, I knew the pain was bad.

The EMS ambulance and the horse ambulance arrived at the same time. The track vet walked NoCashRefund around and inspected his legs.

The EMT ran over and knelt beside SkyMan. His eyes seemed to focus with a faint "thanks for being here" look.

From behind me, one of the calmest voices I've ever heard said, "How is he?"

I stood up and glanced at the badge hanging from her blazer pocket. Her photo ID was better than any driver's license photo I'd ever seen. Her eyes were irresistible, three shades of green and gray. She braced her umbrella against the wind and studied my muddy face. I motioned for her to follow me over to the rail, away from SkyMan.

"I was riding with him when he went down," I said. "Hi. I'm Amos Moon."

"Rixie Ricksland. I work for NESPA." She studied me for a moment. "You're one of the luckiest bettors 'round here."

"It has nothing to do with luck, but some people think I'm the best, as you say, 'round here.'"

"Really?"

"Really." I studied her for a second. "This is the first time I've ever seen you at the track instead of riding shotgun through the barns with cheap-ass W. D. Stamples. Where's Max Hunter? He's the NESPA man in charge of racing."

"Busy."

"Busy? Too busy to be out here checking on us and these horses?"

Of all the days for Max to be "busy." We'd had an accident, and now we were stuck dealing with someone from the NESPA office.

"How long you been here, anyway?" I asked her.

"Since last October, and yes, Mr. Hunter is over racing. I'm filling in for him today." She nodded at SkyMan. "What's his name?"

"SkyMan."

"Last name?"

"SkyMan is his name. Never heard any other name."

A light rain had started again, and she wiped drops off her iPad. "No name even close to SkyMan is registered here at HSD, HorseShoeDowns. That's a violation of NESPA regulations. Which barn?"

"Buster O'Bryan," I said. "Barn7. He's right there, holding the horse."

She glanced at the horse, studied Buster, and made a few notes. "Where's SkyMan from?"

"New Mexico. He's Native American. Been here five days."

"Still not on the list."

She nodded at me and walked over to Buster. From there she watched everything, made a few phone calls, and made a lot of notes on her iPad. She glanced back and forth between SkyMan and me, still taking photos. Evidence?

I heard her tell the EMS ambulance driver she was going to the hospital. I walked over and said, "You're going to the hospital with him?"

"Dr. Winkley has authorized Clink, another NESPA colleague, to sign the accident forms."

Clink showed up out of nowhere. He reminded me of a weak, wimpy weasel with his narrow face and beady eyes. He always wore polo shirts and khakis. He didn't like me either because I knew he was trying to hook up with my ex-girlfriend, Kellsey.

She turned to talk to him. I had to interrupt. "Why would someone who doesn't even know his name go with him?"

She shot me a look. "It's my job and NESPA protocol to document everything that goes on before, during, and after every incident at this track."

"Did you say before? Y'all are not doin' much in the before. Looks like you're showing up after."

She raised her eyebrows and turned back to me. "You're the one who has been complaining about everything from track safety to more security. You, of all people, should understand."

So she didn't just know me from gambling.

"Well." I shrugged. "Today's a good day for you to see what can happen in the rain on a wet track if the drainage isn't done right. I thought since NESPA showed up, these accidents wouldn't happen."

Pointing at Buster and the track vet, she said, "That's the responsibility of the trainers and veterinarians."

"And the track owner, Stamples. And officers of the track. They all have responsibilities too. What about track security? Or lack of security. Anybody can come onto these grounds, in and out of the barns, day or night."

She looked around as if she was trying to find an answer. Instead she asked, "Why? Do you know any suspicious people coming around the track?"

"Just check the security cameras."

"I have some questions for you and forms to fill out. I'll come by your barn later."

I had to get the last word in. "Maybe you should bring Max Hunter."

She closed the iPad. That conversation was over. I left some things unsaid and went over to check on SkyMan.

The EMT had SkyMan's safety vest unzipped and his helmet off. His face was muddy, and his breathing was quick and shallow.

The EMT said, "We need to get this stretcher under your back."

SkyMan's eyes moved from the EMT to me. "How's the horse?"

"He's walking okay."

"Take care of him."

I could only nod and say, "Don't worry, I will." I took his hand, held it for a second, and squeezed it. His eyes never left mine. They picked him up and loaded him into the back of the EMS ambulance.

I stood at the back door, wishing I could be of some help.

He tried to lift his head. "Call Martha, my wife, and have her bring my saddlebags to the hospital."

"Okay."

I glanced up and Miss NESPA was already in the front seat. She turned and looked at SkyMan on the stretcher. She glanced at me, and I gave her a thumbs-up before the EMT shut the door.

Chapter 2

"Max, I'm in the ambulance on the way to Fort Worth General with a rider from Buster's barn who just went down," I said into my phone. "Landed hard on his shoulder. Amos Moon was right in the middle of the entire mess, making sure I knew how serious this was."

His voice was abrupt. "Call me back after you get to the hospital."

The driver went right through traffic. I held my breath a few times. The siren was getting to me, and I could hardly hear him as he said, "We had two people to thank for getting the ambulances about five years ago. Stamples, who finally agreed to stroke the check. And Amos got it done back then, with the help of the Texas Jockeys group. He's always looking out for everyone and keeping the heat on Stamples to get new ones. These babies cost over $250,000."

He looked at me and said, "I heard they may be closin' this dangerous track. Us haulin' guys like him back there off to the hospital all the time. It's only March. I lost track of how many horses already died here this year."

I knew it was two horses. Fewer than this same time last year. The driver phoned ahead, and the emergency room was ready when we arrived. They bypassed reception and took him back to the examination area.

The registration lady couldn't believe I didn't know any more about him except that his name was SkyMan. He didn't have the required medical information card attached to his vest. Another violation. She said, "We need an insurance card or some guarantee for payment before we can admit him."

I handed her my business card. "I'll be your contact at HorseShoeDowns about payment."

She stapled my card to the folder. "Here, take this to the nurses' station. He's in bed three." She pointed to the door marked "NO ADMITTANCE." As I got closer, it opened automatically.

SkyMan was behind the curtain. I didn't know what to expect, but he was alert and calm. He smiled at me in spite of everything. His neck and shoulder were immobilized.

"Mr. SkyMan. I'm Rixie Ricksland, with NESPA. I rode over here with you from the track. We contacted your wife, and she'll be here soon."

A nurse came in and checked the monitor and the IV. "What happened?"

"He was in a riding accident this morning."

She looked again at his chart. "Motorcycle?"

"Oh, no. He was riding a horse."

"Way better than a motorcycle. At least he's got some skin left on him."

My phone rang. Max. I excused myself and went outside.

"Rixie, I'm in here with the stewards. We called the track in New Mexico. They said this guy's a good rider and he was one of the best assistant trainers. They wished he hadn't left." Max sighed. "Assure him the track will do everything we can."

"That's bullshit. I won't tell him that. We'll do everything we can, but the track probably won't do anything."

The phone went muffled, and I heard Max say, "Excuse me, gentlemen. I'm going to step out." Then he came back on the line. "Talk to me."

"It's infuriating," I said, leaning against the wall. "No one's protecting these guys. That's why NESPA hired us. Amos said the horse stopped running, slowed down so much his legs gave way under him, and threw the rider. I'll keep you posted."

I hung up, walked to the concessions, and got a bottle of water. The things Amos had said at the track burned in my ears. Was he right? Was this job more impossible than Max and I wanted to admit? It made me wonder if NESPA really could prevent accidents or if I was just in charge of pushing paper and processing information.

I went back inside. The lights were bright in the hall. I pulled the curtain back, and an attractive Native American woman was with SkyMan. She didn't look up; she was whispering in his ear. The rhythm of her voice and her words was captivating. It was like a prayer and a song.

"You must be Martha," I said.

"Thanks for coming here with him." Her voice broke. "It's all my fault. We only came over here because my sister's sick and I had to come take care of her. I'm a painter. I met a woman at the art show in Albuquerque. Her husband is Buster. So I sorta got him the job. He's really a good rider. Do you know what happened?"

"They said his horse, NoCashRefund, started to slow down and his front legs buckled. They rolled together."

She nodded. "I knew he wouldn't get throwed."

"I'm Rixie Ricksland."

"Martha Drummer."

Drummer. So most likely SkyMan's last name.

"This is the day I have dreaded, when he's gone to work," Martha said, reaching for his hand once again. "Every day I pray he comes back in the door and has a good day riding horses and doesn't get hurt."

Chapter 3

When the red taillights of the ambulance disappeared, I squeezed my eyes shut and prayed for SkyMan as the veterinarian checked over NoCashRefund. Once he was cleared, his nostrils flared, and he let out a long breath. We made a slow walk back to Barn7.

Buster was pacing. "What happened!" he roared, loud enough for the entire barn to hear. "I thought you said he was a good rider. NoCashRefund is supposed to be in a race next week. First it was Dos hanging around, and this guy got dumped on the track. Now NESPA will be breathing down my neck because he wasn't in the system. How'm I gonna explain this to the owner? I don't need any more problems!"

"Whoa, whoa, whoa." I was used to his temper, and I had to get him to listen to reason. "This guy rode NoCashRefund as good as he could. You know when a horse is going down, you have to hold on; you don't bail and jump off. You keep him going forward; maybe he'll get his legs back under him. He did everything right. Another rider, it could have been a lot worse."

He glared at me. "The vet'll be back in a few hours—keep NoCashRefund quiet in his stall." He slammed his office door.

There were still horses to train, and I checked on FlybyNite, trying to calculate when I could get to the betting window. I couldn't put my finger on it, but something wasn't right about the accident.

I pushed that thought away in favor of thinking about that $120 ticket. That's all Daddy would have thought about. He wouldn't have cared where the tip came from. For Daddy it was about money, the only way to keep score. For me it has always been to be better than my daddy.

If indeed four of Dos's long-shot horses came in the top four, his $240 ticket could be worth way over $200,000—each. My $120 ticket would be half that. Then it dawned on me: if BigOilRig came in the top four, Dos's tickets wouldn't be any good.

Right then I said to Lucky, "Maybe I should get a six-horse ticket and add BigOilRig to Dos's numbers…After all, what could go wrong?"

Lucky barked, and that was all I needed to hear.

Priority now, though, wasn't the ticket; it was taking care of NoCashRefund. He spent the morning standing in a knee-high ice boot as a precaution. Every time I walked by, he nickered, but when I held out a cookie for him, he shied away and refused. He was alert; we kept his hay net full, and he drank plenty of water.

I watched him for a moment as he stood in his stall. This place was like a prison. Bars on the windows. Walls around the front so loose horses wouldn't escape. Walls also served as public art for people to either take selfies with or add graffiti. They offered a false sense of protection—kinda like the Alamo.

Moving on, I checked on BigOilRig. I'd always wanted to own a horse like him. Buster and I had disagreed a lot about his races and the distances he had run. The owner had to rely on Buster's decisions. But if I'd owned him, I would have done it differently. He was only four years old and had a lot of racing ahead of him.

Back in the winter, I'd actually contacted BigOilRig's owner and asked him if BigOilRig was for sale. He'd told me he wasn't and for me to keep riding him to see how good he was. He'd thanked me for the call. All I'd done was raise the value. The owner probably felt as though I—being the exercise rider—knew something even the trainer didn't know.

I walked over to BigOilRig. He was eating hay hanging in a net on the outside of his stall. "How are you going to finish today?" I asked him. "If the owner won't sell you to me, unless he drops you in a claiming race—how can I ever own you?"

I had to get over to the betting window. It was 11:50 on the clock by the TV screen. Also had to grab a cup of strong coffee and something to eat.

Lucky, GunShy, and I headed out, cutting by Barn2. Someone hollered, "Lucky, come here." They wanted his presence to give them good luck. Everyone was so used to having Lucky around. They were so superstitious. He was like the track mascot or HorseShoeDowns' poster dog.

He stopped to pee and lagged behind. I had bets to make. From now until the bell went off, when BigOilRig went out of the gate in the fourth race, it was the rush that would keep me going. It's why I was in the game.

"Come on, Lucky, let's go," I called, and he scampered up next to me.

With each step, my anticipation grew. There was that sweet smell of success in the air that only exists at a racetrack when everything goes right. That's why it was such an exciting sport. Hope was the other part. I had to hope Dos's numbers had some validity. Dos always bet on a long shot, but today, he was betting all long shots on an exotic wager. A two-dollar superfecta box was one of the hardest bets to win.

Just like insider information, a tip at the track was a dangerous thing to have. I took out the scrap of paper again, still baffled that 8 wasn't on it.

What if BigOilRig finished in the top four and I didn't have him on my ticket? It would be as if I didn't have any confidence in the way he'd been trained; plus I knew he was ready to go the distance.

I came around the corner and stopped short to see the Preacher. He was the track chaplain and had Cowboy Church every Sunday. He was there every day, a tall man in a green HSD gift shop jacket like the ones the ushers wore, looking like an employee, binoculars around his neck and a stack of cards in his hand.

A tour group crowded in front of him, and I couldn't go around them, so I took out my *DRF* and acted like I was reading.

He handed everyone a card and said, "Luke 6:37: 'Judge not, and ye shall not be judged: condemn not, and ye shall not be condemned: forgive and ye shall be forgiven.'"

The people in the group read the cards and moved away. Their stares compelled me to take a card. I put it in my shirt pocket.

Lucky and I always went to Brenda's window. I stared at her: she had cut her hair real short.

I hesitated, remembering the time I came home from school and Daddy had spent all the money at the track. My mother had cut her hair herself. For a second Brenda reminded me of her, in more ways than just her short hair. She had a sincere way she always handed me my tickets and said, "Good luck." I felt as though she cared if I won. Tipping her when I had a winning ticket always helped.

I had a combined feeling of excitement and fear. The excitement was the rush of placing a bet and maybe winning a lot of money, and the fear came from considering that the source of the tip might be a little dishonest.

Brenda sat there, her hand on the machine, waiting for my numbers. I feared Brenda, of all people, had jinxed my bet by cutting her hair. I stood there, kind of hypnotized.

"Something wrong?" she asked.

I looked up at her hair. She pushed a nonexistent loose strand behind her ear. My betting hadn't been as sharp as it had been back before Kellsey and I had split up. I hadn't focused on the main thing—me and the horses.

Before I could respond, she asked, "What's got you so nervous today?"

"Oh, I was beside the guy who got thrown this morning; he works at our barn. Just been shook since then."

She said in a low voice, "Yeah, NESPA's got the whole place on alert. Who's the other pup?"

I looked down. The dogs were at my feet.

"GunShy. He belongs to the guy who got thrown."

She slid two dog cookies out for them. "Okay, what'll it be today?"

"I've got three bets. Fourth race. Two two-dollar superfecta boxes, 2 6 10 3 7 five-horse box."

She looked up when I finished as though she was totally surprised. "That's $480."

"Yep," I said, and slid Dos's $480 through the window. She gave me his two tickets. I checked the numbers and put his two tickets in the front pocket of my jeans. I didn't want to contaminate my own ticket.

"One more." My voice had been a little sketchy on those first tickets, but now I got a little excited. These were *my* numbers. Well, Dos's numbers plus 8. "Fourth race, one-dollar superfecta box, 2 6 10 3 7, and add another horse, 8."

When I said "8," I got an "Are you sure?" look.

I put the $120 from Dos and added my $240 to make it a $360 bet. I slid the money through the slot in the glass.

The ticket came out, and she said, "Good luck."

The window reflected the puzzled look on my face as I remembered how SkyMan had said luck was neither good nor bad. The preacher's card brushed my finger as I put my ticket in my shirt pocket.

Lucky and GunShy had already walked off, smelling everything on the ground. We passed a few people who stood like statues, holding programs, cups of beer, cigarettes, and hands of empty luck. They had looks of utter despair, as if the whole future rode like a stowaway on the saddle with the jockey.

They were a lot like my daddy. His system had been guessing at numbers. He couldn't admit he had picked the wrong horse or lost next week's rent money. He couldn't accept the truth. One thing I knew for certain: I was better at this than Dos or Daddy.

I couldn't wait to bring BigOilRig over for the fourth race.

Chapter 4

The moment I was back at the track from the hospital, I headed to Barn 7 with a lot of questions. I recognized her from her photo in her HR file. She had a teal flowered scarf around her neck gathered with a silver nut, maybe from a piece of equipment. For March it was still cool, and I had on my blazer, but she was wearing a short-sleeve shirt, exposing her taut, muscular arms. She couldn't have weighed more than a hundred pounds, but I couldn't imagine anyone choosing to mess with her. Her brown frosted hair was pulled back under a dark-green ball cap.

"Charlene?" She never moved, just kept brushing the horse. "Excuse me, Charlene."

"No one here by that name. I am Charlane. "Char" like charcoal, and "lane." Charlane. Say it, so next time you'll say it right. Go on, say it."

I thought this was a joke, but she stared a hole in me, and I must admit, I stuttered a bit when I said it. "Char—Charlane. How's that?"

"Hun. You got it. Only one Charlane."

She kept brushing the horse and gave me a big smile as if she was glad to see me, or probably glad to be seen. Then she took a round plastic tin from her back pocket, opened it, and put a pinch under her lip, showing her slightly crooked lower teeth. "Who're you?"

"Rixie Ricksland."

She leaned over, squinted at my badge, and said, "Ohhhhh. NESPA, I heard about you. I also heard NESPA has delayed implementing the rules and regulations at horse shows, and even rodeos over at the Stockyards. Put off for at least two more years. They ain't got enough doctors and vets. Not to mention inspectors like you. I also heard the fancy DEA labs can't keep up with the samples from the racehorses. NESPA has more rules than they have people to enforce them."

"Yes, so they contracted with the Hunter Group to oversee the regulations here at this track."

"That's why Clink's on the payroll," she said, nodding. "I heard somehow Stamples got him that job."

I filed that away for another time. "He was here when I started."

"Kinda busy. Buster's in the office with Clink, fillin' out the accident report. Amos is making a bet. You know he bets a lot? Course you do. I tell you what I bet…between you and me, we probably know everything that goes on around here."

I smiled. "Most definitely." Keeping up a camaraderie with her was the way in, I could already tell.

She motioned for me to follow her. "Come on, Hun. Let me show ya 'round. Hay and feed room. You know the best thing?" She stopped and pointed at her picture on a box—holding a cookie. "Right there. Miss Ellane's cookies."

"That's you!" I said as she held up the box and grinned. "Great photograph."

"Yeah." She winked. "One of my aliases, a.k.a. Miss Ellane. Short for Miscellaneous. They said they couldn't pay twenty-five dollars for a box of cookies. I told 'em, "Just put it on the owner's bill as 'miscellaneous.'" Pretty clever, huh? Miss Ellane's cookies are in every barn at this track. I sell a lot of cookies."

I picked up the box. "So what's in them?"

"Secret recipe. Mainly oats. Nothing's more natural for a horse than oats. Ever give a horse a treat or a carrot?"

"No, not really."

"You wanna do it? Come on, Hun. Here, grab you a handful."

"They're pretty hard."

"Horses gotta chew 'em up." The closest horse was lunging at us. "See how much they like 'em?"

She reached over and took my hand and said, "Hun, you got nice nails. I'm ashamed for you to even see mine. I scrub 'em every night, but they still dirty and cracked."

She turned my hand over and gently placed a cookie in my palm. "Gotta hold your hand out flat—just like the picture on the box. Thumb in tight. They'll grab it. Can't be actin' like you're hitchhikin' or thumbin' a ride. Betcha never did, did ya?"

"No, not really."

The horse took the cookie almost as gently as she'd placed it in my palm.

I rubbed my hands together and followed her past the office, and she pointed to a huge bulletin board. "You'll like this," she said. "Amos Moon's road map for success. Everything has to be precise. He's meticulous, strict, and stubborn. No shortcuts when it comes to the horses under his care. This goes for the barn, the people who work here, exercise riders, and jockeys."

I stared at the board, trying to take it all in. He was the safety advocate for the entire track. He had the Ten Commandments, the Cowboy Code of the West, the Lord's Prayer, an American flag, Bible verses, and all the track rules up on the board. It would take me weeks to read it all.

"You know what Amos wants more than anything? To be an owner someday. He's savin' up to buy some really good horses. Start his own string and train them himself. Look, you got your own section. Right here."

Big red arrows pointed to a NESPA letter: "NO MORE ACCIDENTS." It was a warning to trainers about how serious the situation had become concerning track safety and the importance of trainers' abiding by the medication regulations.

I looked at some of the winner's circle photos.

"That's Buster's daughter, Kellsey," Charlane said. "She won hundreds of stakes races right here. That's the big boss, W. D. Stamples, right there in the winner's circle every time, giving her the trophy. That's one reason Amos and Kellsey split up. Stamples always hittin' on her. Course her flirtin' with him didn't help."

"Yes, I've heard of her," I said, not wanting to dive into track gossip. "She's a legend around here."

"'Round here? All the way to Oaklawn, Fair Grounds, and California. Jockey of the year, most wins, most money. She has a huge fan base here. People love to bet on her."

She reached up and adjusted her ball cap, tilted it up, and said, "Listen, Hun. I heard she shipped back to HSD this morning. Ol' Stamples was so happy when he found out Kellsey dumped Amos right about Valentine's Day. Amos'll never get over her. He took it real hard. He ain't been the same the past coupla months. Too much stress. Even his handicappin' sufferin'."

"What do you mean?"

"He can't concentrate. Can't pick winners. A guy gits jilted, he starts doin' desperate things. Relying on bad tips. Bettin' too much. Doublin' down. Never git even thataway. He's bettin' with his heart and not his brain. That kinda man only wants to win back what he's lost. He can't see—well, when a woman like you shows up—he can't see past his lost love. And every day, he has to work for Buster, his almost-future father-in-law."

"Why, were they engaged?"

She laughed, "Oh no, Hun. Never got that far. They dated. They were serious. She stayed up there in Amos's apartment when she was here. That didn't work out, what with Amos working for her dad and her gone all the time. Buster vetted Amos when he thought they might get married. You know, psycho tests."

She looked at me as if I believed her. "Come on, Hun. Just kiddin' you. Buster told me Amos has a 'rigorous personality.' He looks at everything to make certain it is correct or safe. That's where him and Kellsey split. He wanted her to retire from race riding, and she wouldn't do it.

"They had a big fight right here in the barn. I heard it all. Amos told her bettin' was a game to him and he could quit anytime he wanted to. She couldn't quit race ridin', ever. Only after she was so broken or banged up or in a wheelchair or worse. There's a real soft spot inside that tough cowboy. His begging didn't work. She accused him of being like his father—a gamble-holic. And an adrenaline junky. We all are, you know. We ain't normal like you."

She didn't wait for a response but said, "Anyway, she's gone all the time. Racetracks are notorious for—well, you know, she's very attractive. Listen, she could have any man she wants, not like you and me."

She laughed again and studied my face.

"Well, maybe you got your choice of guys. Anyway, he took it hard, and she moved on. I even heard she's been goin' out with Clink when she's back here. So who's Amos gonna meet 'round here?"

I wondered if the only men I could meet would be here at the track. Before I could even dream up an answer, she went on: "He's right, you know?"

"About what?"

"This terribly dangerous world we live in. He couldn't convince Kellsey to retire. To quit. You know the Irish meaning of Kellsey?"

"No."

"Brave. Coulda been her middle name. It went way beyond the money. Addicted to the adrenaline rush, the fans, the spotlight, the photo in the winner's circle. She has to ride. And every time she had an accident—every broken bone—it didn't stop her. Oh yeah, she's strong. Jockeys are strong. Probably as fit as any athletes."

She rolled up the sleeve on her right arm, and I couldn't help staring at the dollar sign tattoo as she bulked up her bicep.

"Go ahead, touch it." She kept her arm raised and rolled her clenched fist. She tapped it with her index finger. "Go on."

So I did. I reached over and tapped her bicep. "Hard as a rock."

"Yeah, I guess it is. How 'bout yours?"

"Are you just talking, or do you really want to see my arm?"

That was the first time I stumped her. "If I showed it to you," I said, "you would be the only person here that would know how strong I am. Maybe not as strong as you—I bet I'm spotting you about ten years. What are you, about thirty-five? But for a woman my age who has continued self-defense classes and training, let's say I'm pretty fit. Those were required for me to go to work for Max. Along with being certified with a variety of firearms."

"Hun. You shore don't look forty-five. You're pretty game. I like you. Now, Hun, I'm not lobbying for any favors or anything. Trying to be nice. Some people say I'm too nice. Oh, but I can be tough when I have to be. Gotta be tough around here." Then she got real serious. "You'll see. It'll either make you tough or you'll wish you had stayed—where was it? Back at the bank?"

I wondered how she would know I had worked in banking. What would she say if she knew I was a former IRS agent?

Finally, she laughed. "Hun, you'll be good for this place. You ever throw darts? Shoot pool? What do you do for fun, anyway?"

Fun? Who had time for fun? All I did was work. When I didn't answer her question, she went on.

"Whatcha doing tomorrow night? Wanna grab dinner?"

For the first time, she paused until I had to respond. "I can only get away on Mondays or Tuesdays when there's no racing."

"Okay, Monday it is…You like Chinese? Mexican? I'll get takeout. You come to my place. We can…" She pointed up to the cameras. "We can talk there."

I started to answer, but she put her finger up to her lips. "Shhhhh. This place is bugged, you know." She laughed. "Course you do."

Chapter 5

"Lucky, this could be huge." He looked up at me every time I checked the ticket, as if I were getting him a treat out of my pocket.

I was the only exercise rider for BigOilRig; that's why I knew he was ready for a big race. He got his name because he was big and powerful. He was classified as a dark bay; his coat was almost black.

I walked up to his stall and watched him. He acted as though he knew he was entered in a race today. As he looked at the horses in the barn, he flared his nostrils, sucked in the fresh air. About one o'clock Pepito and I started getting BigOilRig ready. Pepito was one of the best grooms we'd ever had.

Buster said, "Walk him over easy. Don't let him get agitated. Get him saddled, and I'll meet you in the paddock."

We left the barn as soon as the third race was official. Pepito carried the bucket, towel, and sponge, and he backed BigOilRig in the number eight saddling area. Javier, our jockey, came up wearing the owner's blue silks with an orange goalpost on the front and back. He was from Denver and a big Broncos fan.

"Hey, Javier. We really need him to get in the money. Go for the wire, but first, second, third, or fourth would be great."

Javier said, "Si, amigo. Uno, dos, tres, o cuatro."

Buster got there and checked the saddle. He said to Javier, "Keep him close to the front. He's better to be forward almost on the lead."

"Riders up!"

Buster gave Javier a leg up, and he got in line to go out on the track. As we followed the horses through the tunnel, the track bugler sounded the call to post. A seven-furlong race starts in a chute in the far back corner. Buster always stood at the rail next to the winner's circle—his lucky spot. With my having had almost no lunch, and the uneasiness of the accident this morning, my nerves were shot.

When I saw Dos's horses in the post parade, I regretted using his numbers. I looked at the tote board. BigOilRig was still 8-1. The odds on two of Dos's horses were going up. And the favorite's odds were going down. Immediately, I wished I hadn't made my $360 bet. What was I thinking?

My stomach still ramped up to a self-inflicted level of excitement. I love that feeling, and I told myself it was only a horse race. I think excitement and disappointment take turns.

My heart started to beat a little faster. That was why I was in this game. The thrill—and let's be honest, the money—was how we kept score. That was how we measured success.

The announcer came over the loudspeaker.

"They're at the post. Number 1, Old Boundaries, the favorite at 3-1, is in. 2 is a long shot, Thunder Trumpet. Number 6 Foolish Answer, is 99-1 on the big board, loads next. And 7, MoneyTime, is in. 3 is Lost Asset; another long shot loads easy beside the favorite, number 4, Dear Friends. At 8-1, number 8, BigOilRig, walks right in. Next to him is a favorite number 9, Defend and Honor; Majestic Place is number 5 at 3-1 and loads easy, and last in is number 10, the long shot Music Director; they're all in. The bell went off.

"And they're off in the seven-furlong 'Don't Mess with Texas' Allowance. Foolish Answer broke away from the starting gate with the quickest beginning and heads to the front. Lost Asset is right with him in second. Then it's Music Director on the inside. So far it's just these three. Two lengths back BigOilRig, who got bumped out of the gate, is fourth, followed by Old Boundaries, then Thunder Trumpet. Dear Friends and Majestic Place are side by side. Ninth is Defend and Honor, and trailing the field is a long shot, MoneyTime.

"It's still Foolish Answer with the lead, holding off Music Director, now second, as they race down the backstretch. BigOilRig and Lost Asset are side by side, now two lengths off the lead, as they enter the far turn.

"Opening quarter went in twenty-three seconds flat. Dear Friends, a 2-1 favorite, has moved up from seventh to fourth, challenging BigOilRig for third. Old Boundaries, one of the favorites, is losing steam; he's dropped to fifth, now sixth."

I said, "Come on, 8, come on!"

BigOilRig was holding his own. I had the top three on my ticket.

"Next is Thunder Trumpet, and MoneyTime, passing Majestic Place, who is now two lengths behind the rest of the field.

"Foolish Answer is hugging the rail and taking a solid lead. Lost Asset is holding second, while Dear Friends and BigOilRig are now side by side. MoneyTime has gone from trailing the field into the middle of the pack at fifth.

"At the top of the stretch, it's still two long shots who won't quit. MoneyTime is putting pressure on BigOilRig in the blue silks. At the quarter pole, it's Thunder Trumpet gaining ground on the top four. Looks like he's going to catch the other favorite, Dear Friends, and take over that fourth spot."

I kept saying, "Come on, 8!"

I said it so loudly Buster picked up my chant.

"Come on, 8!"

When they got to the stretch, I really felt as if my decisions were validated. I was watching a great performance. Usually in this scenario, the horses with the higher odds would falter and a horse like BigOilRig would pull ahead. At the eighth pole, the only change in the field was MoneyTime. He had come from dead last and was gaining ground.

All I could do was slap my *Daily Racing Form* on the rail and holler, "Come on, BigOilRig!"

"Foolish Answer is neck and neck with Lost Asset. They've got a strong lead on the rest of the field. BigOilRig, Dear Friends, and MoneyTime, the 60-1 long shot, are battling it out for third and fourth.

"Dear Friends has thrown his jockey—as MoneyTime goes by him."

It looked like a replay of this morning. Dear Friends was another favorite. The jockey was up and walking…All the attention from the crowd was back on the horses, who were almost to the finish line.

"At the wire, it will be a long shot, Foolish Answer, who led wire to wire in this one, pressured all race by another long shot, Lost Asset, who was just a neck behind. It's a battle for third between MoneyTime and BigOilRig."

"8, 8, 8," I must have said a dozen times as they crossed the wire. I knew 8 was fourth. On the big screen, the camera angle was perfect. I could see that BigOilRig was on the outside, holding his own. He was a solid fourth-place finisher.

I was ecstatic for BigOilRig's performance. He had held his own with the top two and was driving, getting closer to them at the wire. I figured I had a winning ticket. And in a split second, I knew Dos's tickets were no good.

"Looks like the long shots ruled the field as the favorites didn't perform. Number 1, the top favorite, Old Boundaries, finished last behind the rest of the field, and Dear Friends did not finish. Ladies and gentlemen, hold all tickets until the results are official."

Buster looked over. "Maybe fourth. We got beat by three long shots. Those first two ran the best race they will ever run. And we had to face them both today."

By now the horse ambulance and the EMS ambulance were parked beside Dear Friends. His jockey was walking okay, but as a precaution he had to ride back in the ambulance.

The crowd signaled the results of the photo at the same time as the announcer said, "Here are the results of the photo: third is...number 7, MoneyTime. Number 8, BigOilRig, is fourth, followed by number 2, Thunder Trumpet, fifth. Final order of finish: 6-3-7-8."

"Holy shit." That's all I could say, repeatedly.

"What's the matter?" Buster asked.

I wanted to smile, and I wanted to laugh, but I had to contain myself. I kept glancing at the tote board. I heard the crowd. It was all *oohs* and *ahhs*, grunts, groans, cuss words, people tearing up and throwing tickets in the air.

"Can you believe that photo?" I managed to say. "Wasn't it great that 8 got fourth?"

Buster looked at me and then stared back at the tote board.

"Yeah, I guess it was. All those long shots beat us."

"They sure did."

I overheard a guy say to his gal, "Only a dumbass or the luckiest guy in the world would have that superfecta ticket."

I caught a glimpse of the TV screen: $1 superfecta—$110,264.

I would never forget that number.

I stuck my right hand in my shirt pocket to be sure my ticket was still there. Yup. I shook my head. Closed my eyes, and $110,264 was all I could see.

Javier brought BigOilRig back, and we washed his face. Javier took off the saddle and got weighed in. I was more excited than the people in the winner's circle. My heart was beating so fast I could feel the artery pulsating in my neck.

I went over to BigOilRig and put my hands all over his face. Javier said, "He had some more left in the tank; I thought those first two would quit, but they didn't. At least we beat all the favorites. Amigo, got you a fourth!"

I reached up and put my hand on BigOilRig's neck. He was amazing. To finish fourth in a photo. I was happier than if he had finished first and won. The difference would have been a ticket worth a lot less than $110,264.

You know that old saying "Money burns a hole in your pocket"? Well, that ticket had my shirt pocket so hot that I was worried I would have third-degree burns on my chest. I almost wore the ink off, taking it out to be sure it had the right numbers.

I finally showed it to Buster. "Have you ever seen anything like this?"

He studied it for a second. "How much is it?"

"It's $110,000."

He raised his eyebrows. "No, I never saw a ticket worth that much."

We went to the barn, and Pepito brought BigOilRig back from the spit box and walked him around the shedrow to cool him down. BigOilRig stopped every time by his stall and drank from his bucket. After Pepito gave him a bath, I took him out into the paddock to graze under the big oak tree. I removed his halter and rubbed his ears. He was content, finding pieces of alfalfa on the ground.

He raised his head up, and I looked straight at his deep, dark brown eye. His ears were alert as I said, "BigOilRig, this is what I meant this morning. I'll take care of you. You have a future beyond that wall. Free from training, racing, and living in a stall. Someday you'll go be a horse, free from this, before you go home. You can bet on that."

Chapter 6

The crowd roared as the "Race Official" sign went up.

"Miss Ricksland, come here," the chief steward called to me. We looked out the window at the tote board with the payouts. Win paid $186 for first. Place paid $83. Show paid $62. That 8 came in fourth. The $2 superfecta was $220,528.

We moved to his computer. He said, "Look at this replay. Just like that horse from Barn7 this morning, one of the favorites, Dear Friends, almost went down, and threw his jock. The other favorites finished up the track except 8, BigOilRig. The long shots are out in front and aren't gonna get caught."

The bell went off, indicating there was one live $1 superfecta ticket, 6-3-7-8, worth $110,264. They switched to the security cameras showing the ticket windows and zoomed in. Right there a guy was checking the numbers on his tickets and looked up from under his cowboy hat.

"Amos?"

I don't know if it was the tone of my voice or that I knew his name, but the stewards all looked at me.

There he was, nonchalantly sliding money through the window. I turned up the volume and listened. He was getting three tickets. I went to the computer tracking ticket sales. He'd bought two $2 superfecta tickets without 8.

The chief steward said to me, "Go question Dear Friends' jockey."

Once I was at the jocks' room, I handed the security officer a page out of the day's program with Dear Friends' jockey's name circled. "I need to see this jockey."

He looked at my badge. "Yes, ma'am." Then he opened the door and hollered the jockey's name. Dear Friends' jockey came out; his face was still a little dirty. His eyes were serious, but he smiled under a faint mustache.

Security said, "This is Miss Ricksland, NESPA operations—use this office."

I wished he hadn't said it. Anyone with authority around here was an outsider, but add NESPA, and no one breaks the code of silence.

Once we were seated around a small table, I asked, "How are you doing right now?"

"Good. Dr. Winkley cleared me to ride in the sixth race."

"What happened to Dear Friends in the fourth race?" I asked.

"We were ready to make our move, and he quit running."

"Why?"

"Don't know."

I'd questioned a lot of people, but this guy was pretty good at nondisclosure. I couldn't ask him if he'd held his horse back. Upstairs, I told the chief steward, "He didn't know why his horse quit. Even if he held his horse back, we can't prove it."

He said, "When Stamples found out Amos Moon had the big ticket, he called right in. He said the owner of the horse that didn't finish might file a protest and contest the outcome of the race. He put a hold on paying out the money on that superfecta ticket in the fourth race."

I pressed my lips together, imagining the response from Amos.

"We can't do that. The race is official." It was obvious to me, but I added, "Legally we have to pay out the winnings to the person who made the bet, who has the ticket."

"He didn't say we weren't going to pay it out. I'm telling you Stamples put a hold on paying out the money on that superfecta ticket in the fourth race. That's all."

Chapter 7

There was a big buzz around the track about how much the payouts were for the fourth race. A $2 win ticket on Foolish Answer paid $186. The exacta and trifecta were all huge.

The last race went off at 5:20, and I had to cash my ticket before the windows closed at 6:00. I wanted to take off running over to the grandstand. Lucky and GunShy kept up. Images of SkyMan falling flashed through my mind.

I tensed up when I spotted a guy wearing a Hawaiian shirt like Dos, but it wasn't him. I didn't need to deal with him—not now. Not at the window, cashing my ticket.

Brenda stared at me as I approached the window. She halfway smiled. "We knew it was you. One of the biggest tickets ever."

I nodded and slid the ticket in the window. She inserted it, and the light flashed in the machine. Handing it back, she said, "It's good, but the IRS, you know—get over to the casino IRS office before six o'clock."

"Thanks." I held the ticket up in my right hand, kind of tipping the brim of my hat. I saw the damnedest smile on my face in the reflection in the glass.

I'd been to the IRS window at the casino dozens of times over the years. By the way the guy at the computer looked at Lucky and GunShy, I knew it was going to be confrontational.

"Dogs need to wait outside." I gave him a look and put the dogs in the hall. He put my ticket in the machine and looked up as if I were a bank robber. "Just a minute." He turned and started to walk away.

"Where are you going? With my ticket?"

"I have to get it approved."

"Just let me hold it, and can I go with you?"

He looked down at my dirty boots and dragged his eyes up my jeans, still muddy from this morning.

"Come on." He handed me the ticket and pointed to an office farther in the back, like at a car dealership—the one where all the secrets are kept and only a bona fide offer can be accepted. "The steward's office called. The owner of the horse that didn't finish in the fourth race has made an inquiry. I've been told to give you a voucher for $90,000. We'll withhold $20,264 for the IRS—1099 taxes."

My stomach dropped. "What inquiry?" I demanded. "From the horse's owners? They can't do that. There wasn't an objection from their jockey."

"That's right. But NESPA and the stewards are investigating that accident this morning with the horse in Barn7. Funny, they say you were in on that deal too, and now you got a big ticket with a horse in Barn7."

There was a challenge in his eyes I didn't like.

"In on what deal?" I said, in a pretty loud voice. "What do you mean?"

"They say horses are slowing down and unable to finish a race or gallop around the track without stumbling and throwing their riders. They don't want any bad PR, so you'll get your money. It's a formality." He pointed at the clock, which read 5:57. "We close at 6:00. Either you can take the voucher now, or I'll put it in our safe and you can come get it later."

He put the voucher in an envelope and held it out to me.

Stamples had to be behind this. That kind of man always wins, one way or another. I grabbed it. "Thank y'all."

Outside the office, Lucky looked up. Still in disbelief, I asked him, "Did I just get screwed? Instead of giving me the highest high from the biggest ticket ever, they asked if I was 'in on that deal.' Well, bullshit. I did get screwed."

It was a long, slow walk back to Barn7, and I was totally numb. They'd challenged my integrity. When I saw NoCashRefund, reality set in. It all came back about SkyMan.

Buster was camped out in his office, waiting to meet the vet. The thrill of having that super ticket and winning that much money drifted toward the horizon, which was trying to absorb the soft, setting sun. I watched it sink and leaned against the wall, still trying to get my bearings.

I wondered if Dos was coming back by the barn to get his two losing tickets and $120. He might try and shake me down for three-fourths of the money. He had given me three of the four horses. He should have listened when I told him to put 8 in.

I was thinking about the guy at the IRS office. I remembered back at Hialeah, when Daddy had won a big ticket and I'd been with him. That guy had been all smiles and had paid him his money. He'd known Daddy would be back the next day and lose it all. I had to close my eyes to fight that picture of Daddy's dreams, his excuses, and the sound of him cursing everyone and everything when his horse hadn't won.

I wasn't like that. I walked over to BigOilRig and rubbed his ears. "Thank you." I was talking to myself. I was talking to him. "BigOilRig, thanks for doing your job today."

For a moment after the race, I knew how guys down in Houston—like Stamples—feel when an oil well comes in. And this was how it felt when it didn't. At least I'd gotten my money honest. Not like him. He'd stolen it off the blood, sweat, and tears of the jockeys and horses he didn't protect. I made sure BigOilRig had enough water for the night and gave him some extra alfalfa. I whispered to him, once again, "Thanks."

Chapter 8

What a crazy day. It was 6:30 when I went back to Barn7. I went right up to Buster's office. He sat behind his desk, and I looked at the cabinets and shelves, taking inventory.

"Let's get off to a better start," I suggested. "No matter how much some trainers around here don't like all the NESPA rules and regulations, they are in place. I'm not running a popularity contest; I have a job to do. All I ask is for the trainers to do the right thing, abide by the rules, be honest, and cooperate. It's our job to make this track as safe as possible—for horses and jockeys. And you of all people…" There were ten or twelve win photos of his daughter on the shelf—and the trophies with her name engraved on them. I pointed to a photo and said, "That's Kellsey, sitting on the pony wearing a cowboy hat?"

"It's a long way from the Wise County Fair to the winner's circle."

"What's it like having your daughter be a jockey?"

"Dangerous, scary, and exciting. That's all she ever wanted to be. Guess it's in her blood!"

He laughed a little.

"Must be in everyone's blood around here." I made my tone a bit firmer. "Tell me about this SkyMan."

The mood shifted. "He started Saturday."

37

"I found out he's registered with NESPA, but HorseShoeDowns HR doesn't have his papers."

Buster looked at a file cabinet, then out the small window. "Sometimes Charlane helps out with paperwork, but she's off and on; he was filling in for her."

"Doesn't matter. This is a violation of NESPA rules. Every rider has to be registered in advance before they even go into a barn, much less ride a horse. Too much liability, and now he's in the hospital. Go over to HR first thing tomorrow and explain this to them."

Buster leaned forward and said, "Okay, I got the message. How is he?"

"Couple of cracked ribs and a broken collarbone. After he gets out of the hospital, he'll have several weeks of therapy and rehab on his shoulder and neck. He's a lucky guy."

I made some notes on my iPad, then asked, "How's the horse?"

"He went down on his left knee, and there was some swelling from where he hit the ground, so we put his leg in an ice boot for twenty to thirty minutes a few times. No cuts or anything. He walked okay around the barn, finally ate his hay and drank a lot of water. That's what we want. He's a great horse."

"Did you notice anything unusual around the barn the past few days or this morning?" I asked.

Buster shut the door and took a seat back at his desk. "Nothing unusual. This morning a guy was here talking to Amos."

"You know his name?"

His eyes found the door again. "Dos, or something like that."

"Did he interact with 8, BigOilRig?"

"He thought it was BigOilRig in stall 11, but it was actually NoCashRefund. He walked up to the stall door, and the horse actually tried to bite him."

"That's the same horse that threw SkyMan?"

"Yes."

"Tell me about the fourth race. Number 4, Dear Friends, threw his jockey, and some other horses appeared to slow down. But not your horse, 8. He finished strong, didn't he?"

"Yes, BigOilRig was right there. Those long shots got him. He was fourth."

"Amos Moon had that superfecta ticket, right?"

"Yes, biggest ticket I ever saw. He's a pretty good handicapper and an even better rider."

I handed him my card. "Do you think those other jockeys held their horses back?"

"No, ma'am."

I stood to leave, turned, and said, "I'm going to ask Amos a few questions. If you think of anything, call me."

I walked out, and the barn was quiet. Both those dogs looked up, and one ran to me. Amos said in a calm voice, "Lucky, don't bother her." He looked more sincere than he had this morning, with mud on his face. A little more rugged, but there was a genuine look in his brown eyes. An honest look.

"Oh, he's not bothering me," I said. "Lucky. That's a great name." I reached down and rubbed his ears. He had a beautiful coat for a barn dog.

"Yes," he said as he took off his cowboy hat. "Thanks for going to the hospital with SkyMan this morning. Sorry if you got the wrong impression—I was tore up. Coulda been my horse that fell...Could be me over there at the hospital. That's really bad news about his ribs and collarbone."

"He probably won't have any surgery to deal with. Is there some-place private we can talk? I have a few questions."

He glanced up to the window above the office and down the aisle. "I really can't leave the barn. The only place would be my apartment." He pointed upstairs and said, "Would that be okay?"

I remembered one of Max's interrogation rules: "Try to get inside their office or house; that tells a lot about them." So I went for it.

"Sure." His empathy made me feel safe. I was comfortable around him.

"Give me a minute. I'll take these dogs up, then come on up. Mine is the one on the right."

He whistled one of those catcalls—*sweet sweill*. For some reason, Lucky looked at me when he whistled, as if I were supposed to respond, but he ran up the stairs ahead of the other dog. Amos followed them.

I gave them a minute, then climbed the stairs, and he held the door open. *Sparse* and *clean* were the first two words that came to mind. I stood by a bookcase, studying the photographs and magazines. He had a large collection of books. "You read all these?"

"Most at least once. Not much else for a guy like me to do. I like to read and listen to music…jazz and real country, not that new stuff. You want something to drink?"

I walked over to the refrigerator. "Mind if I help myself?"

I touched two magnets made from shotgun shells that held the Jockey's Safety Award on the door. It was made out to Amos Moon, Barn7. I pointed to the award and raised my eyebrows.

He said, "We have the safest barn anywhere."

Couldn't help myself. "Until today."

He shrugged his shoulders, showing both his hands. They were tan and muscular. Refrigerator was stocked full. Every shelf lined up. I got a bottle of water and twisted off the cap. He watched me from the moment I raised the cold bottle to my lips and took a sip until I set it on the counter. Leaning back against the cabinet, I crossed my arms across my chest.

He pulled out a chair and turned it around backward, sat down, and leaned his arms up on the back of the chair.

"Amos, I'm interested in how you managed to have that super ticket today. Why did you put 8 in your ticket?"

"I'm the only exercise rider who has ridden him since he shipped here a year ago. I knew he was ready to run."

"Where did you get those other five numbers that were on your ticket?"

He looked away and said, "A guy came looking for Charlane. He wanted her to make his bet. She wasn't here, so he asked me to do it."

"That guy's name is Dos, isn't it?"

He seemed surprised I knew Dos's name, but he nodded.

"This morning I said something about you being one of the luckiest bettors, and you said it has nothing to do with luck. What do you mean?"

"When it comes to betting on horses, I believe in skill—not luck. I ride these horses every day; I have knowledge no one else has. So it might appear to be luck. There's no skill in relying on some random system, like letting a computer pick lottery numbers. Luck and skill aren't the same. Over at the casino, those games are all luck."

He pointed at Lucky. "Take him, for example—he's lucky to be alive."

"Why's that?"

"Two years ago he got left behind by a trainer who had to cut and run in the middle of the night. Some of these trainers are like my daddy. He cut and ran and never looked back. How could anyone leave their dog behind? On purpose. A vet had him in the bed of his truck and told me he couldn't take any more stray dogs home.

"'Somebody better take care of him,' he said. 'If he makes it, he'll be lucky.'

"'I got this,' I said immediately. 'What's next?'

"The vet wrote out a list of instructions, gave me a box of medicine, and said, 'Good luck.' Lucky lived in the shower in my bathroom for a week. Every time he threw up, I said, 'Come on, Lucky.' That's been his name ever since.

"SkyMan—he's lucky his accident wasn't worse. They had no choices in those situations. But me betting on a horse—takes a long time to know what I know about horses. Now my daddy...you could say he was unlucky because he had no skill and made bad decisions."

"Did you notice anything unusual around this barn last night or today, before either of the incidents? What about the horses? Anything different?"

"No, everything as usual."

"Anything you can tell me about SkyMan or the jockey on Dear Friends?"

"They're both good riders."

Lucky went to the screen door and barked. Amos pushed his chair back and looked out the screen door. "The storm woke Lucky up about 2:30 this morning. He went straight to the door and barked when the power was off here at the barn."

Buster hollered up, "The track vet has some questions."

Amos looked at me. "Okay if I see what he wants?"

"Sure; I'll catch you later. Okay if I use the restroom up here?"

Amos started out the door and pointed down the hall. I put "2:30" in my notes.

There wasn't even a door to the bathroom. Just a bunch of beads hanging from a rod and tied back with a piece of orange baling twine. It had been a while since I'd been in a man's bathroom. I untied my ponytail, shook my hair loose, and fished around in my purse for my brush.

As I walked down the hall, tying my hair back, I glanced into the bedroom. Now I'm not nosy, but I did have a job to do. I learned a long time ago that clues and evidence are sometimes right in clear sight. Analyzing photos can sometimes help find them. I flipped open my iPad and started taking photos of his apartment.

When I walked down the stairs, Charlane stood by the bulletin board. She looked surprised to see me coming out of Amos's apartment, and she almost laughed. She motioned for me to follow her, and we walked over to the paddock, where horses were grazing. She said, "Lot goin' on, huh? Are you aware Amos could have been set up? If BigOilRig hadda got doped instead of NoCashRefund and finished fifth or worse. And that fifth horse, Thunder Trumpet, or something like that, he's a long shot too—he comes in fourth and…Amos would have had two big superfecta tickets, maybe worth as much as $250,000 each. The other ticket Amos bought…It's good too. About $125,000. They catch him with all three tickets. What's that? You're the numbers lady."

I wondered how she would know any horses got doped or was that just the assumption everyone made? Pretending to count on my fingers, I said, "$625,000."

"Yep. They got some dumbass don't know a gray horse from a dark bay. If 8 gets doped—well, then they got the dopin' *and* race fixin'. What if they find something that could've been planted in Barn7?" She clapped her hands together. "BINGO. Ol' Amos is set up big time."

From the other end of the barn, the vet called, "Miss Ricksland."

I held up one finger. "Yes, sir. One minute."

Charlane's eyes locked on mine. She squeezed my elbow, pulling me closer. "Hun, listen to me; what I'm gonna tell you is between you and me. You know the track tip line? Crime-stoppers deal. It's pretty well-known Amos has called it a lot. He ain't made any friends doin' that. He's got the track to suspend some bad characters, and there's a bunch of trainers and even some vets here that would be glad if this got Amos ran off. Somebody done set Amos up."

I'd questioned embezzlers, bank frauds, tax evaders, all kinds of liars and thieves. I'd learned how to spot the liars, and unless I'd made a mistake somewhere along the way, Charlane wasn't one of them.

I went to join Amos and Buster with the vet. Amos looked at me as though he wondered what I'd been doing upstairs for so long. I forced a smile. If Charlane was right, I had to figure this out. If they'd set him up this easy on a horse race, what else would they do if he was still in their way? And I didn't even know who "they" were.

I'd worked with the track veterinarian almost daily since I'd been there. He'd been at this track for over a dozen years and was one of the biggest proponents of NESPA. He had on a green HorseShoeDowns ball cap. A day-old stubble of gray beard graced his tan, weather-beaten face.

"We're waiting on lab results from the samples we took this morning. Protocol is for me to retake some samples on the 8 horse from race four, too."

The vet began drawing blood on BigOilRig. "The horse looks good. He was clean after the race, and I'll bet he's clean now. He's not involved, as far as I can tell."

"Involved in what?" Buster asked.

The vet sighed. "Well, we've got to find out why NoCashRefund slowed down like those horses in the fourth race. What if there is something totally new that can't be detected? Can't be found in urine, saliva, blood, or even a sample of their hair? It could, in some cases, cause a horse to almost stop or slow down. I need to get some more samples on NoCashRefund to verify that's not the case here."

I considered this. "So it looks like someone gave three horses in the race something, and also maybe NoCashRefund, too? If I had to guess, it looks like NoCashRefund got doped instead of BigOilRig."

Amos's face changed. "That could have been BigOilRig during the fourth race. It could have been a really bad accident if it had happened in traffic at racing speed."

Buster's demeanor changed. "Amos, anything I need to know?"

Amos's face darkened. "Looks like somebody got to some horses."

Buster switched it up. Looking at me, he said, "Any suspects?"

In a way, I was glad Max wasn't there; he would have already jumped to conclusions and had the handcuffs out. "Three names have surfaced."

They looked at me. "This Dos guy," I said. "Does anyone know where to find him?"

Amos said, "Dos Pesos Locos Restaurant in South Fort Worth."

I said, "There's the new guy from New Mexico."

That was kind of an accusation, and Amos jumped in. "Listen, there's not an exercise rider or jockey on this planet who would do anything like that to a horse and climb on the horse and ride. SkyMan wouldn't do that. None of us would."

The vet and Buster both nodded their heads in agreement.

My turn. "The third suspect would have had a financial interest in the outcome of the race. Someone who was either really lucky or had a significant wager at stake."

Again, at the word "Lucky," the dog came over and put his head on my foot. "Someone who had a huge winning ticket, like Amos here."

I studied his eyes, looked for him to flinch or blink. He did neither; he burst out laughing.

"You know what? A guy over at the track said, 'Only the luckiest guy in the world or a dumbass would have had those horses on his ticket.'"

"Amos, I don't think you"—he looked directly at me now, practically leaving the other guys out of the conversation—"would be a dumbass and dope three other horses and NoCashRefund, then let him break down on the track, jeopardize the health and safety of SkyMan, and place a bet on 8, if you were in on this."

The vet nodded, and Buster said, "I agree."

We stood in silence for a moment. Then the vet looked at his watch and said, "Okay, I got other rounds to make. Let's call it a day here and start over tomorrow."

They both scattered. "I didn't say this in front of those guys, but why would anyone set you up? You know, so you would take the rap on the whole deal?"

He didn't say another word, just had a stoic, stern look on his face.

"Come to the office tomorrow at four o'clock," I told him. "To be on the safe side, put that voucher in a safe place. Like hide it in your Bible."

Immediately I wondered if he thought I'd been in his bedroom and seen the Bible on the table. I glanced down. Lucky went over and sat by Amos. They both looked at me. For some reason, I opened the camera on my iPad and said, "I need to take your picture for the report."

CLICK CLICK

Chapter 9

I wrapped my arms around NoCashRefund's neck and pressed him close to me. I didn't know who needed whom the most. Maybe both, I guess. I let go, pushed his mane back over.

"This NoCashRefund's stall?" The voice startled me a little.

"Yes," I said. A middle-aged man in a NESPA jacket stood in the shedrow. He had five or six empty plastic containers on the back of a golf cart.

"Need to get some samples from any stalls he was in. I need his hay, grain, manure, urine-dampened straw, water from his water bucket, and his schedule of medications."

In less than twenty minutes, he had what he needed, and I headed to my apartment. I'd gone up those stairs thousands of times during the highest of highs—and right now, this might have been the lowest of lows. My mind was spinning, my stomach was empty, and I didn't feel like eating. Lucky and GunShy were tired, and both found their spots and went to sleep.

I went over to open the window facing the parking area. Instead of the skyline view of the world beyond the wall, I saw a black SUV sitting with the lights off, engine running.

I lay down, staring at the ceiling. I wondered why Dos hadn't come back. All I could see was SkyMan being hauled away in the ambulance, and the only thing I was guilty of was having that monster voucher in my Bible.

My bet didn't have anything to do with SkyMan's accident. Two unrelated events. The accident had most likely happened because of doping and someone's greed. Like Daddy's obsession with betting. Even if Daddy had won this much money on one race, he would have seen how fast he could try to parlay it into even more money. Right up there with doping horses, I hated people addicted to gambling. I remembered all the times I'd hoped he would win enough money and quit.

I ran my fingers across my name on the voucher as if there were some braille impressions or secret codes embedded in the numbers.

Daddy could only dream about a voucher like this, and here I had one made out to Amos Moon. This proved I was better than Daddy was. But if I hadn't made that bet, I wouldn't be in so much trouble.

I reached down and ran my hand down Lucky's back. He looked up as I said out loud, "Gambling. It must be a family curse."

Sirens wailed and echoed through the open window. I woke up scared and dazed. I was sure the police were coming after me, even after the siren faded into the distance. Everything about yesterday and racing haunted me.

Lucky rolled over in his bed, and I said to him, "I dreamed you chased a black SUV. Are we stuck in the middle of a really bad dream with SkyMan and this Miss Ricksland?"

Her last words: "Why would anyone set you up?"

I wondered the same thing. What if I hadn't switched their stalls, and they'd gotten to BigOilRig instead of NoCashRefund? BigOilRig finishes up the track and doesn't come in fourth, and their tickets are worth over $250,000 each. And what if they'd disavowed even knowing me? I'd have been stuck holding their tickets worth over $500,000 and my one ticket worth over $100,000.

They'd doped the horses, and I'd been left holding the bag. Talk about victims: The horses. SkyMan. Me.

The only sound beside my boots hitting the steps on the way to the barn was the sound of the horses nickering. They looked at me, and I forgot all the worries I'd had upstairs. There was something special about horses and the huge Texas sky ready to welcome a beautiful sunrise.

The dogs and I headed to the track kitchen. The minute I walked in, all eyes were on me. I ordered my usual bacon, egg, and toast sandwich, got a cup of coffee to go, and left my usual tip in the jar. The lady looked at me as if she was expecting me to fill it up.

I smiled and said, "Good morning," and touched the brim of my cowboy hat. She reluctantly smiled back. Whispers and gossip. I knew they all were talking about me. There weren't any secrets on this side of the track. It was such a competitive world. Not much compassion, especially from a jealous angle when big races were won and big tickets were cashed—like the one I had.

I was getting paranoid about the money. Even Brenda would tell them I never bet $840 on one race. NoCashRefund throwing SkyMan, and Dear Friends throwing the jockey. It had to be the same reason.

As I stepped out onto the street, I looked over my shoulder at the streetlights. I listened for a signal. But the quiet morning let me hear only my conscience, and I almost wished I'd never made that bet. I stopped at the paddock where my quarter horse, Chex was turned out. His ears pricked up when I started to vent about what was going on. He understands me. Thank goodness.

A voice way down deep was saying, "Hey, dumbass, there's no connection between SkyMan's injury and your bet. Just two coincidences."

Yesterday had felt like the longest day of my life. Today might be even longer.

I walked into the barn to find Charlane hard at work. Turning, she said, "'Bout time you got here. Buster begged me to come back. First set's ready to go out. Me and the grooms got all the chores done. You're nowhere. Got your ass in a sling. Takin' Dos's tips? Thought you retired after yesterday. Winning all that money. Ain't you lucky."

She had a way to verbally attack a man.

"SkyMan got banged up pretty bad, substituting for you, I might add," I said. "As a matter of fact, Dos was lookin' for you to make the bet."

"If I got Señor Dos's tip, I'd be the prime suspect, not you."

"No, his tickets paid out zero. It was a big payout because I added BigOilRig to his numbers. Cleared almost $90,000 after IRS."

"Whatcha gonna do with $90,000?"

"There's some big medication inquiry going on. Haven't even put it in the bank yet, but I will."

"You're so proud of winning that bet. Shit like this don't happen by accident."

The word "accident" was like a spike driven into my ear.

"*Hello*. Didn't you hear me?" Charlane practically laughed. "You're the prime suspect. You gotta hire me."

"Hire *you*? What for?"

"How you gonna prove you didn't have nuthin' to do with this? And find out who framed you? You gonna put your life in her hands— Rixie? You need me *now*. More than ever."

Who else at the track could I even count on? I had alienated so many people with the tip line and complaining. Being framed was a helpless feeling—and I was afraid she was right.

Chapter 10

Back at the office, I matched the stewards' database of all infractions with the short list of people involved in this incident so far. The other three trainers had a few minor incidents that were actually normal. One of them had hired and fired more grooms than anyone else. One of the jockeys had repeat violations for drug abuse and suspensions. The other jockeys weren't based at HorseShoeDowns, so their files and records weren't as thorough.

I was used to dealing with people involved with banking and IRS situations. Here, it was a revolving door of horses, trainers, and jockeys shipping in and out all the time. NESPA had built a system for chasing data. They had hired me to figure out who was doing it right and wrong, and I was determined to help make sure NESPA was successful.

First up in the files was Jose Martinez Jr., a.k.a. Dos. In his HR file was his photo, his social security number, and in big letters, the word "SHILL." He probably couldn't get away from gambling, so he'd signed up for a salary and floated around the casino making bets and giving the money back to the house. I called him and set up a meeting that afternoon at his restaurant.

I dug into Buster's files. Other than not registering SkyMan last week, Buster appeared to run a tight ship. His grooms had been with him for quite a while. Especially Pepito, whose family all worked at the track.

Charlane, on the other hand, was a different story. Her HR file was full of transfers between different trainers; she sometimes worked for several at the same time. She left and went to other tracks depending on race meets. It seemed she didn't always leave of her own accord, but later she was back at the same barn.

I found more on her police record than I expected. A few unpaid traffic tickets. An unflattering mug shot. Her fingerprints. A photo of her dollar sign tattoo. She had been on probation for a misdemeanor—possession of a controlled substance for distribution. No jail time but placed on community supervision.

I spent more time than necessary on the HR records of Amos Moon. His previous bosses gave him glowing references, saying he was responsible, reliable, hardworking, and friendly. Everyone mentioned he was a good horseman. He had letters of recommendation from some of the best trainers. He'd been around, but in Fort Worth the longest.

I remembered what some of my friends had said when I'd told them I was moving to Texas. They'd thought I was searching for a cowboy. He sure fit that description.

I googled "Amos Moon." The name came up on only one website—Legacy.com. His name was listed in the "survived by" section. Son—Amos Moon. I searched his father's name, Samuel Moon, on the national police records website. Nothing there.

I added the photos, saved all this to my own private file, and gave it a code name: OMERTA. A word I have always found fascinating—the Mafia code of silence.

I followed the GPS to Dos Pesos Locos Restaurant. It was only about fifteen miles southeast of the track. I couldn't miss it. It looked like a huge Mexican flag from a distance. A unique Mexican restaurant with the green roof, the white porch, and the red banner around the bottom.

"BEST TACOS IN FORT WORTH" was painted on the side of the multicolored food truck parked out front. There were a few cars in the front parking lot.

I had my Glock in my purse and my mace in my blazer pocket. I smelled the aroma the moment I climbed out of my car. I pulled open the screen door, and the place was surprisingly respectable. Besides the blaring mariachi music, I tried to take in everything else—lighted votive candles, the takeout counter, and a soccer match on the big-screen TV.

From the looks I got from the five men at the bar, I guess I looked like a bill collector or a private investigator. A man watched me from the minute I walked in. He had on an apron and was wiping down some tables. He motioned for me to follow him. Reaching out to shake his hand, I said, "I'm Miss Ricksland, from HorseShoeDowns."

"Dos." His right hand was clammy and damp. He kept his left hand in his pocket. "We can talk in my office." He motioned for me to go to the back. There, he sat behind an old green table, and I settled in across from him. "So what's up?"

"Just a few questions. Need your full name."

"Jose Martinez the second. They call me Dos. You know, number two."

I nodded, and he confirmed his phone number and his address. "How long have you lived there?"

With a certain degree of pride, he said, "Over ten years. I was born here fifty years ago. My ancestors have been Texans for over a hundred years."

That explained his perfect English with little accent. "I know you work part time at the casino. I need to know where you got those numbers you gave Amos."

He took a paper towel and blotted his forehead. He moved some papers around. He wouldn't look at me; instead he finished the coffee in a beat-up tin cup. I motioned for his answer.

"Can I speak to you kinda off the record?" he asked.

"Yes."

"Let me give you a hypothetical situation," he said, fiddling with the coffee cup. "What if somebody or somebody's family would be hurt really bad if somebody told the source of certain information? Or. What if somebody would rather not divulge that information today, but he indicated that at some future time he would?" He looked straight at me. "If *you* were that somebody, what would you do?" He mimicked me from before, motioning for my answer.

I'd interrogated Ponzi schemers, bank embezzlers, but none of them were as cool as this guy. All I'd get was a promise to "maybe" perform with the info we needed, but I couldn't force the issue—he'd clam up tighter than a prison lock or disappear completely.

"I would assist with that very important information at a future time," I told him. "And I would be very concerned that the longer I sat on that information, the more horses and jockeys could die or be seriously hurt. Do you concur?"

"Concur?"

"Agree?"

"Yes. Agree. I will help you."

It was a relief to hear him say it, but I didn't want him to know that.

"When do you work at the casino?" I asked.

"When it's slow here, I go over there for a coupla hours."

There were pictures of children all over his office.

"This your family?" I asked, picking up one of the frames.

"Yes, ma'am." He proceeded to give me names, ages.

"Dos, do you mind if I take some photos?" He looked puzzled for a second but nodded. The best one was of him in front of the bar with the collection of the dozens of different tequila bottles behind him.

I handed him my card. "Call me if you think of anything else."

"Come back on any Monday for margaritas or tequila taco Tuesdays."

I just nodded.

Outside, I called Max. "What do you think?" he asked. "Is he the guy?"

"No, he's just an opportunist. Where he got his numbers is the link." I paused. "When are you going to question those guys involved in the fourth race?"

"I already did. Nothing there. I'll meet you back at the office."

It wasn't five minutes and my phone rang. "Change of plans," he said. "I have to go to a meeting with Stamples and the stewards."

"You need me?"

"No. Meet me there when I get done."

He sounded stressed. I thought of what he'd once said about his guys at the police department. They could be 100 percent right, and by the time the mayor and the press got through with the situation, all bets were off.

Sure enough, after his meeting, Max burst through the office door. "I have always respected authority, but this isn't a racetrack anymore," he said, tossing a folder onto the desk. "It's just one cog in a big wheel spinning at the whim of the casino corporation. We got a problem. Stamples wanted the stewards to come down heavy on Amos."

Max shook his head, and I could tell he was analyzing what had happened down the hall. He said, "Right now, I don't know what the motivation is behind them wanting to make him confess to anything and make him the scapegoat. I talked them out of that; he's a good man. Honest. Hardworking. Has cowboy values. They finally agreed to let me handle it. He just needs to disappear. I know a ranch west of Fort Worth we can send him to for a while."

"Disappear?" The idea surprised me. "Did you say disappear?"

"We need him out of here so we can figure out what's really going on. I'll have to do some fast arranging. Isn't he due here at four o'clock?"

Max picked up his water and sat across from me. "Here's how this needs to happen. Let's start off smooth and easy. Let him talk about himself, whatever he wants to talk about. The dogs, maybe. Have him meet us at the Hunter office tonight. I'll tell Amos I met with the track owners, we're putting together a plan, and we need to go over it off site. We'll go from there."

One word stayed with me.

Disappear.

Chapter 11

In spite of everything, my plan for the day was to work. I rode the usual schedule, checked on BigOilRig and NoCashRefund every hour, and had a meeting scheduled at the NESPA office. My mind was split between two things: being questioned again and seeing Miss Ricksland. I preferred the latter to the former.

I'd heard a lot of horror stories about the stewards' office. They had to deal with false accusations, trainers' lying, and veterinarians' testimony so technical it was clearly meant to cover up for other vets and themselves. There were times before NESPA that security, stewards, and the track could act on a vendetta or a grudge. They could make illogical decisions and ruin a career on a thread of evidence. They let appeals drag out. They didn't have to be accountable to anyone. So Washington set up NESPA to resolve most of these transgressions and create a level playing field. NESPA was the check and balance we'd needed for a long time.

As much as I hated to admit it, the entire investigation revolved around me. I'd interacted with SkyMan, Dos, Buster, Pepito, two of the horses in question, and even Brenda, who'd sold me my ticket— they might even think she was an accomplice.

The day before, my friends had been elated I had the big ticket, but now they were distant. I could tell by their eyes that they were skeptical, as though they didn't know if it was legit.

Buster said, "I got cornered by Dear Friends' trainer. His owner is planning to file a complaint against me *and* you. I just spent two hours at HR. I had to beg forgiveness because SkyMan's papers weren't turned in. They thought I was hiding something."

"You don't have to hide anything," I assured him. "Neither do I. You just got an HR violation. I'm the one with the target on my back. I'm the one going to the NESPA office at four o'clock."

He shook his head. "Good luck over there."

Something very serious had happened for nothing to show up in the horses' tests. Buster and the other trainers were worried about themselves, not SkyMan and me. We were just small fish in a big pond. Dispensable.

Several times when Charlane passed by, I got the "$90,000" look and she smiled, which was equally sarcastic and seductive at the same time. She was the kind of woman who could simultaneously be happy for you and sad for herself.

She sidled up at one point and said, "Worked my way 'round the track to find out what happened to the horses. Nobody knows anything. Major cover-up, or an outside job. Everybody knows you're going over there at four o'clock. If you'd quit proving what a good bettor you are, you wouldn't get in a shitty mess like this."

She was right, as much as I hated to admit it. I spent some extra time grooming BigOilRig and NoCashRefund. Horses were the great equalizer. Then I brushed the dogs, especially Lucky. At 3:15, I scraped the dirt off the bottom of my boots and went up to the apartment to put on my cleanest shirt.

I was glad Max was involved in this. Ever since he got here, he'd had an eye on the safety measures I was trying to put into place. We'd communicated almost weekly, and even though I barely knew him, I had a hunch he was on my side.

NESPA had several offices on the top floor. I stopped for a moment at the door. The sign said "No admittance without proper ID." Even GunShy and Lucky didn't want to go inside.

Breathe deep, I told myself. With "bronc rider" on my resume, I could surely survive a few questions. Especially when they were asked by a woman like Miss Ricksland.

I was about to step over the threshold, from the racing world to the official, legal, ethical, moral, judge-jury-and-executioner world. Just as I reached for the handle, the door swung open.

"Hi, Mr. Hunter," I said.

He shook my hand. "Howdy. You've met Miss Ricksland?"

"Yes, sure did."

The best thing I had seen in two days sat right there at the desk. At first she stared at her computer screen. Then she looked up.

I smiled, tipped my hat, and took it off. "Afternoon."

When she shook my hand, hers was as soft as I'd imagined it would be. Our eyes met, and she almost smiled, but in a professional way. She looked away only when Lucky and GunShy ran behind her desk. Lucky went right to her, and she lowered her hand for him to smell it.

"We don't get too many dogs visiting us, do we, Max?"

He pointed at the gray-and-black dog. "He's the one they call Lucky, right?"

"Yes, sir."

Lucky went right up to Mr. Hunter, who said, "He has the run of the track. He can get into places even I don't have security clearance for." He laughed. "He's famous. Even in the short time I've been here, I heard about him. What breed is he?"

"Mixture of Australian shepherd and blue heeler."

Miss Ricksland said, "Can I get you something to drink?"

She could ask more questions with her eyes than a man like me had answers for. "Just water."

This wasn't the way I'd thought it was going to be. They were actually being pretty nice. Maybe I'd answer a few questions, get back to work, go to the bank, and go see SkyMan.

Mr. Hunter said, "First, you need to go see the stewards. They're right down the hall."

First?

The stewards' office was intimidating, overdecorated with photos of the famous and not-so-famous people who had to come in begging and pleading for their jobs, or worse yet, lying to protect themselves. They didn't use "exonerated" very often. It was usually guilty until proven innocent. There was a big mirror on the end wall—probably two-way glass so they could record meetings.

Three men sat behind a big table. The man in the middle was the chief steward. "No need to sit down, Mr. Moon. This won't take long. Just a few questions."

The first question caught me off guard. "What did you tell Javier, 8's jockey, before race 4?"

"Just take him to the wire."

"Anything else?" he asked.

"Try to get him in the top four."

"Did you specifically ask or tell him to get 8 to finish fourth?"

"No, sir."

"Ask him to come in."

They opened the door and Javier came in. He acted as if he didn't know what to do. Usually, they would get a jockey on the phone and ask them a few questions.

"Have a seat," the chief steward told him. "We have only one question for you. Did Amos Moon, the exercise rider for BigOilRig and assistant trainer for Buster O'Bryan in Barn7, tell you to be sure

8, BigOilRig, finished fourth in Race 4? Not first, second, or third, but to finish fourth."

"No." He gave me an apologetic look. "He said a top-four finish would be good."

"What did you say?"

He smiled. "I told him, 'Si, amigo—one, two, three, or four. Uno, dos, tres, o cuatro.'"

"Okay, thank you."

The chief steward pointed to the door. Javier jumped up and bolted.

"We're having trouble putting all the pieces together on this," the chief steward said. "Why were you the only person with 8 on a super ticket?"

"I ride BigOilRig every day. I knew he was going to finish strong."

"If you and Javier are in collusion to be sure 8 finished fourth and not first, second, or third, that's a serious violation."

I wanted to say that was the stupidest thing I'd ever heard.

"I didn't do anything. Sir, if I was going to fix the fourth race, I could have just scratched 8, and then all three tickets would have been good. Because here's why—number 2, Thunder Trumpet, finished fifth, so if 8 was scratched, all those tickets are good. Maybe you should find out about those other favorites—why did they all finish up the track?"

Broke the first rule. Not my place to ask questions.

He glared at me. "Yes, and we will find out."

He waved at the door again, and I got my ass outta there.

Outside, I leaned against the wall in the hallway. Holy shit. They were playin' for keeps up here.

Down the hall, she was waiting for me.

"We call this the War Room," she said, after indicating I should join her. "Max is a veteran and a history buff—mostly about the Second World War and Vietnam."

It was a room behind the conference room. The walls were covered with charts and graphs. Arrows connecting circles. Code letters and numbers. Cartoon figures. The back wall was a white erasable board with an overhead projector for computer connectivity. The dogs followed us and scoped out the room, smelling everything.

Max said, "Who's the other dog?"

"SkyMan's," I said. "I'm keeping him while he's in the hospital. He's GunShy."

Max said, "He doesn't like guns?"

"No, his name is GunShy. I don't think he likes gunshots, or fireworks, or even thunder."

She unbuttoned her blazer and put her hand on her Glock. Maintaining eye contact, she said, "Well, if he's gun shy, let's not let him see this."

I nodded. "Yes, good idea."

Max pointed out the door. "So how'd it go down the hall?"

I took a seat even though I didn't know if I was supposed to.

"Javier told them we didn't fix the race to get 8 to finish fourth," I said. "I was going to ask them about the rest of my money—my $90,000, which they haven't bothered to pay out yet—but I didn't."

Max pointed to the big mirror on the back wall. "This meeting is being recorded. Stamples has more rules up here than for the rest of the whole place." He used a red remote and clicked the camera on.

I had my back to the door. She and Max sat across the table.

"Here's the real problem we are up against as it pertains to you, Amos," Max said. "I met with the track owner, Mr. Stamples, and the stewards about an hour ago. They didn't appreciate the fact that Miss Ricksland went to see Mr. Drummer at the hospital. None of them are going to check on him. They can't risk implying the track has some responsibility."

I leaned forward. "Did they ask about NoCashRefund?"

"No, they just wanted to be sure the vet made his report and they got those samples from the barn last night." He frowned. "They asked me how the suspect-roundin'-up phase was going. They didn't even ask who was on the list of suspects. I was prepared to update them on the other trainers and the jockeys, but all they wanted to know about was you."

That didn't surprise me as much as it should have.

"They were hell-bent on singling you out," he said, shaking his head. "They know you're a damn good handicapper, and they know how much money you've won over the years. They thought I was pretty good at conducting this type of investigation and I'd better get it solved pretty fast.

"So I brought you here today to tell you we're not going to stop this investigation until we get some answers. Is there anything you'd like to share at this point?"

"I haven't done anything wrong."

"Well, time will tell." Max picked up the red remote and turned off the camera. "That's all for today."

Miss Ricksland slid a folded piece of paper across the table. When I opened it, several questions jumped to mind.

"Okay," I said. "I gotta take these guys back to the barn. Thanks."

Outside, I opened the paper and read it again.

Meet us at 8:30 tonight at the Hunter Group office.

GunShy and Lucky bolted and ran around chasing each other all the way back to Barn7. Once we were there, I took a deep breath. It was quiet except for horses nickering as I checked on them. The dogs were hungry, but I wasn't.

Meet us at 8:30 tonight at the Hunter Group office.

I had no idea what that was about.

Chapter 12

At 8:25, I stood outside and watched for the headlights in the parking lot. The dogs jumped out and ran up to me. He walked with a slight limp, which I hadn't noticed before. He put on his hat, and then when he saw me, he tipped the brim. "Evenin'."

"Good evening. How are you doing?"

"Oh, I'm doin' just great. I thought about stoppin' at the palm reader and getting my fortune told to see what my tarot cards looked like. But here I am." He pretended to look at a watch on his wrist and said, "Right on time."

"Let's go in and see what Max has put together."

He had on a clean shirt, and he hadn't shaved in a couple of days. I wondered how I looked to him. He opened the door to the office and held it for me to go in first.

I brushed by him as he said, "This office looks more—can I say—friendly? Not like the ones at the track?"

"Friendly? Yes, I guess so. We didn't have anything to do with the offices over there, except the War Room is laid out the same."

Max stood by a blank whiteboard. "Rixie, why don't you and Amos sit over there." Once we were seated, he got right down to business. "When NESPA, the National Equine Safety Protection Authority, got started, it didn't take long for them to figure out they didn't have all the expertise they thought they had. So five months ago, in October, they hired the Hunter Group.

"First, Amos, I want to thank you for showing me around when we got here back in October. You gave me a lot of the information I needed. I will never know all the secrets about what goes on at a race-track. Nobody else will either."

Amos nodded, as though in agreement.

"Here's what I've learned from chasing trainers and veterinarians around," Max said. "It's not only about doping horses. That's a big part of the problem. But then…" He raised his index finger as he said, "Rule number one: follow the money." He pointed at me. "She's here because she's a data-driven gal. Been in banking and spent four years at the IRS.

"Amos, somebody has made this look like you're guilty as hell. They don't have to prove you did it. There's enough circumstantial evidence, right now, as they say, to take you downtown."

Amos shifted in his seat, looking uncomfortable for the first time since he'd walked in.

"Only you had access," Max said, "as far as we know, to the horses in Barn7, and only you have a hint of a motive. It looks like you have been set up." He raised his voice a little. "What the hell happened?"

The dogs got startled as Amos shrugged. "You know more than I do. What'd you find out? You've got all the evidence."

"The evidence points to you. Right or wrong, Stamples has us only looking at you. You're the only one with a motive. And downtown, sometimes that's all they need for a conviction."

Max closed his folder, and Amos shook his head. "Conviction of what?"

"Race fixin'." Max paused long enough to see me close my eyes and tap my fingers on the table. "We know you didn't fix race four," he said quickly. "It doesn't matter what we think, though. What matters is the court of public opinion; they only see what they want to see. Even though you have been a strong advocate for safer races and protecting horses, the image will be of you over at the IRS office at the casino, trying to cash that ticket."

"Yeah, what about my money?" Amos asked.

"Everything is on hold."

"It's *illegal* to not pay out that ticket."

"From where Stamples sits, so is fixing a race that pays out 110 grand." Max folded his hands together and rested his chin on his over-sized fists.

"And he's got my money," Amos grumbled.

I jumped in. "Just so you know—we have an uncashed-ticket account. Your money is there. I put it there myself. The voucher is all you need to claim the money, but not until everything settles down."

I could tell Amos's patience was wearing thin. "Go ahead, Max, and tell him the plan."

"Here's what needs to happen," Max said. "You need to get out of here for a couple of months. Just lie low—let Rixie and me keep working on this investigation."

"What if I don't want to do that?"

Max leaned forward. "You don't have a choice. Here's what will happen Monday morning: you and Buster are going to be suspended. You will be restricted from being on the HorseShoeDowns grounds, and Buster's string of horses will all be put on the stewards' list. Essentially he won't be able to train or enter a horse in a race. He'll have to turn these horses over to another trainer."

Amos stood up, fists clenched. "So Buster and I are both thrown out? No one will be overseeing Barn7. Won't that hurt your investigation?"

Maybe to soften the blow, I said, "Max, he's right. We need Buster, and we need to get his suspension waived."

Max glanced at me, giving me the signal. We could almost complete each other's sentences.

"All they know," I said, getting to my feet, "is that you had that winning ticket. We can't prove who did this, and we can't even prove Dos, Charlane, or anyone else is involved."

Amos sat back in his chair.

Max went on, "So here's what we propose. Since SkyMan isn't even supposed to be working here, the track doesn't want to go after him. But if we can prove his horse got doped, he could come back on the track and claim negligence caused his injury. They already have lawyers working on a big settlement."

Amos crossed his arms.

"Here's where you fit in. We don't need any bad press about horses getting doped while we're trying to gather information. We want an arrangement. Where nobody would know—except you and us."

Amos looked at me. "Know what?"

"It looks like you were set up to take the rap from the start," I said. "That's why Dos had you get his tickets for him."

"Let's be honest: your reputation here is tainted." Max had started out explaining; now he was selling. "Some people think you are involved, and a lot of people hope you're not. It doesn't look good. They know you won $110,264."

I was close enough to hear Amos's breathing change. I turned my chair a little to the side and watched him. I was trained to watch an individual's eyes, the lips, even the wrinkles on the person's forehead. He was calm, collected, and confident.

Max looked at him. "I'm convinced you were set up. Everybody knows this track is on notice about any more accidents or horses put down. If they could set you up to have four horses get doped and make it look like you did it, the next time could be for all the marbles. It's my job to protect you from the next accident. Here's what is going to happen. We're gonna send you out to work at TSPAN—Texas State Prison at Noose."

Amos was back on his feet. "Say that again?"

The dogs jumped up and went to the door.

"TSPAN—the men's and women's prison out in Noose, Texas."

"Noose, Texas? Are you kiddin' me? Shit. Y'all treatin' me like a criminal." He glared at us. "It's not the first time someone in my family was accused of being a criminal. I remember the Davie sheriff came and banged on our front door." He knocked on the table.

Knock. Knock. Knock.

"He came to arrest Daddy for cold checks. Daddy wasn't there, and my mother told him to check the Hialeah racetrack. I remember the sheriff had a pistol and said they'd find Daddy and put him in jail with the other criminals until the debt was paid."

I interrupted. "Amos, you're not a criminal. Everyone knows you are an amazing horse guy. But this superfecta ticket has got you in so deep no one can pull you out. Stamples is hell-bent on making an example of you."

His eyes never left mine. "Your plan is to send me to work at a prison?"

Max leaned forward and said, "You need to get out of here for a coupla months. It's a ranch near the prison. They've got rescued horses, a training track and an equine assisted therapy center. The prisoners come there and work. I called the owner, Mr. Applegate, and got it set up for you to help them out."

Amos never blinked. Max walked over and pointed at a spot on a huge map of Texas on the side wall and said, "You ever heard of Fort Wolters?"

Amos shook his head.

"It has an important place in the history of the army training bases in Texas. Noose was an army town back during both world wars. Fort Wolters was an army helicopter pilot training facility. Thousands of helicopter pilots headed to Vietnam trained there. At the end of the war in Vietnam, they converted the army base into a prison, and that's where TSPAN is right now. Texas State Prison at Noose."

He pointed to a dot on the map. "Just north of Mineral Wells on the west side of US Highway 281 is the ten-thousand-acre Applegate Ranch. It stretches all the way to the Brazos River. That's where we've arranged for you to go."

Amos got up and looked at the map. He shook his head.

Max said, "I know this is a lot all at once."

He came back and sat down, and I put my hand on his arm.

"Amos, this is the break we've been waiting for," I said, my voice quiet. "If you didn't make that bet, we'd have nothing. Now, we've got a case where we know some horses have been doped, and we can launch a full-blown investigation. Under the radar. You're not a criminal. You're a hero in my book. You've gotta trust us. It's our job to investigate this now."

Since he was listening, I continued. "We're just as concerned about the safety of the horses and riders as you are," I told him. "We want to get these guys. So as soon as Stamples releases it, you'll get to keep the $90,000 from the superfecta ticket, and we'll give you another…let's say $250 cash per day. Kinda like a retainer."

He shook his head. "You're paying me to take the rap. You're bribing me. Listen, I didn't do anything to any horse. I think I should stay right here in Fort Worth, not Fort Wolters—or whatever it is—until the truth comes out and whoever is dopin' these horses is arrested." He got to his feet. "I still have chores to do, and I need to get back to the barn."

Max had to get the last word in. "You know, we don't have too many options, and you have fewer options than we do. Think about it. We can meet here again tomorrow morning at nine o'clock."

The air was still fresh when Amos and I walked outside. His eyes were as clear as they had been the first time he'd really looked at me. The dogs were pacing, ready to take off, but we weren't. We both looked up at the moon at the same time, and then at each other.

"You okay?" I asked.

He sorta smiled. "I didn't see this coming."

"Well, it did, and it's coming fast. Be ready to leave Monday."

"Monday? Just like that. Ship out?"

"Yes." I hesitated, then handed him my card. He looked at it and then at me, as if he were memorizing my face. "Cell number's on there. Call if you need me. I can come out there this weekend and update you on the investigation."

"I'd like that," he said, and he turned with the dogs toward the truck.

I walked back up the stairs to the office, but the door was locked. Max was going to have to let me back in.

Knock. Knock. Knock.

Immediately I thought about Amos telling us about the sheriff knocking on their door.

Max let me back in and shrugged. "Successful missions are survival and not surrender. NESPA has an almost unlimited budget for this investigation. At the police department, it was money for information from informants. NESPA is so desperate for a solution, they opened up the cash coffers."

It bothered me that I didn't know anything about that.

"Really? This is how it works?" I took a drink of water and set it on the table with a thud. "Money makes it get solved? Just like money caused someone to dope the horses? Is it always about money?"

"Or the illusion of money." Max rubbed his eyes, looking tired. "The great motivator. You wouldn't believe what I've seen people do for money. I can't sit idly by and see an honest man like Amos take a rap and be exposed to the next round. They could set him up again and destroy him. This way, he becomes part of the solution."

Before I could even muster a comment, he continued, "I also can't sit by and let this guy SkyMan not be compensated for his injury. I got it set up for the track to settle with him for a lot of money. Let's keep the faith, keep pushing forward, and find a good solution. It's about SkyMan and all the other riders. It's about the horses. Tomorrow, you convince him how important it is for him to go. Be prepared for him to try and raise the retainer amount. You just need to get the commitment."

I thought about the Cowboy Code on his bulletin board at Barn7: "Do what has to be done."

Max tapped his watch. "Late for dinner again." He made it to the door and turned. "Police department, IRS, banking, horse racing, it's all the same. Different people, different names. We need this guy to leave Monday to buy us some time. Someone knows something, and we're going to find out what."

Chapter 13

Exhausted from two nonstop days, I did the last barn check, and I settled into bed, where I looked up Applegate's Ranch on my phone. It looked as if it was a lot more than a training center and a horse rescue outfit with inmates helping out. They raised a lot of cattle. There was a photo of the governor's wife cutting the ribbon for the women's equine assisted therapy facility.

The next morning, I was at the barn at 4:45. Charlane was in charge. Giving orders to the grooms, until she saw me.

"You look like shit." She pulled me aside. "You're the target for sure. Making an example of you. If you're smart, you'll take some time off."

Her eyes were sincere, but I knew Charlane also wanted me out of the way so that she could ride the best horses.

Buster's truck pulled up. I met him as he walked in. "Hey, Buster, let's walk over to the track kitchen and get a coffee. Charlane and the guys have everything going okay."

Once we passed the end of the barn, he asked, "What's up with you and NESPA and the stewards? They're not looking at shutting me down, are they?"

I motioned for us to stop by a paddock where one of his horses was turned out. "They're not looking at you. I talked them out of you getting suspended."

He looked off into the corner of the paddock.

"They're telling me it's going to be a long investigation," I said. "It could go as deep as vets and grooms, too. Those other trainers whose horses were part of the incident. This could drag out for months. They suggested I take some time off. Since you never got SkyMan signed in as an official rider, they're on the hook for a big settlement check. If this gets blown up, it could affect other trainers or owners who might not send their horses here."

It was sounding good, so I kept going. "I'm taking a big hit here. A lot of people already think I'm involved deeper than I really am. So on the surface, if I take off for a while, let them do their investigating, I'm sort of protecting you."

"So you're leaving?"

"Tomorrow, you need to round up someone else to go out with Charlane."

"Well, this is just great." Buster frowned. "Not only do I have a horse that could have had a horrible injury, I've got to bring on some new rider. I've got to hope they don't fine me or have me help with this guy's medical bills. And you…you're going to just take off?"

"I don't have much choice, do I? Besides, maybe something good will come of this."

Buster didn't say anything else, but his eyes echoed what I was thinking deep in my heart. Was I kidding myself?

Could something good actually come of this?

Chapter 14

I walked into Barn7 at six o'clock carrying a box of doughnuts. It was a trick Max had taught me—a dozen doughnuts could get you in anywhere. Lucky came to me and then took off. Charlane stood there watching.

"Doesn't Amos worry about him?" I asked.

"No. He stays right around here. Him and Buster off to the kitchen." She had on a well-worn vest, frayed around the collar. "We can talk while I work."

"Doughnut?"

Charlane selected a pink frosted one. "What's goin' on? Something big for you to come around here early on Sunday."

"You know we're investigating the accidents."

"Ain't you arrested anyone yet?"

"Where were you last week?" I asked.

"Ridin' for a new trainer. I told you. New trainer showed up. Plus he's cute; gotta look out for me. Hired me away last week. Buster begged me to come back, and here I am." She polished off the doughnut and licked her lips.

Charlane was entertaining, but I had to put her in one of the textbook suspect classification profiles. She was evasive, not answering questions, and misleading by changing the subject.

"Gotta speed this up," she said. "Got more chores to do. Take my name off the list. Amos's name off the list too. He ain't done nothin'."

"Well, do you have any ideas who else we should put on 'the list'?"

"Lotsa people come through these barns. I'd be last to know who did this. Just put in my time, ride my horses, go about my business." She narrowed her eyes. "Before the track hired the Hunter Group, there was a confrontation with a trainer who shipped in from outta state. He had a veterinarian give his horses some banned drugs. And when he got caught, he threatened the stewards and the NESPA employee. The police had to come and physically restrain the guy after he pulled out a gun and threatened to use it. I'm tellin' you—just be careful."

I didn't say anything. She stared at me. "So who do you think did it?"

Right then, her name moved up on the "list" a notch or two.

"We're sorting out the evidence."

She took another doughnut. "Hun, how's your Spanish? One groom quit Saturday. You'll never find him." She raised her eyebrows. "Maybe. He. Did. It."

"He's got a name?"

"Sure, he's got a name. And a nickname. They got one name this barn. New name next barn."

"What do you know about Dos?" I asked.

She pointed toward the casino. "He moonlights at the casino on the weekends. Restaurant may be a front. Guess Amos past posted him on that bet."

"Past posted?"

She rolled her eyes. "Hun, you got a lot to learn. Okay. Dos had his numbers all picked out, and Amos added 8. So Amos added information after Dos made his picks. Good for Amos. He past posted Dos."

"Where does Dos get his tips?" I asked.

"Who knows?" In a low voice, she said, "Hun, you know what's worse than being the son of a billionaire Houston oilman? The son-in-law. You want a history lesson?"

75

"Okay," I said, curious where she was going with this.

"When all Stamples's rich buddies were buying pro sports teams, he spent his wife's money buying this racetrack. He knew nuthin' 'bout a racetrack. So then Amos came along. He started out as a big help with the track surface, safety standards for the riders and horses, and getting the first ambulances. Stamples took credit for all the info Amos gave him. Three years ago, Austin approved Stamples to build the casino, and last year Washington approved him to add the sports book. That was the good part."

She took a deep breath. "You ready for the bad part? He hates all this NESPA stuff. He hates to hear about what's needed now. He hates the letters to congressmen about track safety. He hates the animal safety groups. And he hates hearin' from Amos about makin' him improve the racetrack surface.

"The drainage is terrible. We got accidents all the time. Amos is a voice of one. WD is tired of hearing from and about Amos. But most of all, he hates Amos because of Kellsey. He couldn't stand that she was in love with Amos."

It took me a second to digest all that.

"Well, I'm just sayin' Amos shoulda protected himself. Someone decided to stack the deck and deal him out. The race was set up for there to be a big payout, and Amos would have all the tickets. It was just a fluke Amos had a third ticket, and 8 didn't get doped, and Amos ends up with the only ticket."

I wondered how she knew all that. "How long have you known Amos?"

"Probably too many long days." She winked at me. "And not enough nights."

"What can you tell me about him?"

"Hun." Her eyes blinked a few times, and she looked away. "On the record or off the record?"

I closed my iPad and put it in my oversized purse.

Charlane suddenly lost her cocky arrogance, and a sadness came to her eyes. "We wasn't together long." She paused, looked all around as if she were searching for words. Then her eyes met mine. "I don't get along with anyone."

I wondered if this was the only true thing she had told me so far.

"I demand too much. Expect too much. He's a great guy. It was me. It's always me."

She nervously messed with a halter, buckling and unbuckling it as she said, "We met in Amarillo. Quarter horse ranch. Nothing happened there. Just friends. Ended up at this dump of a track. He'd come over to my trailer. I'd fix him dinner sometimes. I do a mean vegetable soup. He likes my oatmeal-raisin cookies."

She turned away from me. I had to ask, "How similar are they to the ones you bake for horses?"

"Oh, Hun. Can't be divulging my secret recipes to you. Oats and oatmeal—that's all I can tell you…What was I sayin'? Oh yeah, about Amos…I never wanted to be alone. They tell me I'm too controlling. Can you believe that?"

For a second, I didn't know what to believe. It all sounded convincing. Then I remembered something I'd been told back in my earliest days of training: Lies are spread out in a lot of details. The truth is shorter.

Charlane's eyes finally met mine. "You need to see Buster or anyone else around here? I gotta get to work, but I want you to see something."

She took me over to the schedule.

"Look right there. Amos is not riding today. Or tomorrow."

Back at the office, Max said, "I'm going back over to the hospital to tell SkyMan about the details of the settlement they are proposing.

They don't want to confront him, so they want me to get him to sign off on the deal. Why don't you take over? You can handle this."

I was slowly embracing the concept of informants. It seemed it was how a lot of things got put together.

"Max, I'd like to have you arrange for SkyMan to continue working for Buster," I suggested. "Maybe he can hire him to take Amos's place as his assistant trainer and run the barn. We could present it as a way to keep him from holding ill will toward the track, but in truth, he would be our inside man. Our eyes and ears."

He looked down over the top of his glasses. "SkyMan, the informant. Who trained you, anyway?"

"One of the best."

Chapter 15

I borrowed Buster's truck and talked to Lucky on the way over to the meeting at the Hunter Group. I didn't even know why I'd agreed to come back.

"Lucky, you were there," I said. "What would you do if you were faced with two equally unacceptable decisions? If I stayed, either I would get set up again, and the next time they would make sure I was guilty and my career would be over. Or I would get injured so bad my career or my life would be over."

Lucky looked as though neither of those was a good idea.

"The other equally unacceptable decision," I said, bumping over the ruts in the road past the barns, "is to go the safe and protective route. Go to this ranch and leave my career behind. We're up against the system."

After parking the truck, I saw Max in the parking lot. He waved and got into his car. It seemed odd that he'd leave right when we had this meeting. I was tempted to take off right then, but I went in.

Miss Ricksland was there, sorting through a bunch of papers.

"Is the meeting canceled?" I fidgeted at the door, holding my hat. "I saw Max leave."

"He's the point man to arrange financial settlements with the Drummers. He's off to see them at the hospital." Rixie tapped her pen on the table. "How are you feeling about all this? About our offer?"

I took a seat across from her. "At first, I was taking it personally. I felt as if my integrity and reputation were under attack, but I chose to associate myself with Dos, and now I have to suffer the consequences. I came here today with a resolve to think more about SkyMan and less about myself. But I'm not the guilty one here. The system that protects the wrong parts of the equation is the guilty one. We're the victims."

"Yes, and we're"—Miss Ricksland pointed to herself and me—"going to do something about that. That's why we have this plan in place."

"There are considerable risks if I go ahead with your plan," I argued. "I'm gambling on a different level, with different odds. I'm putting my chips on my own line, then betting I can beat the odds and help the other riders and horses. I'm willing to risk my future to help right a wrong." I stared down at the table, thinking about my past years at Buster's barn. That life wasn't something I was ready to give up, but I had to do what was right.

Looking at her, I said, "Most people would just fold their tents, walk away, and let a guy like SkyMan or me take this entire rap, and have no guilty conscience. They'd just be glad it wasn't about them. I don't want to look back someday and admit to myself I could have made a difference and didn't."

Miss Ricksland watched me, but I couldn't read her expression. "We need you to help us," she said. "We can't do this without you."

"Are you positively convinced this is the best plan? I'm giving up a career being an exercise rider. Assistant trainer. Maybe even the dream of being a trainer and an owner someday."

The reality that I might never own BigOilRig was painful, but I had to do the right thing here.

"It's the best plan," she said.

I looked down at the table again. My stomach was upset. I'd had headaches, and multiple parts of my body ached from injuries over the years. I was too old to do this forever. This would give me the chance to do something important for horse racing.

Miss Ricksland tapped her folder. "What else do you need from us to move forward?"

"You said I'll take off for a couple of months. What happens at the end of two months? Am I supposed to be on the retainer until this investigation is finished?"

"Yes."

"I'm willing to put my time into the equation because this is the right thing to do."

If eyes were the windows to the soul, I saw my true self clearly in the mirror on the wall behind her. I saw a man who could not sit idly by and let this treatment of horses and riders continue.

"If you're sure—if me getting out of Fort Worth for a while helps clean up this sport and make the track a safer place, then I'll do it," I told her. "I'll just leave my ego and my—what did Max say?—tainted reputation behind."

The deep realization of what was going down settled in.

"Here's something you don't know," I told her. "I have had this idea to buy BigOilRig or claim him someday. It can't happen right now. But I know what I won't leave behind—Lucky. And Chex, my quarter horse. What about him?"

She leaned forward. "We can arrange to have him shipped out there. I promise you this. I will do my best to make whoever is responsible pay for what they've done to SkyMan and these horses."

I had to wonder if they already had the goods on somebody and my exiting was just a chess move. Maybe they were sacrificing me for a bigger fish? In the mirror, I saw a man with a new mission. I had to let those questions go.

"Let's do it," I said.

I left and went back to the track to go to Cowboy Church.

Chapter 16

Cowboy Church had just gotten started when I walked in, my mind still moving a million miles an hour. I filled out a prayer card—*SkyMan Drummer, who had the accident on Friday*—and put it in the basket by the door.

The preacher was a devoted pastor, bilingual in English and Spanish. He spent every day on the backside, walking through the barns. He was a resident counselor. Before every race he offered prayers with jockeys in the jocks' room.

When we got to the end of the service, the preacher closed as he always did, asking everyone to become a "warrior of prayer." He read the cards and, when he got to mine, said, "We pray for SkyMan Drummer, as well as the doctors and nurses who are treating him. May he have a steady recovery and return to riding. And Lord, today, tomorrow, and every day, protect and watch over these men and women who ride. Amen."

After church, I loaded Lucky and GunShy into the back seat of the pickup to go see SkyMan. At the hospital's reception desk, the lady said, "The sign says no dogs."

I was determined to take both dogs to SkyMan's room. "Yes, ma'am, but these dogs belong to the man who got injured at HorseShoeDowns yesterday. He needs to see them."

Her face softened. "Check with the nurses' station on the second floor."

"Okay, thanks."

The dogs followed me to the elevator. No one questioned me again. We walked right to his room, where GunShy ran right to Martha. He wagged his tail as she picked him up and laid him on the bed.

SkyMan tried to smile, but the neck brace was tight up against his chin. He had one arm wrapped against his chest, and he tried to reach toward GunShy with his other arm but gave up and laid his arm back on the sheet. I could tell from the tension around his mouth that he was trying to hide the pain.

He said, almost in a whisper, "What's going on at the track?"

I settled into a chair by the bed. "They're investigating everything about the race Friday."

"Don't they know I coulda got killed?" he demanded.

"Yes, they just started the investigation." I hesitated. "I have to tell you something. I put 8 in my ticket with those other horses I got the tip on. Rixie and Max, from NESPA, think I got set up. They told me I need to get out of here for a couple of months. So I'm leaving tomorrow."

Just then a nurse came in. She gave GunShy a look and said, "Visiting hours in this room are over."

I was glad she was not giving me a shot.

"One more minute with my friend?" SkyMan asked.

The nurse stepped out, and he said, "Martha, hand me my saddle-bags." He dug around and pulled a silver coin out of a paper envelope. He read it out loud, as much to himself as to me: "O Great Spirit whose voice I hear in the winds, I come to you as one of your many children. I need your strength and your wisdom. Make me strong, not to be superior to my brother, but to be able to fight my greatest enemy: myself."

He handed it to me. "Here, take this with you."

"Thanks," I said, struggling to speak. "This is special. Get well and get out of this hospital."

SkyMan nodded.

I picked up GunShy off the bed and put him on the floor.

We got into the elevator, and I read the message on the coin. The last sentence resonated with me: "…be able to fight my greatest enemy: myself."

I was standing outside Barn7, waiting for my ride to the meeting with Rixie and Max, when I spotted Charlane. She would now be BigOilRig's official rider, and she started right in. "Amos, Amos, Amos…Jockeys get lenient suspensions. Trainers get second chances. What are they doing? Making an example out of you?"

"I don't have too many choices," I said.

In a low tone, she said, "Mr. Hunter was here talking all private with Buster. I overheard him say you was probably leavin'."

"Tomorrow."

She shook her head. "You better watch out. I wouldn't trust anybody, at this point."

An SUV pulled up. Miss Ricksland. She waved out the window.

Charlane gave her the stare-down before saying directly to me, "Be careful." Then to her, "I'm proud of him, and I'm afraid for him. There's a thin line between courage and crazy. Make sure he comes back."

"Don't you worry," Miss Ricksland said. "He's in good hands."

Charlane gave me a half-hearted wave and headed back into the barn.

Back at the Hunter Group office, we went in with the dogs. Rixie was good with them. I could tell she was compassionate, even though chasing bank robbers had given her a tough outward appearance.

Max peered over stacks of papers. "Have a seat."

Once I did, he said, "Mr. Moon. I used to be a sheriff over in a West Texas county. When I left there, I took some of these blank documents with me." He held up some official-looking papers. "Never had much use for them, until now."

He handed me the first page.

"This document, it looks like it's from the Texas Racing Commission—you don't have to read the whole damn thing, but it says you are hereby suspended from any duties as exercise rider or assistant trainer for a period of two months."

He looked up. "I made all this up. It looks official, if I do say so. Give us two months, and then you'll have your life back."

Relief cut through me. If this really was only for two months and not forever, there was still a chance I'd be able to own BigOilRig.

"We could not have ever dreamed up this type of case," Max said. "Then you made that bet. Got it started. Do you know how valuable your having made that bet is?"

"No."

He opened another envelope and fanned a large stack of hundred-dollar bills. I wasn't impressed. I'd been around card tables when guys had large stacks of chips or money.

"A $250-a-day retainer." He held up the money. "Tomorrow morning you need to be back here. Bring everything you'll need, suitcases, and any of your riding equipment. A driver will take you first to the TSPAN men's facility as a decoy stop, then to Applegate's Ranch. Guys work for him on work release. Minimum-security stuff."

He pulled out a cell phone and slid it over to me, along with a page of numbers. "This is a secure phone registered to this office. These numbers are programmed into the phone. You'll see the Dos Pesos Locos number. Call him and set up a meeting for today. Find out who gave him the numbers on the tip and let him know you are leaving."

This felt like some sort of a test, so I just nodded and dialed the number.

"Hey, Dos, it's Amos," I said, and Max nodded. "You got time to meet today? Got some developments concerning Friday at the track, but I can't go over it on the phone."

A long pause, and a lot of noise in the background. "How about now, this morning? Before the lunch rush."

I hung up, and Max nodded. "Rixie, can you take him over there?"

"Sure." She stood up. "Oh. One more thing. No gambling."

"No gambling?"

She started laughing, but I didn't see anything funny. "Yeah, not a good idea for you to do *any* gambling. Sure enough, if you bought a lottery ticket, it would probably be good, and they would think the lottery was fixed. Not even any scratch-offs."

"Lottery tickets are a sucker's game. I don't do that."

"Okay, just saying. It's kinda buried somewhere in the fine print. Nothing personal."

I just stood there, my life and my future tucked away in some of the folders on Max's desk. I kept telling myself to think about SkyMan over in Fort Worth General and all the other riders affected by the people who caused these "accidents."

I pointed to the door, and Max nodded. I had all my important fake papers, my new cell phone, a box full of money, and more concern in my heart than when I'd walked in.

It was a short drive to Dos Pesos Locos. Rixie let Lucky and GunShy and me out, and I wished I had leashes. They followed me in and immediately both growled and ran toward Dos. He was busy but motioned for me to come to the back, and we sat in his office.

He kept wiping his hands on his apron while eyeing the dogs. "Health department sees them in here, I get an eighty score to post on the window."

"What is it with you and dogs?" I asked.

He rolled up the sleeve on his left arm to show the ugliest scar I'd ever seen. It went from his wrist up to his elbow.

"Over a hundred stitches. They tore up so many nerves, I hardly have any feeling. Teeth went right down to the bone."

His hand had atrophied. I remembered he always had his hands in his pockets, and those Hawaiian shirts. Always long sleeves. Suddenly I felt sorry for him. That was a terrible thing to go through.

"Maybe, somewhere, there's a dog that's been attacked by some other dogs and needs to be cared for. In a way, you both could get over the fear of being attacked."

He acted as though he didn't hear me.

I got to the point of the visit. "Okay, well, *we* are in the deepest shit you can imagine."

"What do you mean, *we*?" he asked.

"It's pretty simple. You're the prime suspect."

His mouth dropped open. "Why's that?"

"Because you were there Friday morning with the tip on *all* long shots. Only one problem. They think either you or someone else was in Barn7 and doped NoCashRefund instead of BigOilRig."

He crossed his arms. "NESPA came here. They asked a lot of questions. Quite a few about you."

"They think you do more than run a restaurant and place a few bets—usually on long shots."

"A lot of people bet on long shots."

"They know you gave me those numbers."

Dos got indignant. "It's your word against mine. You can't prove that ticket was for me."

"The camera shows you giving me a slip of paper and $480. Shows you walking over to BigOilRig's stall. Shows you don't know the difference between a gray and a dark bay, almost black horse. Shows if you don't know the difference with all the lights on, you or someone else wouldn't know the difference at night."

He stared me down. "When they came over here, they sure did a lot of talking about the guy from New Mexico. They must think he was in on it."

"Let me show you something." I pulled out the page with the suspension from the Texas Racing Commission.

He scanned down the page. "Looks like they're focusing on you, not me." His whole demeanor changed, as if he was relieved.

"Yeah, they can wait months to try to figure out if a trainer has done something to win a race, but let a guy like me win a few bucks, and they can move pretty fast. They also don't want any bad publicity. So they came up with this."

Dos looked up. "So why did you say 'we' when you started?"

"Because if I stay around here and fight this, they'll dig as deep as they have to and pin it on someone." Then I played the best card in my hand: "Only difference is that they know I'm innocent."

He handed the page back to me. I stuck it back in the folder and put it on the chair beside me.

"You want a coffee or something?"

"Yeah, sure. Black."

He walked to the kitchen area. I took a few deep breaths, relieved at how authentic the documents looked. He handed me the coffee without making eye contact. "What are you going to do?"

"I gotta get out of town. Month or two. As soon as they get evidence from the lab, they'll be close to making an arrest. I only got one piece of advice for you, mi amigo. The sooner you cough up the source of those tip numbers, the better off you'll be."

I stood up, thanked him for the coffee, and got the dogs.

Before I walked out, he said, "I get instructions. I'm a shill—I get paid to bet. Even if I knew who's behind it, I wouldn't tell you, and here's why: they'd kill me and then you. Maybe you first."

I stared at him and headed out to the car.

"How did it go?" Rixie asked.

Before I could answer, Dos came running out, waving my folder.

"You forgot this." He handed it to me and said to Rixie, "Afternoon, ma'am. Didn't expect to see you so soon."

"Yes," she said. "I thought the next time was for tequilas on a Tuesday, but he needed a ride."

I rolled up the window as Dos gave her a thumbs-up.

She pulled out. "So?"

"He didn't threaten me directly. But I got an indirect threat and a promise. I've never trusted Dos, and after his comments, all I can do is let him keep his information and alert you to tread lightly trying to get the source of his tip."

She said, "Well, in my business, we have to treat suspects, witnesses, informants, and everyone else on the list with kid gloves. We have to bribe them sometimes to speak up or shut up, depending on the situation. I did get a commitment that when the time was right, he would cooperate with the information I requested."

"That's impressive." I held up the envelope with the cash in it. "Does the bribe part apply to me?"

She smiled. "No. You're like an employee on paid leave."

"That's reassuring. I need to get back to Barn7. I have important employee duties to take care of."

She laughed. "Need a ride tomorrow?"

"No, I'll get someone from the barn to take me to Hunter's office. Will you be there?"

"Yes." We pulled up to the barn, and I got out. "See you at nine o'clock."

I had to see Chex and make sure he knew he was leaving soon to be with me. The dogs and I made one last trip through the barn and stopped at BigOilRig's stall. I went in and stayed for ten or fifteen minutes. I was worried Stamples, the stewards, and NESPA were going to require Buster to transfer BigOilRig to another trainer while the investigation went on. I wouldn't be his exercise rider when I came back because he wouldn't be in this barn. Or what if the owner decided to move him to a new trainer at a different track?

"Let's just keep one thought moving us forward," I told BigOilRig. "Someday, I will rescue you from this racetrack. I don't know exactly how but remember what I said: 'There's only one sure thing.' Rest assured; I will be back for you."

I pushed his mane over, wrapped both arms around his neck, and stood there as long as I could. His big dark eyes followed me as I shut the door.

Chapter 17

Max was still there when I got back to my office, but he was packing it up for the day. I ran him through the deal with Amos.

"He's not happy about it," I admitted, "but this is a guy who seems determined to do the right thing."

"Well, Rixie, we're doing what we can," Max said, leaning against his desk. "Buster almost begged me to get SkyMan to work as his assistant trainer and barn manager. I presented SkyMan with the possible settlement terms from the track. I mentioned the job opportunity with Buster and implied that if he took the job, he could help us keep an eye on Barn7."

"Okay, what's next?" I asked.

Max looked tired. We'd had three long days, with no end in sight.

"My stomach's rumbling. Dinner for me at home. How 'bout you? What's next for you?"

"There are still some details over at Barn7 I need to go check out."

"You never get tired, do you?" he asked.

I laughed. "Get some rest, Max."

Once he'd left, I looked at the stack of mail and papers on my desk.

I wished I'd had Amos grab me some takeout at Dos's restaurant. Another Sunday night working at the track with a Delivery Dash dinner. As always, it would be dark when I got home.

Chapter 18

About 5:00 the next morning, I woke to see Lucky sniffing the suit-case. He knew something was up.

Off to the track kitchen for the last time. I thought about getting nostalgic about it, but I was tired of this place anyway—same break-fast, same people. I was kinda glad to be outta there. Who knows? I could have been the next to get hurt.

The security guy, James, stood at the kitchen door. "Bad news— this is off limits for you."

"Doesn't matter, I'm leavin' today," I said, not wanting to give James a hard time. He was only doing his job.

The kitchen door blew open, and Charlane came out, waving her arms.

"Can you believe this bullshit? Banning you from the kitchen is the last straw." She glared at James. "What do you want, Amos? Usual? Wait here." She came back out with a white to-go cup and two brown paper bags. "Egg sandwich for now, ham and turkey sandwiches for later. Everbody knows you're gettin' a bad deal."

James tailed us all the way back to Barn7. Charlane kept looking back, keeping an eye on him.

Quietly, she said, "WD don't mess around, does he? Heard you shippin' out today. Need anything?"

"Can you take GunShy to your place until SkyMan gets out? They're shippin' Chex out this week. You take care of him till then, okay? I also need a ride about 8:30."

"Where you goin'?" she asked.

"I'm just goin' 'cross town—and then Max is sending me out to a ranch."

"Max knows ranchers?" Charlane rolled her eyes. "Remember what I told you: never trust an ex-cop."

"I don't have a lot of choices on who to trust. See you at 8:30."

Once I had my stuff stacked up in the parking lot, I looked up, and here came Clink. He looked out of place, wearing starched khakis, a golf shirt, and tennis shoes. He was a month overdue for a haircut, and I knew he was glad I was shipping out. This jerk had moved in on Kellsey, my old flame.

He said with a sheepish smile, "You need to sign this NESPA form indicating where you are moving to."

"None of your business."

I signed the form and put a checkmark by the line "Unknown destination."

After putting it in an envelope, he said, "Good luck."

About 8:15, Charlane pulled up next to the office. "Gotta make our getaway. More security on the way. Gotta get you outta here."

I put my saddles, a big box with some books, most of the stuff from the bulletin board, and my suitcase in the back of her truck. "What's with all these cookies?"

"For the horses out there. Take them with you. Here's an invoice. They can mail me a check."

Lucky jumped in the middle between us, and GunShy squirmed his way onto the floor by my feet. She put the Hunter office address in her phone. We pulled up, and Rixie came out of the office wearing a jacket and jeans.

Charlane's enthusiasm faded. "You goin' with *her?*"

"No, they just made the arrangements."

"Nice day for a road trip," Charlane called out the window. "You shoulda been there at Barn7. Left outta there like we robbed the place. Me drivin' like I stole this truck, and him just laughin' and eatin' my killer oatmeal-raisin cookies. You wanna try one?"

Charlane hopped out and stacked about twenty boxes of Miss Ellane's cookies on the sidewalk. "Over $500 worth of cookies right there for the horses at Max's friend's ranch," she told Rixie. "See you at my place this afternoon. Two o'clock, right?"

Rixie nodded. "Two o'clock."

Charlane put GunShy in her truck and pulled out. When she looked back, we both waved.

"What's that about this afternoon?" I asked.

"I'm going over to Charlane's. She said you've been over there. She also told me you 'wasn't together very long.'"

I laughed. "Well, we were never together. At all. Here's what you need to know about her: you can only believe half of what she says. The problem is it's hard to tell which half to believe. But we were never together."

Rixie considered the stuff I'd put on the sidewalk, then waved to a guy standing by a truck parked at the end of the lot. "Billy is your driver."

Billy pulled up and parked.

"Howdy," I said.

He just nodded, and Rixie said, "Morning."

"Mornin', ma'am."

I couldn't tell if this was the first time they'd met. Billy knelt down, and Lucky smelled his hand. "What's your name?"

"That's Lucky. Mine's Amos Moon."

"Billy." He reached out his hand. His grip was strong and firm. He took off his state-cop-type sunglasses, and harsh brown eyes bored through me.

"Come with me to the office for a moment," Rixie said.

My pulse quickened. She'd promised to get me my check before I left. Lucky and I followed her inside, and she sat down in the conference room. "How are you doing?"

"The last three days have been a whirlwind," I admitted, pulling up a chair. "I guess I don't need to think about anything except that you will show the whole world all I did was make one hell of a bet."

"I assure you I'll find out who's behind this and prove your innocence." She got to her feet, then opened the door as if we were heading back out.

"I thought I was coming up here to get my check," I said.

She hesitated. "Well, as it turns out…"

I had had little sleep and even less breakfast. I slammed my hand flat on the table. "You said I would get that $90,000 check before I left!"

"I'm working on it." Her eyes were kind, and they seemed to plead with me. "Another promise from me to you. If I can, I'll come out there this weekend and see you. I may have that resolved by then."

Her eyes kept convincing me to go forward. How could I back out now? She dropped down on one knee and messed with Lucky. "I don't think he heard me say I'll come out there this weekend and see you guys—you remind him, okay?" She stood up and said, "Keep the faith," then reached out to shake my hand.

When I let go, I saw she'd put a metal object in my palm. It was a small horseshoe the size of a quarter.

"What's this?"

"Keep it close, for protection." She smiled. "It's an amulet."

"Go ahead, get in," Billy said.

I opened the pickup door, and Lucky climbed into the back seat, sniffing those cookies. On the front seat were a large notebook, a box of shotgun shells, a carton of Merit cigarettes, a thermos, a plastic refillable coffee mug from Allsup's, and a pistol in a black leather holster. Billy moved all this into the back beside Lucky. "Sorry, got a lotta stuff." It was almost ten o'clock, and he said, "I've got several stops to make. Gonna backtrack to Dallas on the way. You ain't in no big hurry to get there, are you?"

I shrugged. "No."

He turned on some classic rock and started talking over it, but I was staring at Rixie in the side mirror, thinking about her coming out to visit that weekend. When the truck turned, she disappeared.

Billy rambled on, "I have to keep track of about sixty parolees and probationers, from here to Phoenix and north to Denver. Have to see them two or three times a year and get phone calls from them every month. So what'd you do?"

"I was either at the right place or at the wrong place."

"Well, now you'll be in Noose, Texas. Way back—hundred years ago—they had a jail with the gallows right on Main Street. Coulda sold tickets when a really horrible guy got hanged. We sure could use some of that now. Like those guys that shoot up a school." He took his index finger and sliced it across his throat above his Adam's apple.

"TSPAN used to be the only maximum-security prison in Texas. All the executions done there. Now just minimum security. You're lucky." I turned, and Lucky looked at him and then at me. "You're going to be working at Applegate's Ranch. They call Mr. Applegate 'APP,' and the ranch is TAPP Ranch. This will just be like work for you, even if it's not as glamorous as a racetrack."

I nodded and focused on the music. I hadn't listened to classic hard rock in a long time. It reminded me of how Daddy had driven with the windows down, rock music blaring on the radio.

Billy kept the gas pedal down. The bleached asphalt was worn down by the sun. A lot of apprehension was in my stomach as I thought about the uncertainty of the next several months. I closed my eyes and imagined how bad TAPP and Noose might be.

I thought praying would help. I clasped my hands in my lap. It was never too late to say, "God?"—and my mind implied a question mark. I waited a moment, as if a quiet, spiritual voice would speak to me. The silence kept me company.

All I heard was the wind in the truck and the tires rolling outside. I thought, *God, this is about that guy over in Fort Worth General. Get him well, okay?*

My mind went to Kellsey, who was still racing every day, and I asked Him to protect her. I opened my eyes and looked at Billy, who noticed me holding the amulet.

Billy's first stop was out of the way, back near Dallas. He had to check on one of the parolees working at a tire store. After that, he stopped at Cousins Bar-B-Q for brisket. I ditched those track sandwiches Charlane had gotten me and got brisket, too—it might be my last good meal. He stopped to see another guy, and it was after four o'clock before we even got to the first part of Route 180 west, the red brick road—Camp Bowie West Boulevard.

The closer we got to Noose, the more I wondered what kind of ranch could possibly be out there. Besides a few abandoned oil derricks from a long time ago, all I could see were mesquite and oak trees. No horses or cattle on this stretch of the road.

Billy pointed ahead and laughed. "There it is. The only honest thing between here and the border."

The billboard had been there so long the paint was faded. It said, "HANG IN THERE—NOOSE."

He glanced over at me. "You hangin' in there?"

I didn't laugh, but he did. We went the next few miles and just listened to the radio. I guess he told the same stories to all the guys he brought over, trying to shock them into being worried.

I knew what worry was; I'd had my share of times I was worried in my life. Worried about my mother and what was going to happen to her. Her safety and security. It wasn't the same kind of worry I had about my father. And I'd worried about riding horses I'd suspected were unsound and unsafe.

I was not afraid of Noose, Texas. I was worried about getting SkyMan well, and the Hunter Group finding out why I was going out there and who was responsible.

"There it is," Billy said. "TSPAN-M. Texas State Prison at Noose— Men." I'd had this picture in my mind: fences, barbed wire, buildings with turrets and guards, and it was almost like that. The sun glared down. "You know all this equal stuff for women? Well, two years ago they completed TSPAN-W, and TAPP Ranch is across Highway 281. It goes all the way to the Brazos River. Prisoners on work release are vanned over there every day. Most of them work with horses over there. They could have built the women's prison anywhere, but the governor's wife—her pet project was creating vocations for them when they get out. Close your eyes and picture makin' a cowgirl outta a jailbird."

The guards opened the outermost gate, and Billy got out of the truck with a handful of paperwork. "Stay here."

Lucky rallied and looked over the seat.

"Who's that?" I heard the guard on the right say, pointing at me.

"I'm takin' him over to TAPP Ranch."

The guard on the left, a tall, thin guy, uniformed, with a black shiny belt holding up his pants, holster, and nightstick, stared at me. Then he broke his sealed lips, not with a smile or word, but instead he spit on the ground three inches from Billy's boot.

"What's he gonna be doin' over there?"

Billy got back in the truck and slammed the door. He stuck his head out the window after he started backing up and shouted, "He's APP's new ranch manager."

He drove fast out of there. "I made that up about you bein' the manager—sounded good, didn't it? They hate everything, everybody."

I kinda thought the same.

Billy rolled the truck up to the TAPP Ranch entrance. I looked up the gravel driveway. A white iron pipe fence framed the paddocks and turnouts. Dozens of horses mirrored each side of the road, and seeing them felt good.

Maybe this was a good solution. Being vindicated would have been better, but since there was a gray line of doubt, it could have been a lot worse. I might as well be okay with the deal. There was nothing I could do about it now.

Billy saw me looking around. "Don't be alarmed about the appearance. APP was the warden over at the prison, and he likes the way this block-and-bar architecture feels. You won't find any favoritism here."

We started to get out, and a pack of dogs rushed toward the truck. I told Lucky, "Stay."

The first dog did not wait for me to get out of the truck. He leapt his way to me, pounding the ground, making big tracks with his huge paws. His eyes, a pair of dark charcoal question marks, moved quicker than his legs. His stare locked onto me.

The truck door slammed shut. The grayish-and-white dog advanced to my suitcase and sniffed the zippers and handle before dragging his nose along the ground. He pulled his chin across the top, smelling the dusty green canvas-and plastic-trimmed bag. He licked his lips to show his teeth and looked at me with the notice I was next. I knelt, offering my hand. The dog ignored this and continued pushing his nose along my pants, smelling my shirt and arms. Then, after looking me in the eye, he sniffed my hand.

I moved my other hand toward the hair on the top of his head, a darker blend of brown and black. He shied away but stopped and moved back toward me. I moved both hands around the dog's face, which he lowered as I rubbed his ears, pulling them long and smoothing the hair on his neck, which was wet from slobbering.

Billy stood by the truck, watching. "Most guys come here can't get within ten feet of Powder."

"Powder?" I repeated.

"He's a sniffer. You know—cocaine, dust, gunpowder."

"You mean drugs and bombs?" I asked, a little naively.

"You got it. He trained with the FBI and army intelligence over at Fort Hood."

"What's the dust, angel dust?" I asked.

"No." Billy looked straight at me, his eyes not flinching. "Ashes to ashes, dust to dust. Dead bodies."

I looked down the road, to the Texas highway that had ended here.

"He's never found any here," Billy quipped. "First time for everything, you know."

I nodded.

"Powder?" I said to the dog.

He raised his head and ears, watching me. I took a handful of biscuits, and he smelled my hand. I gave them all to him, and he cautiously wagged his tail.

"Good thing you're good with animals. They might of sent you to the lumberyard down in Houston. Talk about a lot of dirty, thankless work."

I shrugged and let the other dogs sniff me. I rubbed my hands over a black-and-white mixed small dog. "They got names?"

"She's new; the other one is Popcorn."

The dogs spotted Lucky in the back seat looking out the window. They started barking, and Lucky spun around in the seat. I opened the door, and he jumped out. Well, he herded those two dogs in a circle so fast they got dizzy. He kept going around them; all they could do was turn their heads and watch him.

Billy gave Lucky a look of approval. Powder came right back to me, as though that were his assignment. I looked toward the office and saw a man standing behind a window, watching.

I moved my hands along Powder's chest. Barn dogs aren't usually brushed much, but Powder had a shiny, groomed coat. He lowered his head, shutting his eyes as I ran my fingers through his hair.

"This one's Applegate's dog?" I asked.

The screen door slammed, and a gravelly voice said, "*Mr.* Applegate's dog."

Powder jumped up; he and I snapped to attention together.

APP looked as if he'd just stepped out of an ad for the Texas State Police. He was tall and stout, his barrel chest stuffed into a starched white shirt, his stomach held up by the biggest buckle I'd ever seen. He had a stern face, all business and toughness that showed up in his hands. Had to be size-twelve hands.

"It's good, he likes you. He's a sniffer. Part bloodhound, part lab. You must be Amos?"

"Yes, sir, Amos Moon. Just came out from Fort Worth."

I looked down at his boots, a shiny crocodile type, the heels hiding behind a densely starched pair of like-new jeans. He had a big ring on his right hand, a bigger watch on the outside of the cuff on his left wrist.

Billy turned and got back into his truck without a word and headed out. I looked around, viewing the barns and fences.

"This is one of the nicest ranches in this part of Texas. A section and a half, about ten thousand acres."

"Do you go all the way to the Brazos River?"

"I'm just glad you know how to pronounce it—sounds like 'Brasis.' Most people not from around here say it like it rhymes with 'lassos.' And yes, TAPP Ranch goes almost to the Brazos River."

Powder raised his head, walked over, and sat beside him. APP didn't even acknowledge him. Powder looked back at me, his eyes expressing what I felt. What was it, anyway? I wasn't sure. Maybe a life or a love left behind. I saw it in his face, a longing.

"Put your gear in the back of my four-wheeler. We'll take a quick tour before dinner."

Lucky ran beside us as APP drove to the first building. "That's the equipment shed. The big barn is for the rescued and retired horses, and the other barn is for the ones in race training." He pointed to a building on the other side of the ranch. "Way over there, that's the women's equine therapy facility. Air-conditioned indoor arena. Covered outdoor arena. The barn. The greenhouse for the gardeners, landscapers, florists." He pulled up to a cabin. "There's your new home."

"Really?" I didn't know what I'd expected, but not something this nice.

"Yeah, they built it thinking Patty was going to live here, but she lives down in Mineral Wells."

"Who's Patty?"

"Oh, she runs the women's equine therapy center. Let's take your stuff in there, and then meet me in the dining room."

The cabin was ten times larger than the apartment back at Barn7. It had wood floors, beams, walls with antlers, leather furniture, windows, and a fireplace. I fed Lucky, putting his dinner in one bowl and filling the other with water.

Once Lucky had eaten, he walked around and smelled everything. Then he curled up next to the door and looked at me.

"What do you think, Lucky?" I was still a little surprised at the setup. "You like our new home?"

He looked up as if he didn't care where we were, as long as he was with me.

It was a short walk back to the dining room. More antlers on the walls and oversized Texas-style tables and chairs. APP introduced me. The three men seated by the door didn't jump up and shake my hand, just nodded and waved. They watched as he led me back to his table.

"Here's the schedule, what happens every day. Jessie, in the black shirt over there, takes care of my dogs. That's his only job. The guy beside him in the green ball cap, he's over all the maintenance. Tex, the other guy, does everything else around here, but primarily, he manages the big barn. I manage the racing barn. Got a full-time job doin' that."

We went through the buffet and sat back down. I was wondering where I fit in. He'd skipped through the racing barn pretty fast and hadn't mentioned me.

"Dig in. It's every man for himself around the chow line." He bit into a piece of fried chicken. "I used to call everyone 'convict labor,' but it changed to 'the crews from the pen,' and now I have to call them 'teams.' The maintenance team does the mowing, carpentry, and fences. The ag team of women on Patty's side does all the landscaping, fruits, vegetables, and flowers. The big barn team does everything with the rescued and retired horses, similar to what Patty does on the other side."

He'd mentioned Patty several times now, and I was starting to get curious about her. It seemed she had a big role.

"Racing team has six guys that only work with horses in training," he continued. "They do the barn chores and the grooming."

He finished the rest of a biscuit and said, "If I'da had more lead time instead of this spur-of-the-moment deal, I coulda used a guy like you to help me out." He flipped around a wood pencil and made a few doodles. "Two special guys are exercise riders for the horses in race training. So we don't need you to do any ridin' for now."

I put down my fork. "I thought I'd be working with the racehorses at your training track."

"There was something about them pullin' your trainer's license. We don't need any problems. A gal left last week who was working over there, so Patty's hired you on her side."

He went on talking while I sat in silence, absorbing the news.

"Patty's team started in January. The goal is for the women to receive their equine certificates. The first two months are in the classroom—books, homework, anatomy. She does that to see if they're capable of grasping everything. Then they progress to the hands-on part. Each woman is assigned four to five horses, and they're totally responsible for their care."

He shuffled the schedule papers.

"Patty's all business," he said. "She's focused on these women and the horses she has them paired with. She leaves about 5:30 or 6:00 every day, so you'll be doin' the night check and everything else that needs to be done when she's gone. You'll meet her tomorrow." He took a last bite of his food and got to his feet. "I'm glad you're here."

Glad somebody was. He pointed at the buffet. "Dessert?"

I wasn't even hungry, but I nodded.

"Go ahead. Cook does a pretty good version of fried cheesecake, made famous in Mineral Wells." He slapped me on the back. "Make yourself at home!"

Chapter 19

Once Amos had been sent off, Max and I could get into the real investigation. We had a list of all the people who came around the track at all hours of the day and night. There was no security preventing People from outside coming on the track grounds, delivering equine supplies, hay, grain, feed. The horse owners were entitled to watch their horses train. That was the outside scenario.

The inside scenario included the jockeys, vets, grooms, trainers, exercise riders, and all the HSD employees. That list was smaller, around three hundred to four hundred. We didn't have a suspect list, but sending Amos away bought us some time to build one.

I headed over to Charlane's. So far, she was the only one who would talk and talk and talk. Maybe she could shed some light on all this. I just had to weed through all her chatter and sort out what the truth was.

In Charlane's trailer park, there weren't any mobile homes. They were RVs, camping rigs and travel trailers with a lot of space between each one. Her trailer was a huge tri-axle horse trailer with live-in quarters and side walls that slid out. There were even landscaping and trees.

Her dogs greeted me with a lot of barking. She smiled and started waving as soon as I got out of the car. "Don't mind my dogs. They only bite certain men."

"How's GunShy doing?" I asked.

"Oh, Hun, fits right in." Her eyes swept over me. "'Bout time we got some class out here. Glad you're here—was afraid you'd cancel. You heard from Amos? He get there okay?" Before I could answer, she motioned and said, "Follow me. Hun, you gotta see my garden."

We headed around back, and I had to blink a few times. "Wow." I had never seen anything like it. "Nice greenhouse."

Inside it was a kaleidoscope of colors. An incredible array of flowers and small trees. "Can I take some photos?"

"Sure. What for?"

"I love photography, and this is beautiful."

One of the most interesting photos I took was of a seed bin with dozens of little compartments, all labeled and organized. It was a great shot in the midst of all the wild vegetation.

"Everybody says I have a green thumb," she said. "I put in automatic waterers. Vegetables and flowers. What else does a girl like me need?"

"That's all."

"You know some of the vegetables at the track kitchen? Come from right here. Flowers in the casino? Right here. Hun, looks like I'm feedin' the whole damn place. Cookies for the horses, vegetables for the kitchen. That's almost a full-time side hustle. I get paid—checks or cash—for everything I do." She winked. "You thirsty? You want something to drink?"

"Sure."

"Come on in. Cleaned it up just for you."

Inside, it smelled more like a bakery than a horse trailer. "Let me show you the best part. This is big enough to haul six horses." We went through the bathroom area and through the door. She had taken out all the partitions and converted the area into a kitchen/living room. She had rugs and a couch and a big-screen TV, tables and bookcases full of books and magazines. The very back wall had been converted into a huge kitchen with two big restaurant-type ovens and a full-size refrigerator.

"This is a nice setup," I said, taking it all in.

"It is. Don't get much company anymore," she said. "Kinda taking a break. Men. What about you, Hun? You married?"

She grabbed my left hand. My ring finger still had an indentation from a long time before.

"No."

"Got a steady squeeze?"

"No."

"Hun, you can tell me. I'm good at keeping secrets. Good-looking lady like you. You gotta have 'em lined up."

"Well, I just got rid of one."

"You make that decision before or after you met Amos?" she asked.

"Amos?" Her question caught me off guard.

"Did I stutter? Amos."

"I don't date men from the track."

"That's the only place I get to meet men. What with gettin' there at five in the mornin', I go to bed early, usually alone. Know what I mean?"

I knew what she meant.

"You makin' any designs on Amos? He'd be available now, since you don't date guys from the track." She kinda frowned. "Hun, I got to apologize to you. I implied one day that Amos and I were together. I made that up, trying to make you jealous. He came out here one night straight from the barn. Never took a shower or nothing. That's how you can tell if a man is interested in a little more than dinner and dessert, you know."

I wasn't sure how much of this I needed to know, but she went on. "He said he only had time to eat and get back to the barn. So we had dinner. Here's what happened: I was standing right here, wearing a pretty dress. I untied my apron, pulled it up over my head real easy, so I didn't mess up my hair, and it was getting dark outside a little bit. I thought, 'If he don't get this message now, he has got no interest in me in that regard.' I told him, 'So you're leaving and you don't even notice I've fixed up my hair, put on this perfume, put on this dress. You don't like me.'"

She reached over and grabbed my arm. "Here's what he said: 'I do like you, but…There's no F…U here.' I looked at him. 'You mean as in F-U-?'

"He said, 'No, there is no F-U-T-U-R-E here,' and he started laughing. 'There's no future here.'"

Charlane and I laughed and laughed. She went on, "He said, 'Yeah, we work hard, and we have fun together. Let's keep it that way.' Since then, I have respected the man."

She handed me a photo. "That's me right there, holding the lead rope. I have a nice smile, don't I? Well, when you win, everyone beams with a big smile. That's BigOilRig's win right here at HSD. Last month. See the guy in the cowboy hat? Your guy. Amos."

"My guy?"

"I saw how he looked at you yesterday when you picked him up. The way you put the dogs in your car."

This conversation was going in spirals. "You've got a lot of win photos," I said.

"Oh, yeah. For some people a win photo is all that matters. Got a lot of friends in these photos."

That was my chance. "Speaking of friends. You remember Dear Friends, number 4 in the fourth race Friday? Did you go by his barn that morning?"

She gave me a confused look. "No, I was working over at Barn5. That's not his barn."

"The security camera at Dear Friends' barn had you there that morning. Are you sure you weren't there?"

She squinted at me. I had learned a long time ago to ask the question and wait till hell freezes over for the answer.

"Oh, Friday is drop-off-cookies day. So I probably was there. Now you just check your little cameras, and you'll find me in every barn. That what you need to know?"

"Yes, it is."

"If they need—what do they call it on TV? Expert witness?" She winked. "That's me. Lot goes on at a track that security don't know about. Complicated business."

That was a loose statement. "I'll tell them." I considered her for a second. "Would Kellsey retire and come home and take a job like Amos had now that he's gone?"

It took her a second, but she said, "No, she'll never get into training, but she got back here this morning. Got some big-time horses to ride in the big stakes races comin' up. You ain't gotta worry about her. Hun, here's one minor reason she came back: she's seein' that guy you work with—Clink."

"Clink?" The news was a surprise to me, and Charlane looked pleased that I hadn't known.

"Yeah, Clink. Hit it off right after she and Amos split. Didn't set too good with Stamples. That kinda complicated Stamples from seein' her when he's here. Amos ain't even an AE—Also Eligible. He never was; he ain't even Irish. Now, Clink McMillin—bet he's Irish. You know—the Irish take care of the Irish."

I walked back outside. Her dogs ran up at the end of the trailer where the fence wrapped around. They were a mixed bunch of pound dogs. Yapping and barking.

Charlane followed. "See what I get?" she said. "Leftovers. Don't take me wrong. I love 'em. That one brings back bad memories. His foster dad up and left me with the bills and a lot of problems. That's better than having him still here, know what I mean?" She pointed at me. "Just like this guy you just got rid of. You can't move on until you create a vacancy. The biggest one is the one in your heart. Trust me on this. I know."

"You mind if I take a few photos of your dogs?" I asked.

"Okay. If you want to."

I took my iPad out and took a few. "How 'bout one with you?"

"Oh no, I don't take good photos."

"Sure you do. Just smile like you did in those win photos inside."

She stopped at the trailer window to check her hair. Her blond highlights covered her medium-length brown hair. She said, "Most women have to worry about hat hair. Me, it's helmet hair."

She tried to fluff up the back and picked up two of her dogs. I took about a dozen photos, and she posed and smiled the whole time. Not vain at all.

Charlane kept looking at her watch. It was probably a Rolex knockoff. "I gotta go see a guy. I owe him some money. You want to go with me?"

I knew circling the wagon around her friends would be a good idea, but I always liked to drive my own car. "How about if I follow you?"

"Oh, no, Hun. You ride with me. You can't be goin' where we're goin' drivin' a BMW. You gotta be careful in that kinda car—that'll get you mugged or carjacked."

She scoped me out and got all serious. "You and I are a lot alike. We got dangerous jobs. Me ridin' racehorses. You bein' the NESPA enforcer." She dug in her purse, which was basically a small shopping bag made of canvas.

"I can never find my keys." Finally, she pulled out a plastic horse-shoe on a chain. "You don't mind if Little Piss goes with us? The one you think is so cute. His real name is Pistol, but Little Piss suits him better, don't you think?"

We all piled into the front seat of her old Nissan pickup. Pistol sat on the floor by my feet. After a few tries, the engine kicked over and the radio came on.

She dug a little tin out of her back pocket and put a pinch under her lip. "You want some? The look on your face. Hun, do you think I would put something as dangerous as tobacco in this body? I make this outta shredded dried plums, apricots, figs, and a little CBD oil to keep it moist."

I shook my head no. She adjusted the volume. "You wouldn't have some money I could borrow…Do you?"

Before I could answer, she slapped her leg and said, "Just tryin' you on. You'll figure out I like to joke a lot."

I started recognizing some of the streets as she drove the same route I had taken to Dos's restaurant. Right ahead on the right was a big sign: "Uncle Money's PAWN—Cash for Gold—Guns—Ammo—Jewelry."

She pulled into the parking lot and backed into the last open parking spot, between an old pickup truck and a small minivan full of kids and a dog. Little Piss started barking.

"You want to go in with me?" she asked me, and then laughed. "Gotcha again. Be right back! Watch Li'l Piss."

They had a chain-link-fenced area right in front with everything from lawnmowers to chain saws to bicycles.

This was a part of Fort Worth I'd never been in, but I could tell she knew her way around. She stopped and talked to a couple of guys hanging around the front door. After about five minutes, she came out, stopped again, and gave the taller guy a slight hug. She glanced toward the truck as though she wondered if I'd noticed or wanted to make sure I did.

Little Piss nearly jumped out the window when he saw her.

"That was easy." She slid into the seat and cranked on the truck. "See, when the guy left me with the trailer, I got that place to refinance it for me. I paid it off last year. Guys you hang out with probably got good credit. Me, now, I attract guys that are always looking for the next great thing, and usually the next great thing they find…" She pointed her thumb back at her chest. "Is *me*."

I gave her a reassuring look. She dug in that purse contraption of hers, one hand barely on the wheel, and pulled out a card. "That's my medical marijuana card. I can get you one."

"No, I'm okay on that."

"If you change your mind, let me know. Here's my Uncle Money's Quick Cash Card." She held it up, kinda proud. "I can get you one of these too."

If I had said anything, she might have thought it was sarcastic, so I just shook my head.

"You see it's a debit card? I got money on deposit." She said "*deee*-posit" again, tossed it back into the bag.

I'd never heard of anyone who would have money in a savings deposit account at a pawnshop.

I had to ask. "So it's like a bank?"

"Yeah, Hun. Just like a bank. Where do you think they get the money they loan at 20 percent?"

I shook my head.

"From people like me. People that have C-A-S-H."

She glanced at the iPad in my lap. "You're not recording this, are you?"

"I am." She raised her eyebrows over the top of her sunglasses and looked at me.

I pointed at her. "Gotcha on that, didn't I?"

She had the greatest laugh. "Hun, you hang out with me and you're going to learn a lot. What interest you get on your savings account?"

"Well, it's pretty low right now."

"Bullshit, Hun. Get your money out tomorrow, give it to me, and I'll put it in my account. When they pay the interest, I'll give it to you. Right now it's 7 or 8 percent. What do you say?"

"I say I don't have that much…C-A-S-H, as you call it."

"Okay, Hun; when you get some, you let me know. You want to order takeout and go back to my place?"

"Rain check on that. I have to go to an event at a ranch over in Dallas tonight."

"At the TexaSTARanch?"

"Yes." I was surprised she knew about it. "Are you going?"

"Oh, no—you go and mix it up with all those rich friends of Stamples."

"I have no idea why Max and I were invited."

She looked serious. "They gonna try to get you to lighten up on all these NESPA rules. This accident Friday has tipped the scales in Stamples's favor. He's probably on notice that if there's another accident or another horse is put down, TXRC—the Texas Racing Commission—will shut down the live racing. That's what him and his buddies want, because then, he gets a green light to develop the property and keep the casino."

I'd thought about what the ambulance driver had said on Friday, about how this dangerous track might be closing. Finally, I understood the dynamics in play and behind the scenes. I was not surprised, that Charlane always seemed to be in the know.

"Funny, you gettin' to meet those guys," Charlane said.

"Those guys?"

"Oh, Hun. His investors are always in tow with their fat checkbooks when he needs them. I heard he brought some of them in as investors when he built the casino." She glanced over at me. "They'll all be there. I know why Kellsey came back today. She'll be there too."

She stopped at a gas station. "I need some snacks. Come on, go in with me."

We walked in. Bars on the door, and all eyes were on me. She grabbed two Rambler Texas-limestone-filtered sparkling waters, some pork rinds, and two packages of Texas Outlaw beef jerky. It said on the package, "This will change your life."

Why did I think she might pull a gun and hold the joint up? And ask me to drive the getaway truck?

Since Max and I were scheduled to go to this party, I dug my authentic cowgirl attire out of the closet. A beautiful pair of cowboy boots, a black skirt, and a flowered blouse.

When I got out of my car, Max said, "Wow, girl. You're going to get some guys' attention tonight."

"That's the nicest thing you've ever said to me."

Max drove, and I put the address in my phone.

"Well, I had an interesting afternoon over at Charlane's trailer. How would she know Stamples is waiting for more accidents to let TXRC close the track and keep the casino?"

"There's been rumors about that floating around since we got here." After miles and miles of white iron pipe fences, we pulled through the gate and were greeted by a man in a security uniform. We gave him our names, and he gave us a "What are you doing here?" look but waved us through to a big log building on a creek.

Once inside, we were given name tags. I carried my black cowboy hat in one hand and got a glass of white wine. I scanned the huge room that was filled with a collection of antique cars and trucks and focused on Kellsey O'Bryan, who was surrounded by three or four men. Dressed to the nines. The tightest jeans and a leather fringed coat. Her smile was infectious.

After what Charlane had said, I expected Stamples to be right there beside her, but he wasn't anywhere to be found.

On display were artists' renderings of oil rigs on platforms and maps of the Gulf of Mexico. Max and I went through the food line and got barbecue and brisket. We sat with a couple of guys, introduced ourselves, and told them we worked at HSD.

"That must be an exciting place to work," one man said. "Some tracks around the country are falling away and being developed for other things besides horse racing. I hope that doesn't happen over there—but you never know."

I got up and brought Max and me the warm blueberry cobbler with vanilla ice cream.

"Are you going to invest in the oil rigs?" the man asked when I sat back down.

Max said, "Well, maybe."

"Maybe." He laughed. "That's the most important word. Maybe it will happen. Maybe it'll be the biggest ever. Like over at your racetrack.

Maybe my horse will win. It's the same game. Only these stakes are way bigger than the ones in a horse race."

The guy with him, the one with the big hat, said, "Well, surely you are going to be included in the prospectus if you're here, so welcome. Glad to have you on board."

He got up and glanced at me, giving Max the thumbs-up. I guess Max was right. I got some guys' attention.

I walked over to the man and said, "Mr. Hunter and I work together. We're not on a date."

"Oh, ma'am. I didn't mean anything. I meant it was a signal to get in early on the oil rig exploration. That's all."

He nodded as if he got the message.

I noticed Kellsey was at a head table, if there was one. It was an eight-top, and there were seven men with eyes on her.

A man tapped a knife on his glass. The help took the cue and exited through the side door. Once they'd left, the host thanked everyone for attending, then closed with "Washington is going to auction the Gulf of Mexico oil leases early this summer. We'll have an update at the next event in April. Thanks for coming tonight, and be safe going home."

On the way out, Max and I were each handed a "TexaSTARanch" gift bag. I opened mine in the car. It was a silver oil well on a platform with a black ribbon coming out of the top. I held it up by the black ribbon and showed it to Max.

"So much for Charlane's idea we were set up to loosen the NESPA rules. That never came up. That guy at our table said 'you never know'—and he hoped HSD doesn't close."

Max was always able to analyze a situation. "Looks like Stamples wants us to concentrate on this oil well auction so we divert our focus off the NESPA rules."

Martha wasn't too happy with how things were going. She called about 8:30 and sounded discouraged.

"Miss Ricksland, some additional tests were ordered, and his discharge is delayed."

I hoped they hadn't discovered internal injuries. SkyMan had been through enough.

"Tuesdays are dark at the track—no racing," I said. "Would you like to go to Trinity River Park tomorrow and get some fresh air?"

"Can you bring GunShy?" she said, after a pause. "My sister, Mary, will be here and can take him to her house when we get back. Can you check with Charlane to see if she will bring GunShy to Barn7?"

"Yes. I'll make those arrangements."

Chapter 20

Tuesday morning started off having breakfast with the three guys. An old-salt horseman watched me eat.

"You like the grub?" he said. "Bacon, eggs, pancakes, juice, and coffee. Every day it's the same."

I glanced up. He caught me lookin' at a filled-in scar on his forehead.

"Horse kicked me. I've got a stainless-steel plate in my skull big enough to fry this here egg on. It's why I got no eyebrows—the surgery," he said, digging into the eggs.

"Amos."

"Tex." He shook my hand. His hands had scars and large knuckles but muscular fingers. "I'm from south of Odessa."

"Fort Worth."

"You shoulda stole that horse back there."

I didn't know how much he knew about me, so I just asked him, "Why?"

"Evidence—always destroy the evidence!" He slapped his leg, laughing, showing his narrow lips and crooked teeth. "That's what I did. They tried to pin one on me in El Paso. Wrong place at the wrong time. Know what I mean?"

I shrugged.

"I was inside TSPAN before this," he said. "APP took me in, and I'm just like the layups that need time off before getting back in training."

I didn't comment, just kept eating. My head had hurt since I'd woken up, and I figured the food would help.

We headed outside, and right at seven o'clock, four vans pulled up. The inmates got out and walked through the gate. They sized me up pretty fast, and it became clear that they had a spokesman. His eyes were as cold as a rock on a tombstone.

"We done heard 'bout you. Fancy horse trainer sent down here for fixin' races." He turned to the other guys and asked, "What they call that now, community service?"

They all laughed.

Before I could say anything, Tex told the group, "Sounds like fixin' races is just like the rest of us. We all got caught; that's what we got in common. So what are you gonna do when you get out? Git in trouble and turn around and come back or worse? If you want to learn a trade, this is more than showin' up and shovelin' horse shit. Y'all better listen up and try to learn something about horses over here."

Tex yanked the clipboard down off the wall of the barn.

"If you don't want to be here, I'll have the van take your sorry ass back over there to crawl into your cell. Anyway, Amos ain't gonna be workin' over here—he's workin' with Patty on the other side."

That guy interrupted. "I heard he was gonna be APP's ranch manager. Sounds like that didn't work out?"

I wondered how he could possibly know that. Billy had made that up and only said it to the guard back at TSPAN. Just like the track—no secrets here.

Tex shrugged his shoulders. "If anyone gets to be ranch manager, that would be me."

Another man said, "In your dreams."

Everybody laughed. They got to work, and Tex turned to me. "The vans bring the women at eight o'clock sharp. APP will take you over," he said. "Schedule says you'll be eating lunch back over here. See you then."

Short and to the point. I looked up and saw that APP had been standing on the porch, watching. I waved as I walked up. "Good morning. Tex thought you were grooming him for ranch manager."

"Yeah, I heard him say that. Let's go find Patty." We started to walk, and he said, "If you're like me, you don't know much about equine therapy."

I nodded.

"This all got put together because our first lady got concerned about the conditions of the women's prisons. When the women got out, they didn't have any skills or a vocation. She got the money allocated to build the new prison over at TSPAN, as well the barn, the arena, and even that cabin over here on my ranch. Now, just between you and me, at first, I thought it was a waste of my ranch and my time, but it's all about the contract and the lease I got."

He went on, "Patty's first class finished last year. The women are proud of the certificates they got and the real jobs they got on the outside. The women on the team are up for release at the end of the year. Because of this program, they are new women—changed from the inside out."

I tried to picture the type of woman running all this. "Tell me about Patty."

"She's tough on the outside, but she cares deeply about the prisoners. How they change from when they start the program. She's all business, focused on the women and the horses. It was the first lady's vision—but really, all the credit goes to Patty."

APP pointed at the dust trail behind a black Range Rover SUV coming up the road. It stopped, and out stepped a woman about my age, dressed in jeans and a green denim shirt. Her light brown hair was pulled back in a ponytail under a white sun visor.

APP whispered, "Gov's wife got her that car." Raising his voice, he called, "Good mornin', Miss Patty."

Wow—I suddenly felt a combination of surprise and concern. The surprise was at how much better looking she was than how I had pictured the boss at a prison horse therapy ranch. The concern was that she was probably married or that I could fall for her; it had been only a few months since that ill-fated breakup with Kellsey.

Not to mention that she probably could care less who I was, and she hadn't had much say in hiring me.

"Yes, a beautiful Texas morning," she said, walking up. "Who's this? The famous racehorse guy?"

I studied her face. I didn't want to stare, but it didn't look as if she wore any makeup or lipstick, and she was still alluring. She had a serious, no-nonsense look. I stared at her smile and her soft, bright, bluish-gray eyes. Her jeans were worn smooth, held up with a real trophy buckle—not one bought at a boot store. Her boots looked as though she wore them every day.

I found the smile I'd been afraid I'd left in Fort Worth. "From what I hear, if there's anyone famous around here, it would be you."

"Famous for what?" she said.

"Famous for turnin' out some women who give you all the credit for their new lives."

Patty glanced at APP. "Sometimes, yes, but not always. Not everyone wants to move on. Some people can't leave the past behind. They can't trust their own hearts to move on past their failures and leave behind what kept them downtrodden."

I must have looked puzzled. She said, "Downtrodden. You know—when people are treated badly by people in power."

"Yes, I know about that, firsthand." I glanced at her small but muscular hands. No rings. No fingernail polish.

"Every day, I take a stick and draw a line at the end of the arena." She dragged her boot in front of her. "They know once they step across that line, they're no longer prisoners. They are participants in a therapy program that just happens to be centered on horses, but it's really centered on each woman here. They're here to learn by doing.

And what better teacher on this earth than a horse…and God." She got more serious. "Do you believe in God?"

If this was a belated job interview, she was winning. I couldn't think of answers as fast as she drilled the questions into me, and I kept staring at her mouth and the way she enunciated each word. She wore a small gold cross on a necklace.

"Yes, of course," I said.

"A lot of people we work with answer 'Yes,' 'No,' 'Maybe,' 'Prove it to me,' etc. My job here is not to sell God to anyone. After a few weeks in this program, even the biggest doubters start seeing—and every time they touch a horse, feeling—how God is working in their lives."

I nodded to confirm what she said.

"Sorry, I get wound up, and here I am preaching to the choir." She gestured out to the pasture, where a few of the horses were grazing. "God has created these amazing, beautiful creatures, and not only are they partners in our effort to create a new life for the people we work with, but we are also stewards for their protection."

Patty crossed her arms. "Speaking of stewards—like the ones at racetracks—can't they do their jobs? What about the track owner?"

"That's a whole 'nother story. Talk around the track is he would rather get rid of racing, keep the casino, and develop the property."

"You mean just like those other tracks around the country that have been developed?" Patty squinted at me. "What's up with all these horses getting hurt? Are they getting drugged? Doesn't anyone care about the horses anymore? Horses are defenseless; they have to be protected from people that compromise their health for personal gain."

It felt good to hear the same thoughts from another person who wasn't in the racing world.

"There are a lot of people like me who do care," I said. "Sadly enough, we're in the minority. There are trainers and veterinarians who push the envelope, take an edge—whether for greed, glory, or gold. There's not enough accountability. Racetracks protect the trainers to keep their barns full so the horses are there to fill the races. There's not a moral conscience or a moral compass for guidance."

APP jumped into the conversation. "How about that new government agency? NESPA?"

"It started three years ago, and it's already effective," I said.

"I bet there are some guys that are afraid they can't make it if they have to go the honest route," he said, and I nodded.

"It's a good thing I'm not in charge of that," Patty said. "Catch people drugging horses—I'd build those gallows back in downtown Noose and make them wish they'd never heard of me. I'd tie their hands, cover their faces, and trip the trap door down."

I pictured her as an executioner. Yes, she could do that. Patty pointed at the vans coming down the road. "There's more we need to discuss about how horses are treated at racetracks, but I have one more question for you before everyone gets here: Why did you really come to TAPP Ranch?"

I hesitated, then said, "You don't have enough time for me to tell you all the reasons I'm here. For now, let's just say—do you believe in destiny? Fate? Or consequences?"

"Consequences…I like that word. Are you always this guarded, this vague?"

APP jumped in. "Miss Patty, he's a cowboy. Some of them don't talk much, but when they do, it's a good thing to listen."

"My job—with the help of horses—is to improve the lives of people, betting on their futures." She paused. "You know a little about betting, don't you?"

Her voice was smooth but powerful; her eyes darted almost right through me. I wondered how she'd guessed that about me.

"Yes. Some people think I'm a professional gambler."

"That's interesting."

"Flattering, maybe. People acknowledged how good I was."

The vans were pulling in.

"I want to know how good you are with people," she said.

"Well, I've been working for years trying to protect riders and jockeys to make racetracks safer. That shows I care about people and horses. I worked with a lot of people as the barn manager and people worked for me. I think I did a pretty good job."

"Equine therapy is like that," she said, nodding. "Very hands-on. The women will bring their four to five horses in, and you and I will work together side by side in the arena. That's how you'll learn what equine therapy is all about. People working very closely with horses. Horses are the foundation here. Without them, this would just be another outdoor exercise area where prisoners get fresh air. But in order to work here, you have to be good with people."

"I think I'm good with people."

She considered me for a moment. "I guess we'll have plenty of time to find out about that, won't we?"

"Yes, ma'am."

Chapter 21

Amos texted me on Tuesday, asking about his check and when Chex would arrive. Stamples still had his money tied up, and I wasn't sure when it would be released. I promised to call him back with news about Chex.

At Barn7, all I got from Buster was a list of reasons why Chex hadn't been shipped out yet.

"Amos left me high and dry," he said. "You want it to happen fast, you take care of it."

He handed me a worn piece of paper with a list of horse shippers, but when I called, none of them had an opening.

I texted Amos: *<Buster said shippers are booked up. He turned this over to me. Waiting for a cancellation>*

He replied: *<Guess I should get used to waiting>*

It was a clear spring Texas morning, and I stopped at the track kitchen. I had no idea what Martha liked to eat, so I just duplicated my order. Peanut butter and jelly sandwiches always worked on a hike. Some fruit, bottles of water, and a little plastic bowl from the kitchen for her dog.

I picked up GunShy from Charlane, who had him ready and waiting. At the hospital, it was as though GunShy had a green-light pass. He'd been there a lot in four days. Some of the staff even knew his name.

Martha was glad to see us, and GunShy was the star of the moment. She picked him right up and held him over the edge of the bed to see SkyMan, who looked better but was still in a neck brace. I wondered if they'd completed the additional testing and what it was all about.

His shoulder and the nerves in his neck had taken the force of the fall. I wondered whether it was realistic or safe to have him working in Barn7, but that was a conversation for another time.

Martha asked, "Where are we going?"

"Trinity River Park, hiking trails by the river." I looked over at SkyMan. "We'll be back after lunch."

He motioned for her to go as if he were shooing her out. "Get some fresh air."

"You might want to bring your art supplies," I said. "If you don't want to hike, you can draw."

Martha settled into the front seat, and GunShy jumped into her lap. Smiling, she held him, hugged him, and talked to him. He gazed at her before curling up and going to sleep.

When we got there, she said, "I'd like to stay here and draw, okay?"

"Sure," I said. "GunShy and I will probably hike for about an hour. We'll go out and back. Leave you your lunch and water."

She pulled out her notebook, along with a box of pencils and pens. "I'll be fine here." She smoothed out the pages and sorted out her pencils.

"What do you draw?" I asked.

"Usually, I draw landscapes and flowers. Today, I'm going to draw the future."

I thought about the future, and asked, "How do you do that?"

"With these." She held up a handful of pencils and pens, random colors, and laughed. "Go on your hike. Maybe you'll find your future out there."

The Native Americans I'd met had a way to say the truth in a way we white folks didn't comprehend. Maybe we didn't want to hear the words or didn't believe what they were saying. But today, I heard what she said. The words "my future" settled in my brain and made their way down to my heart. I'd been so wrapped up in my day job, I hadn't stopped long enough to ponder exactly what my future did hold.

Martha pointed off into the distance.

My eyes followed her arm all the way through the trees to some far distant place. There was a silent breeze moving through the leaves along the trailhead.

A Texas spring was pretty special. I was just starting to appreciate it after my time in Virginia. I hooked a long leash to GunShy's collar, and we took off. He sniffed everything on both sides of the trail, up and down the bank to the river. I couldn't smell anything except the fresh air, which was such a great improvement from the racetrack. Those smells never changed.

Out here, it was birds singing and flying. GunShy chased one, and it flew away from him. My eyes took it all in, from rocks to trees to the river to footprints left by people before me on the trail.

The future. What did the future hold for me? Maybe I needed to listen more closely to my own heart. Pay attention to what happened this week and double down on the vow I'd made to make a difference.

After about thirty minutes, GunShy and I turned back. I ate my sandwich as we walked. Martha had found a clearing near the river and was drawing, relaxed, and seemed to be in a very quiet place. GunShy ran up and sat beside her. She didn't look up, but she dropped her hand, petting him.

She had picked a great vantage point; there was a lot to draw here—wildflowers, trees, and shadows.

"Thanks for bringing me here," she finally said. "I needed time to think about myself. I have been so consumed with SkyMan."

"He'll get back on his feet."

It was the right thing to say; I could tell by her grateful look that she needed reassurance. She motioned up the trail in the direction of the truck. "What about the future?"

From somewhere deep inside, I found an answer.

"It has three parts," I said. "What we are afraid might happen, what we hope happens, and what really happens."

"Which one did you focus on?"

"It really is about the last one, isn't it?" She half nodded. "Amos left yesterday. We're going to find out who is behind this and why this happened to SkyMan."

"Most of the time, we don't volunteer for difficult tasks in life. It's a combination of being picked and stepping up. You will figure this out," Martha said, sounding more firm than she had before. "Don't worry about us. Think about the other riders and the other horses. They need you. We need you. And Amos. What do you think about Amos?"

"I liked him the first time I met him," I admitted.

"His heart!" She touched the end of the pencil to her chest. "He's someone who cares. He cares about SkyMan."

Martha stood up, and GunShy took off as if he knew it was time to leave. She gathered her things and walked on ahead, as though she wanted to be alone. We loaded up and started back to the hospital.

Martha shut her eyes, holding GunShy in her arms. They both slept all the way back to the hospital, where Mary met us at the entrance doors.

"We're going to head back up to see him," Martha said as she got out. "Thank you. I needed time away from the hospital."

As I headed back into traffic, I realized I had probably needed the afternoon away more than Martha did. All I did was churn this case around in my mind. Martha had challenged me to consider those other categories in my life. Hope happens and fear happens. And I wondered: Why even think my future might include Amos?

Chapter 22

When I arrived at the equine therapy barn Wednesday morning, I topped off my mug with decaf, which was all Patty had over there.

"You okay?" she asked. "You look exhausted."

I wondered how she could smile so early in the morning. Back at the track, it was all about schedules and deadlines. Nobody had time to smile or be happy. Was she always this happy?

"I'm not used to not having horses to ride," I said. "I already miss BigOilRig. He's that really nice horse that ran in the race Friday. Now, he's going to get transferred to another trainer. He's the one horse I always thought about buying or claiming, and I'm not even there. My quarter horse, Chex, will ship out here soon."

"The minute you started talking about those horses," Patty said, "you relaxed and your face lit up. You smiled just like you did yesterday when we met." She paused. "Let's plan a trail ride when your horse gets here."

"Yes, definitely."

She put a cookie in my palm. "What's the deal with these? It's only been two days, and all every horse here can think about is when the women are going to give them another cookie. Twenty-five dollars a box? This Miss Ellane called the office wondering how my horses like her cookies and when are we going to send her the check. Who's she, anyway?"

I just shook my head and laughed.

Patty looked surprised. "What's so funny?"

"Miss Ellane, well, her real name is Charlane. She rides at my old barn."

Patty got down on the floor and messed with Lucky, whispering to him as if she'd known him her entire life instead of two days. I was starting to understand how down to earth she was.

"How'd you get started riding horses, anyway?" she asked.

"We lived in Davie, Florida. My grandparents had a donkey on their farm. I rode him bareback. We called him Ol' Bad Eye."

Laughing, she said, "How'd he ever get a name like that?"

"A minister came by and told my daddy and grandpa, 'That's Obadiah following Amos.' Obadiah is the next chapter in the Bible after Amos. Daddy couldn't pronounce Obadiah anyway, so he just called him Ol' Bad Eye."

"Did you grow up around racetracks?" she asked.

"You could say that." I took a sip of coffee. "Daddy went to the racetrack two or three times a week instead of going to work, and I went with him instead of going to school. He got tips from the exercise riders on the backside. He left me at the barns, and he went to the grandstand and bet. I was six or seven; it was better than going to school for me.

"They taught me horses, and the track taught Daddy how to lose. Sometimes he'd win, and we'd stop on the way home and he'd buy my mom something nice. That false sense of money and happiness camouflaged his fear that it wasn't going to last."

I'd never said that out loud before. I took another sip of coffee and avoided her eyes.

"But you still went into racing," she said.

I hesitated, then settled in on the floor next to her and Lucky. "Yeah. I've had a hands-on career for the past twenty years and take great pride in being an assistant trainer. Exercising horses is probably the most important job at a racetrack. Exercise riders' pay does not even equate to how dangerous it is."

She was quiet for a moment, then said, "It makes me think of these prisoners. They should get paid for the work they do. Sure, they're serving their time, but is it right for them to come over here and work for free?"

I'd never thought about that.

"Tell me about those 'consequences' that brought you here," she said.

"I was set up in the fourth race last Friday." It still sounded like something that had happened to someone else. "Someone came into my barn and gave something to NoCashRefund, thinking he was BigOilRig. Then SkyMan rode NoCashRefund that morning and got thrown. It was to try and manipulate the outcome of the race. Well, BigOilRig came in fourth and made those two tickets worth zero, but I had a ticket that included BigOilRig. It paid out a lot of money. The person had it planned for me to get caught holding those tickets so it would appear I doped all four horses. With the new NESPA rules, I would have been in serious trouble—even done jail time."

Patty whistled. "Now *those* are consequences."

"So the Hunter Group—they oversee the racing for NESPA at HSD—gave me two choices. One, stay there and get set up again and/ or risk an accident, or two, move out here for a few months, let them find out who was behind this."

"That's so wrong," she said. "Giving a horse dope to affect his performance—I agree with you that being an exercise rider is dangerous."

"You know, I've never wanted to be anything else, except a good husband and a good father," I said. "I haven't had a chance to try either of those."

"Are your parents still together?" she asked.

"No." I set my coffee cup on the floor. She watched me, as though waiting for me to say more. "My father would win and lose. The pattern lasted for a year or two, and then the financial problems got too bad. There was one day he walked in and he had lost everything, after my mother had juggled money for the rent and owed every grocer in town. She told him it was either the track or us."

I avoided Patty's eyes and said, "My sister and I pleaded with him to stop. He said, 'I can't.' Mom just stood there with her hands on her hips. He stood there, crying, and she told him to get out. We knew at that moment, in that little house, the track had won for the last time."

"I'm so sorry," she said.

I nodded. "It showed me that if I ever do get married, I want to be a better husband than my father was and a better father than he was, but at the same time, marriage feels confining to me. Maybe that's why it hasn't happened yet."

She rested her hand on my arm and gave it a gentle squeeze. "Beliefs formed in childhood are protection mechanisms."

"Yeah, well." I cleared my throat. "It all helped me become who I am. I became a horseman, kind of by accident, kind of on purpose. Fate, I guess. Or free choice. I've always believed in destiny. How 'bout you?"

"Do I believe in free choice or destiny?" Patty asked.

We both smiled. She made me feel important, as if that moment with her was the only one that mattered. Sitting in the barn, sipping coffee, and telling her things I don't tell people.

"Either one," I said. "Do destiny first."

She looked at me. "Destiny. You mean like on Tuesday when I opened the door of my car and I saw you?"

That image of her the first time I saw her was embedded in my mind. I had silently thought she might have felt the same.

"So yeah, Amos," she said as she petted Lucky. "I guess I believe in destiny."

"Some people believe accidents cause everything to happen," I said. "That's the opposite of destiny, isn't it?"

"This is too heavy a topic right after breakfast, don't you think? If we both weren't involved with horses, we wouldn't be sitting here, would we?"

Out of the blue, I said, "You know gambling? I could take it or leave it."

"Is that something else you wanted to do better than your father?" she asked.

All those scenes of chaos and shouting spun through my mind, and I was grateful I hadn't turned out like him.

"You know, you're the first person that's ever asked me that question," I said.

On top of that, I could tell she cared about the answer.

"Amos, sometimes just doing the opposite is enough."

I kept my eyes on her. I liked her face, her sincerity. Finally, someone had recognized what I'd been trying to prove all my life. She did it naturally and easily.

"Thanks," I told her.

She nodded, and I could tell she understood the past few moments had been important.

She got to her feet. "Next time, I'll tell you what I think about free choice," she said, as I stood up, too. "You look tired."

"I've had a headache since last week before I left Fort Worth. I'm used to working fourteen hours a day. I went from being 110 percent active, physically and mentally, and now I'm here. Just a long way from…"

"What you used to do." She nodded. "It takes your brain and your body time to adjust to not riding racehorses every day. That's as intense as any job I've ever heard of. This job is not intense or dangerous. There's no adrenaline rush here. It's going to take time for you to get acclimated and slow down."

I looked out at the fields. Silent, still. Completely different from the chaos of the track.

"We rehab prisoners," she said. "That's what we do. We're turning out people who have hit probably the roughest spots in their lives, and we give them horses to connect with and let them adjust their lives based on what horses teach them."

"I feel like I'm a prisoner. Kinda trapped here."

"You'll figure out what we really provide here is freedom. It sounds like you were trapped in that racetrack life. 24/7, like a prisoner. And now you're here, and maybe this is the freedom you need."

True. The only prisoner now was BigOilRig. He was exactly like the prisoners over at TSPAN. I needed to figure out how he could escape.

I took out a bunch of sunflower seeds from my shirt pocket and put them in my mouth.

"What's that?" she asked.

"Shelled sunflower seeds," I said. "One of the women from the greenhouse came over here yesterday and gave me a bag. She said they'd help the headaches."

"Our resident botanist. She raises all the sunflowers over there. They do have a medicinal effect on some people, but I think you need to spend more time with the horses and me." Patty laughed, looking uncertain for the first time. "I mean with me and the job we have to do. That's what I meant."

Chapter 23

I was at work in my office when a number I didn't recognize came through. "Miss Ricksland?"

"Yes." I signed off on another report and half listened.

"This is Agent Johnson and Agent Wyiskosky. We're here at the FBI office in Denver." I pushed the paperwork aside. "About five years ago, one of our team members, Agent N-412, worked with you when you were at the IRS in Washington. Are you at a secure place where you can take this call?"

I got up and closed the door. "Yes."

"Okay, ma'am. After you left the IRS, you went to work for the Hunter Group, private investigators in Fort Worth. We're involved in a big case right now that includes W. D. Stamples, the owner of HorseShoeDowns Racetrack, Casino, and Sportsbook."

I opened Notes on my iPad, ready to record anything important.

"He's always on the edge of lobbyists and political candidates—I can't say mergers and acquisitions, because really, he's on the side of hostile takeovers. Here's the purpose for our call. Washington is going to open an auction for leases for oil rigs in the Gulf of Mexico. It will be soon. This Stamples guy has put together investors, and they have already put almost $100 million in escrow for deposits."

"Yes," I said. "I was invited to attend one of the investor meetings, along with Max Hunter."

"Well, he's been bribing someone at the Bureau of Ocean Energy Management to be sure he is awarded the majority of the leases. We just sent your cell phone a link to the actual prospectus. We think there is high-profile criminal activity going on."

I put my silver oil rig gift from the TexaSTARanch in a drawer.

"We're going to be sending one of our agents to Fort Worth. We'll be in touch. Any questions?"

"No." It wasn't my first time dealing with the FBI. If they were involved, it meant Stamples was in deep. "Let me know if there is anything I can do to help you."

"Keep him focused on the racetrack affairs for the next several months. Those will serve as a distraction so we can work with the folks over at the Ocean Energy Bureau."

"Okay." I hung up and stared at my phone.

I remembered what Max had said in the car after the TexaSTARanch event. Something about how he thought Stamples wanted us to concentrate on this oil well auction so we would divert our focus off the NESPA rules.

At least now I knew what Stamples wanted. I couldn't be misled and chase him along with the FBI, especially for something that might not even happen.

I knew for a fact that some horses had gotten doped. My job was to find out who did it.

Chapter 24

On Thursday Rixie sent another short text with some weak excuses why Chex hadn't shipped out. In spite of my connection with Patty, there wasn't anything appealing about being at the ranch. I needed Chex to keep me sane.

I spent the morning working side by side with Patty. She introduced me around and made light of the fact that I didn't know the techniques they used. The hands-on grooming was universal. I had seen demonstrations over at the Stockyards where they would give hand signals and horses would move and follow the instructors. I was new but I was interested, especially in the way the women were proud of the bond they had with each horse they worked with. The more time I spent with them, the more I started to learn what equine therapy was all about.

A big dark bay thoroughbred reminded me of BigOilRig. I wondered how he was doing and if he'd gotten transferred to a new trainer.

That afternoon, a new farrier came from HSD to trim several horses. Once he'd finished, we went to the office to get him his check. Tex was there, and the farrier started to tell us about the racetrack news from Fort Worth.

He said, "Big controversy at HSD last week. Somehow favorites were given something to make them slowdown in the stretch. Driving those stewards crazy."

Tex stood there acting uninterested. I jumped in to see how much the farrier really did know. "What's that stuff, anyway?"

"Nobody knows, and they don't know who doped the favorites." He continued, "I'd like to stay here and talk all day, but I ain't on the clock like you guys. I got four more horses to shoe tonight and get back to Fort Worth."

We watched as he climbed into his truck. Tex said, "You ever hear about any of those race problems over in Fort Worth?"

"Yeah, some races turned out like that. NESPA is testing horses before and after all races. If they could, they'd test them during a race."

We both laughed and got back to work.

Back at the arena, one of the women was talking quietly, almost singing as she brushed a buckskin quarter horse. He reminded me of Chex, and I wondered when he would actually get shipped. I asked her, "What's the most important thing here?"

She didn't hesitate. "Trust. These horses trust me. And I'm learning how to make an authentic connection with this guy, especially since he's my favorite. He's leading me on my way back to relationships with people. On the outside, before I started over here, I trusted all the wrong people in my life."

Her voice broke as she added, "And nobody trusted me." She looked away for a moment and found a smile. "I get released in January, and because I have this training, I feel confident I'll get a job working on a farm somewhere."

I was impressed with her honesty.

Behind us Patty said, "Horses allow us to forget our past failures and focus on the future."

I thought I was supposed to teach these women horsemanship. I had been there only three days, but I was learning, minute by minute, that this whole experience might go a whole lot deeper than I'd thought.

Chapter 25

I sent Amos a text: *<shipping not arranged yet>*

No response.

<we just started on this Monday…not the only thing on my plate.>

I was busy chasing down the vets and jockeys involved in the race, and I didn't have time to worry about shipping his horse. Back at the IRS and the banks, few people had access to accounts and checks, so building a suspect list could happen much more quickly there than here.

It was Friday before I knew it, and I still didn't have a shipper lined up for Chex. I went by Barn7 to check on him. Charlane started right in.

"You got Chex set to ship out?"

"They're still booked up."

"Well, Hun. How 'bout this? I can borrow Buster's trailer and…" She winked. "Me and you. Load Chex up Saturday after I get done at the barn and head out there. Be back by dark."

My mind spun through three to four hours in a truck with her.

"Hun. What you waitin' on? Ain't goin' out there by myself." She flashed me her con-artist grin. "If I went by myself, I might not come back. You wouldn't want me to stay out there with Amos. Would you? Tell Amos it's arranged. Don't tell him it's you and me. Men don't need to know details. It'll be a total surprise. Don't know who Amos wants to see the most…Chex, you, or me?"

I let that comment slide and sent Amos a quick text: *<Got a shipper scheduled to be there late Saturday afternoon with Chex. I'll let you know exact time.>*

He texted back: *<I'll have to be here and we better not plan to meet on Saturday.>*

I texted him back: *<Let's reschedule for next weekend. I'll come then, okay?>*

He replied back with the thumbs-up emoji.

"What did he say?" Charlane tried to peer at my phone, and I put it in my pocket. I didn't want her to know I had planned to see him Saturday night.

"He's okay with Saturday," I said. "What time?"

"Leave at 2:00 sharp. We need a girls' trip outta this place."

Chapter 26

On Saturday, Patty had me help out with Visitors' Day. The women's kids came to visit, and it was a big deal. Patty briefed me on logistics as we got the water, coffee, and doughnuts set up in the indoor arena.

"Some of these kids will be terrified of horses," Patty said, "so we let them go at a slow pace. We start out with basic grooming and brushing. It's about letting them get used to touching horses. A few were here before, so they'll get to ride—well, walk—on the lead line." She handed me a box of cookies for the horses. "Here, take some of these and teach them how to give a horse a cookie."

"You're giving me a lot of instructions."

Patty smiled. "Sorry; I'm not used to having help. It's all I can do to make sure everyone gets a turn."

They showed up in all colors, from all corners of the world. Spouses, ex-spouses, men, women, and kids.

I had to step in like crowd control. "Whoa there. Slow down around horses; no running. Get a doughnut, coffee, or water, and take a seat on the bleachers."

Patty led me to the center and greeted the crowd. "Good morning. I'm Patty." She smiled at me, mostly with her eyes. "He's Amos. This is an important day; having family and friends here to share our horses is special for us all. Raise your hand if you have never been around a horse."

Most of the kids' hands went up, and almost all the adults. I raised my hand and said, "Me too. I just shipped in Monday, and this is my first time doing this, too."

That broke the ice, and a few people even laughed.

"He might have just got here," Patty said, "but he's been around horses his whole life. Mostly racehorses. We're all here to have fun and learn. Let's get started."

The women each got one of the horses they worked with and started showing their son or daughter how to groom.

We got the other kids fitted for helmets; it was time to ride.

"A couple of you were here last time," Patty said. "Who wants to go first?"

A little girl, about eight, raised her hand and stood up. She looked concerned. I recognized her mother sitting with her. She had told me every day this week how much she missed her daughter and couldn't wait for today.

Patty led her to Minty, whose real name was Peppermint Ice Cream. Patty handed her a brush and led her over to brush his legs. She smiled and almost laughed.

Patty knew her name. "Adrian, are you ready to ride?"

When the girl nodded, Patty motioned for me to come over. I moved the mounting block into place, and Patty said, "Two more steps."

Adrian put her hand on the top step and said her first words of the morning: "I got it."

Patty helped her. "Do you remember what's next?"

"Yes. Left foot in the stirrup, left hand grab the mane, and right hand on the back of the saddle."

Patty guided her foot into the stirrup and helped her up. She leaned forward and put both hands all over Minty's neck. Her smile was priceless. She adjusted her sunglasses, her helmet, then nodded. It was like how a bronc rider nods when they pull the rope to open the chute.

Patty handed me the lead rope. "Mr. Amos will take you today, okay?"

We started to walk, and I asked her, "So you were here before?"

"Yes. Tell me what you look like."

The question surprised me. "I look like a cowboy. You know, jeans, kinda dirty boots. I have on a blue striped shirt, cowboy hat."

"But what do you look like?"

"My face is tan, but kinda rough from the wind and sun—with wrinkles on my forehead and around my eyes. Brown eyes. Regular kinda ears. My teeth are pretty straight. Had to have the front ones replaced. My face went forward, and a horse's head came back and busted my mouth."

"Ouch, that hurt. Riding horses can be dangerous, right?"

"Yes, until you learn everything you need to know."

She pulled the reins and Minty stopped. "Do you think a blind kid like me can ever learn everything? Could I ever ride a horse by myself without someone holding the lead rope? You know, not just walk around, but trot, jog, or canter?"

"You're riding a horse right now."

"I mean by myself."

"Yes, I think someday you could. Minty doesn't know you're blind. He just knows you want to learn. He knows by your touch and soft voice. Horses know if someone cares about them. When you reached up and rubbed his neck—he felt that. He knows you care."

"It's about trust, too, isn't it? Minty has to trust me and I have to trust him. Right?"

"Yes," I said.

"Do you trust me?"

"Yes, why?" I asked.

"Do you have a bandana? Tie it around your face, shut your eyes, and let me guide you around blindfolded. Okay?"

I tied it in a knot, shut my eyes, and said, "Okay, let's go."

She walked him in a circle and then reversed in the other direction, kinda dragging me beside them, and I tried to keep up. She said, "Whoa," and he stopped.

"Okay, you can open your eyes now."

She'd put on quite a show. Soft, respectful applause came from the bleachers, and I helped her down. Her mother was right there, smiling.

Patty was all smiles, too. "Looks like you met your match there. This is what we do, what it's all about. It's not about the money, like at the track."

Money was the only thing that mattered at the racetrack. I realized some people actually have jobs that are satisfying because they love helping people. I remembered what Patty said about the prisoners not getting paid a fair wage and how these people needed all the help we could give.

It was a good point. I'll never forget the smile on Adrian's face. It was priceless.

Chapter 27

Max kidded me about the trip with Charlane, but when I woke up Saturday morning, the reality set in, along with frustration that I was the one who had to handle this.

All I'd really accomplished in ten days was getting Amos shipped out, and instead of hiring a shipper for his horse, I'd become one. Or assistant shipper. For sure Charlane would take all the credit—it was her idea.

Charlane called first thing. "Did you get Chex's health certificate from his vet?"

"No," I said. "I figured you would handle that."

"Hun, look, I'm just drivin' the truck," she said. "I'll text you Chex's vet's contact info; you need to call him and see if he can come here ASAP, examine Chex, and fill out the health papers and get his Coggins."

"Coggins? What's that?"

"Hun. You serious? Every time you ship to another state or facility, every horse has to have a current health certificate and proof of a negative Coggins test. To prevent the transmission of infectious diseases. You gonna get a feel for what we gotta do every day—keepin' up with paperwork."

I spent all day waiting on the vet. He finally showed up at 5:30. I texted Amos and told him the delay on the paperwork meant the shipper would now come out there Sunday about noon.

The next morning, I arrived at the barn at eight o'clock. Charlane and I had planned to leave at nine o'clock sharp. Immediately she started in.

"Looks like you're going to see your boyfriend."

I looked down at my simple, tailored shorts and button-up tank top. "No, this is what I always wear when I haul horses across Texas."

"Well, Hun, you look great. Amos will be glad to see you. Everything's ready."

She loaded Chex into the trailer and pulled up the ramp. We got into the truck, and I noticed dozens of boxes of her cookies in the back seat.

"Hun, you keep track of everything," she instructed. "We got to pay Buster for usin' his trailer. I get paid for my time, and I ain't cheap. Those other shippers were $400, wasn't it? So we're worth $200 each. What you think?"

"I'm just happy to help."

"Hun, I took care of ol' Chex all week. At least thirty dollars a day. Another two hundred. Amos can pay me outta his salary. Heard he got a sweet deal out there. I heard Stamples is tellin' anyone who will listen. Amos will probably end up like his father, since he got sent off to TSPAN prison."

She let go of the steering wheel and pointed up ahead—an electronic billboard flipped. "Look at Mr. W. D. Stamples's mug shot. How many jobs he's created, how much money he gave to Fort Worth charities."

She took the wheel again. "But WD has a history of disregard for human lives. There were numerous accidents, deaths, and safety infractions on those oil rigs in the Gulf of Mexico. He's the kind of man that thinks he can throw money at something and accomplish everything. It's his wife's money, anyway."

"Oh?" I said. "There are photos all over the walls in the executive offices of WD giving checks to charities."

"Yeah, no photos with employees or us on the backside. We make it happen for him so he can give those checks out. You know the chapel at the track where they have Cowboy Church? Preacher got him to donate all the money to build it, just for his ego, PR, and he got a big tax write-off."

I wondered how she would know that.

"Hun, you think he cares about hospitals and kids' camps? No. Photo op. If he really cared, he'd give money to the Official Universal Injured Jockeys Alliance guys. That's what's important at the track."

"OUIJA," I said. "I donate to them."

We drove in silence; then she said, "WD's wife and daughter are horse show girls. He has a disdain for the questionable billing practices of trainers and veterinarians. The entire horse show environment is just about chasing ribbons, schmoozing, and kissing judges' asses. Outside Houston, they have a state-of-the-art, Texas-sized ranch, barns, indoor air-conditioned arenas, outdoor arenas, trucks, trailers, equipment. All he did was try and keep track of the money goin' out. He never goes to any of the horse shows."

She looked over at me, then went on, "WD was a big fundraiser and donor to politicians. You know, Hun, you gotta get special permits to drill them oil wells out in the Gulf? Ain't cheap. All his buddies were busy buying professional football and baseball teams, trying to outbid each other. He thought he knew something about horses because of his wife and daughter. That's why he bought the track."

She glanced over at me. "Hun. Been gossip a long time. You know the only thing holding Stamples up from developing the entire eighty-five-acre property? Live racing. He's gotta keep live racing to keep the casino."

"I'm aware of all that," I said.

It was the reason NESPA hired us. It was a nice idea to think he had us there to improve safety measures, but it appeared that he didn't mind risking the track getting closed. As long as he kept the casino, he could develop the property.

The mile markers crawled by, even though she was way over the speed limit. I said my prayers.

"Hun, you ain't talked much about your big investigation. You ready to arrest anyone, or are you waitin' for the big guns from NESPA to come in and clean house?"

"Off limits."

Charlane made a face. We drove right down Main Street in Noose. She pointed out the Trap Door Saloon. It wasn't too far to Applegate's Ranch.

She said, "Well, there it is—Amos's new home!"

He directed us where to park. I got out, and he said, "Wow, this is a surprise. Welcome."

He seemed genuinely glad to see me. Charlane hollered, "Amos, get that rake and muck basket out of the tack room. Ol' Chex made a mess back here."

When he saw Chex, he seemed happier that Chex was there than that I was there, which was both offensive and endearing. Walking to the back of the trailer, he asked Charlane, "How's BigOilRig?"

"New trainer is giving him a little time off," Charlane said. "He's just goin' out and gallopin' a few laps every day. Just waitin' for him to be cleared off the stewards' list."

Amos finally included me in the conversation as he rubbed Chex's head. "His real name is Kings Chex Mate. He's twenty-five," he told me. "I've had him almost his whole life."

He looked at Charlane. "So how's Chex been doin'?"

"Great. You owe me $120 for the vet reports yesterday, $200 for this past week, and me and her $200 each for bringin' him here. Gave him a bath this mornin' like the good ol' days. I'm gonna miss him.

Ain't much talk about you—only me and her, well, we talk about you all the time."

I glared at her. "I wouldn't say all the time."

"Well, ain't nobody else talkin' about him. Lucky, now, everybody misses *him*." She handed the lead rope to Amos. "Take him. I gotta move some things around, clean out this trailer. Two of you go on. Figure you got some catchin' up to do."

"Let's go turn Chex out. This will make being here a lot better—having him here."

He sounded as though he resented being at the ranch. It was actually a fantastic modern facility. He didn't seem to have much appreciation for what I was doing to clear his name, but to be fair, I wasn't exactly expecting applause. The whole thing was frustrating, and it had to be hard for him to give up his entire life just because he'd made a bet that put everybody's eyes on him.

We walked, and Lucky followed right behind. "I don't guess you brought my check, did you?"

"I have no control over that."

He hardly acknowledged what I said. But his mood seemed to change immediately as a Range Rover pulled up.

An attractive, energetic woman got out, waving. "Amos," she called. "I was hoping your horse would be here." Walking up, she held out her hand. "Hi, I'm Patty."

"Rixie. I work at the racetrack." Charlane headed toward us, and I said, "That's Charlane, also known as Miss Ellane."

Patty laughed. "Do I owe you money? The cookies are a hit."

"Hun, you think I come out here to get my check? I'm tryin' to matchmake these two," she said, pointing between me and Amos. "Shippin' to a prison—couldn't get anyone to do it. So me and her did. Right, Rixie?"

I was starting to get frustrated with her. "Right on about everything except the matchmaking."

"Too bad. You'da made a nice couple." She looked at Amos. "She's gettin' rid of a guy. Put her on your AE list."

Amos pointed at a building. "Charlane, you should go look at the greenhouse."

I said to Patty, "She has one back in Fort Worth."

Charlane had to get in the last word. "Ma'am, you got one of the best cowboys you coulda got, right there."

Patty nodded. "You both should have seen him yesterday with the visiting children. Proud to have him here. As for me, I want to see this horse I've heard so much about."

The three of us headed back to Chex's new paddock, and he trotted right up to the fence. Patty put her hand on his neck, lifted his upper lip, and then studied his eye. "He's a nice horse. I can see why he's so special. I'm glad he got here okay." She looked at Amos, then me, and back at him. I could tell she was wondering about us. "Well, I've got to get back and start dinner. It was nice to meet you."

Patty drove off as Amos and I walked toward the women's side of the equine therapy facility. "I work there," he said, pointing at the barn.

That was news to me. "I thought you'd be working with the racehorses on the men's side."

"Well, Mr. Applegate indicated I was supposed to work for him, but a woman quit last Friday and they moved me over here."

"So Patty's your boss?" I asked.

I wasn't so sure I would have endorsed this if I had known this would be his arrangement. Not that I had time to put him on my AE list, as Charlane liked to say, but Amos shrugged. He went into the office and returned with two bottles of water. "You got me out of the way to do your investigating. How's it going?"

"Not easy. I can see how frustrating it was for you to be the safety sheriff."

"Safety sheriff. I'll put that on my resume. Too bad we missed last night. Maybe next Saturday?"

I figured I might as well cut to the chase. "Do you want an update on the investigation? Or do you want to see me?"

"Both."

At least that was the right answer. "We drove by the Trap Door Saloon. It was everything I imagined on the outside. Can't wait to see the inside. Let's see how this week comes together."

Charlane came back carrying a box. "Look at this. They won't miss these. Gonna sell 'em to the casino. Bluebonnets, red Indian paintbrush, wildflowers, and sunflowers. Boss lady, time to tell your boyfriend goodbye."

Amos leaned back on his heels, looking vaguely amused. I glared at her.

"Shit, y'all. She's bustin' up with some guy, and Amos, you on the rebound from Kellsey. Just sayin'. Why not?"

I just shook my head. "Fort Worth. Let's go."

We all said "Good idea" at the same time.

The trip back felt twice as long. I had to have some quiet time. I put on my sunglasses, put my earbuds in, turned on *my* music on my iPad, shut my eyes, and blocked everything out.

Amos had an interesting arrangement. I'd never imagined it would be such a fantastic facility. I guessed everything about the governor's wife could be true. Patty seemed to have it together, and she had Amos in her life, too.

Why was I even thinking about that? The plans we'd made for next Saturday were to talk business. I could update him on the case, and that was it. Maybe deliver his check. But I had to admit, it did kind of bother me to know he'd be spending the next few months with Patty.

Charlane touched my arm. "You awake? Listen, I've been thinkin' 'bout you and Amos. Hun, you're too much like Kellsey. It'll never work. Amos needs a woman like Patty back there. Did you notice how they looked at each other? Like we wasn't even there, like we were just horse shippers?"

I had never been so glad to get out of a truck in my life.

Chapter 28

On Tuesday, I made my rounds, and I ran into Charlane at Barn7.

"Hun, guess who came by here?" she said. "Kellsey O'Bryan. I got her caught up on everything. First thing, she noticed Chex was gone. So I told her about you going out there to see Amos. I heard Stamples would match any jockey fees she earned for the rest of the meet here. For example, let's say she wins a $100,000 race. The owner of the horse gets $60,000; he pays the trainer and the jockey $6,000 each. And Stamples will kick in an additional $6,000 to Kellsey. That, my friend, is a sweet side hustle."

Charlane added, "Oh, he cuts some trainers deals, too. He will give big-time trainers free stall rent just to keep them here."

I thanked her and excused myself. The information was interesting.

I had planned to meet one of the stewards at Barn7. It was important for a steward to join me when I went on an info search, and Buster motioned for us to go to the office.

"Just one question," I said. "What, besides hay, do you give your horses?"

He handed me the printout of what every horse got. "I gave the stewards a copy last week."

"Can I keep this copy?"

"Yes." He looked at the steward. "It's bad enough BigOilRig and NoCashRefund got transferred to another trainer—for no legitimate reason—but what's taking so long for my other horses to get off the stewards' list?"

The steward raised his voice a notch. "We are still waiting on the final lab reports; should be back any day."

"Any day?" Buster raised his voice too. "This week or what week?"

"You will know as soon as we know."

Buster's patience was wearing thin. I was glad he was taking out his frustrations on the steward and not on me. The steward's phone rang, and he went outside.

"Buster, I need to see Pepito for a minute. Can we use this office?"

Buster went out and sent Pepito back by himself. Pepito shut the door and took off his green HSD ball cap, pushed his short black hair over to the side, and sat down. I showed him the printout Buster had given me. He read through it pretty fast, then looked up.

I said, "Do they get anything else?"

"No." He thought for a minute. "Oh, they get cookies."

"How often?"

"*Todo el tiempo*. All the time."

I frowned. "Even on days they're entered in a race?"

"Yes."

"Friday, when BigOilRig raced. Did he get cookies that day?"

"Charlane made a new batch and told me to give them to BigOilRig. Yes, I gave those cookies to him. They was kinda…*quemado*."

"*Quemado*?"

"Si, burnt. Looked like they got a little cook too much."

"Are you sure you didn't give them to NoCashRefund?"

Pepito wiped his forehead with his shirt sleeve. "I might have mix up. Six o'clock is dark; lights aren't very good. Horses switch all around, different stalls; Buster hollering, and me just doing my best. I do anything wrong?"

"Not if you told me the truth."

"Si. That is the truth."

"Have you told anyone else about the *quemados*?"

"No."

"It's important you don't say anything about this, and don't tell Charlane you told me either."

"Si."

"Anything else?"

"Charlane brings oatmeal-raisin cookies to the barn for me to take home to my kids."

I nodded to Pepito. "One more question. How many cookies did you give him?"

"She had six or seven in a plastic bag. She said for me to give them all to him."

"Okay."

I went to the storage room where Charlane kept the cookies, got a handful, and put them in a paper towel. I took them back to the office and got Clink to send them to the NESPA DEA lab and request a quick evaluation.

By Wednesday SkyMan was out of the hospital and started his new job with Buster. I headed over to Barn7 to see how he was doing.

Martha was there too.

"I'm not sure he should start this soon," she told me, by way of greeting. "Still, you know a man can't lie around the house or be in the hospital very long until he has to get back to doing what he loves. Buster wants him to keep his eyes on everyone and everything. No physical work. He's still got his arm in a sling."

"I have an idea to bounce off SkyMan and you. Could we go up to SkyMan's apartment?"

She said, "His apartment is the one on the left." She motioned for SkyMan to join us, and we went upstairs and sat in the living room.

I said, "I started thinking about the cookies the horses have been eating." I took one out of my purse and asked Martha, "What if these cookies were burnt and given to a horse?"

She said, "Anything burnt and then eaten by an animal could be toxic and cause any animal to vomit, almost immediately. The animal would be sick for a while and drink a lot of water."

"What if a horse ate a whole bunch of them?" I asked. "Can horses eat too many?"

"These horses eat as many as they want, every day. If they ate too many burnt ones, it could be dangerous."

I said, "At first I thought some horses here at HSD had been given burnt cookies that caused them to slow down just like NoCashRefund did when you had the accident. But what if the cookies only looked like they were burnt. What could cookies be made with that would make a horse slow down?"

Martha frowned. "Lots of things would make a dog, or an animal or even a horse be calm and quiet and even slow down. Sunflower seeds, melatonin, red raspberry leaves, and CBD."

"Crushed marshmallow root too," SkyMan added.

I thought for a minute. "So what if NoCashRefund ate a bunch of cookies made out of that stuff?"

SkyMan said, "That might make him do exactly what he did that day."

"Those other horses in Race 4, too?"

"Yes. It could explain why the favorites finished up the track."

"Could those ingredients be detected in a horse's urine or blood before or after a race or training?" I asked.

"I don't know," SkyMan said. "They probably aren't testing for those things."

They looked at me, as though waiting for answers.

"I know what you both are thinking, but for right now, we don't have any evidence. Thanks for sharing your ideas about what ingredients in cookies could cause a horse to slow down."

Max was supposed to go to Oaklawn Park in Hot Springs for a NESPA conference. On Thursday, he decided it would be a good opportunity for me to go instead—and I got a flight for Friday. He didn't know I had planned to meet Amos on Saturday.

On Friday, I headed to DFW airport and texted Amos: <*Max sending me to Oaklawn. NESPA conference. Sorry. Rain check?*>

He sent back several sad-face emojis. I sent him back three emojis—rain, a check mark, and a happy face.

The Southern Airways commuter jet was so small I barely had room to work on the fold-down tray. I tried to review the schedule of topics covered at the conference, but I stared out the window instead. There were few moments where I could slow down and think. It felt as if my life were passing by like the clouds below me.

I looked up the aisle at the other passengers. I wondered what else was in Hot Springs besides Oaklawn. What were these other passengers going there for? What was I going there for? Or the bigger question: What would I be doing with my life when I left there on Sunday?

There were moments where it felt as though this NESPA assignment had more downsides for my career than upsides. At least back as a bank examiner and a criminal investigation IRS agent, I not only chased the crooks—I also caught them and put them away. Now I didn't even have a clue who I was chasing.

The plane landed, and outside the secured area, a tan and attractive man was staring at me. I couldn't look away from his greenish-gray eyes; the left one was greener than the right one. I started to feel flattered until he held up an iPad with "R. Ricksland" on it.

Just my luck, my first time here and I fall for the limo driver.

I reached out, and we stood there shaking hands a couple of times. I never shake hands with Uber or Lyft drivers. What was I doing?

"I have a small bag," I said, pointing at the baggage claim area.

"Sure, let me get it for you."

He picked it up, and we headed outside. The car was an SUV from the track.

"Sit up front if you want to," he said, and smiled when I did. "What brings you to Oaklawn?"

"The NESPA conference. I work at HorseShoeDowns in Fort Worth. Are you familiar with it?"

"Yes, but I've never been there."

"You'll have to come down there and check it out."

I almost said I'd pick him up and show him around. We pulled up to the main entrance. "I'll put your suitcase in my office until you need it later."

I thought he just drove the shuttle.

He left me in the lobby. There weren't many people there, but a man wearing a suit two sizes too big walked up to me, almost in a rush.

"Welcome to Oaklawn. I'm Walter Southton, financial operations director. I see you met Thomas." He pulled his glasses off his bald head. "Keep your eye on him—he's from NESPA."

Keep my eye on him. Might be the easiest part of the trip.

"Let me take you on a tour of the facility."

That hour, just like at HSD, confirmed the biggest problem was how difficult it was to get people to keep their data updated. Walter took me back and said, "Thomas can show you around the rest of the afternoon."

It was a beautiful afternoon. Thomas and I went out to some seats to watch the next race. "Well, did Walter tell you how much he dislikes the whole program? Or did he say they're making progress here?"

"Neither. He said I had to spend the rest of the afternoon with you."

I had no idea why I'd said that. For a second, I thought of how different Thomas was from Amos. I could get used to spending afternoons with him.

He smiled and said, "Here's a copy of Oaklawn's NESPA monthly reports since they started. We track every veterinarian and trainer.

Every medication administered to every horse. The track doctor does random drug and alcohol screening on every employee, groom, rider, jockey."

I was impressed with his knowledge and a little embarrassed I hadn't realized he was with NESPA from the beginning.

"Come on," he said. "I want to show you the barns." He got a golf cart, and we made it to the backside. The barns were much nicer than those at HSD.

"I'm Mister Bad Guy around here," he confided. "Nobody likes rules, especially new rules that uncover problems. But the horses are doing better. You'll see a whole section in your notebook about breakdowns, injuries, scratches, the stewards' list. Another section on penalties and fines to the people involved, and one on stewards' decisions."

We went back to watch the last race. Thomas watched it intently. "Can I give you a ride to the hotel?" he said as we got to our feet.

"I'm in a suite at the casino hotel. Yes, I'd appreciate a ride."

On the way out, I noticed he was right—no one acknowledged we were there. He put my suitcase in the back and opened the door for me.

"I'm glad you're here," he said. "Gives me a break from what I've been doing. Sorry, I didn't mean that's the reason I'm glad you're here. I meant, I'm glad you're here."

"I'm glad I'm here too."

He pulled up to the casino hotel entrance and carried my suitcase to the reception desk. He checked me in, got the key card, and handed it to me but held on to it until our eyes met. "Would you like to go to dinner? Tonight? With me?"

I studied his face and held up the notebook. "I was afraid I was going to have to read through this tonight. So yes. Let's do that."

Dinner date. Glad I'd brought a decent dress to change into.

The restaurant didn't seem fancy, but apparently, it was the best in Hot Springs. The waiter said, "We have a good selection of wines."

"What do you prefer?" he asked.

"If the grouper is good here, I'd like white."

He ordered a bottle, and we talked about first-date topics before he said, "There will be a new NESPA job opening at your track in July. You would surely qualify, and NESPA pays top dollar."

"I have a good job now," I said, but the wheels started turning.

Max had been firm on the fact that the contract position wouldn't last forever, and he talked as if he wanted to retire. I'd have to find something to move on to.

I studied him and said, "Why don't you put in for a transfer? Come check out Fort Worth? You don't seem to be what I imagined the NESPA auditors to be like."

He laughed. "Auditor? Well, I've never been called that before." He handed me his card.

Thomas de Tono
President and CEO
NESPA

"I guess I owe you an apology," I said. "First, I thought you were the limo driver. This has been the most interesting day I've had in a while."

I fished out one of my Hunter Group cards that I was proud of—vice president and CFO. I slid it over to him.

"I guess I owe you an apology too," he said. "I didn't know you're part of the Hunter Group. It's the first private investigation firm we have contracted with, shoring up our shortcomings as a federal agency. What exactly do you do there?"

"I'm responsible for examining all the NESPA forms created by trainers, the veterinarians and the track doctor. When there are violations, I'm involved in administering the penalties," I said. "And by the way, I'm investigating an incident on March 26 that has some serious repercussions for that track and the individuals involved. I may need to bounce some strategies off you as it evolves."

"Absolutely," he said. "I would love to help you."

When was the last time I'd heard "love" and "you" in the same sentence?

He studied me for a moment. "I'm glad they decided to send you here."

We shared a fresh fruit and vanilla ice cream dessert. He drove the short ten minutes, and when we pulled up to the hotel, he parked in a reserved parking spot by the main entrance.

"It's a nice hotel," he said. "Is your room okay?"

"Which one? It's a huge suite."

We walked up to the hotel, and he paused just outside the main entrance. "I have to go back over to my office and finish some work." He smiled. "For some reason I got distracted this afternoon."

"Are you serious about coming down to Fort Worth?" I asked.

"My job is to visit every racetrack. So yes, now I have another reason."

"And what would that reason be?"

"Let's just say you are a very interesting woman."

I faked a glance at my watch. "Let's see. You picked me up at two o'clock. I use that term 'picked me up' with a certain amount of discretion. Now it's almost ten…That's probably the best eight hours I've spent in a long time."

"Me too. Let's regroup in Fort Worth," he said. "I have to go to NESPA headquarters in Lexington tomorrow right after the morning session, so I might not see you tomorrow. So for now, let's say good night."

"Okay, good night," I said, but he still stood there.

"Well, let's see. You accepted the offer to dinner, turned down the job offer, and accepted the offer to have a date in Fort Worth, so let's see if you'll accept an invitation to go to the Kentucky Derby."

I was surprised at how fast this was happening. The Derby was in four weeks. "It's a big simulcast day at the Sports Book, and I usually have to work. But, yes, I would love to."

He smiled. "All right. That's perfect. So it's good night again."

"That's the last good night for tonight. I promise."

He gave me the thumbs-up. I wondered why everyone down here used that as a way to say okay and goodbye.

I couldn't wait to get to my room and google Thomas de Tono. I wasn't disappointed. Two years prior, he'd resigned as the managing partner in a prestigious Kentucky law firm that specialized in an exhaustive list of legal services to take the job at NESPA.

He was impressive, and I was impressed.

The casino hotel had a large conference center, and there were hundreds of people just like me there the next morning. Name tags. I looked all over for Thomas but couldn't find him.

At the ten o'clock break, I looked at the schedule and saw the executive committee was scheduled for a golf outing while the rest of us sat in the conference room hearing panel discussions. That must have been what he meant when he said he might not see me today.

It might not be a bad idea to take up golf. Like I have time for that.

When the morning session concluded, there was a big luncheon. The golfers all came in together and sat at the head table.

As soon as he sat down, our eyes locked across the room. He smiled and picked up his phone. A text came right in: <*Could you give an ex–limo driver a ride to the airport when lunch is over?*>

I wanted to keep it short and sweet, so I texted him a thumbs-up emoji and <*what time is your flight?*>

<*on the NESPA plane—it leaves when I get there*>

I googled "romantic things to do in Hot Springs," then texted, <*Have you been to Garvan Gardens? It's eight miles from here. Do you have time to stop there on the way to the airport?*>

Right there, in front of two hundred people, he looked right at me, smiled, and gave me a thumbs-up. Better than another emoji. The people at my table had to notice that exchange.

My temperature notched up, and I took a drink of water. He finally finished his presidential duties and worked his way through the crowd.

He motioned with his left hand for me to go in front of him and put his right hand on the small of my back. I decided to just smile and act as though I knew what I was doing.

Just when I thought I was stuck here at the races, ready to watch for potential violations, I had something much more pleasant on my plate: I had a date for the afternoon.

We met in front of the hotel, and he already had his suitcase in the car. He said, "I'll drive, and you can bring the car back."

"Can we go to the Gardens?" I asked.

"Of course."

He had already put the address in his phone. When we pulled up at the entrance, I was surprised and a little disappointed to see so many cars. I didn't want to share Thomas with anyone. He got our visitor's stickers and gently stuck mine on my blouse.

I had envisioned the two of us by ourselves, walking on the paths, but we fell in behind a walking tour. The guide said, "We plant hundreds of thousands of tulip and daffodil bulbs."

They were all in bloom, and in spite of the other people, I was glad we'd picked this time of year to be there.

Before we branched off on our own, I asked a woman to take our picture. I wanted to savor this moment. Thomas put his arm around me and stood as close to me as he could as the lady said, "On three. One…"

"I don't know what's more beautiful," he said, quietly. "The acres of tulips or the smile that's on your face."

"…two, three," the woman said, and took the picture.

"What got you involved with NESPA?" I asked, after we'd walked in silence for a moment on the path. I was still thinking about the thing he'd said, about me being beautiful.

"For several years Washington tried to pass legislation to have a federal organization regulate all aspects of equine activities. I started going to the Capitol four years ago and helped them write the language of the bill that created NESPA. My law firm had extensive experience in all aspects of horse racing. Even though the bill is written to regulate all equine activities, it had to start with horse racing because that's where there are the most violations."

I liked that he was athletic, in a different way than Amos, like a man who worked out and played a lot of golf. It was a good thing he didn't have a set time to catch his flight; he never looked at his watch or phone but was intent on just being there—with me. We started to walk slower under the pine tree canopy.

"What was the biggest accomplishment in getting the bill passed?" I asked.

"I had to convince Congress to be a financial partner with the horse industry. Washington matches the money the tracks are charged. This protects the small tracks and doesn't put an unfair expense burden on owners who have a small string of horses. This way it was set up to be successful from the start."

"What was the biggest surprise?"

"We underestimated the shortage of veterinarians and doctors that are required to carry out the rules and regulations."

"So how'd you go from the law firm to NESPA?"

He smiled. "You're showing me your investigative skills with all these questions."

I was interested in learning as much as possible about him, and I had only a short period of time to do that.

"After they did a national search, they kept enticing me with how important this was, and there was no one else that could do this job," he said. We stopped and sat on a bench between the large stone bridge and the waterfall. "I never thought I'd go to work for the Department of Justice. And especially the DEA."

"Don't take this the wrong way, but do you know omertà?"

He laughed and raised his eyebrows. "Why? With a name like de Tono, do you think I'm in the Mafia?"

I laughed. "Of course not, Thomas. I should have said this first—the entire culture at racetracks is like omertà. The Mafia code of silence. We can't get any answers, and everything is hush-hush and covered up. NESPA is supposed to be proactive, and I feel as if we are reactive. I'm not sure even a private investigative firm like the Hunter Group—and it's one of the best—has the training to miraculously infiltrate the systems and culture of a racetrack and do the job we are hired to do."

He nodded, as if to tell me to go on.

"We are up for the first six-month review in a few weeks, and this situation from two weeks ago is serious. So serious, I'm not sure I want to continue."

Thomas thought for a minute, then spoke. "I did a little homework on everything down there in Fort Worth. You are absolutely essential to our organization. Keep the faith, and stay focused on the investigation. You'll figure it out."

He paused and said, "As for me, I have to get back to my day job. Auditor, no. Limo driver, no. Mafia, no."

We laughed as I took some more pictures of the interesting stone bridges and a peacock. Before we left, I got more pictures of us; each time we wrapped our arms around each other tighter than before. It turned out to be a three-hour tour. We walked back and got into his car. I wished he wasn't leaving.

"Okay, after that, one more question," I said, not wanting our time to end. "What's the highlight of your job, so far?"

Our eyes locked again, and he never hesitated. "Yesterday. Last night. Right now…"

I was shocked. Flattered. Intrigued. But also cautiously excited.

Chapter 29

I was disappointed that Rixie had canceled the second Saturday trip out here. She'd only been here for an hour when she'd brought Chex out. I'd decided to go to Noose anyway. I found a Cowboy Church for Sunday. The guys would think it was a waste of time. Maybe, by my example, I could show them a better way. What would they see at the moment? Given what everyone thought about me, I had a lot of reputation repairing to do too.

APP loaned me a truck, a nondescript old pickup with "TAPP Ranch" on the doors. I had to clean it first. When the truck was ready, I went to thank him and ask if he needed anything in town.

"No." He turned and said, "Just be sure to come back with my truck."

Most people who would say something like that would mean it in jest, but he was serious. His eyes put an exclamation point at the end of his sentence.

I nodded, took the keys, and said, "Yes, sir."

Before leaving, I texted Rixie: <*I'm going to check out Noose. Sorry you won't be here for the first trip. How's the investigation going? Update? You said you'd try to bring my money this weekend, but now, you're not coming at all. Have a safe trip to Oaklawn*>

I hoped she'd sense the sarcasm in that text. Lucky sat in the passenger seat and looked out the window most of the way. I turned on the classic country radio station in Fort Worth.

I barely got off the ranch before I stopped for gas at a truck stop that had a big field in the back. Lucky jumped out and found a stick, and he chased it until he wore me out throwing it. It was starting to get hot in the afternoons, even though it was still early spring.

I went in and got an ice cream. The people were either old-timers or people passing through. I was definitely temporary, for sure.

"Trap Door Saloon?" I asked the guy behind the counter. "Where is it exactly?"

"Exactly? You go west out of the parking lot, go back about twenty years, and it's about two miles. Can't miss it. Big stone building right on Main Street."

"Thanks." Going back twenty years made me think of when I started exercising horses at Hialeah Park down in Miami. So much had changed for me, but in some ways, so much was still the same. I drove the rest of the way without a text from her.

Downtown Noose was laid out in an L shape. I checked into the Noose Hotel. I paid extra for Lucky, and after he sniffed around the room, I got him some water, and he found a good spot by the front door to lie down on his old blanket. "Don't get comfortable; we're heading out."

The bar wasn't hard to find. An old, sun-bleached sign spelling out "Trap Door Saloon" hung over the door. I parked under a big oak tree near the back of the gravel lot, and Lucky curled up on an old blanket in the truck bed.

I had on my cleanest shirt and jeans. My straw hat was vintage rodeo. Creases, dirt. The sweat stains on the outside gave it instant credibility. I was wearing my old belt buckle from over in Abilene.

Our eyes locked as soon as I came in the door. She had long, dark hair with a blond streak on the left side. Old half boots, a well-worn denim skirt shorter than it had to be, a red-and-pink flowered shirt—unbuttoned, with a skin-tight white T-shirt underneath. As she walked up to my table, she spat out a small piece of gum into her hand and helped herself to the chair next to me. "Howdy, stranger."

"Howdy."

She looked straight at me, seriously sultry. It was more than intentional. "Raven's my name. What's yours, cowboy?"

I knew it wasn't her real name and I shouldn't give out mine, but I did. "They call me Amos."

"Amos? That's a new one for me. First time at The Trap Door?"

"First time."

"Here's the lowdown on this joint." She leaned in closer, as if she were telling me a secret. "About ninety years ago, they tore down the gallows on Main Street. The platform was salvaged and brought up here, installed right in the middle of the dance floor. Two original trapdoors. This is *the* tourist attraction here in Noose. People come from all over to walk over there and cautiously stand on the trapdoor. How do you plead?"

I didn't expect that question. "Not guilty."

"What did you do, anyway?" she asked.

"Stole a truck and escaped from TSPAN this afternoon."

She backed away from the table. "Come on—you're shittin' me."

"Come on. I'll show you the truck. I parked in the back."

We walked by the bar, and she told the bartender we'd be right back. Lucky was a hit. She messed with him and pointed to the TAPP Ranch sign on the door. "Okay. I thought you said TSPAN? What's the deal?"

"I started working with the horses at TAPP Ranch last week."

"And you just happened to tell me a big jailbreak story. I believed you. That's the best pickup line I've ever heard."

I left that comment outside, and we walked back in and sat down at my table. She lit up half a smile and said, "You're here a little early for happy hour, but I can get you the same prices. What are you having?" She pushed the blond hair behind her ear. Her head moved to the rhythm of the slow country song on the jukebox.

"Surprise me. Thinking about a draft to start with."

"And what do you end up with?"

"Don't know; depends on a lot of things."

"Fair enough." She stuck out her tongue a little, and put a fresh sliver of gum back in her mouth.

It was a saloon, for sure. Big wooden bar on one side. A small stage at the back. Cowboy decor. Old hardwood floor, the trapdoors in the middle, just like she said. It could have been a bank or a feed store many years before.

Raven put down a square paper napkin printed with the trap door logo. "Here's your surprise. My number's on the other side." She set down an ice-cold bottle of Abilene Ale. Now this wasn't the kind of greeting I'd thought I'd get in Noose, Texas. I'd been tied up too long at the racetrack. It was time to see how the rest of the world was doing.

It was pretty good. She circled back around as people started coming in.

"Good choice," I told her. "Thanks."

I wasn't much of a drinker or a guy that hung out in bars. I finished the beer, took the napkin, and put it in my shirt pocket. Left a good tip on the table and walked toward the door.

"Way too early to be leavin'," she called. "What's your hurry?"

"Gotta get some dinner, go feed my dog. I left money for the beer and a tip on the table."

She looked back, as if checking to see if I'd taken her number. Smiling, she said, "Next time bring him in. We like dogs."

I tipped my hat to her. "Next time. Thanks."

Lucky and I drove back to the hotel. We hit the sidewalk and toured the town on foot. Small Texas towns are all alike; only the names change. There was a bar, a bank, a hotel, a feed store, a cemetery, and a lawyer's office or two. A church on each end of town. I fed Lucky and went to the café for dinner.

I finally got a short and pretty vague text from Rixie. She didn't ask anything about me or my trip to town. I wondered what she was up to and turned in early.

It was a rustic Easter Sunday service at Cowboy Church, held in an old converted barn on the outskirts of town. Lucky and I sat on the bench in the back. They had coffee and rolls, but I only tried the coffee.

Lucky was a hit like always, making friends with all the women. We got invited to the potluck lunch, but I declined. Everybody was friendly, and I put some money in the bucket for the offering.

We got back to TAPP Ranch refreshed. I pulled the napkin from the Trap Door out of my shirt pocket, where I used to put my tickets during a race. I couldn't stop thinking about Raven's phone number. I guess I could have found her interesting if I hadn't made arrangements to meet Rixie. Even though I might only be here for a couple of months, I was really fascinated with Patty.

Chapter 30

On Monday, after my fast trip to Oaklawn, the results came back from the NESPA DEA lab on the cookie I'd sent them. It showed nothing they were presently checking for. I'd waited long enough to confront Charlane; as I walked up to the barn, I said, "We need to talk."

"You're right we do," she said, without skipping a beat. "People in this barn and around the track are getting a little irritated that their horses ain't allowed to run. Hun, what did they hire you for anyway? You gotta keep horses racing. Keep the races filled, the barns full. You ain't doin' a very good job of that. WD has to have racing to keep the casino license. Ain't too many clean trainers left. You got Buster barely makin' it, what with those two horses transferred to another trainer. I heard some regular trainers—here every year—might not ship in for the summer. Goin' to Oaklawn instead."

It was time to confront her about the cookies. I fully expected she'd been waiting for me to ask her this and would be quick to sell the first person she could down the river. I said, "Charlane, there's something we need to discuss."

"Oh, shit, Hun. You gettin' serious on me, ain't you? I know what you gonna ask me about. Go ahead." She crossed her arms and leaned back. But she couldn't contain herself and said, "Listen. There are some things you don't need to know about...because if you know certain things, that puts your name on certain lists, and trust me—you don't want that."

"It doesn't matter to me either way," I said. "I want answers."

Charlane sighed. "Hun, I gotta come clean with you. Some people have to do things, and some people get in the way. Here's a little advice for you: don't get in the way. Keep doin' the investigatin'—act on information. When the time is right, you'll get your answers. Now what did you want to ask me about?"

The tone of her voice was threatening, but I was not about to back down.

"We need to talk about the *quemados*."

She wrinkled her forehead. "*Quemados*—what's that?"

"Those burnt cookies BigOilRig was supposed to get."

"Well, I don't know what you are talking about. I don't bake 'burnt' cookies. Must not be mine."

Charlane grabbed a brush, walked over, and started brushing the first horse she could find. I followed her. She was indignant. "That's exactly what I'm talkin' about," she said in a low tone. "Forget about that for right now. That incident was—what—three weeks ago? You need to focus on the next incident and try to prevent that."

She grunted, brushing harder. "Maybe NESPA should have hired a public relations outfit instead of private investigators. You got a lot of people worried. I tell you what—you better be careful. Now I got friends; they'd do anything for me. How many friends you got around here?"

"Not many," I said.

"Exactly." Putting away the brushes, she said, "Without exercise riders, you got no racing. These horses have to train six days a week, rain or shine. I'm one of the most important people at this racetrack. Maybe the most important—to you, anyway. You could treat me with a little respect."

With that, Charlane stalked off, leaving me in her wake.

"Well," I said out loud. "That didn't go as planned."

Thursday evening after work, I was sitting on my back porch; it was almost dark, and I got a call.

I smiled. "Thomas. I have looked at every incoming number, hoping it was you."

"This is your limo driver, trying to make arrangements to pick you up again. Sorry it took me so long to call." I visualized his smile; his voice was warm. "I had a lot of family stuff to deal with on Easter Sunday. How are you?"

"Busy."

So busy that I'd neglected to notice Easter rush by, which made me feel a little guilty. The call stretched out for an hour. We talked a little about our afternoon at Garvan Gardens, and he said he'd get me a plane ticket for the Kentucky Derby, since it was coming up in two weeks.

It sounded like a great opportunity to learn more about the world of the jockeys, horses, and trainers, but more than that, a chance to spend time with Thomas, and I was looking forward to that.

"Tell me about the Derby. I know I need to go shopping for a new dress and hat, but tell me what to expect."

"There will be 150,000 people. We will be in the NESPA suite on the sixth floor. There are a lot of people who want to meet the mystery lady from Texas."

"I guess they know I work for NESPA?" I asked.

"Yes. Everybody here knows the Hunter Group. Not like we will have you on a panel to discuss how this is going. It will be totally social."

"I've heard so many people say the Derby is on their bucket list. I'm getting excited to go be with those 150,000 other people—and with you."

It was probably the best invitation I'd ever had to something like that. "Is everything okay with your family now?" I asked.

"Yes. I've just been spread pretty thin. I need some quality time... with you."

That's what I wanted to hear. I hung up the phone, stood up, and glanced at my reflection in the glass door. I looked flushed and happy, which was exactly how this guy made me feel. It was a welcome change. Maybe he was the man I'd been searching for.

Are you crazy to be thinking like this? You just met.

Still, there was something about him that had drawn me in from the start. I hoped this could turn into something that could last. Too soon to tell, but it would be interesting to see where it went.

SkyMan had settled in his new job at Barn7, wearing a compression vest to protect the bones that were still healing. Everyone knew he was going to get a big settlement. Instead of being happy for him, they seemed envious. Money changes people. Except SkyMan—you'd never have known he expected to get a dime from the track.

On Friday, I ran into Martha at Barn7.

"How are you doing?" I asked her.

"I wish we'd never come to Fort Worth," she said. "As soon as we have the settlement money, we're going back home to help Mary start a children's learning center."

"Really?" That was impressive.

"SkyMan's been talking with Amos about what he's doing—helping the women with horses, and we've decided to add an equestrian center. I'll be so glad when this whole thing is over and we can move on."

When this whole thing is over.

I had this trip out to see Amos penciled in on my calendar on Saturday. I felt as though I was harboring the information from my conversations with Pepito, Dos, and Charlane. I kept logging in to the OMERTA file and documenting the facts as I got them. I sure couldn't tell Max—he'd want us to take drastic action, which would be premature. We were at a standstill on the investigation. We couldn't do anything until another incident occurred. It was my job to make sure that an incident didn't occur, so as always, my hands were tied.

There had been a positive test after a stakes race on a horse in Barn4. I pulled on my latex gloves and got out of the golf cart with the chief steward. We were acting on a call to the tip line. Clink and the head track veterinarian, together with two other golf carts filled with security, had already swarmed Barn3.

I showed my NESPA badge to the trainer, who immediately tensed up and clenched his fists.

"I need you to move outside the barn area," I said. "We're here to do a routine barn check. You can wait out there."

I heard the unsaid words that were obvious in his brown eyes. He grabbed a towel and wiped his hands and tried to take it with him.

"You can leave that towel here."

He tossed it to me. He was rough and tough, and he wanted me to know it. I stared him down until he walked through the opening in the side wall. My background was with white-collar criminals, like embezzlers. It was simple—we knew they were guilty when we had a confrontation like this.

Security and the track veterinarian came out of the trainer's office with a plastic bag containing several vials in plastic tubes.

"Here it is."

I waved to the trainer. "Can you come over here? We just found these illegal substances in your office. Do you want to tell us about this or just pack up and leave HSD grounds?"

"That's not mine. You can't prove that it's mine."

"All we have to do is use the absolute insurer rule. If it's here, you're guilty for it being here. We have filmed every moment since we stepped into this barn and that's proof enough that we found it here—in your office. And right now you are suspended from training. These horses will be transferred to the quarantine barn, and their owners will be notified."

He scanned the barn and all the security personnel swarming it.

I nodded at him. "Probably a good time to go with security and remove your personal items."

"Probably a good time for you to get out of my way," he said. "Not the last time you'll see me." He turned and came at me as though he were going to push me back against the wall.

I used one of my self-defense moves. Pulled his arm, spun him around, and had his arm behind his back in an instant. He didn't know what to do. By then security was right there, and they took him by both arms and led him out.

If I accomplished anything, at least everyone there that saw me handle that situation now had a new level of respect for me. I made sure my Glock was with me everywhere I went.

I texted Amos: *<Everything still good to meet you tomorrow?>*
<Yes. I got the weekend off. Trap Door 6:00>

I kinda wished I'd never suggested going out there to see Amos. At the time, a month ago, I'd been trying to appease him. He was expecting information on who framed him, but I didn't have an answer for that. I also didn't have his $90,000. Now, I'd met Thomas and wished I weren't going.

I headed out late Saturday afternoon. On my drive, I couldn't forget that trainer threatening me. I kept looking in the rearview mirror; a car did pull out and follow me for a while. For the next ten miles, I imagined every car was following me, because of the threats and the altercation. It was the first time I'd taken a road trip away from the track alone. It left me vulnerable.

What if whoever Dos was protecting had someone follow me down to Noose? Everyone had bought into the idea that Amos had been suspended, which in theory would give whoever was behind this a false sense of security. But if they figured out Amos was not actually suspended, that we had gotten him out of town for his protection, that would put both him and me in danger.

In case I was being followed, I reached across and pulled my purse closer, opening it, feeling for my pepper spray and my Glock.

That was the first thing Max had had me do when he'd brought me on—get self-defense training and a concealed permit. I knew I could use both if I had to.

I glanced again in my rearview mirror. No one there. I needed to stop and freshen up some before I got there, so I pulled off the road into a gas station, my worries close behind.

Chapter 31

On my second trip to Noose, they let Lucky into the Trap Door Saloon, as Raven had promised. She messed with him and put a napkin down. "New phone number. Whatcha havin' tonight?"

"I'm meeting someone. Gonna wait and order then."

"Okay."

I put the napkin in my shirt pocket. About ten minutes later, the front door blew open. The Texas sunlight turned Rixie into a silhouette. Nice tight jeans, a white blouse, boots. She carried a cowboy hat. She never looked around but walked straight to my table and sat down. Raven gave me a look. Rixie ordered a Dallas daiquiri on the rocks. I was going to have a beer but said, "Two."

She excused herself and went to the restroom. When she got back, she updated me on how SkyMan was doing at the barn.

"So how's everything else at HSD? How's the investigation going?"

"It's like a puzzle that keeps getting changed and more pieces added. We got you out for protection, not only from riding but also from any unknown adversary that had it in for you. I'm starting to feel whoever has it in for you has substituted me for you. Yesterday, we canned a trainer, and he threatened me. In my other jobs, I've dealt with some really bad people, but now I'm on the front line."

I had no advice to give her. She was the investigator. When I didn't react to her comments, she got serious.

"I went to Oaklawn last week to a NESPA conference," she said. "How did you like that track?"

"Oh, it's a nice track. There was a big stakes race on Saturday. I met some nice people over there. How's it going at the ranch?"

"I'm fitting right in. It seems I have a lot in common with the prisoners. We're all on a work release. Just puttin' in our time, waitin' for the sentence to run out."

She looked sympathetic. "Sounds like you miss the track?"

"I don't miss it at all. But I promised BigOilRig I'd come back for him, someday. Maybe he'll be in a claiming race. I need to check on my trainer's license and get an owner's license."

She brightened. "I know everyone at the state racing office. I'll get to work on that Monday—for you." She looked at her watch.

"You gotta get back to Fort Worth?"

"Yeah, pretty soon."

Raven circled and caught my eye on every turn. Rixie noticed.

"She's cute. Your type?"

"My type? What is my type?"

"Well, I sure don't know." Her eyes told me that topic was over. She swirled her glass, the ice clinking, and glanced toward the door.

Raven moved in. "Two more?"

Rixie looked at me. I looked at her.

"Sure."

"You staying for the band tonight?" Raven asked. "Or just happy hour?"

We looked at each other again. Kind of at the same time, we said, "Happy hour."

Raven looked a little disappointed. She brought the two drinks, and I gave her a twenty-dollar bill. Rixie watched me looking at her.

"I'm going to take Lucky outside and feed him," I said. "Be right back."

Rixie pulled out her phone. There was a poster by the door about the band that was going to be there at seven o'clock. The Ex-UBERants were a twangy Texas band, probably ex–taxi drivers. I looked at the clock on the wall—6:45. The parking lot was getting busy.

The band was warming up when I returned. We couldn't really hear each other anymore, so we settled in and relaxed.

Our eyes met frequently. I picked up my phone and texted her: *<You staying for the band or just happy hour?>*

Rixie read the text. She studied my face before looking back down at her phone. She started to touch the screen but instead turned it off, looking back at the band.

So I did too. We sat there, two people on the fringe of the Trap Door Saloon. The guys in the band put down their guitars. Sound check was over, and they split up. Two guys went to the bar and the other to the restroom. They each had their own versions of a black shirt, belt buckle, and cowboy hat.

A slow song came from the jukebox, not near as loud as the band, and a couple slid onto the dance floor. They were pretty good.

Rixie tapped the table with her fingernails and moved her head. When she closed her eyes and pursed her lips, as if for an imaginary kiss, I couldn't help but watch her. Just as quickly as her eyes opened, I looked back at the couple sliding around the floor.

She was animated, fiddled with her glass and the stirrer, but acted uneasy. She studied my face. "There's something I've got to tell you." She leaned in close. "Never share this with anyone. I went back and asked Dos point blank where he got those numbers. He said he couldn't tell me. He gets 'instructions'—that's what he said. If he knew—and if he told me—it would be very bad for him. He implied that I shouldn't want to know where he got the tip numbers, because if I did, I would be putting myself in a lot of danger." She paused. "And Charlane. She told me to be careful. The whole way down here, I felt like I was being followed." She took a deep breath. "We have to be careful. I really feel, with a little more time, we'll get the information we need."

"Sounds like you are covering the bases. Coming out here like a parole officer—checking on me."

"Well, they're both still on the suspect list."

"And maybe they are just trying to deflect the attention off them and frighten you to distract you."

She looked off to the empty stage and back to me and said something totally unexpected. "We're just getting to know each other—you know, how to work together. This is kinda like a first date."

I wondered what she meant. I'd thought she was just the messenger, coming out here with reports. I liked her terminology—the "first date" part.

"You miss Charlane?" she asked.

"Sure, she's my friend. She's the kind of woman that if you make the approved short list, she'd do anything for you."

"What if you don't make the list?"

I shrugged. "Watch out."

"She told me about you and Kellsey splitting up."

"Yeah. It's called a conflict of careers."

"You miss the track?" she asked me again.

I'd learned one thing: Private investigators ask a lot of questions.

"Some aspects, but I'm actually enjoying this new job, working with the women prisoners. Do you know they get paid pennies for what they do?"

Rixie looked back at the stage. The band started the seven o'clock show. She nodded to the dance floor, the thing I was equally afraid of and kinda excited about. "You dance?"

"No." My answer was abrupt, and she looked disappointed. "You wouldn't call what I would do out there dancin'."

"Me neither, but I love to watch a couple that knows how." She pointed. "Like them."

My eyes followed the pair as they moved in a planned routine. "I don't have the rhythm."

She looked at me. "I feel exuberant—you want to try it?"

I couldn't help but laugh. She'd come all the way out here to have a drink, maybe get picked up by a cowboy with a dog in a bar and listen to a band named the Ex-UBERants. She reached over and touched my hand.

"What do you say, Mr. Amos? Happy hour's over."

We stepped onto the dance floor. Instead of dreading it, I decided to just give it a try and not be self-conscious. She took my right hand and put it in the small of her back, took my left hand and interlocked our fingers. We fell in behind that couple that was pretty good and followed them, trying to imitate what they did.

"Just try to feel the music, and don't look down at the floor or your feet," she said.

If someone had told me that morning I'd be doing the Texas two-step at 7:30 that night, I would have thought they were talking about someone else. She smiled and kept her eyes on mine as we—no, she—moved across the floor. I just held on.

It wasn't as if I'd never done this. I had. But it wasn't my favorite activity, and she made it easy. The more I relaxed and listened to the music, the more I could kinda let myself go. The song came to its end, and everyone stopped and clapped.

Rixie said, "You got a five?"

I nodded and dug in my front pocket, pulling out my bills. She chatted with the singer for a few minutes and shook his hand, slipping him the five-dollar bill. He tipped his hat again and put the bill in his pocket.

He turned to the other members of his band; they nodded, and they started back into another song.

She grabbed my hand and led me to the edge of the dance floor. They slowed it down. The steps were similar, but the real difference was we were closer together. I had to look at her eyes, still in between the shadows. She put her face close to mine, and so I responded, pulling her closer.

"You request this song?"

"No, just asked them to play something slow. I don't know who's luckiest. Me or Lucky. Maybe we both are." She moved her face closer to mine. I had no idea what type of perfume she had on, but it was nice.

That song ended, and we stopped and clapped. It was probably after eight o'clock, and we stood there looking at each other.

"You want to get something to eat?" I asked.

"No, I need to get back to Fort Worth. Better head out."

All I could say was, "Okay."

She went back to our table and got her purse, pointed to the restroom, and said, "Meet me at your truck."

Lucky and I headed to the door. Raven, who was leaning up against the bar, held up another napkin and kinda waved it. She had a smile that was hard to forget.

I took Lucky over to the field behind the bar. It was getting dark; the long shadows played with the remaining light. Rixie knelt down and roughed up his ears and rubbed his chest, and he lay down. She scratched his stomach. She stood up, adjusting her blouse and her jeans. "It was like we were the only ones on the dance floor. I think we did pretty good."

"Yes; thanks for 'staying for the band.'"

"It wasn't about the band."

"What was it about?"

She looked me straight in the eye. "Being lucky."

Lucky walked over and put his face down on her foot. Anchored her there, as though she couldn't leave. She knelt back down and said to him, "We are lucky."

She got to her feet and pointed to the east. "Fort Worth is that way, one hour."

Once she left, all I could see was an almost-dark Texas sky and the faint memory of her taillights as her car pulled out onto the highway. Lucky made the first move. He took off for the grassy area, and I threw his bowl in the truck.

It was too early to go to the hotel, too early to do anything else. Maybe get a little dinner. There was only one café near the hotel, and the door stood wide open, only two tables occupied. The waitress gestured toward a table by the window. I took off my cowboy hat, turning it upside down on the chair. She handed me a menu and said, "Brisket is the best anywhere around here."

I said, "Sure, and water."

I took the napkin from the Trap Door and smoothed it out on the table. That was something I didn't need to get into right then. I folded it up and put it back in my shirt pocket. I was a little worried about Rixie. I decided to call her after I finished dinner.

Chapter 32

The sun was almost down when I left, and a car pulled out and followed me for several blocks. I could barely drive for looking at every car that seemed to follow me. My mind started to think crazy thoughts.

Did he go back to the Trap Door Saloon?

The bar girl had been extra friendly to him. I almost laughed at the worry. Here I was alone out on some Texas road, a semi-disguised cowgirl, sorta hooking up with a…cowboy.

I'd never thought I'd be interested in a cowboy, especially a cowboy that had had a scrape with the law. I wasn't, really. I was interested in Thomas, but there was something about Amos that intrigued me.

He'd been single-handedly trying to save the horses at HSD, and now it looked as though I was his accomplice.

My phone rang—Amos. He said, "Everything okay?"

"Every car looks like it's following me and is filled with thugs or escapees from over at TSPAN. I speed up—they speed up. They look at me when they pass, like they're going to kidnap me." I laughed. "What are you doing? What's Lucky doing?"

"I'm at the café. Lucky's looking out the window."

"I wish I had a dog like Lucky to protect me." It wasn't a bad idea. Maybe I should look into getting a dog, especially since I had this unexpected sense of danger. "I wish he was with me."

"You want to turn around?" he asked.

My heart said yes, my mind said no, but my instinct said maybe. It felt like a trick question, with no right answer. "I'm going to pretend you didn't say that, Mr. Amos."

I looked at the suitcase in the back seat—the one I'd packed for emergencies—as though I wanted to be sure it was there. Turning down the radio, I waited to hear his reply.

"I meant I would let you take Lucky back with you."

Well, that was the quickest nonreply. This guy made me feel safe. He was easy to be around. I looked at my eyes in the rearview mirror. Besides a few wrinkles, I liked what I saw. Was this cowboy responsible for the peace I was now feeling?

"Are you serious about me coming back?" I asked. "Or I can just call you when I get home?"

"Turn around. I'll be at the hotel. You want me to get you something from the diner? I ordered brisket. You want that?"

"Okay. Probably thirty minutes unless I get run off the road and kidnapped."

I had to roll down the window and get some cool, fresh Texas air when we hung up. "Phew."

The next half hour, I played out every scenario imaginable. He'd get me some dinner and I'd have to eat it in his room? It was after nine o'clock. I should make the handoff quick, because it would be almost midnight when I got back home…unless…

Finally, his hotel. I pulled in and parked by his truck.

Lucky came running, barking, jumping on me. I had never been so happy to see a dog. I wanted to pick him up and hold him. Or cry. It was an elation I hadn't felt in a long time—this feeling that someone was watching out for me.

I hoped that I'd get to that point with Thomas, but I didn't feel ready to show him a weakness. I didn't want him to think that I couldn't do my job. With Amos, I felt safe. He had his arms opened, walking up to me, and I grabbed him and buried my face in his chest.

His shirt was soft, and his arms and hands were strong. He held me as long as I let him.

"It's been a long time since I had a hug like that." I had no idea why I'd said that. I hoped he would say "Me too," but he didn't.

Then, as I pulled back and looked into his eyes, he said, "I remember what someone told me one time: 'If I ask you to look after my dog—even for a minute—know this is *the* biggest compliment I will ever give you.' Come on, I can heat up the brisket in the microwave in my room."

We went into his room, and he locked the door. Was he locking me in or keeping anyone from breaking in? It was interesting. I was acting vulnerable, and he was still guarded.

We made small talk, and he had a whole list of instructions about Lucky. When and how to feed him. He wanted me to get a special GPS tracking collar first thing tomorrow. Special dog food, treats, brushes. His bowls. He had them all in a box. The dog bed looked as though it needed to be dry-cleaned.

"Is that all...?" I asked. "I mean is that all I need...for him?"

"Don't use a leash on his neck. It chokes him. Get him one of those harnesses."

"I got this," I said. "We're a team. I better go."

We all walked to my car. Lucky knew something was up when all his stuff went in the back seat. He went to pee, and Amos picked him up.

"Be a good boy," he said, and he put him in the back with his bed.

We were at that awkward stage. I wanted another hug, but I just pointed east again the way I had the last time. "Fort Worth. One hour."

I held out my arms. As he wrapped his arms around me, a truck drove by and honked its horn. I jumped and squeezed him. We both laughed.

"Sorry, my nerves are shot," I said. "I got my pepper spray, my Glock, and now I have Lucky. What else do I need?"

"You need to get home safe and call me when you get there."

"I can do that. Thanks, for everything."

I shut my car door, grateful that Amos had been so kind. Anybody who rode thoroughbreds for a living couldn't have an ounce of fear in his body, so I knew Amos had no fear. I pulled back onto the main road. Lucky made his way up to the front seat. I reached over and rubbed his head. I could get attached to him pretty fast. Amos had said he had some protective genes, and I was glad about that.

Lucky curled up and went to sleep as I drove into the quiet night. I pulled onto my street. It was dark; my house was dark. The rear-view mirror was now my best friend. Nothing there but a quiet Texas Saturday night.

My call to Amos went to voice mail as I pulled into the driveway. Lucky jumped out and found his way to the bushes.

"Amos, I just got home; getting out of the car now. I've got a flash-light in my left hand, Glock in my right hand. If I get jumped—this would just be practice. Nobody would mess with me again. Lucky is great. Thanks for sending him with me."

It was almost midnight, and I'd had a long day. I wanted to ask him to let me know when he'd come to see Lucky but hung up instead.

Chapter 33

Where's Lucky? I wondered, first thing on Sunday morning.

Had I really let her take him back with her? What had I been thinking? She'd wanted Lucky for protection. At the time I'd related to that because that's what Max had said about me coming out here. For my own protection.

I was tempted to go straight to Fort Worth to get him but headed to Cowboy Church instead. I didn't hear much of the message because I thought about everything that had happened the night before with Rixie, and what hadn't happened. On the way back to TAPP Ranch, I kept looking for Lucky sitting in the empty seat. It was the first time we hadn't been together, and I wondered when I should go get him.

I texted Rixie: *<You want to come next Saturday and bring Lucky back?>*
She texted back *<Okay>* and a happy-face emoji.

I drove by the main entrance to TSPAN-M, and a bunch of people were picketing and protesting. I slowed down and read a sign that a woman was holding. It said "Pay the Prisoners."

The minute I pulled into the ranch, APP met me. "Come to the office; we gotta talk."

In three weeks, I had been in APP's office only a few times. "What's up?" I said once we were seated. Him behind his desk, me in an uncomfortable chair in front of it.

"There are about twenty 'pay the prisoners' protestors in front of TSPAN-M," he grumbled. "Callin' for them to get paid for working here. Seems like every year this comes up, but the only difference now is you."

My stomach dropped. "What do I have to do with it?"

"You're more famous than we thought, and not in a good way," he said, glaring at me. "I'm gettin' calls from newspapers in Dallas and Austin. TV stations, wantin' a statement from me about how you got this job out here. They've found out how much you're gettin' paid, and people are wondering why wasn't it offered to one of the 'rehabilitated' prisoners."

His face started to turn red. "Here's the worst part. I got another call—some judge issued a decision to stop every prisoner from going to the work sites off prison grounds. This will go into effect in a few days unless Austin can get some legislation pushed through and find enough surplus money to start paying prisoners. Or the governor can authorize an emergency executive order.

"The public is all for this; it's long overdue. There's a wage scale for every job—they'll go by that. It doesn't matter to me; it's not out of my budget."

I finally realized he wasn't actually angry, just fired up.

"Governor's wife has been behind this as long as she's been the first lady. So now I bet it gets done. How are you gonna handle this, since it looks like you're responsible for getting this stirred up again? You need to have your story ready."

"My story?" I was still trying to catch up. "It sounds like my story is already out there. I'll just go with it."

Over at Patty's office, I got a coffee and tried to process everything. She walked toward me, smiling. The minute I saw her smile, I regretted that whole scene at the Trap Door with Rixie.

First thing Patty said was "Where's Lucky?"

Instantly, I realized I'd made a big mistake sending Lucky to Fort Worth.

"I had to meet Rixie yesterday and go over some details about the doping investigation," I said. "Some of the suspects have her scared. She wanted Lucky for protection. He's in Fort Worth for a few days."

A look I hadn't seen before crossed her face. "Oh, really?"

It was like she was trying not to pursue the topic right then. I'd made a lot of mistakes in my life, but at that moment, sending Lucky felt as if it might be the biggest. Changing the subject, I said, "What else do I need to know about me getting this job?"

Patty paused. "On the Friday before you arrived, I let a woman go who had your job. She was in the first group that went through the women's program, and I hired her when she got released from TSPAN. To be honest, I was afraid she would go postal when she got fired, so I had APP and Jessie here when I did it. She wouldn't sign the termination papers."

Patty was uneasy but went on. "Sure enough, we got a notice from the corrections department that she filed a wrongful termination grievance. She claims I fired her so I could hire you. Somehow, she found out how much you're getting paid, and she was making a fraction of that. She claims she was trained by me and you don't know anything about equine therapy. Something about me not advertising the job opening, not taking applications, and not offering it to a rehabilitated prisoner instead of you."

She glanced at her phone. "There could have been a lot of publicity about her claim, but the first lady, who is a very good friend of mine, got involved. She's responsible for everything here and didn't want any bad press. She arranged for a settlement with the ex-employee. The first lady feels the prisoners should get paid what the job is worth. The prisoners could have that money when they got out or—more important—transfer it to their spouses or their children."

Patty shrugged. "So the first lady took matters into her own hands. Now it doesn't matter how you got this job; everybody wants to be on the record for prison reform. She tells me they can fund it with all the new money the casinos and sports books are sending to Austin." She smiled at me. "With this newfound fame, you've become some kind of a hero. With you here under these circumstances, they got the exposure they needed."

I knew nothing about politics and how it worked. One minute there was a problem, and the next, the government either fixed it or made it worse. I couldn't help but wonder—could this newfound fame, as she called it, help me change the horse industry for the better, or was it just going to lead to more trouble?

"So what happens now?" I asked.

Patty rubbed her hands against her arms, and I realized she was nervous. "I'm sorry this put you in the spotlight. Once we get the prisoners' pay instituted, it will be a good thing. Seems like dealing with 'consequences' is becoming more important than being lucky."

When she said the word "Lucky," I saw that whole scene at the Trap Door really had been a mistake. I'd been here only three weeks, and I felt as if I had known Patty my whole life.

Chapter 34

The first lady was all over the Monday morning news. She had become the loudest advocate for the prisoners' pay to be instated, and she focused on Patty's program as an example.

"The women at the TAPP Equine Assisted Therapy Ranch do the same work with horses as women on the outside. They need to be equally compensated." She went on to discuss the importance of equine therapy for the women and mentioned Patty and me. The first lady made it appear as though they'd hired me away from horse racing to bring my experience and expertise, justifying the pushback she got for how my pay was put together.

Once the segment aired, Patty and APP had meetings all morning. Calls from Austin and the corrections officers. They worked fast to keep everything in place. It was a win-win for everyone. Everyone except Lucky, since he wasn't there.

It didn't take long for Patty to start to push for him to come back. "We kinda got used to having Lucky here, especially on the visitors' Saturdays," she said as we cleaned the stalls. "He was great with the kids. When's he coming back?"

"I got a text about him this morning," I said. "He's okay. He'll be back soon."

No use getting into any details about me meeting up with Rixie and getting Lucky back. Still, I got that sideways glance again.

That afternoon, Patty got a text from the first lady requesting the two of us get on a conference call with her and the governor. We took the call in Patty's office, and I tried not to be overwhelmed by it all.

The first lady started the call with praise for our work. Then she said, "The governor has approval to issue an emergency executive order for all this. He has something he wants to tell you."

A smooth voice rang through the line. "Well, y'all makin' me look good. When I thought this was gonna be just another Monday at the capitol, I got to do the kind of work the great people of Texas elected me to do. Prisoners haven't been taken care of enough for years until now. Thanks to you both. Now Patty, I want to meet this cowboy you got out there to help you. I hear it's because of him we got this done."

Patty nodded at me, and I said, "Sir, thanks for sayin' that, but I think you and the first lady can take credit for this."

"Amos, this is how we do things here in Austin," he said. "We share the credit when we do something as great as this. When things don't turn out like we plan—then we blame the other political party." He laughed. "I want to invite you both to come to Austin when I sign the order on Wednesday. I'll send my plane out there to pick you up. We'll put you up at the Four Seasons and take you back Thursday. How's that sound?"

Patty said, "Yes, sir. We accept."

The first lady said, "That's great. Amos, I've heard a lot about you and can't wait to meet you. See you both on Wednesday."

We hung up the phone. "What about that?" Patty said, nudging me.

"Which part?" I said. "Going to Austin or what she heard about me?"

"The Austin part is a major accomplishment for these women here. And you—well, I did tell her how different everything is now that you're here. Different in a good way." She smiled. "I'm having some friends over to my house tonight for a cookout. Six o'clock. Use my truck and come over."

When I'd started at the ranch, Patty had suggested I get my lunch at APP's kitchen and bring it over to eat with her in her office. It had become a daily event. Now I'd moved up to an invitation to her house for a cookout.

I put on my cleanest jeans and found a shirt that still had the laundry tag on it. Grabbed my cowboy hat and started her truck. Probably the nicest truck I'd ever been in. White F-150 King Ranch. Of course.

I called Rixie on my way over to the cookout. "I just wanted to check in. Lucky good?"

"He's sitting right here with me."

I cut that call short and pulled up to the cookout. There was already a pretty decent crowd there, and I spotted Patty. She had her hair up in a loose ponytail and wore a blue silk skirt that seemed to move with the breeze. It was held up with a nice leather belt with silver conchos. She had on a newer pair of boots than the ones she wore at the barn. She smiled at me the minute I walked up.

"Excuse me," she said to the group she was talking to. Then she grabbed my hand and gave me a slight hug. She walked me around and made sure she introduced me to everyone.

I eyed the table with the casserole dishes, salads, fruit, flowers, and every vegetable from the gardens at TAPP Ranch. I thought a cookout would be barbecue, burgers, and brisket, but this was it.

When Patty noticed me looking over the tables, she said. "Next time you come over, I'll have you some real food here."

"Oh, this is all on my diet." I smiled at her and popped a radish in my mouth, trying not to wince. "I need a break from APP's kitchen anyway. The cook has limited ingredients and limited imagination."

"He was inside TSPAN for a while," she said. "Everyone there is an ex-this or an ex-that. Even you—you're an ex–exercise rider, ex–assistant trainer, ex-gambler, and maybe some exes I don't even know about."

She smiled with an inquisitive look, studying everything about me. I wondered what was on her list of exes. I mentally made a list of some that were possible. Some that were definitely not. And some I probably didn't want to know about.

On the drive back to my cabin, I kept thinking about what she'd said. "Next time you come over…"

On Tuesday I called Rixie. Lucky was doing okay, and she said she was thinking about adopting a rescue dog. She confirmed that Saturday would be a good time to meet up and get Lucky back to me.

Wednesday was travel day. I showed up at Patty's office as planned, and she started to laugh. "You can't go to Austin and represent TAPP Ranch wearing jeans and an old Ariat shirt. Let's leave early and go shop at M. L. Leddy's in Fort Worth on the way."

I had never been there, but of course, Patty had good taste. She had fun helping me pick out a new sports coat and real khakis. In the back they had a guy who shined boots, and she insisted I get mine done.

"I like them like they are."

"What about a new pair?" she mused, studying them.

"No, I don't need a new pair of cowboy boots."

"Amos, you are going to be the governor's guest; you can't go to Austin wearing those old boots. Get a new pair. I bet they're really comfortable. What size do you wear?"

"Ten and a half wide. Okay, I'll get a pair of boots, but I have to pick them out. I don't need any more help," I said, laughing. "Go over there to the ladies' department."

Well, she was right, they were the most comfortable boots I'd ever had. I walked into M. L. Leddy's looking like I was on work release and walked out with my old clothes and boots in a shopping bag. I glanced at our reflection in the store window.

"Come on, cowboy." She took my arm. "We got a plane to catch."

On the way to the airport, we were twenty miles from the track, and I kinda muttered under my breath, "Wonder how Lucky's doing."

Patty picked up on it. "When did you say he was coming back?"

"I'll get him Saturday."

"Or how about if we go get him tomorrow when we get back from Austin?" she suggested.

"No, Saturday works okay for me."

She sat there as if she was waiting for me to ask her to go with me, so I did. "Do you want to go with me to get him Saturday?"

"Saturday is the kids' visitation day. We can go in the afternoon, okay?"

I nodded. "Yes."

As we got closer to the airport, we passed an enormous brand-new electronic billboard for HorseShoeDowns Casino with W. D. Stamples's spray-tanned face and fake smile. He was holding up a big check for the children's hospital.

Patty said, "That's all for show. Do you think that would entice someone to go to a casino and lose money so the casino can donate money to a charity?"

"No, big charity donations are just a tax deduction to him."

We pulled up through a gate that said, "Welcome to Meacham Airport," and I was glad I'd brought my best cowboy hat. I got it out of the back seat.

Patty pointed to the left where the plane was waiting. A guy who could have been security met us in the parking lot and helped with Patty's luggage. I carried mine, but at the stairs to the plane, he took it. He showed us where the beverages were and squeezed into the copilot seat. Patty and I had the entire plane to ourselves.

We settled into the two seats facing each other with a table in between. Patty and I kept up an easy banter as the plane taxied and took off. Pretty soon the pilot said we were at ten thousand feet.

"I've never been on a plane like this," she said. "How about you?"

"No, me neither. I've never flown much. I like to be close to the ground, like on the back of a horse. That way I know how far it is to fall."

I looked out the window. It was a long way down. Patty laughed, and we talked all the way to Austin.

We attended the signing of the emergency executive order. The governor was seated at his desk, the first lady right behind him. Patty stood beside her, and I stood next to her, holding my cowboy hat. After at least a dozen photographs, each of us got a really nice ink pen.

The press conference was on the steps of the capitol with the media in full force. Patty did a great job. I liked how she introduced me: "This is my new partner at the TAPP Ranch Equine Assisted Therapy Center, Mr. Amos Moon." Then she touched on my past involvement in safety efforts for horses and jockeys. I held my breath, waiting for some smart-ass journalist to ask me about why I'd left HSD, but no one did.

I met a lot of people who wanted to talk about horse racing, which was exactly what I'd hoped for. I steered the conversation to the doping of horses, and several legislators were adamant that something had to be done not only in racing but in all disciplines as well. They asked what they could do, and I said, "You need to lock arms with the National Equine Safety Protection Authority and work to protect horses, exercise riders, and jockeys."

I showed them my OUIJA card, and they were impressed there was a grassroots organization advocating for safety. I came away from the conversation with a greater appreciation that some politicians were truly advocating for the horses and riders, which gave me hope that it was possible that there could be change.

That night there was a huge reception at the Austin convention center. Probably over a thousand people. Judges, lawyers, prosecutors, lobbyists, people on probation, people with prior time served, and dozens of human rights activists. I had to keep up with Patty as the first lady moved us through the crowd, making sure to introduce us.

Patty knew how to work the crowd, especially thanking the legislators who'd been instrumental in approving the funds for the TAPP Ranch Assisted Equine Therapy Center.

I had brought only a few business cards and had to be selective about who I gave one to. Patty noticed and laughed.

"I should have brought more," I admitted, "but I had no idea what you were getting me into."

They chauffeured us around to the Four Seasons. The concierge and I stood with the luggage, chatting. "Would you like for me to take some flowers to your room for your wife?"

"Yes. Thanks, but take them to *her* room." I gave him an inquisitive look. "Does it seem like we're married?"

"Oh, sir, I apologize. But yes, you look good with her."

"Good thing you didn't say something like that to her; she would have thought I put you up to it!"

"Where'd y'all meet, anyway?" he asked.

"In prison."

We laughed as Patty walked over. "What's so funny?"

"He told me y'all met in prison—that's the best one I've ever heard."

Patty shook her head.

He led us to the guest elevators, then held out our keys. "Ma'am, here's your room key. Sir, here's yours. I'll put the flowers in her room, just like we discussed."

"As a matter of fact, I'll take them. Thanks."

She gave me a lingering smile as he handed me the flowers. The elevator door shut, and we looked at each other. It suddenly felt hard to look away.

She pushed the tenth-floor button. Then she held out her arms and quietly buried her face on my chest. I fumbled with my hat in my left hand. I had wrestled with it all day. The flowers were in my right hand. I awkwardly tried to put my arms around her. She unwound from that entanglement, and as the door opened, she took the flowers.

"This your floor too?" she asked.

"No," I said. "We went by my floor, just a-flyin'. I guess I gotta get used to these high-speed elevators. I was hopin' for a power outage, or that it would get stuck."

Patty smelled the flowers and as the door closed, she said, "Maybe next time."

The whirlwind of the two days in the limelight in Austin still had a smile on my face when we got back to the ranch. I had flashbacks of her last smile when that elevator door had closed.

Maybe next time.

Those two days had been more rewarding than any winner's circle photo I'd ever been in. The people that had thanked me were the most sincere people I'd ever met. Not like some of the racetrack people who were destroying the sport.

Friday morning, thunderous applause greeted me when I walked into the barn. Between the applause and the tears, all the women wanted hugs. It was "Mr. Amos" this and "Mr. Amos" that. The thank-yous and graciases were echoing in my ears. I felt a little guilty, knowing that I really didn't have much to do with it, but I was touched to see how much this change meant to them.

Patty stood by the office, watching. "I didn't even have to suggest they do that."

Adrian's mother said, "Go on, Miss Patty. You too." She circled her arms. "Go on. You know you want to."

So I took off my hat, and Patty said, "The last time, he had his arms full of flowers for me."

We held our hug about as long as the unforgettable elevator hug in Austin. Then we both bowed. More applause erupted and a few whispers.

Later that morning Rixie texted me. *<Guess you forgot about Max telling you to get out of here and just lie low>*

I ignored that. But she sent one more. *<We don't need any more photos of you and Patty all over the news with the governor and first lady. This kind of publicity can disrupt the investigation>*

I wondered after that comment if they were using me for something that they'd "forgotten" to tell me about. I didn't respond.

Patty motioned for me to come into the office. "I got a call this morning from the first lady. She said to tell you how grateful she is that you're working with me."

"I appreciate that, but I don't feel like I've done much."

"Amos, you made the decision to come here. It might feel like a small thing, but if you hadn't done that, none of this would have been possible. Allowing prisoners to continue on work releases and start a structured pay system affects thousands of people."

It hit me then that I really did have a part in this. The decision I'd made to step out of my old life, to leave it behind with the goal of improving the sport of racing, had ended up prompting a chain of events that changed these women's lives for the better.

My father's face popped into my head. I said, more to myself than to her, "My father would actually have been proud of me for this."

"The money is going to make a difference for all the people we work with," she said. "I'm proud of you too."

Chapter 35

Lucky was fitting into my routine, or maybe I was adjusting my schedule to his. Charlane gave me a weird look when I took him to the track on Monday morning. Lucky pulled me to her, and she started right in. "Well now, Hun, you got a lotta explaining. You and Amos hook up over the weekend?"

"No."

"Well. Why you got his dog?"

I thought of our last discussion and the way she'd told me to watch my back. Crossing my arms, I stared her down. "Two things. One: none of your business, and two: it's a long story. Lucky's going back to Amos Saturday. That's all you need to know."

She looked down at Lucky and walked away.

Between the excursions around the grounds, he was happy to get back upstairs to a bed in my office, his water bowl, and the air-conditioning.

He'd been away from the track for only three weeks, but everyone at the barns was glad to see him. I was really getting attached to Lucky. We made the rest of the barn tour without incident. I felt a little safer with him. He got me into the barns that we were scrutinizing without a lot of pushback. The questions about Amos never ceased. Everyone thought I was lying about being involved with him, and Charlane's gossip didn't help. When Amos was on the news running around Texas with Patty, Charlane was busy creating more drama about that situation.

The next time I saw her at the barn, she said, "It looks like he's doing a better job helping prisoners in—what, a month?—than he did here in years."

I made a few calls about Amos's trainer's license. It was still valid. It had never been suspended. All I had to do was to ask the racing commission to register him as an owner. They already had his fingerprints and photo from when he'd registered with NESPA three years before, so at least I felt as though I was helping him while he waited to see some results. The lab reports finally came back on the four horses from March 26. Nothing showed up, which was frustrating. It validated the suspicion we already had that whatever was being used to dope horses was undetectable.

On Thursday Mr. Stamples asked me to come to his office. I had been there only a few times. I knew to stand until he offered me a chair, but he never did. He looked as if he could do an ad for hair gel, or dental implants, or spray tans. His sports coat was on the back of a chair. He wore a colorful tie. And probably had a Mont Blanc pen in the pocket of his perfectly starched white shirt.

He acted busy, seated at his desk, and looked up as if he was annoyed I was even in his office. It was like a sports bar with TV screens—some were tuned in to the stock market channel. His office was almost as big as my house.

"How can I run a racetrack with all these rules?" he asked. "None of which increase the handle or purses. All they do is cost me a lot of money to pay the likes of you to try to enforce them."

I was used to this type of man exercising his authority over me, since this was the type of man I'd worked for in banking as well. And I knew never to argue, just to take the abusive diatribe and hope it didn't get personal. I wanted to tell him the Justice Department had created the laws, but I had to bite my tongue.

He went on, "What if everyone brought a dog, cat, or pet goldfish here? What, are we running a daycare center for animals?"

He leaned forward in his big leather chair, as though he were waiting to pounce on anything. "No, sir. I'm just keeping that dog for a friend. He goes home Saturday."

"Friend? I heard he's more than a friend of yours." Without hardly taking a breath, he went on, "I also heard from a good friend of mine up at Oaklawn. You made quite an impression at the NESPA conference. Just a little advice. Don't get too chummy with that guy you went to dinner with."

"Sir, who I go to dinner with is my business—not yours."

He stood up. "That might be true, but don't forget my contract is with Max, not you."

He waited for me to argue with him, but I said, "Is that all?"

"I have this whole Ricksland/Hunter/NESPA/HSD first six-month contract review coming up next week. It will be interesting to see how effective you have been."

I nodded. "Is that all?"

He motioned to the door and said, "Yes."

I walked down the hall to my office. So much for hoping it didn't get personal.

I gritted my teeth and texted Amos:

<Lucky is good. NoCashRefund and BigOilRig were transferred to a new trainer, off the stewards' list. Cleared to race. Your owner's license is being processed. No progress on your $$$$. Still banned from the track.>

After that confrontation with Mr. Stamples on Thursday, I was stressed out all day, and I steered clear of him on Friday. Everything was going smoothly until about three that afternoon. I walked back to my office to find the door open. Lucky wasn't behind the desk and under the credenza where he usually slept.

I went down the hall, asking everyone, "Lucky. Is he with you?"
All nos.

A few curse words I never used came out of my mouth.

"*Lucky*," I shouted. "Lucky! Where are you? Where is he?"

Everybody came out of their offices, shaking their heads.

"Nobody saw him, heard him? He just disappeared?" I demanded. "Who opened my door?"

More heads shaking.

"When I find him, I'll never leave him here again with all of you." I was furious at the lack of urgency. I'd seen this group move faster at the idea of free pizza in the break room. "I'll lock my damn door."

I wanted to find him *and* find out who left my door open.

The quiet was deafening. Picking up my phone, I called security. "Lucky is missing," I said. "He had to go down the stairs. I need everyone to help me find him."

"Yes, ma'am," the dispatcher said. "We'll get on it."

I'm sure I made quite the sight running through the racetrack calling, "Lucky—Lucky!"

Everyone must have thought I was crazy, which was exactly how I felt. I couldn't believe this was happening. Remembering the tracker that was on Lucky's collar, I came to a halt, and my breathing steadied. That would find him. Pulling it up on my phone, I hit the "locate your dog" icon.

It said: *Charge battery now.*

My stomach dropped. I knew I should have charged up the battery on the GPS the night before. It would have taken no effort at all, and I could have avoided all this.

I raced to Barn7.

No.

Track kitchen.

No.

He had to be at the track. I felt sure he would come running around a corner at any moment, but I was worried. What if he had eaten something and gotten sick and couldn't move? Or gotten hit by a truck? He was used to running around with Amos, but I was responsible for him, and I had to find him.

When word got around that Lucky was missing, SkyMan drove up next to me in one of the track's golf carts. "Here, get in," he said. "I'm caught up; I'll look with you."

His tone was reassuring, and GunShy seemed to kinda know that we were looking for Lucky—every time we hollered his name, GunShy barked. An hour passed before I knew it. I was starting to get panicked again, and that's when we bumped into Charlane.

"Hun, calm down," she said. "I've chased after loose dogs my whole life. They're just like men; the good ones come back. There's some I hoped never came back. Know what I mean?"

She waited for me to smile, but I couldn't. "Don't you worry; we'll find him. I called my friend at the print shop; he's printing 250 flyers. I sent him Lucky's color photo. Hun, I used my number, 'cause you don't want every dognappin' ransom chaser to be callin' you. I told him '$1,000 REWARD' in big letters."

"A thousand dollars?" I echoed in disbelief.

She grabbed me and gave me a girl's hug, holding both my hands. She was incredibly calm about it all, which I appreciated, since I was feeling panicked. "A thousand dollars is a lot of money, especially for these people around here. Me and the guys will go around and put 'em up. We'll canvas this whole area around the track."

She said, "Somebody at the track could've taken Lucky home because they were desperate for him to change their luck. People here are so superstitious."

I felt sick.

"Or someone might hold him for a day or two and swap him for the C-A-S-H—know what I mean? Does Amos know?" she asked.

I wasn't ready to tell him yet, especially since there was still a chance Lucky would come back. "No, I'll call him at seven o'clock. Maybe by then Lucky will have shown up for dinner."

Mentally, I ran through the list of people who had an ax to grind with Amos or me. There were too many to count. I had to settle on two scenarios: Lucky had run off on his own, wandering around the track, or as Charlane had suggested, somebody had taken him.

SkyMan and I circled the entire property at least a dozen times. I was almost hoarse from yelling "LUCKY," hoping he would come running around the corner of a barn. Finally, SkyMan had to call it a day.

"He'll be back," he said, but now he didn't look convinced. "I'll watch out for him tonight. I live upstairs."

At seven, I stopped searching and called Amos. He picked up after the fourth ring, and the words rushed out of me.

"I can't find Lucky. I've been searching all afternoon. He's not at the barn. He's nowhere. He's…" My voice broke. I could hardly get the word out.

"He's…What do you mean?" Amos sounded shocked. Then, he shouted, "He's what?"

"Gone…I left him in my office with the door shut, and when I went back to the office, the door was open. I can't find him anywhere."

"Don't worry," Amos said, sounding relieved. "He'll come back. He runs around that track all the time."

"Amos, I know, but no one has seen him. SkyMan helped me look; Charlane's made flyers, but I don't know what else to do. I'm afraid somebody's taken him for ransom or revenge."

The idea was too cruel to consider. There was silence on both ends of the line. We both waited for the other to say something, say anything.

Then, Amos spoke. "When I left there, I still had a few friends. Now it feels like I have no friends, and enemies all over the place."

Everything that I saw from the corner of my eye looked like a dog.

"I just hope he hasn't run off and got hurt," Amos said. "If someone took him at the track, they knew him, and he knew them. He has a big reputation as a good luck charm. Some of those guys are so superstitious."

I headed out of the office, saying, "I'm getting in the car to go look for him. Please keep talking."

I laid the phone down on the empty seat beside me. One car's headlights were spraying diffuse light on the ground and then in my face. I had to look down. Tears burned my eyes, and my cheeks were wet. I didn't want to cry, but I did.

"Are you okay?" Amos asked.

"Yes, I'll call you back."

I sobbed the moment I hung up. My voice was gone, and my heart raced. I was going to need some serious strength, hope, and faith to get through this.

I drove around all night, screaming "Lucky!" every time I stopped the car. I finally had to go home and get some sleep, which was nearly impossible. I dreamt I was chasing shadows of little dogs, woke, dozed off again, and woke up ready to shout his name.

The next morning I called Amos once I'd had a cup of coffee and had set up a plan with Max.

"We are doing everything we can," I said, trying to sound much more professional than I had the night before. "Max has the entire police department in Fort Worth looking. We've got Lucky's picture all over social media. We printed flyers and put them up. Even the TV and radio have picked up on all this. It's now everywhere—"LUCKY IS LOST."

The phone was silent.

"You okay?" I asked.

"No. Not okay."

I was trying to be positive, but I felt the same. We were both heartbroken. Such an emptiness, and my mind practically exhausted thinking about all the possibilities. Lucky had to be just as scared as we were.

Finally, I said, "Amos, we're doing everything we can."

"I just don't know what I would do if something happened to him," Amos said. "I love Lucky."

"We're in this together," I said. "We have to have faith that Lucky will get back safe."

My guilt was so strong. Amos had given me his dog to help me feel safe, to feel protected, and I'd let him down. Just like I had with his winning check. Just like I had by not having one scrap of evidence about what had happened in those races—to clear his name. I couldn't begin to imagine what he thought of me, or why he'd decided to trust me, because I kept failing him.

"I'll text you as anything develops."

We hung up. I had gotten so used to Lucky being there with me, even for just a few days. If I didn't find Lucky, how could I ever face Amos again? Or anyone else there at HSD? I needed to start looking for clues that didn't seem obvious—like, what if I had been set up, just like Amos?

I sat down on the couch. For some reason, I remembered back when I was little and we had searched for my dog. My mother had said something about St. Francis of Assisi, the patron saint of animals.

I pulled up the picture of Lucky on the iPad and prayed.

Chapter 36

I couldn't sleep. I had made up my mind to take the day off and go straight to Fort Worth and search for Lucky. I went over to Patty's office.

"Lucky is gone. Disappeared."

"What!" She'd been drinking a cup of coffee and set it down so fast some of it spilled onto her desk. Wiping it up, she said, "Oh no. How?"

After hearing the quick version, she gave me a sympathetic look. "Are you doing okay?"

"It's bringing up things I don't like to think about. Like when Daddy left—when I was little and we had to move to an apartment where we couldn't take our dog, we gave him to the people who bought our house. We left him in the only house we ever had as a family together. Daddy had lost all the money betting on horses over at Hialeah Racetrack in Miami. Yesterday, I felt like it happened all over again." I paused. "Even though I'm not allowed back at the track yet, I'm going to go help look for him."

Patty hesitated. "This could be a trap. Especially if someone stole him—as a setup—thinking you would run back to help out. They could get you for trespassing or who knows what else. Remember our word 'consequences'? Don't be tempted to go there."

My heart was heavy with disappointment. "I'm afraid you're right."

"You know who would be perfect to help in this situation?" Patty said. "Powder! Maybe APP would send him with Jessie?"

It was worth a try. I found APP sitting at his table in the back in the dining room. I sat down at his table without an invitation, which I'd never done before. He looked up, and I could tell he was surprised.

"Sir, I have a problem back at HSD. Lucky has been missing since about three o'clock yesterday. We don't know if he ran off and is lost or if someone stole him or dognapped him for a reward."

I had his attention. "I need a favor. W. D. Stamples has me banned from the track—not forever, but right now. Sir, I was wondering if Jessie could take Powder back there and assist in the search. I'll send some of my clothes drenched in my aftershave. Lucky knows that smell. They've got flyers up all over town. I'll pay you for his time."

He took a big gulp of coffee and said, "Anybody who would steal a dog, especially a dog as good as Lucky, ought to be taken to downtown Noose and strung up. Hell yes, we'll send Powder, and if you want me to go, I'll go too."

"I appreciate that, but I don't want to take up your time."

He nodded, then hollered, "Jessie, come here! You gotta go to Fort Worth and help find Lucky. Amos, don't you worry. Not a man alive loves dogs more'n him."

"Thank you."

"When we find him, it may be a good idea to bring him back here."

"Yes sir, I will."

I called Rixie. "Good news. APP is sending Jessie and Powder. He's a sniffer, part lab and bloodhound. He's leaving soon, probably be there by eleven. I'll tell him to go to your office—the last place he was. Maybe he can pick up his scent there. I'm going to send you an audio copy of my whistle. It sounds like a catcall—*sweet sweeill*."

"What do I do with that?" she asked.

"Turn up the volume and replay it while you are out looking."

"Okay, record it and send it now."

We hung up.

I skipped breakfast, got a cup of coffee, and went over to the barn. Patty was working with the horses, but she stopped as soon as she saw me. I gave her the update. "Thank you. Jessie's going to Fort Worth."

"You'll get Lucky back," she said, and hugged me. "You just have to have faith."

Chapter 37

The receptionist called my cell phone. "Miss Ricksland, you have a visitor here with a big dog. WD said this one had better stay on the leash. He's going to start enforcing the track policy of NO dogs allowed after this deal with you."

I gritted my teeth. I continued to get on WD's bad side.

"We want to see if his dog can pick up Lucky's scent," I said. "I'll come meet him."

Jessie was easy to spot, being pulled by the big dog, who was slobbering and smelling everything in his path. "We'll cover this whole place," he said. "If Lucky is still here, this dog will find him."

I started using the "*sweet swell*" whistle while we walked toward the kitchen. Other people began whistling.

"Sorry," I told him. "It's embarrassing when men start using the catcall as a joke toward me."

As Powder raced toward the kitchen, people stared as though they'd never seen a sniffer at work. I had no doubt they were afraid we were doing a sweep of the barns, looking for drugs and so forth. We went out toward the front gate and then around all the barns. Powder hardly stopped, but he did slow down as we passed through Barn7.

Powder went right toward Charlane, who seemed a little startled, but he eased into the room where she kept the cookies. She came out shaking one of her boxes, never looking at anything but Powder's eyes.

"Sit." She put a cookie in her palm.

Powder waited for Jessie's permission. On Jessie's signal, Powder took it, and Charlane rubbed his head. He looked at her until she put three or four in her hand, and he took them all in one swipe. He smelled her pants, her arms, her shirt.

Jessie said, "Those are the same ones we have back at the ranch. He loves them. And that's you right there on the box!"

"Yes, sir," Charlane preened. "So the horses like my cookies?"

"Our horses and dogs won't even eat the old ones we get at the feed store. They'll only eat these."

She took out her pocketknife and opened a box. "Guess I got a whole new marketin' opportunity. There's more dogs in the world than horses anyway. Here's some more for him." She squatted down, and he lay down right under her feet as she rubbed his stomach. "My kinda dog."

We stayed there for at least ten minutes. Finally I said, "We need to move on."

"Wait a minute," she said. "I've had more than a hundred likes on my Facebook. My friends are sharing Lucky's sweet little face. The new "$2,500 REWARD" flyers are in my truck. I'll go get them. I think we should put 'em up tomorrow."

I was tired. "Sure, do it tomorrow."

Powder followed her. When she opened the truck door, he practically jumped in. He went frantic.

Charlane laughed. "Damn dog is crazy about my cookies. Get him outta here. I got fifteen boxes in there I gotta deliver tonight."

Jessie had to pull him out and let him drink from the water bucket back in the barn. "Sorry, Powder's got all hot and worked up about those cookies. He could have lost the scent he got in your office. We can try again in the morning, but if he's been gone twenty-four hours, we're probably running out of time."

I walked back to the parking lot. The heat had gotten to me too. I was a little delirious, thinking about that show Charlane had put on at Barn7. What if Powder was smelling Lucky's scent on her clothes and in her truck?

Everywhere I looked was Lucky's picture on the flyers. "WANTED— LOST DOG—$1,000 REWARD." Soon to be $2,500. Was it possible she was behind all this? No, even she couldn't be that conniving.

My stomach was in knots, my throat sore from hollering his name, my feet tired from walking miles and miles, but I didn't want to give up until I found him. Finally, I had to.

I woke up on the couch about midnight from a dream of posters everywhere that said, "WANTED FOR LOSING DOG," with my picture instead of Lucky's.

Chapter 38

The next morning I hadn't heard if Powder had found Lucky. I'd been hopeful but didn't want it to lead to another dead end. I shook my head. Not a dead end—it couldn't end like that.

I headed out to the horses right after a quick cup of coffee.

Once they were fed, Patty walked up. "Any news about Lucky?"

I shook my head. "Nothing yet."

"I'm grilling burgers tonight at six o'clock. Bring the truck."

I spent the whole day worried about Lucky and waiting to hear from Rixie. She finally called when I was walking out the door, headed to Patty's house. "Charlane got a call from someone who claims to have Lucky; he's okay. We changed the reward to $2,500, and the person wants us to come up with a better number than that. He's going to call her back sometime tonight. She wants to meet me at my house and map out a strategy. Amos, how high can we go? I'll pay half. Even Charlane said she would chip in, and Buster, and Max too. Are you available to patch in the call?"

I hesitated. "It's too emotional for me. Go as high as you have to. Just get a commitment for delivery. Get proof he is okay. Have them send a photo of him. Going to dinner now; call me back."

Her voice was almost a whisper. "Thanks. We'll give it our best shot."

I drove to Patty's house. In spite of the stress of Lucky being lost, I was starting to think I might have added years to my life by slowing down at this ranch. It was amazing how peaceful it could be to not worry every time I got on a horse that it might be my last ride. I went to bed at nine or ten and got up at six-thirty or seven. I'd even showered and shaved again, and it had been a long time since I'd done that twice in the same day. No worries at all—except about Lucky. At least the idea of the call filled me with hope.

Patty had a table set for two on her patio. Flowers again from the ranch. The grill was ready to light.

"Any news about Lucky?"

"Yes. A call came in from someone claiming to have him, and the person wanted a new reward number. Rixie is waiting on a call now."

"Would you like the best sangria in Texas?" she said, starting to pour. "But I don't add alcohol. Do you know how bad alcohol is for the human body? And mind, and liver, and marriages, and everything. You'll like my sangria."

Patty handed me my glass. "Here's to finding Lucky and bringing him back here safe. And for a good life…together."

We touched glasses.

"Okay, I won't be able to eat dinner until I get my cowboy boot out of my mouth," Patty said. "I meant a good life for Lucky and *you*…together."

She touched my glass again and took a sip. She turned and lifted the cover on the grill and said, "How does that look? I hope you're hungry. I cook everything on the grill. Burgers, asparagus, green chilis, baked sweet potatoes. And I have a few surprises for you."

"What can I do to help?" I asked.

"No, relax." She worked for a minute, then said, "Adrian's mother is so grateful for everything we did. I got her a new bank account, and they're doing a direct deposit for her paycheck."

"That's such good news."

"It made my day." She set the two plates on the table and grabbed my hand. "So does this. I'm glad you're here. I've been wanting to do this."

I guess I could have sat there all night and stared at her, but she broke my gaze. "Better dig in; don't let it get cold."

"It looks fantastic."

"What about the burgers?" She smiled. "Looks like meat, tastes like meat. Do you like it?"

"Yes, it tastes almost like real food—as I call it. I'm planning to vegetarian...gradually."

"Really?" She smiled. "Once we're done, we're going to have the best peach cobbler you have ever tasted."

As soon as we finished dinner, she served the cobbler. I ate every bite and she said, "Well, is that the best you ever had?"

"Racetrack kitchens serve what they call cobbler, but it's just berries cooked in dough, and I have had cobbler at places like Cracker Barrel. So your peach cobbler is definitely the best I ever had."

"You're comparing *my* peach cobbler to the cobbler at those places?"

"No, *your* peach cobbler is the *only* peach cobbler I hope I *ever* have."

"Say that again," she said, and walked over to the couch.

I settled in next to her. "The only peach cobbler I ever want to have is *your* peach cobbler."

We looked at each other, and the mood in the room turned serious.

She smiled. "I know you think I want you to kiss me. You're right—so we are going to do that in a minute. But I need to tell you—I am becoming more fond of you every day. Let's take it slow. We have our whole lives ahead of us. Let's just promise each other we will respect each other, and let's give this time. It's like the peach cobbler—if we put the stove on too high a temperature, it will cook too fast and won't taste good, or it will burn, and then it will be gone. But if we use the same recipe and instructions every time, we can make a lot of peach cobblers."

She moved the pillow and kicked her legs up on the couch, putting her right arm behind me.

I started to say something, but she put her index finger on my lips. "Shhh. My plan is quality time, good conversation, some laughter, and lots of cuddling. I've been waiting for this for quite some time now, and therefore I will not back down so easily for something that means so much to me. I now understand clearly why women love cowboys!"

I brushed a piece of hair out of her eyes, and we looked at each other.

"Smile, my cowboy. Your rope has caught me and is slowly tightening."

Even though the thought of living without Lucky was unbearable, Patty still had the power to make me smile. Her voice was quiet. "Oddly, I'm really enjoying it…especially since I know you like my peach cobbler. I'm going to shut up now. *Kiss me.*"

Chapter 39

Charlane and I sat at my house, watching her phone. Finally, at 10:30, she said, "He ain't gonna call this late. Hun, get some sleep. If he calls, I'll handle it. There's nothing else we can do. Just gotta wait."

Right after she left, I called Amos. "No call yet. Charlane said he'll wear us down until we're desperate and pay whatever they demand."

"So what's next?"

"We wait and hope this is a legitimate deal, not a hoax. How are you doing?"

He had started to speak when Charlane's name lit up on my phone. "Amos, it's Charlane—let me patch you in."

Once we'd clicked over, I said, "Amos is on, too. What's up?"

"He wants to meet tomorrow morning in the back of the parking lot of the Fort Woof Dog Park next to the Gateway Park at 6:00 a.m. I said I needed a photo of Lucky or no dice. He said if you want the dog, bring $5,000 cash, and he'll be there. He hung up before I could say anything else. Probably a burner phone."

We all sat in silence; then Amos spoke. "So what do we do?"

Charlane said, "I got that much cash. I'll go and get your dog. Rixie and I are exhausted. We're on his clock, and time is of the essence."

"Okay."

"No, wait a minute," I said. "I want to go. Max should get us back-up. We could have the police standing by in the shadows."

"Hun, you been watchin' too much CSI. We'll be lucky if they don't show up or call me tomorrow and change it up."

"I agree," Amos chimed in. "Let Charlane handle it."

"Okay," I said, feeling frustrated. "Let's finish this."

I had fallen asleep on the couch. My phone rang from down on the floor. It was Charlane.

"Hun, it's 5:30. You up?"

I headed to the kitchen to make coffee. "Yeah, barely. You on the way?"

"I came by Barn7 about 5:00. Kellsey was there, and she'd seen the flyers. Got a soft place in her heart for Lucky. Going to pieces. Hysterical. She asked who the hell you are and why did you have Lucky, anyway. Why were you so stupid to let him get away? I told her it wasn't your fault."

The words stung. Before I could speak, she said, "Let me get off this phone. I'll let you know what happens."

I paced and watched the time on my phone until it was almost 6:00. Minutes passed. I almost called Charlane but changed my mind. I should have insisted on going. Her name came up on my phone.

"You got him?" I said quickly.

"No."

My stomach clenched. "*No?* What happened?"

"I got a call from a new number at ten after six. He said he saw me there, but now he wants another $1,000."

Unease clawed at my stomach. "You said that might happen."

"No kidding," she said. "I know what I'm talking about."

But how did she know? I didn't want to doubt her. Charlane was a lot of things, but she loved animals, and on some level, Amos. She wouldn't put him through this.

Would she?

"He still didn't give me any proof about Lucky. I told him to send me a photo and I'd get the rest of the money together."

"When?"

"Noon today. Same place. He said there is an information desk at the entrance and for me to put the money in the bottom of a flower vase and put a bunch of flowers in it—but no water—and set it on the desk behind the counter. Wait…He just sent me a photo of Lucky. I'll forward it to you. It all looks legit. I like noon better. It was scary out there in the dark this morning, all by myself."

"I told you I'd go," I said. "I'm going today when you pick him up."

"No. He said come alone." Her voice was kinder this time. "As soon as he picks up the money, he'll tell me where to find Lucky. Hun, I got this. He's gonna be fine. Trust me on this; have I ever let you down?"

"You're the only one I can trust to do this," I admitted, thinking of her gold card and the ease with which she'd moved through that world. "I'll call Amos and give him the new plan."

"You tell Amos if it all goes as planned, he'll have his dog back safe and sound. When you takin' Lucky out there?"

I thought it was a little presumptuous for her to assume that she was getting Lucky back, for her to ask when I was taking him back to Amos, but I said, "I'm leavin' as soon as you bring him to my house."

Finally, at 12:30, the phone rang. Charlane was screaming, and I was never so happy to hear a dog bark in my life.

"Shit, Hun." She was crying and laughing hysterically. "I got him. I got him."

I could finally breathe. "Thank you, Charlane, and thank God he's safe. How does he look?"

"He looks good."

I could hear her breathing hard. "Are you okay?"

"Just gotta tell you how it went down. I put the flowers on the table. He called and said if the money was there, the dog would be at the dog park, and hung up. So I'm walking—no, I start running, and my phone rings again—he's watching me. He said, 'Do not run.' I stopped, and he said the money was all there and in five minutes the dog would be in the dog park.

"I put my timer on my phone and stood there. I bit my fingernails; I would have bummed a cigarette and smoked it, I was so nervous. Shit, that was the longest five minutes of my life. That bell went off on my phone. I started whistling Amos's catcall. So then I turned on my camera and videoed him running up to the gate.

"Oh, Hun. I wish you was there. I already put that video up on Facebook announcing Lucky was FOUND!!!! Happy ending."

"I'll call Amos right now."

"Oh. I called him first—he already knows."

Amos called the moment I hung up. "She got Lucky back!"

"Amos, our prayers are answered," I said. "Miracles do happen. I'll bring him out there to you."

"No, I'll come there."

"Really?" I said, surprised. "Okay, I'll go get Texas brisket and all the fixin's from that place we went with Lucky."

"Damn right; let's have real Texas brisket," he said. "It's one o'clock now. I'll get away from here as soon as I can, probably get there about six o'clock. Text me your address."

Charlane's truck pulled in, and the two of them got out on her side, and she smiled her fake smile. Lucky stopped to pee, and then he saw me. She unsnapped the leash, and he ran and leapt in my arms, almost knocking me down.

I'd never been so glad to have a dog lick my face. Inside, he dove into his bowl. It had about a third of his normal portion. He'd have to take it slow for a while. Charlane threw herself down on my couch and leaned back.

"You and me," she said, sounding a little too pleased with herself. "We're a damned good team. Don't let anyone tell you any different."

"Don't get too comfortable. I have a lot to do."

"Of course." She swung her legs over and stood up. "Come here. You look like you need a hug."

I put up my hands. "No. Stop. I really need to save my hugs."

"For Amos…Hun, I understand."

I was not about to tell her he was coming here.

"Thanks again, Charlane."

"All in a day's work. Oh, Hun…" She wiped her hand across her mouth and said, "I made up an invoice for you. I kicked in $500. I'll get Kellsey's, Buster's, and SkyMan's money from them. So yours is $1,900. Here's one for Amos. His is $1,900. You can give it to him when you give him Lucky back." She handed me the invoice with a triumphant smile. "Tell Amos I heard BigOilRig is off the stewards' list, and—did I tell you?—I got a gig with BigOilRig's new trainer. We got him pointed for a nice optional claimer next week."

"Okay," I said, still processing the part where she'd handed me an invoice.

Charlane pointed at me and then at Lucky. She didn't have to say a word. I knew she meant for me to take care of him, as if all this could happen again.

The moment she left, I pushed the door shut, leaned up against it and hoped she hadn't forgotten anything. Her old truck started, and she honked the horn twice. I filled the tub and finally relaxed. I almost fell asleep as the water got cold. I shivered under my towel. Lucky followed me everywhere—room to room.

Then, because Lucky was back and I couldn't stop seeing Charlane's knowing smile, I called Amos again. I had to tread lightly with this, given his friendship with Charlane.

"I've been thinking," I said when he picked up. "None of the cameras around the kitchen and Barn7 recorded a dog loose. You know he would head there looking for you. I'm starting to think that Powder didn't just go to her cookie room because cookies are in there. He was following Lucky's scent. The way he smelled her—if she had him, and that was before he went in the room—and the way Powder jumped in her truck and she claimed it was the cookies."

Amos was silent. When he spoke, his voice was sharp. "I wondered how she could give out suggested scenarios, and sure enough, like you said, that's how it would happen."

"I wish I'd gone out to her house to see if he was there."

He was silent again. "I don't know what to think. Can we talk about this when I get there?"

"Yes. Hurry."

Chapter 40

I hollered, "They found Lucky!" as I ran over to the barn where Patty was. The women in the barn cheered, and I waved to them.

Patty held out her arms, and my hug almost smothered her. Laughing, she grabbed my hand and led me over toward the office.

"Oh, Amos, that's great news," she said. "Wow. What a relief."

I nodded and looked up into the clear sky, silently saying a thank-you prayer. A gentle breeze felt good on my face, and I looked at Patty. "I'm gonna have to take the rest of the day off and go get him."

"Yes," she said. "Take my truck."

"Do you need anything from Fort Worth?"

She smiled. "Just bring my truck back."

"The first time I borrowed his truck, APP said that. What's that mean?"

"That's a Texas way of saying 'Come back safe' and 'Don't wreck my truck.'"

We both laughed. Then she got serious.

"You know, Amos, I've worried about something you said when Lucky got lost. You blamed Rixie—but down deep you said you blame yourself. How are you going to handle it with her? You can't go through life like this, blaming people for what happens. Life isn't like that. You have to try and figure out what your part is in all this. What do you think?"

There she was again, ending her comments with a question.

"How do you know all that?" I asked.

"I've been around women who are prisoners, and they tell me the damnedest stories. It's a combination of my psychology training and therapy training."

I heard what she was saying, and it made sense. She gave me a long kiss. I wanted to stay there and go get Lucky later, but she eased back and said, "Now go. Bring Lucky and my truck back! I've thought a lot about last night. That was just a preview. I want you to have this."

She held up a key and gave it to me.

I held that key in my left hand. All I could think of was what she'd said: "*That was just a preview.*"

I turned up the radio and took a deep breath, and my phone rang—Charlane.

"Hey there, Amos. Whatcha think about me gettin' Lucky back for you?"

Rixie's suggestion that Charlane could have been behind all this had me worried, but now, hearing her voice, I really couldn't buy into that. Yes, Charlane loved money more than anything, but she had lots of side hustles and no reason to try and cause me pain. She'd stepped in and fixed things, Charlane-style.

"Can't thank you enough," I said. "I'm headed there now to pick him up."

"You know, I been riding BigOilRig for his new trainer. The owner isn't happy with the last race, and he wants to enter him in an optional claiming race. I heard there's one maybe this week. I know you have talked about trying to claim him."

My heart skipped a beat. "Yes, that's interesting," I said, slowly. "Thanks for the heads-up."

"Okay. You gonna send me a check for the ransom? I gave Rixie your invoice. $1,900."

I almost laughed out loud. She was such a hustler.

"Yes. I'll send it to you. Goodbye."

I started to whistle. Everything was good. Lucky was safe. BigOilRig might be available. I also took some time to think about what Patty had said, about forgiving Rixie. I'd trusted her with Lucky, and she'd let me down. I needed to let that go, and in my heart, I found the forgiveness to do it by the time I pulled up to her driveway.

Lucky burst out the door, dragging Rixie. When I saw him, I was overcome. I was all smiles. Lucky's butt wagged, and he barked and jumped up on me. Rixie gave us a few moments, then handed me the leash. "Let's take him for a walk."

We walked in silence, then she said, "Amos, I'm so sorry this happened."

"Things happen. We can't let the consequences rule our lives."

"What can I do to make this up to you?" she asked.

"I'm starting to think I won't ever get my $90,000."

"Oh, as soon as WD says 'Okay,' you'll get your money," she said, waving her hand. "To him, everything is a game. He's winning as long as he has your money, and you're losing until you get it. At some point, he'll have no choice but to hand it over."

We walked down the streets in her neighborhood. People came out, and once they realized Lucky was with us, there was applause and cheers, which showed me how big the search for Lucky had gotten. We waved and thanked them.

Back at her house, we sat at the table, and I dove into the brisket. It was really good. I'd almost forgotten how much I missed it. She got out the mint chip ice cream, and I waved it off. "Mint is not my favorite." She put it back in the freezer, and we went in and sat on the couch. It made me think of the night before, with Patty, and how much I looked forward to using that key.

"Well, Miss Investigator," I said. "How are you going to find out who is behind Lucky's disappearance?"

She hesitated. "I still think it was Charlane. This was intentional; this was a direct threat. He didn't run off. He was stolen."

"She wouldn't do that."

"It had to be her," Rixie said. "It was so contrived. I mean, she knew how it was going to play out before it happened, like she was making it up as she went. I went back and reviewed the security tapes at the track, all around the office entrance. That day, there were some people moving furniture in and taking out big boxes. Big enough to put a dog in."

She looked at me. "No one anywhere saw Lucky. If he had run out through the grandstand toward the barns, someone would have seen him. The cameras would have seen him."

I sat in silence for a moment, thinking it through. "Charlane wouldn't do this on her own. Only if she had to—if she had instructions from someone. If that's the case, she'd be too scared to tell us. Who could have put her up to it?"

"That's what we're trying to figure out. Amos, there are always trends in investigations. Repeated instances. They get more daring each time they think they get away with something."

"What are you saying?" I asked.

"I'm saying I think whoever set you up on March 26 with those tips is also responsible for Lucky being gone. I've been putting together some evidence on those four horses that obviously got doped. Pretty soon I'll be able to identify the key suspect."

She was being cautious about what she was sharing with me, so I just listened, a little startled by what came next.

"I hope Charlane's not in too deep," she said. "People get caught in the middle—thinking they can get out. It doesn't work that way. Case in point: back in Northern Virginia, outside DC, a bank vice president got involved with the owner of the bank. He had her alter bank documents under the guise that 'we'll never get audited'—except they did, and you know who went down. The reason I'm telling you is this: if Charlane is on the front line, she is expendable. In a way, I feel like I need to get this solved to protect her if I can."

I pulled Lucky over to me and said, "Well, Lucky, whoever took you won't be a threat again, because I'm not going to let you out of my sight."

Rixie studied me for a moment. When I didn't say anything more or comment on what she'd said about Charlane, she nodded. "Besides finding Lucky—there's other good news today. I got notified all the lab results came back, and BigOilRig was cleared. He came off the stewards' list today. His new trainer has already entered him in a $50,000 optional claiming race on Wednesday."

My heart started to beat with anticipation. "I've been talking to Mr. Applegate about having him put a claim in for BigOilRig."

She got to her feet. Then she smiled, for the first time in two hours since I got there. "Here's what I want—to get you completely cleared. I want to find out who doped those horses and who's behind stealing Lucky. I also want you to know I'm one of your biggest fans, and I hope you can claim BigOilRig. I know how much he means to you. And this guy…"

Lucky rolled over on his back, and she scratched his stomach. "One last request before you head out. I want a photo of you and Lucky."

She got her phone and said, "Smile like you did when you saw him out in the front yard."

It was a great drive back. All I could think about was BigOilRig in a claiming race. Lucky sat right up there in the front seat and watched me the whole way. I sang along with the songs on the radio. It was one of the happiest days of my life.

I called Patty. "Hey, Lucky and I are halfway back to the ranch. He's all good. I am so glad to be out of Fort Worth. Too many bad memories there."

"What time will you get back?" There was a smile in her voice.

I hesitated, thinking of the key she'd given me, but I had to do what was best for Lucky.

"Late," I said, reluctantly. "I'm going straight to the cabin to settle in with Lucky. I need to watch him and be sure his stomach is okay. Let's catch up in the morning."

"Okay, be safe," she said. "You got valuable cargo there."

"You mean your truck and Lucky?"

"And the cowboy driving that rig home."

"Home?"

"Yes. Bring it on home."

Chapter 41

Monday night after all the Lucky commotion was over, I called Thomas to figure out a game plan for the Derby.

After a few pleasantries, I said, "Thomas, I hope your weekend was better than mine. I have had four of the worst days of my life. Last week I was keeping a friend's dog, and on Friday he went missing."

"Your friend or the dog?"

We both laughed.

"The dog."

"Did you find him?"

"Oh yes, after paying a $6,000 ransom."

"I'm in California. How about if I come through Fort Worth tomorrow, probably arrive late afternoon? We could fly together to Louisville on Thursday."

"I can't think of anything I'd like more."

We hung up, and on Tuesday I had to go shopping. I'd been so busy I hadn't put my Derby outfits together for Friday and Saturday.

I called Max and told him that after this lost-dog debacle, I had to take some time off, then headed straight for my favorite dress shop. It wasn't often I had a chance to go there.

The owner said, "Rixie, what brings you in?"

"The Kentucky Derby," I said. "I'll need two outfits."

"One moment." He came over and assessed me with a trained eye. "I have just what you need. Don't worry. You'll be beautiful."

I'd been so stressed the last few days that at this point, it felt as though I could use all the help I could get. He pulled a handful of dresses, all of which were nearly perfect. When I tried on a light green leather dress and walked out of the dressing room, he did a double take.

"Wow" was all he had to say.

So far, so good.

"Try this one," he instructed, handing me a dress with little red roses. "This would be perfect for Saturday."

Sure enough, it was. For the first time in ages, the tightness in my shoulders started to relax. I hoped the weekend would bring the same feeling.

"I'll take them both," I said.

"Do you like these boots?" he asked, holding up a beautiful pair of hand-tooled black boots. He had a pair in my size. "They go great with both dresses." He caught me looking at the price tag and said, "Let's put it all together, and I'll work up one price for everything."

I was already over my budget. Then he handed me a cowboy hat that went perfectly with both dresses.

I hesitated. "A cowboy hat for the Derby?"

"You want to make a statement. Darlin', you can't go up there from Texas and wear one of those little fascinators."

I laughed and he added it all up. I cringed when he turned the ticket around.

"That price is retail," he said. "I can give you 25 percent off."

Once he'd rung it up, he gave me a fatherly smile.

"Darlin'—I don't know the lucky man you are going with, but I do know you will be beautiful."

Thomas arrived around 5:00. I met him at Meacham Airport, his name in big letters on my iPad. When he walked out, he spotted the note and laughed.

"I see it's your turn to be the limo driver."

We headed to dinner and talked about the Derby. His smile had me staring at him over the candlelight, imagining what the rest of this night was going to be like. I wasn't even at the girlfriend phase yet. Not to mention being on display as his date and spending the weekend with him in Louisville. The topic of his children came up over dessert.

"I told them about you," he said after taking a bite of the chocolate soufflé. "They want to meet you."

It was easy to picture Thomas as a father. He seemed as though he'd be a good one.

"What did you say?" I asked.

"I told them I was cautiously, anxiously anticipating spending more time in Fort Worth. They both said, at the same time, 'Fort Worth?'"

"Well, for what it's worth—no pun intended—I'd like to meet them too. Tell me about them."

He gave me the family geography lesson. It was clear he was proud of them both. A son and a daughter, both in college.

"They'll be at the Derby," he said. "You'll meet them there."

I was still thinking how he'd told his children about me when we returned to the HSD Casino Hotel. His suite overlooked the entire track from the top floor, and I hesitated as we walked in.

"Can I suggest one rule?" I said, my hand resting on the door. "I have to go home to my house every night. There was already some track gossip all the way back here from Oaklawn. You and I leaving the conference together probably wasn't wise if we plan to fly under the radar."

"I know. When I got back to NESPA headquarters in downtown Lexington, some of my golfing buddies from the executive committee texted me. I didn't tell them anything. I want you to be comfortable."

Even though I had set the rules, I couldn't help but feel happy knowing that my drives back home each night would keep getting later and later.

Chapter 42

Lucky was staring at me when I woke up, and I knew it would be a great day. I looked at the calendar—April 26. We went to the TAPP kitchen, and everyone was glad to see him.

I pulled APP off to the side. "Sir, I want to thank you for letting Jessie take Powder back to Fort Worth. He was there Saturday and Sunday, and we got Lucky back on Monday. They are going to write a $50,000 optional claiming race on Wednesday for that horse I told you about—BigOilRig. Would you be the registered trainer and claim him for me?"

He peered at me. "Fifty thousand dollars? That's a tall number at HSD. You got that kinda money?"

I lowered my voice. "I've got a coupla hundred thousand in a bank in Fort Worth. More than that, invested."

I got the strangest look from him.

"You look surprised at that," I said. "I made good money exercise riding and being an assistant trainer, barn manager, and gambler. I've never had a house or car payment. Now, living in a barn isn't as fancy as living in this cabin here, but it was free. So yes. As you said…I got that kinda money."

"Well then, absolutely. Get me the papers and a check for the $50,000, and I'll go claim BigOilRig for you."

Everything was falling into place. I whistled as Lucky and I walked to the barn, and he ran straight to Patty. She rubbed his ears, back, and stomach. "Looks like my boys are back home, all safe and sound. How'd it go?"

"Lucky and I made a pact on the way back. I told him that would never happen again. I wish he could tell me where he was for those three days." I hesitated. "Rixie's convinced Charlane had him."

"Why would she do something like that?"

"If she's acting on orders. Rixie thinks whoever set me up is behind it all."

"I've heard some outlandish tales, but this Lucky caper is right up there with the best ones."

My phone rang—SkyMan. I put him on speaker. "Hey there, SkyMan, what's up?"

"Well, Rixie told me all about how Charlane rescued Lucky."

"At least I got him back and he's safe."

"Yeah, she told me about you driving up here and getting him. Rixie said she never saw a man tear into brisket like you did. She said you must be on a special diet out there."

I regretted having the call on speaker, and I glanced at Patty, who was putting hay in a stall. She acted like she wasn't listening.

SkyMan went on, "BigOilRig is off the stewards' list. The owner is going to enter him in a race this Wednesday."

"Mr. Applegate is going to put a claim in for me. Don't say anything about that."

"Good," SkyMan said. "Let me know if I can do anything for you."

We chatted for a minute. Once I hung up, Patty looked at me.

"Were Lucky and brisket all you got in Fort Worth?"

We both laughed.

"Yes. You know they were."

She studied me for a second. "Is claiming that horse something you are really going to do?"

"I've thought about owning a racehorse my whole life," I said. "BigOilRig is the most special horse I've ever been around. For me to get him on a claim would be fantastic."

The enthusiasm in my voice was silenced by her concern. "Are you going to retire him out here or put him in training?"

"I guess to own a horse like him that has a few more years and a lot of races in his future overshadows the temptation to retire him. I've always wanted to own a thoroughbred horse that is racing."

Patty looked surprised. "So if you claim him, you're going to get back into racing?"

"There are a lot of ifs in racing. But yes, if everything went okay, I would race him—at least for one race—to prove to myself I could do that."

Patty looked away for a moment, then leaned against the wall. "This is just my observation. The prisoners and BigOilRig have a lot in common. The only difference—these women get out ten hours a day. BigOilRig lives in a stall twenty-three hours a day. Maybe you were more like a prisoner back there at the track than you knew."

She was right. When I was there, I never went anywhere, and I never did anything else. I worked 24/7.

Patty looked hard and long at me before reaching down to mess with Lucky. "Sounds like a done deal already. It sounds as if your pride is taking over and you are neglecting what you set out to do. A word of caution about temptation. I don't think it's a good decision to race him. For you. For me. For us."

Chapter 43

Thomas and I met at the track kitchen for breakfast. By now everyone was used to seeing us together, but I still wanted our relationship to fly under the radar as long as possible.

"What's all this buzz about Kellsey O'Bryan?" he asked once we were seated at a table. The western omelets were huge, so we shared one. Interesting how we had similar tastes.

"This is her home track. Her father is Buster O'Bryan. You know the dog I kept last week? Lucky belongs to her ex-boyfriend, Amos Moon. She's seeing a NESPA employee now, Clink McMillin. And guess who else?" I lowered my voice. "Stamples."

"Really?"

"Really." I took a bite of the omelet. "Kellsey's agent got her to ride BigOilRig in the $50,000 optional claiming race this afternoon. Since Kellsey is back, Stamples is here. This morning, he found out Amos is trying to make a claim, and he had the racing director put a hold on his claiming application. Of all days for you to be at HSD—you'll get a chance to see how the dynamics play out in something that should be simple. But nothing's simple around here."

The news had frustrated me, because no doubt this failed claiming race was another thing that would make Amos think I'd let him down.

Once we were finished eating, we walked outside. "I need to call Amos and head him off before he drives here for the race."

Letting out a breath, I put the call on speaker. "Hey, update on the race today. One glitch."

"Glitch? What glitch?"

"Your two-month suspension from the track. Stamples thinks it was for real. So you aren't eligible to claim a horse at HSD until May 26."

Silence on the line.

"Amos, there's nothing I can do. Just let this pass."

"That's easy for you to say." He sounded furious. "What if he gets claimed by someone else?"

"If there was another claim in the box and yours was there too, you might not catch the draw and get shut out anyway."

"You can rationalize everything. Call me when the race is over and let me know what happens."

Thomas raised his eyebrows. "The more I see at the track, the more I realize how much negotiation and diplomacy there is." He looked at his watch. "I have meetings with the stewards before the races start."

"I'll get some sandwiches from a great deli sent to my office and meet you there at noon," I told him. "The track kitchen is only good for one meal a week."

Thomas and I walked through the crowd to the paddock. BigOilRig was the favorite on the tote board. I spotted Stamples and pointed him out.

Just then Kellsey came out of her jocks' room and met Charlane and Stamples. He was all smiles. They looked across the hedges, and Charlane pointed me out to her, not once but twice, to make sure I saw them. They acknowledged me with laughter I couldn't hear but could see. Thomas noticed but didn't comment.

We headed up to the stewards' office to watch the race. They didn't know Amos had sent in the check and papers to try and claim BigOilRig. I felt sick inside, knowing that it wasn't going to happen.

Kellsey got a leg up from the new trainer, and she walked BigOilRig out onto the track. Once everyone was in position, the starting gate opened. Kellsey moved BigOilRig right behind the leaders. She stayed with the front group all the way around but never could gain on them. She finished fourth or fifth, and I wondered how much not winning bothered her.

"Well, let's see if anyone claimed him," I said.

Thomas and I went down to the claiming office, and thank goodness, no one had.

I called Amos. "The good news is there isn't another claim in the box. We'll send the $50,000 back."

"While you're at it, send my $90,000."

"I would if I could."

Next, I had to call the owner. He was upset because he'd been told there was an interested claimant. I could only tell him there would be another race late in May.

The moment I got off the phone, Thomas said, "A jockey just got pulled off a horse in the Kentucky Oaks undercard on Friday. Kellsey O'Bryan's agent got her the mount. She'll be there too."

It seemed I couldn't get away from her.

On Thursday Thomas and I were the only ones on the NESPA plane. The weather was perfect, and we arrived in Louisville at Bowman Field early in the afternoon. Thomas had his own parking spot with his name painted on a sign.

"Let me drop you off at the Brown Hotel and get you settled in the suite," he said. "I'll go to my house and change, then bring back the clothes I'll need for the weekend and stay with you. Is that okay?"

I paused. "I've been concerned about what message this gives to everyone up here. I have never been involved with someone I work with or for. Now, I am."

"Nobody cares if I'm at my house or with you."

"Maybe not yet." Still, I wasn't sure I was ready for that. Maybe I wasn't ready for all this. "We can't do anything to jeopardize our jobs."

It was a short trip downtown. When we got there, Thomas took my hands. "Technically you aren't an employee, if that's any consolation. I want to be with you."

"Yes, and I want to be with you," I admitted.

What would it hurt to give myself permission to feel something for him?

"Let's have a great weekend," I said.

I opened the door to the suite, and flowers were everywhere. I unpacked and took a long bath and daydreamed about what I was getting myself into.

He came back at seven o'clock with a box wrapped in Derby-themed paper and bows. "Open it. Something special for your first Derby weekend."

It was a beautiful pink-and-white equine-themed scarf. I knew pink was the official color for Oaks Day, and I modeled it for him.

"It's beautiful," I said, noticing in the mirror how the pink brightened my cheeks. "This will go great with my dress. Thank you."

Even though the hotel was crowded, we had a quiet dinner at a table for two in the grill. I was starting to worry this had already started off too fast, and I was curious if he felt the same. At the track, they called that early speed. I'd only met him three weeks before, on April 8. That said, I could overthink every situation. That's what I'd done my whole life. My jobs had always been about finding out what people did wrong. So far, this guy had done everything right.

I couldn't help but admit that in a few ways he might be too good to be true. But I also promised myself I would give it a fair try.

On Friday morning, we woke up early, and he said, "Welcome to the Oaks."

"I am so happy to be here," I told him. We had an early schedule for arriving at Churchill Downs for the NESPA brunch reception in the Derby Museum. I didn't have to look in a mirror once I got there to see if I looked great, since I got compliments from men and women. Best of all, Thomas beamed with me beside him.

We walked through the crowd and made our way to the elevator. The NESPA suite was elaborate. The NESPA employees and guests were all mingling and having Bloody Marys and mimosas. It was only ten o'clock, which was way too early for me, I got a coffee. Thomas was in his element, introducing me and telling everyone I was from Texas.

As if they couldn't tell that by my cowboy hat and boots. But the looks I got from several women who wore those fascinators validated the look I had. I could tell they wished they looked as good as I did, a thought that surprised me in its confidence. My investigator's mind also wondered if they wished they were with Thomas. So I tucked my hand into the bend of his elbow.

"Let's go down to the paddock before the race the jockey from Texas is in," he suggested.

Back to the elevator and through the crowd. Security and ushers cleared a path for us as soon as they saw Thomas. He didn't need the four different badges on lanyards; everyone knew him.

Kellsey walked into the paddock with the other jockeys like she owned the place. Her attitude and confidence backed up her demeanor. For a second, she scanned the crowd and caught my eye with a "What are you doing here?" stare that lasted two seconds. We looked away.

When the race started, her horse broke out of the gate and stayed close to the front, third or fourth, gaining ground. When she turned for home at the top of the stretch, her horse changed leads and stumbled for no reason, and unseated Kellsey. She landed hard on her shoulder.

Thomas and I rushed down to the first aid facility. She walked from the track ambulance holding her left shoulder. The NESPA team kicked into high gear. Thomas checked with the track doctor and made a call to the hospital before she got there.

"Of all days to have an accident," he said.

The glitz and glamor of Oaks Day had evaporated. He was genuinely concerned about her and relieved when he found out the horse was not injured at all. I could see firsthand why he had this job. For a moment, I saw a trait he shared with Amos. They both were compassionate about the welfare of riders and horses. He called the hospital and got an update on Kellsey. She had broken ribs and they wanted to keep her there for a few days for observation.

Saturday was as glorious as I ever imagined the Derby would be. I didn't have to hand my phone to someone to take photos of Thomas and me. There was a professional photographer that followed us around taking photos all day and told me I would receive a complete file with all the photos and I could transfer any I wanted. Plus the photos would also be in a hardbound book sent to my house.

If yesterday's outfit was a success, the Saturday ensemble was over the top. The minute I walked in, I was asked by several women where I got the dress. I could tell the men were curious who I was—the new woman in Thomas's life. I met all the NESPA brass. Along with my official Kentucky Derby credentials, I had my NESPA badge and access to every area with him.

He introduced me as "Miss Ricksland, one of our NESPA representatives from the Fort Worth track." He was pretty much Mr.

Important. I must say I felt important being with him. Even in Kentucky, with all their horses, people loved to talk about Texas.

I met his son and daughter and their friends. They had a box on the third floor at the finish line. His daughter gave me a nice warm Kentucky hug and pulled me aside to chat. She had the same mesmerizing greenish-gray eyes.

"I'm glad you were at the conference in Oaklawn. He's talked about you for the past three weeks. Now that I've met you...I can see why he's so excited you are here. He's the happiest we've seen him in quite a while...We are happy he's happy with you."

We went straight to the paddock for the saddling of the horses in the next race, the Kentucky Derby. There were a lot of introductions, and several famous people were there. We made it back up to the suite barely in time for the horses to step onto the track and for the singing of "My Old Kentucky Home."

The other guests put up $20 and drew numbers out of a hat to participate in the $400 pool. Winner took all. NESPA board members and employees were not permitted to place bets on horses or even participate in the $20 pool—which was okay by me; I didn't need to win a pool and be under suspicion that Thomas or I had rigged the pool. I had enough unresolved problems back in Fort Worth with races getting fixed.

Immediately after the race, Kentucky's governor made sure we got across the track for the trophy presentation to the Derby winner. Thomas and I held hands as we walked across to the winner's circle. The excitement was contagious. Once the governor had given the trophy to the horse's owner and recognized all the connections, he pulled Thomas beside him on the podium and said, "And special thanks to Thomas de Tono and NESPA for being fantastic partners for horse racing."

The governor and Thomas held up the trophy. They both beamed as though they owned the horse. That moment, seeing how genuine and respected Thomas was, made me proud to be in the NESPA organization. And even prouder to be with him in the winner's circle. That was the highlight of the day.

Sunday was an extension of Derby week. We got invited to a brunch at an exquisite horse farm in Lexington. I immediately realized why it was such a beautiful area. Bluegrass, brunch, and bourbon served all day. I was slowly acquiring a taste for it. The people at this event were really in the horse business. The accolades bestowed on Thomas came from owners, trainers, veterinarians, and retired jockeys who were in attendance.

A few of the women sized me up right when I arrived. Good thing I'd brought my TexaSTARanch outfit: black skirt, flowered blouse, cowboy hat, and my custom boots. It was a casual, dress-down day. I had heard this was one of the toughest crowds to break into, but the people were gracious, especially when they realized I was part of NESPA, and not just Thomas's new…new what? Date for the weekend? Girlfriend? What was I?

A lady reminded me of Martha Drummer, and I thought about that day she'd challenged me about my future. I had known Thomas for only three weeks, but if this was my future, I was okay with it.

I flew back to Fort Worth on Monday, and the first thing I did was go to Barn7 and see Buster. The look he gave me when I walked into his office was slightly wary, as if he expected to run into trouble once again.

I held up my hands. "Mr. O'Bryan, I just wanted to say I was there at the race when Kellsey fell. They have a great staff there, and the NESPA connection to the hospital is one of the best. How's she doing?"

His face softened. "A coupla broken ribs. It didn't seem too serious. She got discharged this morning. Probably on a flight back this afternoon. She was so excited about being there Derby weekend. It could have been a lot worse. Maybe now she'll slow down. You only get so many warnings in this game." He paused. "She said she watched all the races and Derby coverage in the hospital. She saw you on TV and said at least someone got in the winner's circle. She was glad it was you."

That sounded sarcastic and not sincere. But I let it slide.

On Thursday, NESPA had scheduled an event in conjunction with the stewards, the track doctor, and veterinarians. We got a private dining room at Billy Bob's Texas Honky Tonk.

I made all the arrangements. The invitations included spouses or guests. Since Thomas was back in Lexington, I had two choices: go alone or ask Charlane. I drove, and we got there at six o'clock sharp.

I had expected Clink would be there alone, since Kellsey had been back from Louisville only a few days, but they both walked in, Kellsey in a white monogrammed compression vest. Everyone crowded around her. I stayed out of the way. She was definitely star caliber. A celebrity, even in this group. People were even getting their photos with her.

Charlane came over to me. "Kellsey doesn't want to stand around very long. I asked her and Clink to sit with us."

We moved to a four-top table. Charlane brought them over and introduced me to Kellsey. She sat down beside me, sorta smiled, and said, "I was surprised to see you up in Louisville. Everybody kicked in gear when Mr. de Tono came into the first aid room. I wish we had that kind of medical staff here at HSD."

"It's always about funding. The tracks need to put more money into the medical requirements."

"So how do you like horse racing?" Kellsey asked me.

"I'd like it a lot more if it was safer."

"Wouldn't we all. Look at everyone here," she said. "We have no-where else to go. Horse racing is all we know—all we can ever do."

She pointed at her shoulder. "Just a little detour. We ride. We fall. We get back up."

"Come on, Clink," Charlane said, getting to her feet. "Let's go hit the buffet line. You two sit tight and get acquainted. We'll bring you both a plate."

"So tell me about you," Kellsey said.

I gave her the short version of what I did at the track. Out of the blue, she said, "Did you ever find out who dognapped Lucky?"

"We have a pretty good idea, but no concrete evidence."

"Well, I hope you find out. Lucky is one special dog. I always loved him."

Charlane returned with plates, and we all enjoyed dinner, talking and laughing. Eventually, Charlane started table-hopping, and Clink moved to the bar with the guys.

After about ten minutes, Kellsey looked at her watch. "I need to get home. Dr. Winkley said to go from the couch to the bed. He read me the riot act when he saw me walk in here. It was nice to meet you."

"Likewise; get well soon."

She walked out with Clink, and I couldn't figure out what in the world she saw in him. On the surface, she seemed so sensible and practical.

In the car, Charlane asked, "Well, you and the guest of honor seemed to hit it off. What did y'all talk about when I was floating around?"

"Mostly we talked about you and who dognapped Lucky."

"Why?" she asked. "Did you find out? And not tell me?"

"Be assured you'll be the first to know."

She didn't say much else on the drive.

Chapter 44

I was worried my chance to claim BigOilRig had evaporated. It was frustrating that Patty wasn't exactly sympathetic. We sat out on her front porch, and the mood was somber.

"Looks like more consequences caught up with you," she said as she poured me a glass of iced tea. "Maybe you didn't need to claim that horse."

"Maybe I don't need to, but maybe I still want to. BigOilRig's owner will probably run him back in another claiming race."

The whole thing had me on edge. I was afraid owning BigOilRig would be a dream that wouldn't come true.

"So you're still going to try to claim him. Are you going to retire him or race him?"

"If I want to give him one last race or if I want to retire him, those are my decisions, aren't they?"

She just said one word. "Consequences."

That one word worried me. A lot could go wrong, and I would hear about it for the rest of my life. A bad day racing could cause Patty and me to have a major crash and burn. I was worried she would not let me forget she was right and that I had made a big mistake. But if we got a clean trip and he came out of the race okay, then I would have accomplished one of my lifelong dreams.

I knew Patty was worried that if he won and I had a great time, I would want to keep him racing and maybe claim another horse and then be gone all the time to races. So as much as I wanted to own BigOilRig, having one race for him loomed like a dark cloud on the horizon of my mind.

Chapter 45

Max had me circling back around our suspects. I called Dos on Friday, and we set up a meeting at his restaurant.

"Come over today. I'll fix you a special lunch."

"Okay, surprise me. You do something special for me, and maybe down the line I can do something special for you. How's that sound, Mr. Martinez?"

"Señora, *muy bueno*."

It was kind of a hangout, guys watching soccer and horse racing. Dos was in a good mood, and I wondered why he was being so charming. He wiped his hand on his apron.

"*Bienvenida*, señora." He moved his arm toward the back, where there was a private dining room.

The room smelled wonderful. There was an aroma unique to Mexican food. He set down a steaming plate of enchiladas smothered in green chili sauce and cheese. He hovered over me, watching with an eager smile.

I'd never tasted anything like it. "It's delicious." I was truly impressed. "Gracias."

"I fixed my mother's favorite recipe for you; I'm glad you like it. This is why I have a restaurant. It's important to share food with friends and family."

Visions from a long time before swept through my mind.

"My sister and I used to go to Mexican restaurants, and she would always order the green chili sauce," I said. "Probably not as good as this."

"Bring her over sometime. Does she live around here?"

I shook my head. "No, she passed away about ten years ago."

His eyes met mine. "I'm so sorry."

"It was an accident." I looked down at the plate. "Just like the accidents over at the track I'm trying to prevent. That's why I need that information. I need you to help me protect those horses and riders."

I ate in silence, and he rubbed his left arm as if he was massaging it, lost in thought. Finally, he said, "When I was about twelve years old, my sister almost got attacked by a big dog. Instead, the dog attacked me and tore up my arm…But she didn't get hurt."

I looked up at him.

"I know I'm a part of this," he said, his voice quiet. "What you told me the last time you were here made a lot of sense. When the time is right, I'll have that information you were asking about. But I can't do it today." He took a sip from the same beat-up coffee cup. "If we're playing cards, I need a card that will get me out of trouble."

He was just a pawn, and he hadn't done anything wrong. He was genuinely protecting himself and wasn't going to take a rap for anyone. But I had to get his attention.

"This isn't a card game, because people's and horses' lives are at stake." I wiped my mouth with a napkin. "Thanks for lunch, and you promised to give me that information. Right?"

"Yes."

I got up and started toward the door. Turning back, I said, "You did the right thing protecting your sister. And I trust you'll do the right thing with this."

Charlane was next. I pulled up to the barn and motioned for her to come over to my car. "You got a minute? Get in—I have a question for you."

I moved my notebooks to the back seat, and she dusted off her jeans, stomped her boots, and hopped in.

"What's up? You got that dangerous, serious look."

"So, Charlane, ever since I got here, you have undermined me. You have ridiculed me. You have manipulated me."

She reached for the door handle and stopped short of jumping out. "You bein' a little harsh on me, ain't ya?" she said, her voice mellow. "Are our days bein' friends over?"

I wasn't going to get sucked into that sympathy hook. "We're at a crossroads right here. The police and a judge might not look too favorably on someone who has intentionally fed cookies to horses to make them slow down. I'm going to call them *quemados* until I find out what's in them and who caused a man to go down with the horse you were supposed to be riding that day."

Charlane looked out the window.

"If you'd like, I could pick up the phone and call Max, and he'd have the police here in ten minutes. I don't think you want to go down that road again. Do you?"

This was the first time she didn't have anything to say.

"Pretty soon, I have to know who is behind these *quemados*."

"Hun, you got the goods on me, don't you?" Her voice was quiet. "You know I'm gonna cooperate with you. 'Cause if you fail at this, the whole place goes down. We can't let that happen. For right now, I can't divulge the answer to the big question. Who or why. But when I have to, I will. You have my word. Fair enough?"

Then, as usual, she changed the topic completely, "Here's some hot news. Kellsey's going to stay in Fort Worth until her ribs heal. She moved out of her fancy suite over at the casino hotel—moved in with Clink."

"Clink?"

"Yeah, Hun. Go figure. She's slippin' down the ladder here at HSD. I gotta get to work."

She jumped out of the car.

At least she knows I can have her arrested.

Promises…two for two today.

I caught up with Pepito in the barn. No one else was around, and we stepped into an empty stall.

"I just want to make sure you haven't told anyone about the *quemados.*"

"No."

I put my finger up to my lips, and said, "Shhhh. This is important for only you and me to know."

"Si, I tell no one." There was still a worried frown on his face, and he said, "Is everything going to be okay?"

I nodded and said, "Let's hope so. Thanks."

Chapter 46

On Monday I called Buster. "Have you got a minute to chat about claiming BigOilRig? Can you get me an update on what's going on with him?"

I'd decided not to use Mr. Applegate again—Buster was better connected at HSD, so it made more sense to have someone who was there and had his ear to the ground.

"Let me find out, and I'll call you back," he said.

Buster called back in a few hours. "The owner of BigOilRig was very upset with the stewards and NESPA. He threatened to ship the horse over to Oaklawn. The last one was a $50,000 optional claiming race. They'll write it for an identical race pretty soon. I'll send you my bank information; go ahead and wire me $50,000."

My heart pounded. This was more exciting than having a live ticket on a long shot. "That's great news."

"What I care about is helping you, son, because you have been a big help to me over the years."

"Thanks," I said, quietly.

Two hot, dry late spring weeks had passed since I had tried to claim BigOilRig. The shutout at the claim box wasn't brought up again between Patty and me. We got back into the routine, and Patty could disguise vegetables to look like real food. I quit asking her what it was.

One night at dinner, she said, "I've been thinking a lot about BigOilRig. I thought if you claimed him and shipped him out here, he was going to be turned out in these big fields and spend the rest of his life just being a horse. So why race him?"

"It's an option. He's a thoroughbred, and that's what he does—races. Just one race. See how he does. That's all."

She set down her fork. "What if he gets hurt? What if the jockey gets hurt? You used to be concerned about how dangerous it is. What about that?"

"What if this is my decision and my horse?" I asked.

"Sounds like you've decided to put him back in training." She looked down at her plate. "You're not going to ride him, are you?"

"I'll get APP's guy to be his exercise rider."

"So if he gets hurt, he's just an inmate from TSPAN and he's dispensable?"

I didn't understand why Patty was giving me such a hard time about this.

"No, that's his job over there," I said slowly.

"So why risk it?" Her eyes locked onto mine. "What would that prove to everyone at a racetrack if you did this? What would you prove to yourself?"

"It would prove I did something I always wanted to do."

She was steadfast in her opinion. "Claim him, own him, race him. That's what you're going to do, isn't it? Seems like that racetrack is still in your blood."

"It will always be there. That's who I am."

"No, I thought that's who you were. I see a different man living here…Doing what you're doing…This is your life now. Not that."

"Well, maybe I have to prove to myself I can do this. I can put him in training and see how he does. Horses should have a chance to never be in a stall, stay out in a big pasture, train, ship to the track, and race. That's how some big farms do it. Maybe that's what he needs to perform better."

"No, this isn't about him at all, is it? It's about you. You're still trying to prove something to yourself. You like to live in that lie you have told yourself your entire life. When are you going to face the truth? That's not you now."

Daddy. Daddy always wanted to own a racehorse. I hadn't thought about that until now, and I didn't want to think about it further. Picking up my plate, I put it in the dishwasher.

For a long time, I'd wanted to be an owner. Not because my father wanted to, but because I'd promised BigOilRig I would rescue him from the track.

It was no more and no less than that.

It was May 26, exactly two months after the day that had started this entire debacle. Patty hadn't brought much else about me claiming BigOilRig, but she let me take her truck. My bank wired Buster the $50,000, and I met him and SkyMan at the track kitchen.

SkyMan said, "I don't think I ever properly thanked you for everything you did when I got hurt. So thanks. There. Got that done."

"You would have done the same for me."

It was great to see SkyMan. He said, "I'm back to 100 percent. Ribs healed—like new. Glad I'm not riding anymore, though."

Buster overheard us and said, "I never thought I'd have an assistant as good as or better than you. But SkyMan does a great job."

We stepped into the food line, and I gave the choices a suspicious look. I'd been weaned from this type of "real food" for two months. The coffee was still track kitchen coffee. It didn't taste as good as I remembered either, but that didn't matter. What mattered the most was working on this claim with Buster.

Before we headed to the track, Buster called the claiming clerk and verified the office had received his check and everything was in order. BigOilRig was in the second race.

As soon as the first race was over, we decided to go to that special spot by the winner's circle where we used to watch the races. SkyMan begged off and went back to Barn7.

Buster said. "He doesn't go over to the track and the spot where he fell. He stays at the barn. Which suits me just fine."

I leaned on the rail and looked out over the track. I was starting to get as excited as if I had a big bet on one of the horses and knew I was going to finish in the money.

"Did you make a bet on BigOilRig?" Buster asked.

"No. I think $50,000 to claim him is a big enough bet."

Buster nodded. "Are you going to race him?"

Patty's expression at dinner went through my mind, but I pushed it away.

"First, I want to get him out to the ranch and evaluate him," I said. "I don't want to disrupt everything at Barn7, but if it all works out, SkyMan wants to come out there and help me train him. Could you let him have a couple of weeks off?"

"It's possible."

We both looked at our *DRF*s and chatted about the race. Out of nowhere, the announcer said, "There's a late change in the second race. Scratch number 2—BigOilRig."

My stomach dropped. "What the hell is going on?"

There were a lot of boos in the crowd.

Buster immediately called the steward and put him on speaker. "Mr. O'Bryan, BigOilRig was scratched by the track veterinarian. I can't tell you why."

Buster called the track veterinarian. He said, "Sorry. I got instructions to scratch him."

"You know, without cause, that's against the NESPA rules," Buster said.

"Yes, and you know there's one layer of track rules above NESPA that we have to abide by. Don't you?"

I wanted to grab the phone and tear into that man. But Buster hung up before I could. Good thing.

Buster looked at me. "BigOilRig's owner was expecting to be done with him after this race. I trained BigOilRig for a year after he arrived here. I'll call the owner."

He turned on the speaker so I could hear. "This is Buster O'Bryan down here at HSD. I guess by now you found out your horse got scratched. Let me run something by you. I'm standing here with the guy who was the exercise rider back in March when your horse was at my barn. Would you sell BigOilRig? Right now, for the $50,000 tag?"

The man said a few curse words directed at the entire HSD track. "No, I'm going to hold on to him while I file a complaint with TXRC and NESPA. This is the second time they stopped me from having my horse claimed, and today they probably cost me a share of the purse. Someone at that damn track has a lot of explaining to do. After the first one, I heard it was because of that exercise rider, Amos Moon."

Buster looked at me.

"BigOilRig is not for sale until I get some satisfactory answers."

Buster hung up. "Best thing for right now is to let him cool down."

I was so frustrated I couldn't even speak. The second race was about to go off without BigOilRig in the starting gate. I looked at the tote board where it said 2 was scratched. There I was, standing at our special spot by the rail. All I had in my hand was a useless *DRF* and the quickly evaporating dream I would ever own that horse.

Chapter 47

The horses hadn't even gotten to the paddock for the third race when my phone rang. It was BigOilRig's owner calling from Denver. After the first claiming race, I figured there would be more trouble today.

He hardly let me say hello. "Miss Ricksland, they assured me there wouldn't be any problems for my race."

I leaned back in my desk chair. "Sir, all I know is the track veterinarian scratched your horse."

"I just got off the phone with Charlane, my horse's exercise rider at my new trainer's barn. She said there's a vendetta against Amos Moon and you knew his check was sent in, and the track owner—this damn Stamples—stopped that claim from happening."

"Sir, I don't know what Charlane told you. It would be difficult to prove what Stamples did or didn't do."

"I should have gotten paid $50,000 for the first claim that didn't happen. And then—just now, if he had won—I would have gotten 60 percent of a $50,000 purse, which is $30,000."

"Well, he might not have won," I pointed out. "If he didn't hit the board, you wouldn't have gotten any purse money."

"My horse didn't even get a chance to run." His voice was thick with anger. "This is total bullshit. I might have your job over this. What about my other horse—NoCashRefund? He doesn't even want to run anymore after he got doped. Charlane told me he doesn't even like her cookies anymore." He stopped to take a breath and went on, "O'Bryan tried to get me to sell BigOilRig, probably to this Moon guy. I should have shipped him out to Oaklawn. I don't trust anyone down there. Stamples, Moon, and from this point, *anyone* that has anything to do with HSD."

"Sir, there's no one on this earth who cares more about your horse than Amos Moon. That's why he's tried twice to claim him. I know you are upset. But please keep an open mind and let me help you come up with a solution that is satisfactory to you. Will you let me?"

"This whole ordeal cost me $80,000," he said. "You better get me a check for $80,000 for BigOilRig or the next call will be from my lawyer."

He hung up. My phone was hot.

I didn't know what to do or who to call. How had I gotten in the middle of this? I dreaded a call from Amos—who was probably still here. Everyone wanted explanations. I was going to have to implicate Stamples soon. All fingers pointed to him when it pertained to Amos.

To cut to the chase, I called him. "I have to see you. Can you meet me down by the winner's circle after the next race?"

"Can't we talk on the phone?" he asked. "No offense, Rixie, but I'm pretty much done with clandestine meetings and trusting you to get things done."

"Drop the attitude. If you only knew how many times I have kept you out of the crosshairs and deflected the attention off you. Like I said, meet me down by the winner's circle after the next race."

I hung up the phone.

Chapter 48

I stood there with Buster, looking at the crowd.

Two months before, I'd gotten banned from HSD. And today was the first day that I was technically allowed to return to the track. Talk about the highs of possibly claiming BigOilRig and the lows of my claim not being allowed.

BigOilRig got unsaddled, and I followed him back to Barn5. Charlane was there, and she said, "I talked to BigOilRig's owner. He is some kinda pissed. What you gonna do now?"

"I'm going to hang around here tonight over at Barn7 and figure out what to do tomorrow."

I didn't want her to know any details about what Rixie had planned. I texted Patty with a quick version of what had happened. I told her I was gonna hang around and see if I could find out what had happened to cause me to get shut out on the claim and if I had any recourse against the track.

I couldn't go back and admit to Patty that more consequences were controlling my life. I felt as though I'd just lost the biggest opportunity I'd ever had.

It was a long walk over to the winner's circle. I didn't know anybody there. The next race was over, and I watched them take the win photo. All I could think about was the dream I had of being there someday with BigOilRig. I was afraid that was just always going to be a dream and never going to become a reality.

The same calm voice I'd heard two months ago was behind me. "Are you okay?"

I tried to find a smile. I had an immediate flashback to her house, when I'd picked up Lucky and the brisket dinner. But she said, "I want you to meet Thomas; he's the head of NESPA."

We shook hands. I could tell they were a couple. There wasn't much of a crowd, and we walked away for a little privacy.

"I'm sorry about all this," Rixie said, sliding her sunglasses back on her head. "BigOilRig's owner just threatened to get me fired about the race today. He's adamant Stamples, HSD, me, and you can't be trusted. I don't have anything to do with it—except at some point I have to disclose everything I know about all the illegal activity that has been going on here. Your $90,000, for starters. There are enough NESPA violations I know about to close this track down. And at some point, if I don't turn in this evidence, I am complicit in and guilty of withholding information that is jeopardizing the safety of every horse and rider at this track. And on every turn of the card—right there are your name and your fingerprints. That said, I'm the only person who has a line of communication with BigOilRig's owner and can help you buy him."

She had my attention.

"He gave me the conditions and the terms. Let me go to work and see what I can do. I'll call him tomorrow."

All I could say was "Thanks. What can I do to help you?"

"Just be available when I need to discuss the arrangement."

I went over to Barn7 and said to Buster, "I need to meet with Rixie tomorrow when she gets BigOilRig's owner on the phone. Can I spend the night in my old apartment?"

Buster said, "SkyMan took the other one. I figured you'd roll back in here someday."

"I knew I'd either come back or I'd come back for my books. Just need it for tonight."

I texted Patty: *<It's not been a good day. BigOilRig got scratched by the track vet and he couldn't be claimed. Gonna stay here at my old Barn7 apartment tonight. And figure out what to do next>*

<Okay. Let me know what you find out>

She was probably relieved I hadn't claimed BigOilRig. And to be honest, as that realization set in, I was starting to think it was not meant for me to do that.

Back at the barn, it was like old times. I helped SkyMan with a few chores. It took my mind off the disappointment I'd experienced after the second race. SkyMan said, "Martha brings me dinner every night. I'll have her bring enough for you. She'll be here about six o'clock."

"Okay, thanks."

Martha was a great cook, and I enjoyed a meal with them. We talked about the missed claim, and SkyMan said, "Today was a turning point. We have those in our lives. Have faith Rixie can accomplish this for you. If it's meant to be, it will be."

Martha said, "I hope you're not planning to come back here. Your future is out there at the ranch. Not here. You got out safe. Be thankful for that. And just by the grace of God, SkyMan's accident could have been a lot worse. I'm glad he gave up riding."

SkyMan said, "I know you are disappointed the claim didn't work for you today. Have patience."

All that sounded good, but not as interesting as a familiar voice downstairs. I looked out the door, and Kellsey was on her phone, standing at the bottom of the stairs. She was still wearing a protective vest and waved for me to come down.

Martha motioned with her hand and shooed me out the door. As I walked down the stairs, I wondered what she was doing here.

"Hey there. Charlane said you might be here." She looked nervous. "I just came by to tell you I'm sorry about everything that has happened to you. I want you to know there are a lot of people that appreciate what you have done around here to make things safer."

I nodded. "Thanks."

"I heard you gave up gambling. But isn't buying a racehorse a much bigger gamble than betting on a race?" She studied me for a moment, and when I didn't answer, she reached out, put her hand on my arm and held it there for a second and said, "Anyway, I'm proud of you for always doing what is right. Don't give up trying to own BigOilRig."

"I'm not going to give up on that dream of owning him. I've given up on a lot of things around here."

I stared at her. *Including you.*

There was no point in saying it. She knew, we both knew, that we weren't meant to be together. That hadn't made it hurt any less, but now it felt good to talk to her again, without those expectations.

"Based on what I've heard—and I've heard a lot—it sounds like you've found everything out at that ranch we didn't have," she said with a smile. "I'm happy for you. At least some of your dreams have come true."

"What about you?" I asked. "Did your dreams come true?"

She hesitated. "I'm still searching." Her face got serious. "Amos, I'm happy that you were able to escape and get out of this trap here at the track. I wish I could. I feel trapped."

Every time she said the word "trap," it reminded me of the Trap Door. I realized this infatuation that I'd had with Kellsey and what we'd once had was definitely over.

"I'm still grateful, though," she said. "For you. For all this."

I nodded. "Me too."

She smiled. "Okay, that's it. Goodbye."

She walked away. The only thing she left in the barn was silence.

This meeting with Kellsey proved to me that I was on the right path. After she said goodbye, I couldn't stay in that apartment. Kellsey's words pushed me in a direction I hadn't been in a long time. I told SkyMan I was going back to the ranch.

It was the second time I'd driven back toward the ranch from Fort Worth in two months. Once with Lucky and today without BigOilRig. I was more dejected than I'd been when I'd left two months before. I passed through Weatherford and took the turn on 281 toward the ranch.

Kellsey's words about how trapped she felt echoed in my ear. For some reason my hands turned the wheel toward Noose. I thought I'd go to the Trap Door. Maybe Raven was there. I knew that was a bad idea. Why would I risk what I had with Patty? There were only a few cars in the parking lot.

I walked in, and the first thing she said was "You alone tonight?"

I was lost and alone. I just nodded my head and said, "Yes."

She sat down. "Do you want some company?"

"I just want a beer."

"If you want anything else besides a beer, you let me know."

She came back and sat down again.

"What time do you get off?" I asked.

"Trap Door closes at one. But on Wednesdays I can leave at nine. Hang around till then."

I laughed.

"What's so funny?" she asked.

"Hang around at the Trap Door."

She brought me another beer, and just as she set it down, I heard, "Amos, by damn, what are you doing here? I thought I recognized Patty's truck outside. I thought you were in Fort Worth claimin' that big horse."

It was Mr. Applegate and another man I didn't know.

"I got shut out again on the claim. BigOilRig got scratched by the track owner and I'm back to square one on that. Just came by here on the way back to the ranch."

They sat down, and I got the look from him as Raven said, "You don't come in here much anymore. Now you got Amos workin' for you—you could get away and come see me."

"Well, I'm here tonight," he said. "Bring my friend and me my usual. Amos, what are you drinking?"

"This is my last one; gotta get back to the ranch pretty soon."

Raven gave me a sideways glance as she got up to get their drinks.

APP kinda chuckled and said, "We're not interruptin' anything, are we?"

"No, sir. She's just friendly." I got to my feet. "Keep your fingers crossed. I'm trying to buy BigOilRig from the owner. Save a spot over at the racing barn for him if I do. I'm gonna head out. I'll go settle up with her."

"Okay, too bad about that claim not happening. Maybe the third time's a charm."

She was at the bar, and I said, "So much for me stayin' till nine. Boss caught me here."

"I'm flattered you're interested...Listen, cowboy. I put on this act for tips. Remember the first time you were here and you told me you escaped from TSPAN? I was kinda available then, but you never called..." She still had that sultry look. "To be honest, I'm not really available now, anyway."

"I'm not really available either," I told her.

I gave her a fifty-dollar bill and said, "This'll cover my two beers and whatever is on Mr. Applegate's tab. Keep the rest and make sure he gives you a nice tip."

The music was loud. The only thing I could hear was me telling myself maybe I wasn't supposed to own that horse or hang around the Trap Door.

Why risk everything here because I was dejected, despondent, and depressed? It was late, and I was tired and didn't want to complicate my life. I left the Trap Door and drove straight to the cabin.

The next morning I started thinking in a positive way—maybe Rixie could get it done. I even thought I was happy for her and Thomas. He was probably a good contact to expedite negotiating protested claims.

I drove down to Patty's house, and Lucky ran right to me. All I wanted was a hug from her. Sure enough, she held open her arms and buried her face on my shoulder.

"What did you find out about why the horse got scratched?" she asked.

"Stamples pulled a fast one on me. Rixie thinks she can find a way for me to buy BigOilRig from the owner."

"You saw her there?"

"Yes, and I met the head of NESPA…the new man in her life. I'm hoping he can help her negotiate the purchase."

"That sounds like a good plan."

"I didn't stay in the apartment at Barn7 last night. I came back through Noose and bumped into Mr. Applegate at the Trap Door Saloon. Since he tried to help me on the first claim, I updated him on what happened yesterday. Also we discussed some training details if I ever get to own BigOilRig."

"Sorry that didn't work out for you." Patty was always upbeat, even if she wasn't overly excited about me claiming BigOilRig. Her voice was the most reassuring thing I had heard since I'd left yesterday. "Let things settle. The future is ours—to make the most of."

I had to digest that. *The future is ours—to make the most of.*

"You always have such a great outlook on everything," I said. "Where do you get your confidence?"

"The women I work with have taught me how to deal with set-backs, and I've learned how to not let a setback dictate my future. We make our own futures." She paused a minute, then hooked her arm into mine, leading me up to the house. "Remember that first day? You asked me if I believe in destiny? Yes then and yes now. I may not agree 100 percent with you claiming a horse if you are going to race him, but that's just my opinion. If it's done right, racing is a good sport. I also liked the idea of seeing if a horse is never in a stall, if he could ship one hour to a track and have a good race. So I am quietly warming up to the idea of helping you chase this dream you have."

On Thursday afternoon while I was at the barn, I got a call from Rixie.

"I'm sorry for the other day. You caught me at a bad time," I said, before she could speak. "I appreciate everything you're doing for me."

"Well, thanks. I don't know whose ass I'm covering. Yours or mine. As for mine, I'm sitting on a lot of undisclosed evidence. The track veterinarian has broken at least four NESPA rules and jeopardized his license.

"Of all the people I mentioned—you are the only one that has done nothing wrong. If anybody has a claim, you sure do. You are the man who has been damaged in all this. Two months ago you were a free-wheeling gambler. Now Stamples has made sure you don't get any slack, but he didn't count on what I have to tell you."

Her voice got a little excited. "The owner has agreed to sell you BigOilRig for $50,000. Also, as settlement of all his claims, he's agreed to accept $30,000. You will pay the $50,000. The $30,000 will come from a NESPA contingency fund. Don't ever repeat this…Thomas arranged that. Someday you need to thank him."

My heart started to pound with excitement. "This is for real?"

There was a smile in her voice. "Yes."

I had to ask: "Why doesn't HSD or Stamples have to pay?"

"Time is of the essence. We can't let Stamples find out about this until it's a done deal."

"What do I need to do?"

"We'll deposit Buster's check—that's your money—and send the owner in Denver an HSD check and the NESPA check. You don't need to do anything except come get him. We will have all the papers ready. How does tomorrow sound?"

"Fantastic."

The moment I hung up with Rixie, I called Buster. He agreed to let SkyMan come out to help train him for the next few weeks.

I walked into Patty's kitchen, and I couldn't contain my excitement. "Really good news. BigOilRig's owner agreed to sell him to me. We're going to pick him up tomorrow. Are you still warming up to the idea of helping me chase this dream?"

Patty's eyes widened. Then her face lit up in a smile. "I said yesterday I wasn't 100 percent in agreement for you to claim him. But now that you own him, I am 100 percent all in with you. I want you to be happy. I can be your silent partner. How's that sound?"

"You don't have to be a silent partner. I will always value your opinion."

"How 'bout if we do it together?" she said. "I've never owned a racehorse either."

I realized she cared more about me than about all the repercussions of claiming, owning, and racing. That was the kind of partner to have.

Chapter 49

I knew Friday, May 28, would go down as one of the best days in my life. Patty, Lucky, and I all went together to get him. We hooked up her trailer and got away about noon.

When we parked the trailer by Barn7, it felt real. Buster had already gone over to Barn5 and brought BigOilRig back to Barn7. The excitement may have been one of the greatest feelings I'd ever experienced. I walked up to BigOilRig's stall and ducked under the webbing. He looked good.

I was as happy as if I had won the lottery. Now that I had been banned from gambling for a while, I realized I didn't have to gamble anymore to prove anything to myself or anyone else.

Once word got around that I'd arrived, I was surrounded by a complete menagerie of everyone who had been involved with BigOilRig. Charlane brought flowers and her special oatmeal-raisin cookies. She helped Martha, who brought a complete dinner for everyone at the barn, including a special order for Patty. Rixie brought the most important things—the ownership papers signing BigOilRig over to me. We all sat at picnic tables and enjoyed the fellowship that comes with sharing a special meal.

After we were through with dinner, Buster offered a toast. "The most important part of this business is who your partners are. I want to thank everyone here for everything you have done to help facilitate Amos's purchase of BigOilRig."

He nodded to me, and I stood and echoed his remarks. "I need to thank everyone here. But first, here's a big shoutout to Rixie. She's only been here seven or eight months, but she has almost singlehandedly guided this racetrack in the right direction."

She smiled at everyone as we all applauded. I said, "And to Buster. I couldn't have done this without your help. But most importantly, a great big thank-you to Patty."

I reached my arm toward her, and she climbed off the picnic bench and joined me. There was a sincere round of applause. I finished with this: "Like he said—a partner is the most important part. And I have the best partner in the world."

She wiped a tear and put her arms around me. Everyone clapped until I took a deep breath. This was a special moment in my life. I wanted to savor everything about it.

"Hey, cowboy," SkyMan said, pulling me off to the side while everyone helped clean up the tables. "I got all BigOilRig's tack in his trunk. Martha and I will be there tomorrow afternoon. What's his training schedule?"

"Going to turn him out with Chex and let him settle in there for a few days." It felt almost unreal to be saying those words. "Start light work with APP's rider on Monday."

We loaded up BigOilRig and headed back to the ranch. Patty had put on some good country music and sang along with almost every song. She might have moved up to 110 percent on the partnership scale.

As she said, we were all in.

I looked forward to the arrival of SkyMan and Martha. On Saturday, when I heard their truck pull up the drive, I headed out to the front porch of the cabin with Lucky. When GunShy jumped out of the truck, they ran in circles, chasing each other.

"So this is where they ship complainers and whistleblowers," SkyMan said with a smile.

I said to them, "What do you think?"

"Well, Charlane talked about the greenhouse, and Martha wanted to see that," SkyMan said. "I want to see the horses. Rixie told me about the barns and the arena and said you have your own cabin."

"That's where you and Martha will be staying." Turning to Martha, I said, "There's the greenhouse over there. You can go check it out."

I saddled Patty's horse for SkyMan. "Let's go finish that ride we started back in March. Come on, old man. See if you can stay on today."

Lucky and GunShy went on ahead. We took off and went west out on the ranch. The sun dropped behind a few clouds.

We turned back toward the barn. Martha had her easel set up and was painting. Patty met us on the porch, and we both took off our hats. She gave SkyMan and Martha each a big Texas hug and said, "Amos, fix us four private-label sangrias—all-natural, no booze."

Once I'd handed them each a glass, SkyMan said, "Here's what happened after my accident. NoCashRefund doesn't want to train or even go out to the track. Those other three horses—the ones NESPA is following—none of them are interested in racing, either. We can all be glad BigOilRig didn't get whatever it was that made the other horses slowdown in that race. That would be terrible if he lost all interest in being a racehorse. We'll get him over on the track next week and see how he works."

Patty got to her feet. "Everyone ready to eat? I made veggie burgers. And salads."

Everything was wonderful, and when we got finished, Patty said, "Okay, what's the verdict?"

SkyMan said, "Almost as good as beef burgers?"

Patty said, "Maybe so, but we don't eat animals."

"Amos, you gone vegetarian?" SkyMan asked.

"Well, when he's with me, he is."

Martha's voice was solemn. "Really?"

I said, "We adapt to our surroundings."

Patty brought out a tray of coffees. "Hope you like decaf."

The sun was starting to set when SkyMan said, "Did you ever hear about the settlement we got from the track for the accident? It's supposed to be—what do they call it?—sealed, but we want to share the details with you."

I shook my head.

"There's one thing I want you to know about me and my heritage: I don't believe in accepting anything I don't deserve. Like getting a lot of money because I had an accident. Stamples didn't care if I was laid up in the hospital. Or if my career as an exercise rider was over."

"Our ancestors passed down the story that European conquerors came into our land and searched for the seven cities of gold," Martha said. "They were fascinated by the sunflowers—the closest thing they found to gold. My ancestors called that expedition 'seeking false riches.'"

I immediately thought about that $90,000 voucher still in my Bible.

"About a month ago, we signed the papers for the settlement from the track for the accident," SkyMan said.

Martha raised her hand. "He always starts a story at the end. Let me go back to the beginning. When he was in the hospital, Rixie and I went to Trinity River Park. I told her I was going to draw the future and mentioned to her what our dream was: to get my sister Mary well and go back home and set up a children's learning center with her."

SkyMan said, "So Rixie told Mr. Stamples we wanted to build the school. So Mr. Stamples arranged for us to go there and talk to the people who owned the building. I told them about an opportunity for them to sell the building and we would make it into a school with Wi-Fi and computers."

"So listen to this," Martha said. It was like a tag team, they were so excited. "Rixie knew an attorney who said this was the only way to do it. Instead of taking a big amount of money, it's better to get real estate. The track bought the building out there and paid to fix it up. The remodel is already underway."

"Driving back on that first trip," SkyMan said, "I was thinking about seeing you on the news talking about this place and how happy you are doing this horse therapy with the women and children. By the time we got back to Fort Worth, I decided I would only settle after the accident if they bought the land next door and built a barn and a covered arena."

He laughed. "Amos, they went for it all. Somehow, if Stamples built it all as a school and donated it to us, he got a big write-off tax deduction. Rixie said he does a lot of tax deductions. The lawyer helped us set it up—the Children's Learning and Equestrian Center. A nonprofit."

Martha stood up, came over, and gave me the biggest hug. The moment my arms were around her, she started crying. When she could pull some words together, she said, "That's from Mary and me. Amos, we can't thank you enough for buying that ticket."

"Ticket?"

SkyMan said, "Yeah, if you didn't buy that ticket, you would still be there, fighting to save the people and the horses and the track and everything but yourself. Look at you out here—not a care in the world."

All eyes went to Patty. She just shrugged and said, "I give all the credit to the veggie burgers. I knew if he liked them, he'd like me. Any more coffee?"

"No more coffee," Martha said, "but thanks for asking us to come out here."

SkyMan shook my hand, and we walked with him to the truck to help him get their suitcases.

"Call us if you need anything," Patty said. "We'll be at my house, twenty minutes away."

We got into her car. "Most people would hire a lawyer like the ones with their pictures on the sides of buses. That's a great testimony to their humanity and compassion. I had a great conversation with him about equine therapy. He asked me to think about helping them set it up. That's something to look forward to."

Back at her house, she said, "Let's see how good the peach cobbler is tonight."

She came out of the kitchen carrying one bowl with a huge piece of warm peach cobbler hiding under a scoop of vanilla ice cream.

"That's too much for me; I'm full from dinner."

She had one spoon in her right hand, tapped it on the bowl, and said, "We're sharing…partner."

Chapter 50

SkyMan and I mapped out a plan for BigOilRig. In the mornings we groomed him, and one of APP's riders rode him on the track. We were happy with how he adapted to the new environment. My job was to take time off each morning to go over to the track and supervise the rider. He appreciated the tips SkyMan and I gave him.

BigOilRig spent every other hour grazing in the huge pasture. I enjoyed watching him relax in his new freedom. Even though I had a green light from Patty, I guess I still had to convince myself that sending him to a race was the right thing to do.

Patty and I also enjoyed the company of SkyMan and Martha, but as a couple, we continued to grow closer as the days passed.

Patty said, "You know, we haven't been out of town, or even on a road trip. Let's go to Abilene Saturday for the Cowboy Heritage Days. We can get someone to cover for us and come back Sunday."

SkyMan was going to be back at Barn7 helping Buster for the weekend. Martha was happy to have Lucky stay with her and GunShy.

We left right after breakfast. The town was pretty much sold out, but she finally found a room cancellation.

I'm not too big on trade fairs, but the saddle displays and the antique spurs and farm equipment were fun to walk through. She specifically wanted to visit the holistic booth, where she bought several special soaps and things I couldn't even pronounce.

She packed a special dinner, which was better than what we could have had from the food trucks. Several local Texas country bands were featured in the outdoor bandstand.

Sunday morning we went to the Cowboy Church services back at the bandstand. One of the bands from last night made up the choir. We stood and sang the first hymn, "I'll Fly Away."

Patty put her left arm around me and held the hymnal with her right hand. She could have been in the choir.

"You have a nice voice."

"Shhhh," she whispered.

There was a long prayer, and the pastor began the sermon.

"In Genesis, we all know the story of Joseph. Sold into slavery by his brothers—thrown in prison. Later he forgives his brothers for what they did." He looked up. "Maybe you have a list of people that you wish you could reconcile with. Everybody's story has pain. Part of maturing as a person is learning how to respond to life's disappointments. Reconciliation happens because one person is willing to forgive.

"The world today says get all you can. People are all out for themselves. Look out for number one."

He held up his Bible. "This tells us Joseph lived his life by a different script. The word 'forgive' in the Bible means to pardon. It's the idea of canceling out, wiping the slate clean, and letting go.

"Disciples asked Jesus how many times to forgive like that. Jesus says seventy times seven times. Forgiveness doesn't mean you condone what happened. Forgiveness is the experience of finding peace inside. The hardest person in my life to ever forgive was the father that walked out on the family when I was six years old."

Patty reached over and put her hand on top of mine. My mind froze on what this man had just said. Our stories were the same, and he was talking about forgiveness.

"When I chose to forgive my dad, I saw him differently." His eyes caught mine. "He wasn't necessarily different, but I was."

A hundred images of my father spun through my mind. Some good, but most were bad memories.

"The result of forgiveness is freedom. It takes away the power of the one who hurt us, and we get our lives back again. Today as you leave, I ask you to answer one question: Who do you need to reconcile with? Granting forgiveness may be the most difficult thing you will ever have to do. It may be the very thing that's missing in finding true peace in your life."

My eyes closed, and I don't think I heard the prayer or the last hymn. I had avoided dealing with this my whole life. He made it seem so easy, such a simple solution.

Once the service ended, the cloudy skies indicated rain was on the way. As we left, I put some money in a small barrel and a short man in old jeans and a big smile was handing everyone cards. "God bless you," he said.

The card read:

WHO DO YOU NEED TO RECONCILE WITH?

Grant Forgiveness and find True Peace in your life.

I put my hat on, folded the card, and put it in my pocket. Patty grabbed my hand, and we ran to the truck in the light rain that had just started. We sat together in silence.

"Who would you put on your card?" I finally asked.

She turned the radio down. "My mother. I'm glad we went there today. I know all the old hymns. I was in the choir. Piano lessons. I was even in a band once." She paused. "How 'bout your card?"

"I should have gotten more than one."

"No, really, tell me."

The windshield wipers went across, and I turned the radio back up higher.

She turned it down and said, "I'm going to do it…Will you do it? Let's both do it. Life is better together."

Chapter 51

The emergency alarm went off. I was in the stewards' office when the chief steward answered the phone. His eyes went wide. He said, "Kellsey O'Bryan is in the jocks' room. She has to go to the hospital ASAP."

My heart caught. "I'll be right there."

I raced down the stairs. The ambulance had been summoned to the side entrance. I jumped into the front seat. There were two EMTs in the back. Kellsey had an oxygen mask on her face and an IV bag dripping fluids into her arm.

"What happened?" I demanded.

The driver's eyes were focused on the road. At first he didn't say anything, just shook his head. "Something about her shoulder," he said. "She didn't get thrown. You know any prayers? If so, we better pray as hard as we can."

"Blood pressure's dropping," the EMT called from the back. "Breathing's labored. Gonna lose her before we get to the hospital."

Chills went up through my neck—my entire skull went numb.

The driver ran red lights. "Not on my shift. We're gonna get her there."

We pulled in, and she was out of the ambulance in record time.

I ran beside her. "Give me your hand."

Kellsey reached out, and I gently squeezed her hand. She stared at me until I couldn't go any farther with her. They kept running, and I watched her disappear. My eyes flooded with tears.

I was numb and tried to tell the first person I found who she was. A nurse took my arm and led me to a chair, and I buried my face in my hands.

"Stay in the waiting room," she said. "We'll advise you with any information."

I called back to the office and told Max we'd arrived. "Based on what I overheard the EMT say, it doesn't look good."

Twenty minutes passed, thirty minutes passed, but it felt like hours.

The doctor came out with no expression on his face. "Miss Ricksland?"

"Yes."

He motioned for me to step into an office. His eyes were wise behind his glasses.

"How is she?" I asked.

He shook his head. "While she was in the ambulance, Dr. Winkley called to tell me about the rib injuries from a month ago. Could have just been a nick in a vein or artery. That's what did it."

The words took a moment to sink in.

"There's no two ways about it," he said. "She should not have been riding a horse today. Dr. Winkley advised me in confidence that he did not authorize her to ride. I'm sorry."

He handed me a small plastic bag. "Her cell phone was down in her riding boot. Will you notify her parents and give them her jewelry?"

A thousand thoughts went through my mind. I stuttered and said, "Yes."

I didn't want to be the one to have to tell her parents. But I went outside and, through my tears, found Buster's number in my contacts. The phone rang and rang.

Just before it went to voice mail, he answered. "Please, dear Lord, tell me she's okay."

"Mr. O'Bryan. I just spoke with the doctor, and…"

"She's gone, isn't she?"

"I'm so sorry, sir. Yes." There was nothing but silence. "Are you still there?"

He was sobbing, and it sounded as if he was pounding on a table.

"Mr. O'Bryan, is someone there with you?" I asked.

There was a fumbling sound, and Max came on the line. "I came immediately when you left. I'll drive him up to his farm, and we'll tell her mother."

"Oh, thank God you're with him." Max had been in countless situations like this, helping traumatized parents deal with death. "Is there anything I can do?"

"No. I'll send a car for you, and I'll call you when I get back. Buster told me, 'At least someone like Miss Ricksland was with her.'"

We hung up, and I texted Max: <*Big problem. ER Dr here said Dr W told him he didn't authorize her to ride*>

Max texted right back. <*Yes. Same thing—Buster heard right before the race that she agreed not to ride*>

To say we had a crisis would be a drastic understatement. There was nothing more upsetting to the public than a human being who perished doing his or her sport. We had to reach out to the family and the fans. This story would be on *TV Racing*, ESPN, the *Today Show*, FOX, GMA, and every possible social media platform. Kellsey was a national athlete, very well known and very well respected as one of the best jockeys, not to mention a female jockey. The fact that negligence could have contributed to her death was going to be devastating for the track, not to mention everything I'd been working toward since I'd been with NESPA.

Immediately, I called Dr. Winkley. "The ER doctor said you told him you did not authorize her to ride today. Is that correct?"

When he spoke, he was choked up. "Yes. I can't believe she did that. She signed the form that said she was not going to ride and went ahead and rode. She broke every rule in your NESPA book."

"Let me get back to the track," I said. "Meet me at the office beside the jocks' room in thirty minutes."

On the way, I called SkyMan to see if he could get in touch with Amos. That was one job I didn't want. It was not for me to do.

Winkley was right there waiting for me. He looked the way I felt.

I pulled out the NESPA forms for today's races. I hesitated when I found Kellsey's form. It had two signatures—Kellsey O'Bryan and Dr. Winkley. The "cleared to ride" box had been checkmarked.

Looking at him, I said, "I'm sorry, but I think you're in shock, like I am. I know how much you cared about her. Kellsey's form, the one you signed, is right here."

He looked at it. "That's not my signature."

"You didn't sign it?"

He took his pen out of his shirt pocket and wrote his name on a scrap of paper. "That's my signature in blue ink." He tapped the other jockey forms sitting on my desk. "My signature is in blue ink on all those. The one on Kellsey's form—it's not my signature; it's in black ink. The check marks—black ink. Someone forged my name."

I took his pen and wrote this on a pad and showed him:

Don't say another word here. Meet me and Max at the Hunter Group office in an hour.

Chapter 52

Lucky saw us as soon as we pulled up to the cabin. He and GunShy ran right up to the truck.

"Look at those muddy dogs," Patty said, laughing. "They've got to have a bath."

We walked up to the porch, and Patty got a text. "It's SkyMan." She read it and looked up at me. "Here, read this." She wrapped her arms around me, so I had to put the phone where I could see it.

<Patty—are you with Amos? We want to be sure someone is with him right now before he sees it on TV Racing. *Kellsey collapsed after a race. It must have been one of her ribs…cut a blood vessel…she didn't make it>*

Patty held me as long as we both could stand there. A light drizzle started. I dug in my back pocket and handed her my red bandana. She wiped her eyes. "I couldn't read that to you…I'm so sorry."

Lucky put his paw on her foot, and she gave me back the bandana. It was damp from her tears. She hugged me tight. I took several deep breaths.

"Let's go inside," she said. "We should reply to him. What should I say?"

"Tell him thanks, we'll call him back."

"Is there anything I can do for you?"

Outside the window, the sun broke through the thin clouds.

"Go on a trail ride with me."

"I'll fix two coffees to go; you get the horses ready."

Seeing Chex—brushing him, checking his legs, wrapping my arms around his neck—kept me from falling apart. I held him until I had to let go. The dogs barked—they were ready. BigOilRig followed us.

"I turned my phone off," I said, as Patty approached. "I can't talk to anyone."

"You can talk to me. At a time like this, it's better to get your thoughts out in the open. I know you have more questions than answers. It doesn't matter who it is—when we lose someone that has been a big part of our lives, we have to start grieving."

I shook my head, trying to find the right words to accept this heartache. "I can't believe this happened. Well, yes, I can. Just like we all predicted. She would ride in races till the end." An image of Buster beaming at her made me nearly choke up. "I can't imagine what her parents are going through."

I focused on the ride, trying to think about the good times Kellsey and I'd had, but visions of her collapsing at the track were all I could think about. Patty, the hoofbeats, a few dog barks, and silence.

"It's about five o'clock," Patty finally said. "We should head back."

I turned Chex around. He always sped up going back to the barn, but today I was in no hurry to get back. We unsaddled the horses, and Patty hugged me again in silence. Finally I said, "I'll turn the horses out. Let's call SkyMan when I get back."

As soon as I got back from the barn, Patty said, "Let's go to my house. How's scrambled eggs sound? I'll fix Amos's bachelor omelet."

That made me smile, even if it was a little forced. "Yes."

We loaded Lucky into the truck and headed to Patty's house. We went into the kitchen, and I called SkyMan and put him on speaker. He picked up on the first ring. "Oh, Amos. How are you doing?"

"I had to go on a trail ride. Patty went. GunShy and Lucky went."

"Chex knew you needed that. Horses always know when something is pulling on our hearts."

"What happened?" I asked.

"In the stretch, she took her right fist and grabbed her left shoulder. Didn't gallop out. Got down, handed off the reins, and went straight to the jocks' room. They took her out on a stretcher to the ambulance.

"Rixie went to the hospital with her, and she died at the hospital. A rib cut a vein. Buster never got to say goodbye or anything, because he was at the barn when it happened and couldn't get there in time. Max Hunter took him to tell her mother. Here's the most important thing for you right now…spend time with Patty."

I hung up the phone, and I'm not sure who started to cry first, but we buried those tears in each other's arms.

Chapter 53

I met Max at the Hunter Group office. The news about Kellsey's death had already broken, and we needed to be quick with a statement from the track.

Once I had Thomas on speaker, I said, "Here's the story we are going to spin for right now. Kellsey agreed to not ride. She and Winkley signed the form. In spite of that, she rode anyway. In the meantime, we have to find out who forged Winkley's name. The only person who touched the form besides Kellsey, Winkley, and me was Clink."

We mapped out the strategy before Winkley got there. When he arrived, he looked more distraught than before.

"We have Thomas de Tono on the speakerphone," I told him. "He's the CEO of NESPA."

Winkley sat down. "Before I could get in my car, I got summoned to Stamples's office, and he jumped all over me. He said he was in a hurry. He had to get to the airport because there was a storm coming in and he had to get back to Houston. All I told him was that she must have defied the rules and went out there and rode that horse. He was upset."

Max nodded. "Everyone is upset right now."

"I shared with these guys what you told me about the blue ink," I said. "Do you have anything else to add?"

Winkley took off his glasses and set them on the table. "I have been a track doctor for almost thirty years. Probably evaluated thousands and thousands of exercise riders and jockeys. Now, more than ever with the NESPA rules, this shouldn't have happened. But it did."

Thomas's voice broke in, "The NESPA form has a signature that looks like yours."

"Somebody forged my name."

I closed the folder and exchanged a brief glance with Max, who said, "Let's talk off the record. Who would have forged your name on that document?"

"It's a short list. The only people who had access to it were Rixie, Kellsey, and Clink."

"Here's what the NESPA rules say," Thomas said. "You will be suspended immediately, based on this initial piece of evidence, until this gets cleared up."

Winkley got up out of his chair and paced around the table. "Should I have a lawyer?"

Thomas sounded very diplomatic as he said, "Yes, probably a good idea."

Once Winkley left and Thomas had signed off, Max shrugged. "It's got to be Clink," he said.

I wasn't convinced, and we agreed to reconvene in the morning.

The only thing I could think about as I left the office was how I'd failed. The original mission when I'd arrived at the track was to save those jockeys, save those horses, and save the track. Instead, on my watch, a jockey with her whole life ahead of her had died.

I had unfinished items on my to-do list. I drove back over to the track. When I drove up to the front entrance, Kellsey's fans were already setting up a memorial with candles and flowers. I pulled over and parked. Two teenage girls were setting up a jockey's saddle with boots turned backward on a black metal saddle rack.

At first they thought I was going to interfere with them, but I said, "Thanks for being here and doing this."

The taller girl said, "I have cried all day. I had to come over here. I can't believe she is dead."

My eyes filled with tears. "I'm sorry. The memorial you set up is beautiful."

She started to cry, and I went closer and hugged her. For some reason I gave her my card.

She looked at it and said, "Ma'am, will you find out why?"

How could I let her down? But how could I have let Kellsey down—and what could I do to avenge this?

The answer was apparent: work.

Solve this.

Chapter 54

It was hard to believe that Patty and I'd had a nice long weekend at the trade fair only for the O'Bryans' world to collapse like a house destroyed by a tornado. I tried to sleep but tossed and turned. My mind was like a tape that rewound with images and thoughts of Kellsey. The times that were good, the times that were a challenge, and the times that didn't work out at all.

I finally got up, fixed some coffee, and sat at the kitchen table.

Patty walked in. "Did you sleep at all?"

"Off and on. Mostly off. Come here."

She sat on my lap and wrapped her arms around my neck. "I can get breakfast together and head to the barn. You stay here. Take care of anything you need to."

"I need to go to the barn, too. I have to go to work today, with these women. I'm not going to sit around and brood."

"If I can do anything, let me know. We'll get through this, together."

I went to the arena and tried to block out the fact that yesterday, a woman I had once loved had died at the track. I wanted to forget about it, but the story was all the women wanted to talk about. They'd seen her on the news. They hadn't been to the races, but they knew about her.

Adrian's mother came up and said, "Oh my gosh. Did you hear about that accident up there?"

"Yes, I did. She was a friend of mine."

"Your friend? I'm so sorry."

She must have shared that with the others, because after that, they gave me a little space. Still, I made it a point to interact with each woman. That kept my mind focused on them instead of grief.

When there was time to check my phone, I saw a missed call from Rixie and SkyMan had sent me a short text. *<Hope you're doing okay. The visitation is Tuesday.>*

"Amos, just a quick update from here," Rixie said when I called her back. "Dr. Winkley got suspended because there was a discrepancy with Kellsey's medical forms."

"Really?"

"We watched the tapes, and there's nothing there. Amos, how are you doing? I can't imagine what you're going through."

"Trying to keep busy here and not think too much. But it's tough. I feel for her parents. That's the tough part to wrap my mind around. I'll be there tomorrow. Are you going to the visitation?"

"Oh yes. I am the official representative from the track," Rixie said. "This is the saddest day ever, a lot of quiet reflection. Preacher is making the rounds, gathering up some small circles, holding hands, and praying."

I hung up, and Patty fixed lunch. We sat on the porch. I couldn't even imagine what Buster was going through. I barely knew how to face the next few days.

Chapter 55

Once again, I couldn't sleep all night. The ambulance ride and the moment the EMT said "We're gonna lose her" echoed in my ear. The painful expression on her face, as if she knew it was over, and how helpless she was. That brave soul. And Buster's last comment: "She's gone, isn't she?"

It made me think of my parents and wonder how they were able to get through my sister's funeral and endure these ten years. Car accident. I had distanced myself from my nieces because it was too painful to stay in touch.

I went to the bathroom and stared at myself in the mirror. My eyes looked so distraught, so sad. I should have done a better job keeping up with my parents, my nieces, instead of numbing the pain with work; my life was like a jockey's racing silks of chameleon colors.

When I returned to the office, Max was there. "I just got off the phone with the director of the Fort Worth Criminal Investigation Division. He'll be here at 10:30. He wants to review the security tapes, copies of all the documents from Kellsey's race, and copies of her medical records."

I called the track's lawyer. He sent me back an email with the bullet points of the track's position on Kellsey's accident. Because of what Winkley had told me, I made sure the copies were made in color.

Max got a call from the front office, and he put it on speaker. "Mr. Hunter, one of those mobile TV news trucks is setting up back by the barns. We got a request that someone meet them there for an interview. We prefer someone from NESPA to do it, okay?"

"Yes," Max told them.

He hung up the phone and pointed at me. "Nobody better than you to represent the track. You were the last person to see her. You'll do fine."

I thought the first thing would be for the track to issue a statement, and that would suffice. Instead, I rehearsed a few talking points: we didn't know a lot of details, and our thoughts and prayers were extended to the O'Bryan family.

I turned the corner of the barn, and several horses had their heads out through the open windows. The cameras were set up in front of the barn with bright lights shining right on Charlane. She was mic'd up and ready to start an interview.

The cameraman held up his hand, "Quiet, everyone. Four, three, two, one." He pointed to the reporter who stood with Charlane. I thought they'd sent me over here to be the spokesperson—and who jumped the line? Charlane, of course. She saw me in the crowd and gave me one of her condescending sneers. She knew I was on to her about the cookies and Lucky, but that didn't seem to slow her down.

The reporter started, "Yesterday, here at HorseShoeDowns racetrack, Kellsey O'Bryan—one of thoroughbred racing's best-known jockeys—rode her last race. According to a statement released by the family, she was involved in an accident over a month ago when she fell in a race and fractured several ribs, which contributed to her death yesterday. We have a few questions for the last person who talked to her—Charlane, the assistant trainer of the horse she rode yesterday."

She put the mic up to Charlane. "When did you know something was wrong?"

"I knew when she came down the stretch. I could tell something had happened. I saw her take the reins in her left hand and reach up and grab her shoulder with her right hand, like this."

Charlane contorted her face into the most painful expression possible and put her hand up to her shoulder. "I immediately called Dr. Winkley. After the wire, she was supposed to ride the horse out—but she didn't; she came right straight back to me. I was right there by the rail, waiting for her; my job was to take the horse back to the barn. I grabbed the reins, and she eased down…walked behind me and said, 'I'm hurt bad—I'm hurt bad.' I told her I'd already called the doctor. She walked through the crowd with her head held up high and her hand on her shoulder."

Charlane paused. She pulled out some Kleenex and wiped her eyes. "She was my friend—I can't believe this happened to her. I'll tell you this—all you fans and friends of Kellsey O'Bryan—she went out like she wanted to go out. She was damned, damned determined to ride in that race. Can I say 'damned, damned determined' on TV here? And she did. She finished that race and her life exactly on her terms. She gave this sport hope to do better. She's an example that there are a lot of good people in this business. Sometimes, bad things happen to good people—and this is one of those times. We need to honor her with respect and dignity."

The reporter pulled the mic back and said, "The arrangements are being finalized, and we will update this story as information is available."

It was the most coherent thing I had ever heard Charlane say. She made it through the crowd and stopped in front of me.

"That was nice, what you said," I told her.

"Call me later. Maybe we could go to the visitation together tomorrow?"

"Okay."

I went back to my office, closed the door, and sat down in my chair. Then I put my face in my hands and cried. I had to shake it off, since I had a meeting in less than twenty minutes. Then my mind jumped to a place where only someone like me would go. She was on medication for broken ribs. An autopsy would tell that…Surely she wasn't covering up any pain with drugs—she just wanted to go out there and ride.

The clock hit 10:30, and the director of the Criminal Investigation Division walked in with four officers behind him. I directed them to the conference room. We exchanged business cards.

"As you know, one of the nation's premier female jockeys died yesterday," I said once everyone was seated. "Eight months ago, NESPA hired Max Hunter and me to come here and enforce its rules, in hopes of preventing something like this from happening."

The director raised his hand. "Explain exactly what NESPA is and how much authority it has?"

"The National Equine Safety Protection Authority was established by Washington under the Department of Justice. NESPA has total authority, with the DEA, to establish and enforce the rules and regulations. This applies to every activity that includes a horse. Every participant who works with horses or rides them is also protected."

"There was pushback from some of the horse groups and states when this started," he said.

"Yes, there were the usual complainers and the people who don't like rules. And the perpetrators who never abided by the rules. They don't like to fill out forms. Every state has the same set of laws and rules; now there is a level playing field. There's still a national shortage of equine veterinarians and doctors, so they hired us because they didn't have enough people to enforce the rules. Dr. Winkley and the track veterinarian were here. And a few NESPA employees were here when we got here; one is Clink McMillin."

I handed him the personal information for Dr. Winkley and Clink from HR—home addresses and phone numbers.

"We were hired to enforce the rules, to protect horses and riders. This is personal for me."

I held up an eight-by-ten color photo of Kellsey and looked around the room and made eye contact with each person there.

"We are going to find out why. If someone is responsible for her death, we are going to find out who."

I pointed to her photograph, "This woman was not protected. Last night we met with Dr. Winkley, the track doctor. Our protocol in place is that he was supposed to certify Kellsey's fitness to resume riding after her accident in Louisville. He unequivocally told us that he and Kellsey agreed that she would not ride yesterday and they both signed the appropriate NESPA form. And he turned it in to the official in the saddling area."

I walked over to the whiteboard and diagrammed the sequences. "This is as important as checking the horse's digital tattoo to make sure the right horse is in the race."

I held up the blue marker. "This is where this investigation is hinged. We reviewed all the jockeys' forms that he signed yesterday, and they were all signed with blue ink—except Kellsey's. When she showed up in the saddling area and was questioned about the form, she had it folded up and handed it to the official. Right there is a breach of the rules that control the chain of custody of the evidence. That official is authorized to accept forms only from the track doctor. Not a jockey."

I held up the folded piece of paper. "This is the form she handed the official. It was filled out and signed with black ink. Dr. Winkley was adamant that someone forged his signature. He has an impeccable reputation, and his work with NESPA has been exceptional. I'll bet my career that Dr. Winkley is telling us the truth that he did not sign this form."

I paused long enough for the director to ask, "Who had access to the forms?"

"Three people we know about. Kellsey, who is deceased; Dr. Winkley, who is suspended; and Kellsey's boyfriend, who is a NESPA employee—Clink McMillin. He collects the veterinary and medical forms and turns them in to me at the NESPA office. I also had access."

Everyone with the CID director made a few notes. The man sitting next to him took out a document and laid it on the table.

The director said, "This is the CID search warrant. We've ordered a mobile unit that will serve as a lab for us to use to evaluate the evidence. We will use that facility to interview any individuals. We need security tapes of the areas yesterday where she and Dr. Winkley were on the property. Also, we need the NESPA documents."

He looked at me. "Is there anything else I need to know about?"

I quickly said, "At this point, you know everything I can tell you without impeding the success of another investigation we are conducting."

I was sure he meant anything related to Kellsey's death, but my mind went immediately to my OMERTA file. It was full of evidence about Dos's tips and the *quemados*. My silence made me guilty of covering up racetrack safety violations, and that made me complicit in an antidoping rule violation.

I had to do it this way; it was like a mathematical equation. I had to isolate the variables. Three key witnesses/suspects all had to be nurtured and coddled. Each step had to be in the proper sequence. If I acted on one element, that would shut down the rest of the equation, and word would get out about how close I was to putting the responsible parties behind bars. I had to be patient, wait, and wrap this all up at the same time.

"We'll contact the doctor and set up a meeting this afternoon. I'd like for you to go with us."

"Yes, sir. I'm at your disposal."

"Where can we find Clink McMillin?" he asked.

"He didn't come in today," I said. "He took a personal day to grieve his girlfriend's death."

I called Thomas during lunch. "I'm on the way to meet CID at Dr. Winkley's house."

"I finally get to talk to you without an audience," he said. "How are you doing?"

"Not great," I admitted.

"This was the last thing thoroughbred racing and NESPA needed to have happen," he said. "Our checks and balances are full of holes. This is an outright violation of the protocols. I'm coming to Fort Worth tomorrow afternoon."

That put a smile on my face, but it didn't last too long, as I'd arrived at Dr. Winkley's. The Criminal Investigation Division was right behind me.

We filed into Dr. Winkley's house, and he introduced his wife. Their dog checked us out. Their dining room table was set with glasses and three pitchers of water, iced tea, and lemonade. Everyone took a seat except Dr. Winkley.

He stood at the end of the table. The first thing he did was pull some X-rays out of a folder and hold them up to the overhead light.

"This is the X-ray of her ribs taken in Louisville after her accident six weeks ago," he said, getting right down to business. "You can see the three ribs that are broken. They weren't displaced."

He held up another X-ray. "This is the one I took Friday. You can see the ribs are almost healed. I evaluated her for the purpose of deciding whether she could even be listed as the rider. On Friday, she and I agreed she wasn't ready to ride, but she convinced me to wait until Sunday morning to make that final determination. The trainer had already entered the horse and he optimistically listed Kellsey as the jockey. He knew it was questionable for her to ride, but she was listed as the jockey when this information was sent to the *DRF*, and the track program to be printed."

He held up the third X-ray. Quietly, he said, "Here's the one I took yesterday morning—there's no change from Friday."

Dr. Winkley put the X-rays on the table and took a seat. "It's not about a bunch of forms being filled out. It's about a human being who, even if she got a forged document, still had time to make the right choice and not ride."

"Sir, where were you before her race?" the director asked.

"There was an incident in the race right before hers. I was attending to a jockey who had cut his hand. I was in the track clinic, stitching him up."

"When did you realize she rode in the race?"

"I got a call from a woman who works at the barn, Charlane. She said Kellsey was hurt really bad and was walking to the jocks' room. I met her there and helped them get her into the ambulance."

"Which jockey was supposed to replace Kellsey in that race if she had signed the form to not ride?" the director asked.

"The process is for me to notify the stewards," he said. "They go to the jocks' room and tell the designated substitute jockey he is going to be named for the jockey change. That part's out of my hands."

It was the piece of information I'd learned earlier that morning, and I raised my hand and asked if I could make a comment.

When they nodded, I said, "It was Jack Fielding. Today, I followed up with him. He told me that ten minutes before the race, Clink came to the men's jock room and said she got cleared and was going to ride. So he took off the owner's silks and gave them back to Clink. He took them to her."

The director held up a copy of the form and said, "This is a copy of the 'black-ink form' signed by Miss O'Bryan and the one you claim is a forgery. Correct?"

Dr. Winkley nodded. "Yes."

"Where is the real one that you and she signed in blue ink to start this whole situation?" he asked.

Dr. Winkley said, "Clink McMillin gathered all the jockey forms together for that race and turned them in to her." He pointed at me.

"But as soon as the ambulance left for the hospital, Clink jumped into his car and left the track. I assumed he headed to the hospital."

"For the record," I said. "Let me clarify a few things. Clink never came to the hospital. The saddling official told me Kellsey convinced her to swap out the second form for the first form, which Kellsey folded up and took. That was a violation. She should have only accepted the form from Dr. Winkley. And she turned in all the forms."

The director said, "Dr. Winkley, we reviewed the documents, and I assure you, we will expedite this part that pertains to you. As soon as we resolve the status of this missing document, we will notify Miss Ricksland. We can clear you then and request that you be reinstated to return to your duties at the track."

"Thank you, sir."

The woman with them had been taking notes all day on her laptop. "I put Clink's cell number in our tracking system, and his location is pinpointed for us on our CID map," she said. "He's on Route 180 west."

She turned the screen around and showed us a little dot.

"Call the state police," he said. "Have them go after him before he and the 'blue-ink form' disappear."

"We need Kellsey's phone to trace her calls," the woman said.

"It's in my office; you can get it there," I said.

Dr. Winkley held the door open for us as we left. "Please, give me an update when you have it," he asked me. "I cared about her too. Just like everybody else."

Chapter 56

I hadn't talked to Buster since he'd helped me claim BigOilRig. I wished I'd kept in touch. What would I say to him? He had to be in shock. She was their only child. I tried to think of what I could say to him and her mother at the visitation. I dreaded having to do that. I stayed busy all afternoon, isolated from the news about the track.

My mind scrolled through images of Kellsey. It was like leafing through a photo album. The weight of everything was building up inside me. Her death. Their loss. How I really felt about her. Or how I'd once thought I felt about her.

Even when Lucky ran up to me, that reminded me of the times he'd done the same thing to Kellsey. I had to admit, most of the way through our relationship, I'd wondered if it was love or the illusion of love. We'd never talked about marriage. It was too much of a commitment to even discuss. So the easy thing had been to avoid that and go on with our lives.

I'd been stuck at the track, and she'd traveled all over the country, chasing her dreams. The sad thing, in my opinion, was that her dreams were a rolling schedule of the next races. Every time she came back to Fort Worth, and I brought up how dangerous race riding was, she would throw out to me how dangerous being an exercise rider was.

Which only put our relationship on edge and tore down any bridges we had toward a life together.

Just let me get through the next few days.

The afternoon dragged on until I heard "Want some company?"

Patty put her arm up and across my back and rested her hand on my neck.

"Let's go for a trail ride," I said.

"Sure," Patty said. "Let's go."

I thought back to all the times Kellsey and I had talked about going on a trail ride but never did. Our lives had been wrapped up at the racetracks. There hadn't been any time to trail ride.

I got the horses ready, and we went out. Lucky ran ahead and chased birds. I glanced at the hot June sun that tried to find the horizon. I reached and caught Patty's hand, locking our fingers together. It was a beautiful evening.

When we got back, a strange car was parked by the barn, and a man was curled up beside it on the ground. Lucky started barking, and he sat up.

It was Clink. He looked totally disoriented.

"Clink, what happened?" Quickly, I slid down from Chex and passed Patty the reins. Helping him up, I said, "What are you doing here?"

"I got nowhere else to go," Clink said. "The Fort Worth police were coming to my house to question me."

A chill cut through me. "What do you mean?"

"Don't you know?"

"All I know is that Kellsey is dead."

"I was one of the last people to see her alive." Clink looked behind him as though to see if he was being followed. "We started dating right after she and you broke up. When she came back after that injury at Churchill Downs, she moved in with me. On Sunday, she said the racing vest was just like the compression vest to protect her ribs. She told me she was going to ride, and I told her that wasn't a good idea."

He wiped his eyes and went on. "We were in the sitting room adjacent to the women's jock room. Kellsey had already met with Winkley and signed the form agreeing not to ride. But when the bugle sounded for the race right before hers, she grabbed her phone and said, 'Call Stamples. Tell him to get Winkley to change his mind and let me ride.' I shook my head. Then she said, 'If you love me, you'll call him,' and she dialed a number. You know her temper—she insisted I do that for her."

His voice broke. He coughed and cleared his throat, looking from me to Patty.

"Stamples called back and said he got Winkley to sign the NESPA form clearing Kellsey to ride—and for me to come get it. When I walked into his office, Stamples handed me the signed form and said, 'Get your ass back down there.' I did, and she signed it, folded it up, and said she would give it to the official in the saddling area. And now she's dead. I couldn't believe Winkley would do that. He never changes his mind. Now, he claims he never cleared her." He got real serious. "Charlane told me this was just like the time they framed you and railroaded you out of town. She heard there was talk that I signed Winkley's name and turned in the form. I did not do that. Do you believe me?"

"If everything you told us is the truth," I said, "then I believe you."

"That's exactly what happened." Clink ran his hand through his hair and looked around once again. "What do I do? I'm so afraid, I didn't sleep last night. I wish I was the one dead instead of her. Shit, Amos. I'm so scared that I'm being set up here, that I'm getting framed and I got no one that will be on my side. That's why I'm here."

I took a deep breath and said, "Let's go inside." I handed him a bottle of water while Patty waited at the door. "Here. Sit down at the kitchen table. We need to take the saddles off and turn the horses out. It will take us fifteen minutes. Stay right here."

Clink agreed, and Lucky went with us. Patty was silent on the walk to the barn. Finally she said, "He would be complicit in the fact that she rode the horse, because he was in on getting the forms changed."

"Yes. He could have prevented her from riding if he didn't help get the form changed. She could only have ridden with a form signed by the doctor."

Patty said, "Amos, the police are looking for him; he's skipped town, and he's under our roof. You go back inside. I'll call the Fort Worth police and tell them he is here."

She was right. I felt sorry for Clink, though. He was in a lot of trouble. He must have been desperate to come here.

I was back in the cabin when Patty came to the screen door and motioned for me to come outside. "The state police have been monitoring Clink's phone," she said. "It shows he's here. They're ten minutes away."

I went in and sat down across from Clink. "Look. I'll be straight with you. The state police will be here in less than ten minutes. If you keep running, you look guilty."

"You called the cops?" He stood up so fast the table centerpiece shook. "What the hell?"

I got between him and the door. "Clink, I believe you. If you tell the cops what you told us, they'll believe you too. Tell them the truth. Don't get talked into anything else."

They pulled in right then, lights flashing. Clink walked out with his hands up. They spoke to him beside their car as Patty and I watched in silence. He waved before getting into the back seat. The other officer left in Clink's car.

Patty, Lucky, and I walked down to check on the horses. I said, "Can you imagine riding for an hour in the back seat of a state police car? They'll either believe him and take him home, or if they don't—they'll take Clink to the clink."

She tried not to laugh. "That's not even funny. This is a serious deal. Do you believe him?"

I hesitated, then said, "The truth will come out."

Chapter 57

Tuesday morning the obituary was all over the news and social media:

KELLSEY O'BRYAN

DIES at HorseShoeDowns Racetrack on Sunday, June 13, in Fort Worth, Texas.

Jockey Kellsey O'Bryan, a popular Texas jockey who won over 1,000 races in her storied career, is dead at the age of 39 after a race at HorseShoeDowns Racetrack in Fort Worth. She suffered a major injury to her chest.

Kellsey O'Bryan is the daughter of Mr. and Mrs. Buster O'Bryan; Buster O'Bryan is a Texas thoroughbred trainer. She was Texas Jockey of the Year and the recipient of numerous awards and records for female jockeys. Visitation will be today at 4:00 and funeral services will be Wednesday at 1:00 p.m. at Ride for His Brand Cowboy Church in Wise County, Texas. Interment to follow in the Garden of Remembrances. In lieu of flowers, a donation to the Permanently Disabled Jockeys Fund is suggested.

At breakfast, Patty said, "I keep thinking about what happened with Clink."

"Yeah, they hauled his ass right out of here, like in the movies. I wonder what happened? I bet he told them his story, and without any reason to detain him, they took him home. He'll probably be there today," I said, picturing all the familiar faces that would be at the visitation.

The morning passed too quickly, and after lunch, Lucky, Patty, and I got into the truck and headed to Wise County. The first lady called on our way up, and Patty put her on speaker.

"How are you all doing?" Her voice was warm. "Are you with Amos?"

"Yes, ma'am, we're on the way to the visitation."

"I'm so sorry about what happened at the racetrack, Amos. I wanted to ask if you think it would be all right if I come to the funeral tomorrow. This family goes back so far in Texas history, ranching and horses and cattle. I'd be coming out of respect for them. Do you think it's okay?"

Patty looked at me, and we both nodded. "Yes, ma'am," I said. "I think they would appreciate you being there." Once we hung up, I said, "That's interesting."

Patty said, "She's doing her job. She's the face of the government. Sometimes more than the governor, and especially when there's a tragedy. When there's floods and hurricanes down on the Gulf, you name it. She'll pack up and go." She glanced over and raised an eyebrow. "Did you bring that sports coat to wear?"

I smiled. "Yes."

She said, "Do you have a suit for tomorrow?"

I laughed. "No, don't have a suit."

She went to work on her phone. "I'm going to do it right now. M. L. Leddy's. What size sports coat was it that we got you?"

"Forty-two regular."

"I need your waist."

"Forty-two."

"Can't be forty-two."

"Oh, I thought you said age."

She laughed. "I said waist."

"Thirty-four."

"Okay, and what's your inseam?"

"Forty-two."

"Inseam can't be forty-two. You'd be six foot five. Okay, now what is your inseam? The inseam is from the crotch down to the cuff, crotch to cuff."

"Well, it's thirty-four. But I don't want no damn cuff."

"Forty-two, thirty-four, thirty-four? That's all I need to know. It's a nice pair of black pants and a cowboy's black coat. It's got the yoke on the back and on the pockets. We can pick it up on the way to the funeral tomorrow. You'll go in there and try it on and make sure it fits, and you can change there. Like Superman, you go in one way and come back out another way. You can't go up there in blue jeans and a sweatshirt."

I had to admit, if it weren't for Patty, I would have probably dug out my cleanest jeans and shirt and gone up there straight from the barn. If it had been cool out, I might have worn a sweatshirt. But not today or tomorrow. I had a different position than everybody else did—I was almost like family, and Patty was right: I needed to get dressed up to show respect.

We drove in silence for a moment. Then she said, "There's got to be something that we can take up there tomorrow for the O'Bryans. You know them better than I do."

I took her hand.

There was a traffic backup, and I realized all the cars and trucks were in a line to find places to park at the church. We signed the guest register, and I glanced around at the photos of Kellsey. I didn't want to look at her in the casket, but I did. I couldn't believe she was gone; she looked as if she were peacefully asleep. She had on the O'Bryans' white racing silks. The ones with the two green shamrocks on each sleeve. I glanced at all the photos and flowers and sympathy cards. I hadn't sent flowers. I planned to send a donation to the PDJF in her name. The line moved slowly, and I wanted to get out of there. We finally got outside, over to the building where everyone was, a pole barn that was like a covered arena.

I wore out my smile shaking hands. It set in on me: it would take all afternoon to make it up to the front of the line to speak to Buster and Mrs. O'Bryan. I caught Buster's eye, and we both nodded. I took my fist and tapped my chest a couple of times, and he nodded again. The people in line noticed Buster's gesture for me to come to him. They moved to the side and let us through.

I shook his hand. I didn't know what to say, and I don't remember what I did say.

We went over to the tables set up with lemonade and cookies. It was still early, and I didn't have much appetite either. I caught a glimpse of Clink, who was lurking around, lost in the shadows. He was white as a ghost. He looked as if he were going to pass out. I couldn't help but imagine myself standing there, weak-kneed and still in love with Kellsey.

Patty said, "Do you want to head out?"

"Good suggestion; let's go."

I looked at Patty. Her eyes told me what I already knew: I was glad I'd moved to TAPP Ranch.

Chapter 58

Amos was pulling out of the parking lot as we pulled in. We got there late, after being backed up in traffic. Finally we parked, got out, and walked through the church to the covered outdoor building. It was amazing how fast posters and photographs could be found and put up next to the Texas tulips.

Charlane walked in like she owned the place. Wearing her pretty dress and wanting everybody to know she was there. She tried to go one on one and be solemn and sincere. Then she'd talk to people soft and easy as she said, "Oh, gosh. I'm so sorry." She was an actress. She could have been on stage. Anyway, she worked the crowd. She knew everybody there.

A woman in a thrift store dress came up to me and said, "How do you know Kellsey?"

"I really don't know Kellsey."

"Then what are you doing here?'

"I represent the racetrack."

Her eyes narrowed. "Oh, you mean the racetrack where she got killed? Well, let me tell you about the racetrack. I think it's a dangerous place to work. If y'all don't get that place straightened out, there will be more people…We don't want to go to any more funerals."

She looked around and raised her voice. "These are good people here. Most of them work at the racetrack. We don't need any more people getting killed."

"Ma'am, I'm sorry," I said. "I'm sorry that it happened, and we are working to try and make the track safer. We've been working on it for a long time. They hired me…"

"Well, you ain't been doing a very good job, then." She stared me down with ice-blue eyes. "That girl got killed down there."

"Okay. Thank you, ma'am. Have a nice day."

I looked for Charlane. We stood in the line and gave our condolences to the O'Bryans. Charlane said to Buster, "I got everything done at Barn7 today, and I'll take care of everything tomorrow, so I won't be here for the funeral."

I was at a loss for words, but I said, "Mrs. O'Bryan, I was with her Sunday, and the doctor asked me to give you her jewelry."

She studied the items and, through her tears, was barely able to say, "These mean a lot to me, and it means a lot to us that you were there with her."

The drive back was another long dissertation from Charlane. The rare seconds she was silent, my mind kept replaying that woman practically accusing me of killing Kellsey. All I wanted to do at this point was to get home, freshen up, and meet Thomas for dinner to discuss what we could actually do to make the track safe or if it was hopeless, which was how it was starting to feel.

Thomas had landed by the time I got back, so I asked him to come to my house for drinks and takeout from the Italian restaurant near my house. I got everything straightened up and had a couple of bottles of his favorite wine. My email alert chimed, and in disbelief, I read through the message right before the doorbell rang.

I tried to not break down when I opened the door, but all I could do was cry and cling to Thomas.

He held me in silence. When I couldn't cry anymore, he said, "Long, sad day, huh?"

Thomas made me feel comfortable in a way I hadn't for so long. There was no need to hide my emotions or pretend to be strong. He was there and willing to listen.

"Longer and sadder than any day I've had in a long time," I admitted.

Once inside, I poured him a glass of wine, and we sat down at the table. Thomas asked me all about the visitation. I gave him the update and my observations as we made our way through our chicken parmigiana. When we were about finished, I pulled out my phone.

"I saw Clink at the visitation today," I said, "I got an email right before you arrived, from the director of the CID. Are you ready? Here's a copy of Clink's statement. He claims he got the form with the black ink from Mr. W. D. Stamples—the owner of the whole damn track and casino and sports book. What do you think about that?"

Thomas read the email. "That is so far-fetched he couldn't make shit like that up."

"Do you know what this means?" I asked.

"Yes, they are going to make absolutely, positively sure that Clink's story is solid. If it is, then they will proceed to charge Stamples with at least involuntary manslaughter."

"He's not making something like that up to save his ass." I shook my head. "The track's in a PR free fall. They were already lawyering up because of the implied liability. The track has dozens of policies for every contingency. This may slip through a crack, into the track's negligence category."

Thomas raised his eyebrows, and said, "Not just the track. NESPA has some exposure depending how involved Clink is. Our lawyers are already on it. NESPA has the ultimate responsibility to have in place protocols to ensure a forged document cannot be used to circumvent the regulations. Even more important, if Stamples did indeed forge Dr. Winkley's signature, he could end up holding the entire bag." Thomas grimaced. "People like Stamples seem to have a gift for sidestepping this sort of thing."

"Thomas, if Stamples is responsible for this, we can't let him get away with it."

"I agree," Thomas said. "We'll take him down together."

I took his hand, brought him closer, and kissed him. "Would you stay here tonight?"

"I wondered when you would ask." He got to his feet. "My suitcase is in the car."

He came back in and handed me a small envelope.

"What's this?" I asked.

"Open it."

It was an invitation to the opening day at Del Mar in July.

I can't go to the funeral today.

It was still dark outside. I curled up in bed and pulled myself close against Thomas. Kellsey was younger than I was. And gone. Life was way too short.

I couldn't bring myself to go back up there and have a confrontation with that woman or anyone else. I was not the enemy here.

Thomas woke up and pushed a hair out of my face. "Are you okay?"

"How does a special breakfast sound?" I tried to keep my voice bright. "How do you like your eggs? And fruit. Juice, coffee. I can do all that."

"Sure—or do you want to stay here in bed a little while?"

"Yes," I said, quietly. "Let's stay here. I can't go to that funeral today. There was a consensus among the CID, NESPA and the track that racing should be canceled for the day, in honor of Kellsey. I don't know what's going to happen over there today, but I guess technically—indirectly—I work for you. If you are my boss and you tell me I should stay in bed…then that's exactly what I'm going to do."

Chapter 59

Patty and I left at 9:30 to allow enough time to go by M. L. Leddy's. We walked in, and a man unzipped a monogrammed garment bag and took out my suit.

Patty took the coat off the hanger and handed me the pants, and I went to the dressing room. I had my black boots all shined up and wore a white dress shirt. When I looked in the mirror to tie my tie, I was surprised to see how exhausted I looked. I couldn't believe that I was going to Kellsey's funeral.

When I came back out, Patty helped me with the coat. It all fit, and Lucky looked as if he wanted to stay there with the little Leddy lady dog, he was the last one to go out on the hot sidewalk when we opened the door.

Patty said, "I like you better in jeans and a denim shirt. But I have to say—you are handsome in that suit."

Back in the truck, Lucky looked out the window, as always. We were almost to the church in Wise County, and the traffic was backed up. Patty put her hand on my arm, took my hand, and interlocked our fingers.

Once we parked, I grabbed my black cowboy hat and tried to find a breath of fresh air as Lucky jumped out. He was the only dog there and ran up to the first lady, who waited by her car. She hugged Patty.

She pulled me close for a hug. "We are here to support you."

"Thanks for coming. I know it will mean a lot to the family."

A big screen was set up for the overflow crowd in the open-air building. The only sound was a soft instrumental version of Garth Brooks's "The Dance."

At the front door of the church, I shook hands with a couple of jockeys waiting to go in. Flowers and photos of Kellsey were on several tables in the small foyer. A woman whom I recognized reached down and let Lucky smell her hand, then motioned for us to follow her.

"We reserved three seats in the second row right behind Mr. and Mrs. O'Bryan. That's where they want you to sit."

The muscles in my throat tightened. I drew a deep breath as I walked up the center aisle and stared at Kellsey in the casket. Buster and Mrs. O'Bryan were the last ones to come in from a side door. He walked straight to me. I stood and shook his hand as he said, "Thanks for coming." He nodded to Patty and the first lady.

Mrs. O'Bryan forced a smile and sat down.

The preacher said, "Gathered here today are her mother and father and so many of the people who loved and cared about this special young woman. Kellsey O'Bryan has made an impact on the world. Let's all begin by saying our own prayers for Kellsey."

After a minute, he continued, "I have struggled since Sunday—trying to find words. I met her in her jocks' room on Sunday, right when I found out she was going to ride. She and I have prayed hundreds of times before races. This is the last image I have of her; it's the one I want you to picture in your mind. She fiddled with the cross on her necklace."

He paused and gave us time to visualize that. "It's a beautiful thing that horses bring people together. And that is also a pathway to God. In Genesis, at the start of the Bible, on the sixth day God made every kind of animal—and next he made humans. Kellsey's life began thirty-nine years ago when she took her first breath at Fort Worth General. She grew up on her family's farm right here in Wise County. She was baptized here at this altar. Kellsey was an accomplished rider;

it was only natural for her to become a jockey. And what a jockey she was. Her life was one of abundant accomplishments."

He went on for several minutes, but I didn't hear anything. My mind wandered as I closed my eyes and had an avalanche of memories. Lucky woke up and walked right up to the casket, sniffed, and sat down, looking at it and then back at me. The preacher noticed and, for a moment, looked as if he was about to cry too.

There was silence.

Everyone remained seated as a song played softly. It was "Irish Prayer": "Going home, set my soul free. Going home. I'll be waiting to greet you. Here in heaven is where I shall be."

He said, "Please come up front and pay your respects. We will proceed to the Garden of Remembrances Cemetery in the back."

An instrumental violin version of "Amazing Grace" began to play as we walked out; the sun glared down on us, and my shirt started to get uncomfortable from the heat. I tried to loosen my collar—I wasn't used to wearing a tie.

The pallbearers carried the casket on rollers back to the small cemetery behind the church. A mound of dirt covered with a green tarp was under a canopy of cottonwood trees that shaded a creek. Nearly everybody had stayed and stood around the small tent.

The first lady, Patty, and I were escorted to three seats under the tent, right behind the O'Bryans. After a few more prayers and echoes of "Amazing Grace" wafted through the cloudless Texas afternoon, I put my hat back on and wiped my eyes one more time. Patty let her hand drift out of mine as I walked up to the casket.

My knees ached from riding, from the surgery I had back when I was a crazy rodeo guy. I couldn't tell if it was my legs giving out or if my heart was so heavy with grief that the blood was blocked somewhere between my heart and my knees. Each step was dreadful to take. The white roses in a basket resting on the top of the casket were beautiful. She had been so beautiful.

I fumbled in my coat pocket and pulled out the bag SkyMan had given me on Tuesday. It was sand from the spot where she'd dismounted that last time on the track at HSD. I poured it into my left hand.

Tears ran down my cheeks as I started pouring it out on top of the casket. It flowed down, like time draining out of an hourglass, until the last grain fell. I reached down and took a white rose from the casket, putting it in the breast pocket of my new black suit. I turned, thinking everyone had already left. But the others had waited; they watched me with respect for her and my final tribute. The love we'd had once was evident. I buried my face in my bandana.

When I looked back up, my eyes found Patty. I realized what I had suspected for a while: she was the love of my life. She reached for me and took my hand. We left, leaving a big part of my life behind.

June 16 in Texas is one of the hottest places to be in a black suit. I was sure all the men would ditch the coats at the O'Bryans' house. I put the suit coat on a hanger and hung it in the back seat of the truck. Patty put the white flower in a bottle of water in the cup holder. It was a short trip from the cemetery to their house, but I drove slowly, in no rush to get there. Even Lucky looked sad.

"I'm thinking about a good cup of coffee," I said. "I know they'll have some there, and the Irish will probably have the bar open, and some of them will bury their grief in the bottom of a bottle."

We all know the Irish are great people, some of the best. But I wasn't Irish enough, Kellsey had told me, when she'd tried to justify leaving me.

Their farm was Texas rustic and well lived in. It had been in their family a long time. Patty pulled a box out of the Yeti cooler, and we walked up to the front porch together.

The minute we walked in, Mrs. O'Bryan motioned for me to come over to her. Her eyes were red, and she gave me a slight hug. She had changed from the black dress she'd had on at the church into a pair of jeans and a pink flowered blouse.

Patty held out the box. "Ma'am, I made this peach cobbler especially for you and Mr. O'Bryan."

"Thank you. I understand you have a nice barn out there at your ranch. I'd like to show you mine," she said. "Come on; we can put this in the refrigerator on the way."

They walked through the paddocks, and Lucky went with them. He knew his way around, even though it was the first time he'd been there in a long time.

I spotted a big stainless restaurant-type coffee urn. Then I shook my head. I couldn't wrap my mind around the word "urn"—especially the ones for ashes. I couldn't think about Kellsey's body being cremated and her ashes put on the mantle. I was glad they didn't do that.

I got a large plastic cup and filled it with ice and coffee. I turned and, in a sweeping glance, saw so many of Kellsey's friends from school, rodeos, church, and racetracks across the country.

I had to endure the "I'm so sorry" comments. That's all anyone knew to say. I escaped to the den. It was a library full of trophies and family photos. Some of my pictures used to be there. Texas tulips in planters were scattered throughout the house.

Scattered like my thoughts.

I wondered how much longer we had to stay. I didn't know how much time an ex-boyfriend was expected to spend there, or if I was in the way. I headed outside to find Patty.

Buster was outside. I caught his attention, and we walked away from the crowded patio toward the paddock, then leaned on the fence.

"How are you doing?" I asked him.

"Not good. I feel worse than if I'd been drunk for three days," he said, rubbing bloodshot eyes. "I want a drink. No, I want to go get drunk. But I can't do that. I've made a lot of promises in my life—kept most of them—but there is one promise I made probably thirty years ago. I promised myself, my wife, and Kellsey I would never drink again."

I was surprised that I didn't know that about him. Buster let out a slow breath. "Look at all these people…You are the only person who seems to care if I'm okay."

"You're more than okay. I'm grateful for your help with BigOilRig, and I've been thinking a lot about our time together at the track. I know I kinda left in a hurry…"

"Hurry? Shit, son…"

He had rarely called me *son*.

Buster cleared his throat. "Son…they shipped your ass outta there so fast."

We laughed. "That's the first time I've even laughed since Sunday," he said. "Be glad you weren't there. It was terrible. Horrible. Awful."

He wiped his face on both sleeves of his wrinkled white shirt. "I never got to say goodbye to her."

We stood in silence.

"Yeah. I've missed you," Buster said. "I don't guess I ever properly thanked you for trying to make the track safe. All these NESPA rules, and I'm the one with a stubborn daughter who got the rules side-stepped. Look at what happened. We were a good team. Weren't we?"

"Yes, sir. Barn, horses, you name it—we were the best. We didn't make up our own rules; we did things right. I'm proud to have been part of your team at Barn7."

He stared out at the fields. "It's peaceful out here," he said, lowering his voice. "This is my home. Been livin' here my whole life. Never wanted to go nowhere else. Some Texans are like that. I am. A lot of memories here…She learned to ride right there."

He pointed with his right arm as the faint sound of a violin in a country song drifted from the patio. He made swinging, flowing gestures with his arm. It was as if he were conducting a performance. An orchestra.

"There she is. I see her. I see her. I see her," he said. "Can you see her?"

The flood of tears erupted. He leaned down, buried his face in both arms on the top fence board, and between every sob said every curse word in the book.

Once he'd gone quiet, I said, "Damn right, Buster."

He pushed back from the fence, took a deep breath. "There. Got through that. Son, don't you tell anyone I broke down that bad."

"Buster, you can call me *son* anytime. If anyone was ever like a father to me…it's you. Not just at the track."

He shook his head. "I don't know when I'll be able to go back there."

"Oh, you'll go back," I told him. "When you're ready."

Mrs. O'Bryan and Patty walked back from the barn. Spotting us, they walked over.

"Amos, well, I hear you have a brand-new career, and…" She stopped, grabbed Patty's arm, and held it tight. Then she sniffed a proud Texas woman's sniff and said, "Patty tells me she's the luckiest girl in the world."

Mrs. O'Bryan took the edge of a silk scarf that had been wadded up in her hand and wiped her eyes. She studied Patty for a second and said, "Amos, she's special. You both are welcome here anytime. I always liked you…well, I still like you. During the service today, I had a lot of thoughts of you and Kellsey. I remember the first time she met you. She was sitting there at the track signing autographs on the big posters, with her foot in a cast, propped up on a chair, and you were in the line to get an autograph. She called and said she thought she'd met the guy she was going to marry someday. Did she ever tell you that?"

I glanced at Patty. "No, ma'am."

"Well, that's what she said." Mrs. O'Bryan wiped her eyes again. "I want you to know we have zero regrets about how many times we tried to get her to quit race riding."

We stood in silence for a moment, and I nodded at her. "We'll be thinking of you. Call me if you need anything at all."

I motioned at Patty that it was time to leave, and she nodded.

"You both come back sometime, okay?" Buster said, shaking my hand.

"Yes, sir, we will."

Mrs. O'Bryan pulled me aside. She lowered a gold cross on a gold chain into my hand and closed my fingers around it. I looked back at her eyes, full of tears. All I could do was hug her and whisper, "Thanks."

Patty was solemn and quiet walking to the car. She still didn't say anything when we pulled onto the main road. I broke the silence. "Funerals are so humbling. Everyone turns out and reflects on the person we leave behind. So different from these 'celebration' services. It's like people deny there's a God—or are afraid to trust God or believe in God. But I do. I'm afraid not to. I'd rather believe in something than nothing. What did you and Mrs. O'Bryan talk about?"

She reached over and took my hand. "Mrs. O'Bryan told me you treated Kellsey better than she treated you. Kellsey was hell-bent on winning races and getting into the winner's circle. It's an addictive sport. But she loved it. Then..." Patty let out a breath. "Amos, she looked at me and cried. She bawled. I just held her. She kept crying."

Patty let out a shaky breath. "She said Kellsey loved to ride, she lived to ride, and she died riding. Then she perked up. She said, 'Something happened. He didn't stumble. He didn't fall. Her rib severed that vein, and that was it. We buried her wearing the O'Bryan white racing silks with the shamrocks on both sleeves.'

"I told her I saw it and it was beautiful. Then it was like she wasn't talking to me anymore. Her voice got down to a whisper: 'She never suffered. I thank God for that because it could've been worse. A mother is not supposed to bury a child and I had to do that this afternoon. I'd rather she had been paralyzed than she passed away. At least she would still be alive and I could take care of her.'"

I winced, and Patty shook her head. "She started crying again. She's a hell of a woman, to go through what she's going through. She'd just met me yesterday, and out of all these people that she knows, she picked me out of the crowd and said, 'Hey, come on. I want to show you my barn.' She didn't want to show me the barn. She wanted to...I don't know. We just connected."

"You showed up at the right moment, when she needed you," I said. "I mean, you care. You care about people. You care about horses. She recognized your compassion. You share the same values. Yeah, she lost a daughter, but she may have found a friend. Maybe you have too. They're good people." The words caught in my throat, and I said them again. "They're good people. They're good people."

Patty got a Kleenex out of the console and handed it to me before getting another for herself. Then she blew her nose, wiped her eyes, and shook her head. I drove on, and after a few minutes, a song came up on the screen.

"This is that song," Patty said. "I downloaded it. 'Irish Prayer.' Michael Hearne and Shake Russell. Play it. Play it soft. Play it low. I want to hear that song again."

We listened to the words:

> There's an unfinished painting on an easel
> There's a half-burned candle in your room
> An empty chair that sits at the table
> Tears that fall from a bittersweet tune
> Now your voice and your laughter are missing
> It's an absence felt throughout the house
> I watched as you fell all the way from this world
> Beyond the vale into somewhere else
> Beyond the vale into somewhere else
> I had a dream I heard the coach rolling
> Down the mountain and up to the door
> I looked away and you had been taken

Now the world's not the same as before
We seem to appear out of nowhere
Or from wherever we come
Then we just disappear back into there
When a life is lived and is done
When a life is lived and is done
So fly away; I won't try to hold you
Just fly away; it's time to leave
No sad farewells, no tears of sorrow
"I'm going home," I heard you whisper
"Going home, set my soul free
Going home, I'll be waiting to greet you
Here in heaven is where I shall be..."

Chapter 60

Thomas stayed in Fort Worth to assist with the investigation into Kellsey's death. It was as if he'd moved in, and I'd adjusted my schedule accordingly. Instead of jumping up to fight the early morning Fort Worth traffic, I was settling into the shared life we were creating. We still drove separately to the track but, were barely out of each other's sight. He was invaluable helping navigate through the legal aspects of the NESPA rules as they pertained to the medical regulations and the protocol.

Thursday morning, on the way to the track, I was appalled to see banners had been hung on both sides of Camp Bowie Boulevard for a half a mile all the way up to the track. "The Kellsey O'Bryan Memorial Stakes Race," Sunday, June 20. I called Thomas and asked him, "Did you see those banners?"

He said, "Stamples is only doing that to deflect attention off himself."

They had raised Kellsey up on a pedestal of martyrdom, with banners everywhere. It wasn't right to portray someone's accident for the benefit of the track and Stamples. He wanted the grandstands full to get people here so they would buy popcorn, hot dogs, and beer and make a lot of bets. Get the handle up so that he got his percentage.

It should have been out of respect. It should have been a quiet thing. But no, her pictures were everywhere. It wasn't the right thing to do. It wasn't ethical.

It was gloomy out at the main gate, where Kellsey's fans had added candles, flowers, and posters to the memorial. "Rest in peace" signs made with horseshoes, along with other homemade *descansos*, littered the sidewalk. The track gift shop was selling embroidered hats with "KELLSEY" stitched on the front and a horseshoe on the back.

I held one up and showed it to the attendant. "Who gave you permission to sell this?"

The vendor looked at me in surprise.

I showed him my badge.

"Stamples," he said, looking sheepish.

Stamples had commercialized her death. It angered me—but it didn't surprise me. The accusations Clink had made about Stamples had me worried. It was evident he was more ruthless than anyone could imagine or prove. And he had flown out of Fort Worth on his private plane Sunday night.

The director of the CID met Thomas and me in my office, and I briefed him about the visitation and funeral. "I'm going to call Stamples and ask him to come here for a meeting."

Stamples picked up on the third ring. The director introduced himself and said, "I'm the director of the CID and the contact person from the Fort Worth Police Department. I'd like to meet with you to chat about what happened here at your racetrack last Sunday. How does tomorrow sound?"

He didn't have the call on speaker, but I could tell Stamples was being evasive.

"Well, we need to meet before that," the director said. "I'm asking you again: Can you be here in Fort Worth tomorrow?"

He went silent and drummed his fingers on the desk, shaking his head back and forth as though he were listening to his favorite jazz song. Finally he said, "Yes, if you want to. Good, let's meet at my office. I'll text you the address. One thirty sharp. Thanks."

He ended the call and looked at me. "He asked if he should have his lawyer present. I'm sure he will bring one or two, even. Before we meet with him, I want to go into his office and look around. I want to get a feel for what his interests are."

I had been in Stamples's office only a few times. He was an absentee owner. The director went right over to a sidewall that held dozens of photos of Stamples with Kellsey in the winner's circle. Scattered around were photos of him with politicians and famous sports stars. Golf foursomes. His airplane. A few awards from the charities he gave the big checks. One photo of his wife and daughter over in the corner of a cluttered bookcase.

The director sat down in Stamples's chair and put on a pair of vinyl gloves. He picked up the only pen that was lying on the desk by the end, where the clip was. He drew a few circles on a scrap of paper and showed me. He said, "This is a Mont Blanc pen. Black ink. I'll leave right now and take it to the forensics lab. We'll check fingerprints and see if it matches with the ink on the form we think is forged."

We thanked him for his help and called it a day. I left my car at the track, and I rode with Thomas. My stomach was full of anticipation about the meeting with Stamples, but Thomas insisted we stop and grab a quick takeout from the deli near my house. I worried about everything that could go wrong, but Thomas was more practical. I was learning he had patience to deal with facts. I guess lawyers have to have that approach. But me, I have always had to assemble evidence—just like in this case.

On Friday, rumors and gossip were rampant at the track about Kellsey's accident. Thomas and I were at the track early, going through all the information we had compiled in the last few days. At 8:30 I looked at him.

"You ready?"

He nodded, and we both got to our feet. "This should be interesting."

I drove us to the precinct police station. Dos, Pepito, and Charlane had all been brought in for questioning. I'd given them each the heads-up the day before and had let them know the time to hold back had ended.

They were put in separate holding rooms by themselves. Thomas and I joined the director and another police officer in a small room.

They brought Dos in first. He nodded to me and scoped it all out. We sat behind a table at one end of the room. Dos sat in the chair by the door.

Once he'd been sworn in, the director said, "We are investigating the accident on March 26 where four horses were doped. Regrettably, we are also investigating the death of the jockey last Sunday. Let's start with March 26. Who told you to give those numbers, 2, 10, 6, 3, and 7, to Amos Moon?"

"I'm a shill. I work for the track and get instructions from burner phones." Dos held up his hands, and I saw a scar on his wrist. "Look, I have a family—I don't ask questions. I don't know who it is. It could be different people each time. I don't know who."

"Don't withhold information from us," I said. "And worse for you—don't lie. Being involved in a scheme that includes doping horses is bad enough. But on March 26, your tip also impacted the outcome of the fourth race. Both of these are serious violations of NESPA rules. And they carry fines and prison time for guilty individuals. We could arrest you right now for withholding evidence and issuing a false statement—you're under oath. One more time. Who is the person who instructed you to give that tip to Amos Moon?"

Dos glanced at me. "My instructions were to go to Barn7 and ask where Charlane was but get Amos to make the bet. It was from Mr. Stamples."

I took in a sharp breath. "Is that the truth?"

"Yes."

The director handed him a piece of paper, instructing him to write out his statement and sign it. Thomas and I exchanged a quick look.

I could tell he felt the same way I did, relieved to get answers and mentally planning for our meeting later that afternoon with Stamples.

Dos wrote out his statement and signed it, and I witnessed it. He wiped his forehead with a small white towel.

"For right now, don't say a word to anyone about what happened here today," the director instructed. "You are free to go."

I walked out with him. "You didn't do anything wrong. Keep quiet about this."

Pepito came in. He didn't look at anyone but me. "I told you the truth, didn't I?"

"Yes," I said. "But I need you to say again exactly what happened on March 26."

After the introductions, he was sworn in by the director, who made a brief speech explaining why he was there.

Pepito seemed nervous, but he went into the story. "Charlane told me to give the new cookies to BigOilRig. I must have given the new ones to NoCashRefund, because he slowed down like the horses in the fourth race."

"For the record, are those new cookies the same as *quemados*?"

He laughed. "Yes, I called them *quemados*. They looked burnt."

Thomas gave an appreciative laugh.

"Did you give those new cookies to those other horses too?" I asked.

"No. They are all in different barns. I didn't do that."

The director handed him a piece of paper and a pen. "Can you write down what you just said—and sign your name on the bottom?"

I witnessed his statement.

After a quick break, Charlane came in.

Charlane walked in as though she was right at home in a police station. She had on an old pair of clean jeans tucked into her boots and a white shirt with the sleeves rolled up, showing an authentic-looking turquoise bracelet. Her hair was pulled back, tucked under a straw cowboy hat, and around her neck was tied a flowered red silk scarf.

She looked at each person in the room, and when her eyes settled on me, she said, "If I need a reference, ask her. Better yet, if I need bail money, Rixie, you got my back—right?"

I shook my head, hiding a smile. Even at this moment, Charlane didn't disappoint. Everyone tried not to laugh.

The director asked her name.

"Charlane," she said, settling into the chair. "No last name. Mom wasn't sure who my father was, so she put Char Lane on the birth certificate. So I put it all together. There's a lot of famous people that only have one name. Reba, Diana, Beyoncé…After today, y'all will never forget me. Rixie. She's one of a kind too."

He swore her in and gave her the same speech he'd given the others. Then he said, "We are also investigating the disappearance of a canine, Lucky Moon, on Friday, April 23, the doping of horses on March 26, and Kellsey O'Bryan's death on Sunday. Let's start with the dog's disappearance. What do you know about that?"

"I know Amos got him back safe."

"Did you have him the whole time?" I asked.

Charlane looked away. "Yes."

Thomas gave me a sympathetic look.

"Let's talk about the accident that sent Mr. Drummer to the hospital," the director said. "So you're the cookie queen?"

"Well, I sell a lot of cookies."

"Did you give anything to NoCashRefund on that day that could have caused Mr. Drummer to be thrown?"

"No, sir."

"Do you know who did?" I asked.

"Pepito."

I nodded. "Why did he do that?"

Charlane stared at me with a Fifth Amendment look. "A lotta people in this world do things not because they want to but because they have to. I'm one of those people. Yeah, I put on a front and disguise myself to fit in anywhere with anyone, but I'm not a free woman. I bake cookies, I ride horses, and I make a few bets for guys like Dos."

She sat back in the chair and fidgeted with the knot and the ends of the scarf.

"I have obligations—the worst word in the English language. I wish I didn't, but I do."

"It says here in the notes," the director said, "some new cookies, now known as *quemados*, were given to NoCashRefund. Why did Pepito give those *quemados* to that horse?"

"Pretty simple. I asked him to give them to BigOilRig. He gave them to the wrong horse."

"Was that an attempt to fix that race?" the director asked.

"Once it was all over," Charlane said, "I figured out Amos was set up."

"Why would that happen?" the director asked.

"I don't know."

He glanced at me, and I said, "Doping horses and any actions that impact the outcome of a horse race are serious violations of Texas laws and NESPA regulations. Both carry fines and prison time for guilty individuals."

"Yes, but I'm at the bottom of the food chain," she said. "I get instructions. Powerful people don't have any regard for people like Pepito and me. We are used. Disposable. If we get caught, do you think they will come to bat for us? No."

"You said you get instructions. Who from? We don't need a long, stretched-out dissertation—just say the name."

She stood up and didn't act as though she were going to leave but stretched and leaned down, and I imagined her pulling a gun out of her boot.

"My back," she explained. "I can't sit very long. As a matter of fact I never sit down. Not one minute. If I tell you—what's in it for me? Ain't this valuable information?"

I looked at the director, and he nodded.

"We are prepared to offer freedom for your cooperation," I said. "With your sworn statement today, you will not be charged with a crime. However, withholding evidence *is* a crime."

Charlane fidgeted in the chair. She took a deep breath, then said, "Riding thoroughbred racehorses is the most dangerous job in the world. There is only one thing more dangerous: the repercussions I face if I tell you. How can I be sure this man is going down with my statement?"

"Charlane, you have to know the connection between when Lucky was lost, the *quemados*, and the person who forged Kellsey's document on Sunday. Let me ask you—is the same person responsible for all three of those?"

She pulled the scarf up to her face, hunched over, and cried—real tears. Not a put-on. She blew her nose into the scarf and wiped her eyes.

"I didn't have a choice." Her voice was almost a whisper. "I've been involved with him since my days back in Houston. I owe him my life. I had to do everything he wanted to pay him back for saving me from a bad relationship I had with a pro football player. But I despise that man. He forced me to take Lucky to my house and pretend he was stolen. He was so vindictive toward Amos because Kellsey loved Amos. I don't have too many friends, but she was my friend—and now she's gone. He did it all."

The director said, "Who?"

"Stamples. There, I said it. Take him down."

Her confession would make it possible to do that. We now had hard evidence that proved those four horses were doped. We all looked at each other. I was startled, then filled with relief.

Charlane looked at me. "I thought you'd never get anything else on him."

The director gave her the paper and a pen and said, "We need you to write out your statement; also write down the name of the person who gave the cookies to those other horses. That was you, wasn't it?"

She nodded.

"When you're finished, sign it," he told her.

I witnessed it.

Chapter 61

We took a break, and they had lunch brought in. We had about an hour until Stamples was supposed to be there, and the director walked us through several scenarios. He opened a box with an official label and held up a plastic bag with Stamples's pen in it. "Here's all we need. Our forensics lab verified the black ink on this form is from the pen we found in his office. We cross-referenced his fingerprints with those on file when he registered with NESPA."

He read from his notes, "This was a reckless act. He was aware of the risk if she rode, and he chose to disregard that. Which recklessly caused her death. Ultimately, he's guilty of involuntary manslaughter."

"Do you think he's going to show up?" Thomas asked me in a low voice.

It was the same thing I'd been thinking. "He'd better."

The director called him about 12:30 and put the call on speaker. "Mr. Stamples. Just confirming our meeting."

"Yes." His voice was tight. "My attorney and I will be there at 1:30."

Thomas and I stepped outside. We needed some fresh air, but it was already a steamy summer day for the middle of June. We walked and talked, which helped me get rid of my nervous energy.

"That went as planned," he said. "You did a great job getting three signed statements. That plus the lab report on the ink pen is enough corroborated evidence to charge Stamples and put him away for a long time."

When we made our way back to the building, I saw my reflection in the glass door as we walked back up the steps. My whole career had been compressed into this one week. I'd sent men and women to prison for embezzlement and income tax evasion, but I'd never thought I'd be involved in a case with a total disregard for the lives of animals and humans.

Stamples had caused SkyMan's accident, but he'd pushed it under the rug with a huge settlement. Today would be a different story. He was also responsible for Kellsey's death, and there was nothing he could do to deny that. I hoped it wouldn't end up being a situation with lawyers going back and forth for months or even years. The publicity would be disastrous for the horse industry and NESPA. He needed to take responsibility for his actions and let this come to a close.

The door to the room was open, and the director brought in another chair. He put the seats for Stamples and his lawyer at the back of the room.

"Should be soon," he said, glancing at his watch.

"I'll keep an eye out for them," I said.

Part of me still wondered if they would show up. But at 1:20 they walked up the front steps. Stamples had on a perfectly tailored tan suit with a triangular silk handkerchief in his breast pocket, a color-coordinated tie, and shined shoes. He looked as if he could have just flown in from LA, what with his spray-tanned complexion and white-on-white teeth.

I greeted them at the door and motioned for them to follow me down the hall. Everyone shook hands and did introductions while standing inside the door. Once Stamples was sworn in, he and his lawyer went around the table and sat down.

The lawyer had a leather folder. He opened it, spread it out on the table, and sat back. "You wanted to chat with my client. What about?"

"Mr. Stamples, tell us what took place on Sunday, June 13, at HSD Racetrack," the director said. "We have a signed statement from Mr. McMillin that he got this document from you. Here is a copy of that document. We also have a sworn statement from Dr. Winkley that someone forged his signature on this document."

The director slid it across the table. The attorney picked it up, read it, then handed it to Stamples.

"Have you ever seen that document?" the director asked.

"Don't answer that question," his lawyer said.

The director pulled his chair up close to the table. "Again, we have a signed statement from a credible individual that this document was handed to Mr. McMillin by you. Let me remind you that you are under oath to tell the truth. Your lawyer can tell you what the consequences are if you don't."

The director pushed his chair back and crossed his arms.

Stamples started to speak. The attorney touched his arm, saying, "Before my client answers your question, can you give us what charges you might bring against him?"

The director took out a folder. "We have signed affidavits and statements that implicate Mr. Stamples in a variety of activities and behaviors that violate the laws of Texas and the rules and regulations of NESPA. These violations are listed on these two pages."

The director handed one set to the attorney and another to Stamples. Identical copies. He handed the policeman, Thomas, and me copies and started reading.

"Number one: Mr. Stamples forged a medical document that led to the death of a jockey on Sunday, July 13.

"Number two: Mr. Stamples instructed certain individuals to administer substances, a.k.a. *quemados*, to four horses at HorseShoeDowns Racetrack on March 26. Subsequently, NoCashRefund unseated his rider, who was injured. Case in point of Mr. Stamples's guilt: court documents show that he settled with that rider for an undisclosed amount.

"Number three: Mr. Stamples was the mastermind behind the fourth race on March 26, where Mr. Stamples attempted to use the *quemados* to affect the outcome of the race.

"Number four: Mr. Stamples instructed an individual to dognap a certain canine on April 23."

The director paused, leaned back in his chair, and said, "Oh, we are prepared today to charge Mr. Stamples with several crimes. I don't have to tell you his admissions may go a long way toward asking for any leniency any judge in any court in any jurisdiction could possibly consider."

The attorney said, "Would you excuse us and let my client and me have a moment in private?"

The director nodded, and we went outside into the hall.

"So much for building rapport and asking him about his golf game," I said. "You went right for the jugular vein."

"That was for Miss O'Bryan," the director said. "Even if he confesses, he'll never get any leniency. He knew forging that doctor's name was wrong. Not to mention fixing a race and having Charlane get Pepito give those *quemados* to a horse in training, and a rider was injured. And anyone who would have a dog stolen is as low as anything I have ever heard of."

The door opened, and the lawyer motioned us back in. I expected to see Stamples all arrogant, sitting there stoic, ready to deny everything with a "prove it" attitude. But to my surprise, he was standing, his coat and tie crumpled on the chair.

I noticed a Mont Blanc pen in his shirt pocket and glanced at the director, who seemed to have spotted it as well. Stamples didn't look at anyone. He stared off into space, as if in a trance.

The lawyer took off his coat and hung it on the back of his chair and stood behind the table as if he were in a courtroom preparing for his closing argument. He was holding what looked like typed notes.

0

After loosening his collar, he said, "I'd like to share a summary of endless hours and conversations. My client, W. D. Stamples, is genuinely and truly sorry. He did not intend to harm anyone or any animal. Not a single time did he intend for the result of his actions to inflict harm or injury on any person, dog, or horse. I'd especially like to speak to this first item on the list, the event last Sunday. Never in my client's wildest dreams, and now nightmares, did he think filling out a form would result in such a horrendous outcome."

He looked at me. "As you, Miss Ricksland, can attest, it was no secret he had a genuine affection for Miss O'Bryan. He never would have knowingly done anything that would lead to an injury or her death. Mr. Stamples called me Sunday afternoon, and I could tell how distraught he was. He said, 'Instead of Kellsey flying back with me on the plane, she was in an accident and died.' I met him at the airport, and we have been in constant communication since."

He pointed at Stamples, who had sat down and buried his face in his hands. "My client has instructed me to tell you he acted out of desperation. When she called him, she told him if he didn't get Dr. Winkley to clear her to ride, they would never see each other again. I quote: 'If you love me, you will have him clear me to ride today.' And yes—he got a form and signed Dr. Winkley's name. Now we all know this was a series of bad decisions and worse consequences."

He went over and put his hand on Stamples's shoulder. "Mr. Stamples is fully aware of the seriousness of this entire list of allegations. He wants to assure you and everyone affected by his actions that he is truly sorry and that the last six days have been the worst days of his life. He knows he has acted in a dishonorable, dishonest, and despicable manner."

The lawyer looked up from his notes. "This will probably surprise you all. My client agrees to make a guilty confession to these allegations on one condition—that Dos and Charlane will not be charged, since he coerced them into committing these crimes. He will subsequently sign a written confession statement of guilt."

The air went out of the room. Chills went up my neck. Staples looked at me, and the pain behind his eyes nearly broke my heart. I'd never felt so sorry for another human being in my life. I went over and did what no one else in that room could do—I held out my arms and hugged him.

Staples cried hard and shook his head. "Tell Amos I'm sorry," he said, in a whisper so low that I might have been the only one that heard it. "I was so envious that Kellsey loved him. I let my jealousy take over. I finally got my chance to love her. So what did I do? I destroyed everything and everyone I love."

His guilt was worse than any punishment. He took the silk handkerchief out of the breast pocket of his $2,000 suit and wiped his face. It occurred to me that all the money in the world wouldn't change the fact that he was going to prison. He used his pen and started writing out his confession.

When he was almost finished, Staples said, "Wait a minute."

I thought, *Oh no, here we go.* But he said, "Do you have another piece of paper? I want to send a note to her parents."

He wrote a few lines, stopped, looked around, and then wrote some more. Signed his name, folded it up, and handed it to me. "Will you make sure they get this?"

He finished the confession and signed the paper; I witnessed it and handed it to the director.

The police officer took Staples out. The lawyer gave a nod and took his leave; then the three of us sat for a moment in silence.

Thomas, who appeared to be in awe, said, "The NESPA lawyers were prepared to charge him with a whole list of violations if he bucked up and forced us all into a long, drawn-out legal battle. No one wins if that happens. This was impressive. Great job."

"I don't think it was the meeting any of us expected," I said.

The director shook his head. "No. It wasn't." He cleared his throat, then recapped the day and thanked me for the evidence I'd shared with him.

"You've been working with those three suspects/witnesses for three months?" the director asked.

"It wasn't easy," I said. "I guess they were afraid of reprisals from Stamples. If Kellsey's accident hadn't happened, we might have never gotten to this day. They would still be carrying this in their hearts forever—without any resolution. They trusted me enough to do the right thing. They are all basically good people trapped in a difficult situation."

"I want to thank you for an excellent job," the director said. "Juggling evidence is like a chess game. Our opponents think they know our next move."

I laughed. "Sir, there were many days I didn't even know what my next move was going to be."

"Well, you are to be commended on having this case and the evidence structured so professionally that when we showed up, it only took you five days to get these confessions."

Thomas and I got into my car and called Max. His sources from the police station had already filled him in on the success of the day.

"Can you believe we got a confession?" I asked Thomas.

"You mean you got the confession," he said, and took my hand. "You did a fantastic job. Stamples could have dragged this out forever."

I sank back against the car seat. "I need a vacation. We have to have this memorial race on Sunday. How about next week—can we go someplace? Maybe up in the mountains of Colorado—rent a cabin where it's cool?"

Thomas didn't hesitate. "I'll make the arrangements." He looked down at his phone and laughed. "News travels fast. I don't know how they got my number, but an outfit called Dos Pesos Locos texted me and said they were sending a complete dinner for two to your house tonight, a special dinner that you would remember." Thomas looked at me. "Dos also said to tell you thanks."

"I'm glad he didn't take the fall," I said. "For once, justice wins."

I called Amos, and he said, "Charlane has already called me and bragged about how important her testimony was. Stamples was behind everything, and she apologized for the ordeal with Lucky. She told me she'd give everybody back their money."

I said, "Speaking of money, I guess I can finally get yours released."

There was a long pause. "I'm not sure I'll take it," he said. "I'll tell you my plan in a few days. Let me get through this race Sunday."

"Maybe I'll see you there," I told him.

Dos's enchiladas were better than the time I had them at the restaurant.

"I'm exhausted," I told Thomas. "All I want to do is finish dinner, take a nice warm bath, and go to bed."

He held me in a great hug and kissed me. I was so tired I could have fallen asleep in his arms.

"Okay," he said. "I'll clean up the kitchen."

Chapter 62

On Saturday morning, all the news was about Stamples's arrest and about Amos's shipping BigOilRig in Sunday for the Kellsey O'Bryan Memorial Stakes Race. What a turn of events. Stamples out and Amos in. I was happy for him.

Thomas arranged a golf game on Saturday, and I had what I needed—some quiet girl time. I had to decompress. As luck would have it, there was a cancellation, and I got my hair done. Saturday night, we finished Dos's enchiladas and curled up on the couch. Thomas had on the golf channel. I was so relaxed I couldn't stay awake.

Sunday morning, Thomas left early and played golf again until noon. I was moved by the preacher's message at Kellsey's funeral and went to Cowboy Church. Afterward, I hung around until everyone had left the building and then approached him.

"I want to thank you for the kind words Wednesday. Can you help me deal with this guilt I have about Kellsey's death? I've carried the mantle of grief and guilt on my shoulders all week since the funeral. I feel I should have done something more to protect her. We've got this race for Kellsey this afternoon, and I want to go see Mr. O'Bryan and tell him how sorry I am that in spite of all of our protocols and efforts, I couldn't make a difference last Sunday."

"Follow me," he said quietly.

We walked up to the front of the church. I could still smell the smoke left behind from the extinguished candles.

He looked in the back of his Bible, leafed through the pages, and said, "Right here. Psalm 32: 'Yes, what joy for those whose record the Lord has cleared of guilt, whose lives are lived in complete honesty.' That's exactly what to do. Be honest with him and apologize. But first you have to forgive yourself."

I can do this.

I thanked him, and the brightness of the June sun greeted me as I stepped outside.

The preacher's insight made it easier going to see Buster. I had that folded-up letter Stamples had written to the O'Bryans in my pocket. Twenty minutes before the race, I walked over to Barn7. The office door was open, and I knocked on the doorframe. "Good afternoon, Mr. O'Bryan. Want some company during the race, or do you want to be left alone?"

He laid down the program with Kellsey's picture on the cover and forced a smile but didn't say a word. I handed him several of the shamrock stickers, and I went ahead with the simple speech I'd rehearsed a dozen times. "Sir, I am truly sorry for what happened to Kellsey."

At the word "Kellsey," it was like he swallowed the color of his lips.

"I am truly sorry for what happened. But even more than that—the *P* in NESPA is for protection—horses' and riders'. I'm sorry I couldn't have done more."

As I wiped a tear off my cheek, he said, "You're a real hero, because you persevered and sought justice for my daughter. I think you did everything you could have. You can't prevent something like a forged document that circumvents the system." He nodded at my expression. "You are key to the NESPA operation. Let this be the fire that motivates you to continue and finish the work you started. That way, her death won't be in vain. It will be a long-lasting legacy in her memory."

He gestured out at the stands. "Look over there—thousands of people, friends of mine that I've been racing with my whole life. You think they came over here to check on me? No, they didn't. But here you are—like an angel. You didn't have to come over here. You've given me some hope that there are still good people involved in this racing world."

"Thank you," I said. "I wanted to help you get through this part of the day. I try to think about what you and Mrs. O'Bryan are dealing with."

I took out the letter and handed it to him. "Last Friday, when we got Stamples's confession, he wrote this to you and Mrs. O'Bryan."

Buster tossed it—folded up—onto his desk. His shoulders slumped, and he glanced at one of the framed photos on his desk.

"Sir, I know Stamples didn't intentionally mean to harm Kellsey. You know he loved her. I'm not sure what he wrote to you, but I saw him, and he is truly sorry this happened."

He opened the letter, started to read it, and said, "Let's go outside."

We walked through the barn and went out toward the turnout paddock. He stood in silence, reading it, then folded it up and put it in his shirt pocket and said, "Yes, the words on the paper show his remorse."

"I don't go to church every Sunday," I told him, "but I think I'm a religious person. I believe in God, I believe in Jesus, and I believe in humankind. I believe that we're here for a purpose. I have been praying for you and Mrs. O'Bryan. God will give you guidance, sir, give you courage and strength and love. He's got a plan for you and me, and we don't know what our plan is. But we're going to have to live it out."

We walked in silence for a moment; then he said, "You're right. I don't have a clue what that plan is now."

"Sir, horse racing needs men like you that are honest and honorable and want to do the right thing. To be an example. When you are ready, it would be great to have you back full time."

He nodded again and said, "You went to the hospital with her, and we are grateful for that. For her not to be alone, when she…"

"Yes, sir. I know in her own way she said her goodbyes. She loved you and her mother."

We all deal with tragedy in our own ways. I wanted to tell him about my sister, but it wouldn't have added anything to the conversation. Still, the pain remained.

Tears welled up in his eyes and mine. He reached out and engulfed me in his arms. I didn't know who needed to be hugged the most, me or him. Maybe both, I guess.

Chapter 63

The Kellsey O'Bryan Memorial Stakes Race on Sunday was going to be a traumatic event for the racing world.

Headlines were all over the news about Stamples being arrested. His charges were explicit. He was a dognapper and a race fixer, and illegally doping racehorses was animal cruelty and abuse. He was charged with involuntary manslaughter for forging a medical document that had led to Kellsey's death. Rixie was quoted about being the key investigator.

There was not one mention of Dos or Pepito or Charlane. Or that the guy with the big super ticket back in March was innocent as hell. Well, when I showed up with BigOilRig, everyone would finally know.

About eleven o'clock we loaded BigOilRig and Chex into the trailer, and I headed around to the front of the truck where Patty and SkyMan were waiting. Martha stayed there at my cabin with the dogs. I said, "Everyone ready?"

Patty nodded. "My only request is for the jockey to not even take a riding crop out with him for the race." I had already told Javier about that. She was reminding me.

The Kellsey O'Bryan Memorial Stakes Race was not the race where I'd expected to run BigOilRig for the first and only time, but now it felt fitting. Full circle, somehow.

"BigOilRig should be an example of how to train and run a horse," Patty said. "No matter what happens, we have to take care of any consequences, be prepared, and be alert."

"Is this our prerace motivational speech?" I asked with a smile. "The horse is going to do okay. We're going to run. We're going to do the best we can for him and honor Kellsey in the meantime."

We all agreed and put on some music. I drove. Patty sat shotgun. SkyMan settled into the back seat. My thoughts were going faster than I could drive.

When we got there, it was like being at the state fair. Long, vertical Kellsey O'Bryan Memorial Stakes Race banners were hanging out on Highway 180 leading up to the track. There was a big crowd. We pulled in at 12:30, and they had a guy at the gate. "I need to see your papers and see the horse."

I got out. "There he is."

He looked through the side trailer window. "Where are the papers on that other horse?"

"He's not a racehorse. He's a quarter horse. I don't need papers on him." I knew I sounded short, but I was getting nervous that even though Stamples was behind bars, something could still ruin this for me.

He made a call, came back, and said, "Well, they said, yeah, he don't need papers."

I shook my head and I said, "Okay."

"Oh, wait a minute," he said.

I wondered what now—but he gave me three green shamrock stickers.

We took BigOilRig up to the receiving barn, where they checked his digital tattoo. The track vet came by and said he'd heard Javier was sick and might not feel good enough to ride BigOilRig.

I was not about to let them assign some house-picked jockey to ride my horse, so I called Javier. "Are you okay to ride? It's gotta be you, Javier."

"I stay in sweatbox too long—got dizzy. Dr. Winkley saw me and took me off the mounts I had in the third and fourth race. He said he would come to the jocks' room at four o'clock and check me out, and if he clears me—I am good to ride your horse."

"Get some fluids in you. BigOilRig needs you today. Oh. Remember—you can't ride with a riding crop. Right?"

"Okay."

I turned off the phone, wondering if Stamples still had a plan to sabotage me. SkyMan and I checked him and made sure he was not stressed from the trailer ride. SkyMan stayed right with him the whole time. He did his magic with his hands. He rubbed BigOilRig's legs. I mean, he was all over the horse. The horse loved it. I looked at my phone every minute, hoping to hear from Javier. Finally, he called.

"Doc cleared me. I'm on."

SkyMan looked up, and I gave him a thumbs up. "Javier cleared to ride!"

We went over to the saddling area, and the veterinarian assigned to us came over and checked BigOilRig all over. He nodded, wrote something on his pad, made a phone call, and everything was good. No problem.

BigOilRig looked around. There were people everywhere. Almost everyone was wearing a shamrock sticker.

"It feels like an exciting day," Patty said, "which is nice."

I nodded. "They haven't had a crowd here like this in years. Buster hasn't been down to the track since the accident. I'm going to call him."

Patty squeezed my hand. Buster said, "I'm going to stay back here at Barn7. I'm not going over there to the track. I can't do that."

"SkyMan will saddle him," I said.

"Sounds good," Buster said. "Good luck, son."

Javier came up all decked out in the new gray silks I'd had made with the green initials AM-PM on the front and on the back. We went with him to the winner's circle, where he joined all the other jockeys.

The track announcer said, "There will be a moment of silence before the next race to honor Kellsey O'Bryan." The jockeys formed a horse-shoe-shaped formation in the winner's circle and bowed their heads.

On all the TV screens was a reel of hundreds of photos of Kellsey. There wasn't a dry eye anywhere. I had my own reel of memories, and a genuine sadness pulled at my heart. I took a lot of deep breaths.

Patty reached for my hand, and we walked through the crowd to the saddling area and did what owners do—stood around and watched SkyMan and Pepito get him saddled.

"Javier, BigOilRig is a special horse," Patty said. "Thanks for not riding with a crop today. Safe trip."

Patty, SkyMan, and I made our way over to the rail where I always used to stand. I got a lot of good luck wishes and people hollering at me; it almost felt like old times. I'm not superstitious like Buster, but I think it was a good idea. SkyMan and I got a lot of energy there. Out of habit, I got a *DRF* when we arrived. I didn't even look at the past performances of the horses in this race. I needed something in my hand.

This was a whole new type of excitement. I wanted BigOilRig to do great, but I also had a new deep-seated fear that tragedy could strike at any moment. I had a flashback to Kellsey's funeral four days before. My conscience tempted me to pull him out and not risk anything bad happening to him or Javier. I took a deep breath and said a quiet prayer for their safety.

I glanced behind me. The crowd was huge. Right there in his green jacket, standing by the big popcorn machine, was the preacher. He caught my eye and gave me the thumbs-up. I nodded.

"You doing okay?" Patty asked, linking her arm in mine.

It felt as if I had my entire life savings bet on BigOilRig to win. What I wanted more than anything, though, was for him to start, finish, and come back okay.

The horses loaded into the gate. SkyMan said, "I'd say 'Good luck,' but I remember you don't believe in luck…"

My heart raced as they all broke clean and BigOilRig settled in behind the front runners. I was so proud—those were my silks out there on my horse. For a second, I thought I was living out a dream for Daddy too. I glanced up in the sky, just in time for the announcer to say "BigOilRig." Every time he said his name, I said it too, like an echo.

When the horses thundered down the stretch, even Patty started yelling his name. BigOilRig was ready to make his move and be in position to challenge the front-runner. All of a sudden, a horse drifted out to the right and cut in front of BigOilRig. Javier had to check BigOilRig, and he stumbled a little, lost his momentum.

Patty grabbed my arm. "What happened?"

"He clipped heels with that horse." I went silent. I knew his chance of winning was lost when that happened, and I felt numb as the horses flew past the finish line. BigOilRig finished second or third.

"At least Javier was able to keep him running," I managed to say.

"I'm sorry," Patty said.

"That's horse racing. Javier will file an objection." The excitement I'd had less than two minutes before had been replaced with disappointment that he hadn't won. "That other horse could get moved back because he interfered with BigOilRig. BigOilRig will probably be moved up to second. Which is where he would have finished."

Javier brought him back to the rail, jumped off, and filed an objection.

SkyMan lifted BigOilRig's left front leg and showed Patty and me the shoe was gone. He said, "That's a good thing; a loose shoe is worse than one coming clear off."

The numbers on the tote board kept flashing for a few minutes while the stewards made a decision. Finally, the objection light went off. BigOilRig finished second. It was over.

Chapter 64

Patty, SkyMan, and I walked back over to Barn7. Over at the track, they were getting ready for the next race. I'd been in the winner's circle with somebody else's horse hundreds of times. But today, I wanted to be in the winner's circle and hear the announcer say, "BigOilRig's owner, Amos Moon."

It helped me realize something. Turning to Patty, I said, "Well, I just failed. I wanted to win, and that didn't happen, so I feel like I failed. I realized how futile those 'false riches' are that SkyMan and Martha talked about. The allure. The glamor. The greed. I have to be honest with you—I didn't enjoy any of it. There's too much pressure owning a horse. I didn't like it. I'm never going to race another horse."

"That's not a failure in my book," Patty said. "That's success. You accomplished your lifelong dream—you own BigOilRig, and now he will be turned out for the rest of his days. That's a success story to be proud of."

She took my hands. "I figured that you'd get up here and see being an owner isn't what it's all cracked up to be. But you had to prove to yourself you could do it. You bought him, trained him, and raced him. And you were willing to accept whatever the consequences would be."

Patty and I led BigOilRig back to the spit box to get his samples for NESPA. SkyMan waited for him to be cleared. When Patty and I went back to Barn7, I heard a familiar voice. "Will you let an old guy give your horse a bath?"

There was a small crowd of familiar faces, and for a minute it felt like old times. "Only if you promise me one thing," I told Buster. "If I ever think I'm going to race another horse—you'll kick my ass up between my shoulder blades."

Javier came back with my gray silks draped over his arm. He handed them to Patty and said, "You were right: I didn't need a crop today. BigOilRig almost wins!"

"Thank you," she said. "We'll always remember this first and last race."

She held up the silks, looked at me, and asked, "What's the deal with the initials?"

"AM-PM we're partners, right?"

"My last name doesn't start with *M*."

"Well, not yet. *M* for 'maybe.' Let's just say it's Patty…Maybe."

"Maybe what? Maybe when?"

"Maybe why not?"

Patty took my hand and pulled me to her. She hugged me, giving a sigh of relief that the race was over. My lips found hers.

I walked Patty through the barn, showing her the details of where I'd once spent so much of my time. Buster approached a few minutes later and pulled us aside.

"One more thing," he said. "Amos, I want to tell you how much you have meant to Mrs. O'Bryan and me. If God ever put a man on this earth that was like a son to me—it would be you."

Sir, you have been like a father to me. We both loved Kellsey. Let's keep that…"

I couldn't finish that sentence, so he helped me. "Memory," he said. "Let's keep that memory. Thanks for running your horse today to honor my daughter." Turning to Patty, he said, "Ma'am, I want to tell you how much it meant for you to share your time with my wife. And that peach cobbler—she wants your recipe."

"We would be very honored for you to come out to the ranch and visit Amos and me."

Buster put his hands in his pockets. "They asked me if they could make the Kellsey O'Bryan Memorial Stakes Race an annual thing. Next year, they want me to give out the trophy. I don't know how I feel about all that. I don't know when I'll be able to make it back here."

"Mr. O'Bryan," Patty said, "I think Kellsey would want you to get back into training. If you wait too long, you may stay in that grief mode, and it's important to get back into what your life has always been—training horses. The horses need you; you need the horses. When you show up, tell yourself you are here to do your best for these horses. They will bring you out and keep you out."

SkyMan and Pepito walked in with BigOilRig, and they paused right beside Patty. She rubbed her hands on BigOilRig's muzzle and said, "I've worked with horses my whole life. You and I both know horses are the ultimate healers."

Buster held out his arms, and Patty hugged him. "You're right," he said quietly. "Today was—is—as much about me as it is about Kellsey." There were tears in his eyes. "Barn7. My home away from home. I dreaded today, but I'm glad I'm here."

He looked at the group in the barn. "I couldn't get through this by myself. You are all family to me. And this guy right here, he's like the son I never had. Amos has been my rock." With a nod, he said, "Now, what are you all waiting for? Let's get this barn squared away."

"Is there a place we can be alone, away from all these people, before we have to go back?" Patty asked. "What about the track kitchen?"

"Oh, I ain't going to the track kitchen. They threw me out of there four months ago."

"Well, is the chapel open?" she asked.

"Well, yeah, it's open right now."

"Let's go over there."

It was quiet when we walked in. The light filtered through the stained-glass windows as if through a prism. Patty walked up to the front and got a Bible.

"I was reading your Bible one day and you know what I found? A ticket from Hialeah Racetrack. An old two-dollar win ticket. The old style with a red stripe on the side."

"Yeah, that is the last reminder I have of my father. A bet he made on a horse. Ironically it was on a horse that was number 8. Same as BigOilRig back on March 26. Number 8."

"I also found this card. And you know what this card says?"

"Yeah, I look at that card often. Preacher gave it to me that same Friday, March 26."

She read the card: "Judge not and be not judged: Condemn not and be not condemned: Forgive and be forgiven." She looked at me. "I believe what this card says. You've got to forgive yourself; you've got to forgive your father and anyone else you need to forgive. Why not right now?"

I had dodged and denied dealing with this most of my life; I was afraid to dig that deep. But I'm a rules kinda guy. So I figured this might be a road map that would give me the peace I had always wanted.

"You mean—right now?"

"Yes. Leave your hat here. All you do is you walk up to the front right there, bow your head, and say, 'Daddy, I forgive you for everything you did, for walking out on our family.' And whatever else you want to say. You also need to express a little gratitude. You need to thank the man that he was able to show you racing, because this is your life, these horses. I think it's important for you to get in touch with yourself, because this is where you and I are. We've had this couple of weeks where we have been sort of living together..."

I wondered what she meant by "this is where you and I are," and I immediately thought we were at a crossroads. Was this an ultimatum? I hoped not.

She said, "I am so personally grateful for what you said. Today was one of the worst days of your life because you realized what you thought was something great isn't great at all. You had to make decisions about Javier, BigOilRig. And now it's time to make decisions about yourself. We are going to take off on a whole new ride here, Amos. Life is going to be good."

Patty walked outside.

I sat on the front pew in complete silence. I'd never done this, and I wasn't sure how to start, but I closed my eyes and kind of talked out loud. "Well, God, here I am. I've gone all the way around, and I'm back here today. It's about—not condemning and not judging. I have been judgmental about people in my life and condemned their actions, and was judgmental about my father and Kellsey. I guess I'm asking you to forgive me for that. And I'm going to forgive them for what they've done. I think that ought to be sufficient, because that comes from my heart."

I sat for a second, kind of reflecting on what I'd said. It was quiet, but I thought I heard something in the back. I kind of turned, and out of the corner of my eye, damn if the preacher wasn't standing back there. I cleared my throat and nodded to him. He nodded back. "Good afternoon, Preacher."

"Good afternoon, Amos. I knew this day would happen for you."

I got my hat off the pew and walked down the aisle, ready to leave, but I stopped and asked him, "How did you know that?"

"Amos, race day," he said. "That's the only day I think you have ever cut through the grandstand like that before the first race. I gave you a card: Luke 6:37."

I nodded. "Yes."

"I also remember that was the order of finish of those horses—6, 3, 7, 8—because your horse came in fourth. That day is branded in my brain. Would you like to repeat the verse together? I think we should."

Well, I did. I said it right there with him: "Judge not and be not judged. Condemn not and be not condemned. Forgive and you will be forgiven."

"Thanks for being here today," I said. "I have to get back to the barn. We have to get the horses back home. I'm done with racing. I plan to turn BigOilRig out; he's going to go be a horse."

"You've made a big turn in your life. God bless you, son."

The sunlight blasted my face when I opened the door. The sun was low in the Texas sky. The burden of the regrets and guilt I'd held onto had been left in the chapel. I smiled at Patty sitting on a green bench. Her smile was already addictive.

The minute I saw BigOilRig back at Barn7, I thought about the women back at TAPP Ranch and how their time at the prison was like his in his stall, bars on the window, him locked in at night. I went in, and he had this "don't leave me here" look in his eyes.

"When I leave this time, BigOilRig," I told him, "you're going too. We're not coming back."

I snapped the lead rope onto his halter, and we walked out that door. It was such a relief—I felt proud and victorious. I reached out with my left hand, and Patty pulled it behind her. She reached her right arm around me and pulled us together.

"Something I want to tell you," I said. "I love BigOilRig…and you."

She smiled at me. "In that order?"

"Two different kinds of love."

"I don't really know that Amos Moon who was at this track four months ago. But I know the man who has his arm around my waist right now. That man I love. I love you, Amos."

I whispered, "I love you, Patty."

We held each other. She leaned back and said, "Do you remember that night I said, 'Now I understand clearly why women love cowboys'? Smile, my cowboy. Your rope has caught me."

"Yes, that was right after I had your famous peach cobbler and you said, 'Kiss me.'"

Chapter 65

NESPA and the Texas Racing Commission had stepped in to take over the operation of HorseShoeDowns. Max and I got a letter from the oil well lease auction group informing us that Washington had postponed auctioning off the oil leases in the Gulf of Mexico indefinitely.

Mrs. Stamples and WD got a quick prenuptial-enforced divorce. She and her daughter had her lawyers put a deed restriction on the property so it could never be developed. It would always be an equine facility, racetrack, and showground. The casino and the sports book were extremely valuable; she had some interest from some of the groups that owned racetracks and casinos, and she planned to sell the entire facility.

Besides her initial $5 million donation to the Children's Equine Learning Center in New Mexico, she also made a pledge to support it going forward.

When Max and I finally had the chance to talk about the case in depth, he was amazed I was able to keep the information in the top secret OMERTA file. He admitted his patience had worn thin and his old police approach might have ruined the entire investigation if he'd known all the details behind it. Then he confided in me that our gig at HorseShoeDowns was winding down. He'd had the opportunity to extend the contract with NESPA but decided he was going to concentrate on the Hunter Group's other clients, slow down a bit, and think about retiring.

"We had a good run," he said. "But now you'll be off to greener pastures too."

I'd put myself on the map with the conviction of Stamples. It propelled me to receive an offer for a new VP position at NESPA, plus liaison with the DEA. In three short years, NESPA had become a huge success. Accidents were down, horses and jockeys were being treated as they should have been treated all along, and I was proud of the opportunity to join the organization.

Del Mar opened in July. Thomas and I went there for opening weekend. I was afraid this was going way too fast, but I wasn't complaining. Thomas had convinced me to move to Lexington. I was grateful that I'd leave Fort Worth knowing I'd accomplished what had become my two main goals. The first was to prove Amos was innocent. The second was to negotiate and facilitate his purchase of BigOilRig, which I was more than happy to do.

Even though I got all the credit for the investigation and getting Stamples sent to prison, the real hero was the example I learned from Amos. He was right about the bulletin board of success, the values that were incorporated into all those elements. And he was right to fight the system of the status quo of the trainers and the veterinarians that broke the rules. He was the only one to challenge the corporate structure and the owner of the track who had established his own rules.

I'd learned all that in three and a half months. It's odd to go back now and look at how little time I really spent with Amos. Three days in March, one day dropping off Chex, one short spin at the Trap Door. Two hours at my house when he picked up Lucky. His values and approach to challenging the system were invaluable when it came to influencing me and motivating me to continue to make racing safe.

Chapter 66

That night when Patty and I returned to the ranch after Kellsey's memorial race, BigOilRig and Chex walked through the gate. As soon as I took off their halters, they ran together in a straight line as far as they could go until they were out of sight. It's been like that ever since.

Every day when we went on a trail ride—Patty on her horse, me on Chex—BigOilRig tagged right along. Even when I went out on the ranch in a four-wheeler, he followed me everywhere I went. I'd told him I was going to get him out of that stall, and he was exactly where I'd told him he would be. Still, it didn't seem like enough.

One day I said to Patty, "I only saved one racehorse from the track. I feel like I should have done more."

Patty said, "You were able to successfully expose what can happen to horses and riders at a racetrack. Because of your unselfish sacrifice, you succeeded. You saved BigOilRig, and you also set an example to never quit. Because of you and the enforcement of NESPA rules, a dark, dark chapter in the current history of horse racing is closed. You've accomplished a lot."

SkyMan and Martha joined Patty and me for dinner at the ranch. Patty grilled her veggie burgers and made her sangria. The big finish of the meal was, of course, her peach cobbler.

I said, "She entered it in the peach cobbler baking contest at the Parker County Peach Festival. She won a blue ribbon—first place in the first-year entry division."

"I can see why," Martha said, taking a bite. "It's delicious. Congratulations."

The sun was starting to set, and it was a beautiful night, watching BigOilRig and Chex grazing out in the huge open pasture.

Patty said. "I want to come out and see the Learning Center arena and barn. How's that going?"

"It's on schedule to be ready in September," Martha said.

"Did you ever get that money from HSD for your winning ticket?" SkyMan asked.

"No, not yet." Patty and I looked at each other. It had been something the two of us had discussed, and it was the right time to bring it up. "What would you think about me having them send the entire amount, $110,264 to your Children's Equine Learning Center?"

He studied me for a minute and said, "Why would you do that?"

"Because I want to. You told me you didn't feel right about taking the settlement money because you didn't do anything to deserve it; I feel the same way about this. I think it was a byproduct of someone's greed. I feel bad NoCashRefund got the *quemados* and you got hurt. You talk about fate or destiny—if BigOilRig had gotten the *quemados*, we wouldn't be sitting here right now; none of this would've ever happened."

I was compelled to tell them, "I've learned a lot from Luke 6:37, but the next verse—Luke 6:38, 'Give to others'—sure got my attention."

SkyMan said, "Yes, we have a similar saying in my native language. On behalf of the children at the Learning Center, we thank you for everything you and Patty have done."

"It made me think of your humility. You believe in and practice placing others first. You both have taught me a lot about false riches and the power of greed, which I've seen my whole life. I know what happened to my daddy and what happened to Stamples. So for me the decision was easy. I wanted to help out because it was the right thing to do."

SkyMan said, "You don't know this, but that day I got hurt, I was in the next stall, and I heard what you told BigOilRig—that there was only one sure thing, that nothing was going to happen to him and you'd go out together. And you did what you said you were going to do. You are a hero in my book. You went out together. You learned what false riches are, but what you really learned is what true riches are. You are living what true riches are."

After they left, I thought about what SkyMan had said. But the real hero in all this was Rixie. Without her perseverance none of this would ever have been possible.

Patty, Lucky, and I walked down to check on the horses. I took her hand. For most of my life, my love had been reserved for dogs like Lucky and horses like Chex and BigOilRig. Now I had to learn to give myself permission to love Patty, and I was enjoying every moment.

What SkyMan said about true riches resonated in my mind. I put my arms around BigOilRig's neck and held him as close as I could. "We went out together, didn't we—just like I told you. And that was the only sure thing that's ever happened."

Epilogue

I figured I was going to spend that night in the slammer. I don't pray much. Go to church less. That afternoon I said a few prayers—thanking God I'd gotten out of that police station.

That was the last week of June. Stamples waived a trial, and his case got expedited, and by the end of an extra-hot July, he was convicted of a whole string of crimes; the worst was involuntary manslaughter. He was sentenced to eight years in a federal prison over in Louisiana.

The O'Bryans were poised to file a huge lawsuit against Stamples. Mrs. Stamples and her father, the patriarch of the entire oil dynasty in Houston, did not want any more bad publicity. They were genuinely sorry and embarrassed about all he'd done, so they settled before a lawsuit was filed. Regardless, no amount of money could offset the pain and suffering the O'Bryans had been through.

I got a lawyer who thought he could argue that Pepito, Dos, and I were victims and were coerced into carrying out Stamples's atrocities. He met with the Stamples Family Foundation attorney in Houston. Sure enough, they wanted to settle the claims before a lawsuit was filed.

To make a long story short, Dos, Pepito, and I all got pretty nice checks. Details were never made public, which is a good thing; people don't need to know my business.

As for the rest of it, Dos and I set up a large bakery for Mexican specialty pastries right behind Dos Pesos Locos. Pepito helps us part time at the bakery and drives the food truck. We sell sopapillas all over town.

That doesn't mean I've given up on cookies. No, Miss Ellane's Horse Cookies are now world famous. And the deal with that dog Powder got me looking into cookies for dogs.

I refunded the ransom money and apologized. I hope they all felt like I was sincere. I also send free cookies out to the TAPP Ranch for the horses, and cookies for those children who visit their parents on Visitors' Day. I'm planning to do the same for SkyMan and Martha's Children's Equine Learning Center. It's now fully operational. Good for them.

I have to admit, at first I thought NESPA was going to be another bureaucratic layer, but it proved to be successful, and horse racing is getting cleaned up. Attendance is up, and people are having fun again going to races.

I heard HSD was going to establish the 'AMOS MOON STAKES RACE'. He's still a legend around here. I watched Amos fall in and out of love with Kellsey. I tried to fix him up with Rixie. But when I saw him with Patty, I knew they were meant to be together. Good for him.

I think about Rixie a lot. She ended up being a damn good investigator. She proved me wrong all the way around. Got a big-time job with NESPA, and I hear she travels all over the world with Thomas. She deserves that. I wish for only one thing: that she would have gotten the goods on Stamples sooner. Maybe my friend—Kellsey—would still be alive today.

I still ride a few horses, but I'm the only one from our original crew left at HorseShoeDowns. I guess that's probably a good thing. Look what happened to everyone else. Funny how things turn out.

Acknowledgements

I would like to acknowledge the characters in this novel I have lived with, laughed with, and cried with for over twenty years. Funny how twenty years of hard work can end up going into a story that takes place over four months.

Writers have a lot of heroes—not in a sense of mythical or sports heroes, but we are privileged to create heroes from our own hearts and life experiences. So it is with Amos Moon and Rixie Ricksland, who came to life in this story.

I owe special thanks to my wife, Judy; my family; and my children, Leigh, Mary, JP, and Taylor. At times, they believed more in the publication of this novel than I did. They reminded me to keep the faith.

Taylor Miller, who signed up, never gave up and encouraged me as every scene came to life on the page. If this is ever made into a movie, she gets all the credit.

Cynthia Ellingsen has been a stalwart partner in editing every draft. Her steadfast words of encouragement were invaluable: "Let's keep working hard to create the most brilliant draft ever of this wonderful story you've created."

Dr. Francis Skipp, my English professor at the University of Miami, Florida, told me, "Writing opens doors of imagination and hope in a world where neither had existed before." He ignited in me a passion for literature and writing.

Nancy Wood shared her compassion for Native Americans and the Taos Pueblo. She told me, "Follow your heart!! No bullshit! No excuses! Do it!"

I thank Sean Murphy and Tania Casselle for all the writing workshops in Taos; at the Ghost Ranch; at the Murie Center in Jackson, Wyoming; at Francie's cabin in Colorado; and especially during a week writing and riding horses in the Canyon de Chelly. Sean fell in love with Rixie's "irresistible eyes…three shades of green and gray."

Thanks to Natalie Goldberg and her workshops at the Lama Foundation, San Cristobal, New Mexico. She told me that "a writer's job is to give the reader a larger vision of the world."

Thanks to Kathryn Mapes Turner, a Wyoming artist who inspires me every day as I enjoy her paintings in our home. She taught me that "talent is not God-given. What is God-given is a deep passion that motivates you to learn something"—great advice that I applied to riding horses and writing.

Thanks also to Kent Kramer, Lynn Palm, and Cyril Pittion-Rossillion, whose patience taught me everything I know about riding horses.

Thank you to my friends Jane and Steve Beshear, Kathy and Bob Beck, Carol and Tracy Farmer, Jane Winegardner, Donna and the late Johnny Ward, Jessica Normand, Katie Ward, Lesley Humphrey, Dr. Bob Copelan, Tommy Drury, Hank Zeitlin, and Catherine Parke. Thanks for sharing with me your compassion for horses and for the people who love them—and allowing me access to your world.

A special group of friends - Helen Alexander, James Nicholson, Chris McCarron, Staci and Arthur Hancock, who let me include, 'I'll tie their hands, cover their face and trip the trap door down' from his song - Ashland Woman.

My beta readers, Judy Miller, Taylor Miller, Marian Zeitlin, and Hank Zeitlin helped keep my fiction as accurate as possible.

Thanks to the early typists who learned to decipher my not-al-ways-legible handwriting. Ashley Humphrey Clark, Ellen J. Bickel, Liza van Dissel, and Paige Paxton Snyder.

A big thank you to Caroline Cassin and The Brand Thread team for being a fantastic marketing partner; Stephanie Kenyon and the team at Palmetto Publishing; Derek Price graphic design.

Thanks to Susie McEntire's Cowboy Church. Susie, you know my favorite song: "Always. Always." May you continue to spread God's word through your music.

To Michael Hearne and Shake Russell. Thanks for allowing me to include the lyrics for "Irish Prayer." It resonates in this novel as more than a song.